Dear Reader,

I am thrilled to have this opportunity to share with you the exciting return of *By Love Unveiled*. Long out of print, this historical romance from early in my career is finally available once more from Pocket Books, revised and refurbished throughout. How many authors get a chance to revisit one of their early works, to tighten and sharpen the characters and dialogue, bringing to bear everything they've learned in the years since it was first published to make it a richer, deeper reading experience than ever before? I am one lucky writer!

The eight novels I wrote some years ago under the pen name Deborah Martin are distinctively different in tone from my more recent Sabrina Jeffries releases. Where my five lighthearted Hellions of Halstead Hall novels, for instance, are packed with witty, sexy repartee and sensual romantic entanglements, my Deborah Martin novels are steeped in history and brimming with passionate action. Of course, whatever author name appears on the cover, one thing I am sure to bring to all my novels is heart-pounding sexual tension—and plenty of it!

I hope you enjoy this reissue of *By Love Unveiled*, whether it's one of your past favorites or a new reading adventure for you to relish.

Sincerely,

Sabrina Jeffries

"ANYONE WHO LOVES ROMANCE MUST READ SABRINA JEFFRIES!"

—*New York Times* bestselling author Lisa Kleypas

THE HELLIONS OF HALSTEAD HALL

Praise for the "sparkling" (*Library Journal*)
New York Times bestselling series!

A LADY NEVER SURRENDERS

"Jeffries pulls out all the stops. . . . With depth of character, emotional intensity, and the resolution to the ongoing mystery rolled into a steamy love story, this one is not to be missed."

—*RT Book Reviews* (4½ stars, Top Pick)

"Wonderfully refreshing characters, a surprising resolution, and a sizzling, emotionally satisfying romance make this another must-read from one of the genre's best."

—*Library Journal* (starred review)

"Brimming with superbly shaded characters, an abundance of simmering sensuality, and a splendidly wicked wit, *A Lady Never Surrenders* wraps up the series nothing short of brilliantly."

—*Booklist*

TO WED A WILD LORD

"Wonderfully witty, deliciously seductive, and graced with humor and charm, this clever, well-conceived romance treats readers to a compelling story peopled with remarkable characters."

—*Library Journal* (starred review)

"The fourth installment in Jeffries's exceptionally entertaining Hellions of Halstead Hall series delivers another beguiling blend of captivating characters, clever plotting, and sizzling sensuality."

—*Booklist*

HOW TO WOO A RELUCTANT LADY

"A delightful addition to the scandalous Sharpe family saga. . . . Charmingly original."

—*Publishers Weekly* (starred review)

"Richly imbued with steamy passion, deftly spiced with dangerous intrigue, and neatly tempered with just the right amount of tart wit."

—*Booklist*

A HELLION IN HER BED

"A lively plot blending equal measures of steamy passion and sharp wit."

—*Booklist* (starred review)

"Wonderfully original. . . . Jeffries's sense of humor, her engaging characters, and delightfully delicious sensuality spice things up!"

—*RT Book Reviews* (4½ stars)

"Jeffries's addictive series satisfies."

—*Library Journal*

THE TRUTH ABOUT LORD STONEVILLE

"Jeffries combin[es] her hallmark humor, poignancy, and sensuality to perfection."

—*RT Book Reviews*

"Lively repartee, fast action, luscious sensuality, and an abundance of humor."

—*Library Journal* (starred review)

"First in captivating new Regency-set series, [with] delectably witty dialogue, subtly named characters, and scorching sexual chemistry."

—*Booklist*

SABRINA JEFFRIES

WRITING AS
DEBORAH MARTIN

By Love Unveiled

Pocket Books
New York   London   Toronto   Sydney   New Delhi

Pocket Books
A Division of Simon & Schuster, Inc.
1230 Avenue of the Americas
New York, NY 10020

This book is a work of fiction. Names, characters, places, and incidents either are products of the author's imagination or are used fictitiously. Any resemblance to actual events or locales or persons, living or dead, is entirely coincidental.

First Pocket Books paperback edition March 2013

POCKET and colophon are registered trademarks
of Simon & Schuster, Inc.

For information about special discounts for bulk purchases, please contact Simon & Schuster Special Sales at 1-866-506-1949 or business@simonandschuster.com.

The Simon & Schuster Speakers Bureau can bring authors to your live event. For more information or to book an event contact the Simon & Schuster Speakers Bureau at 1-866-248-3049 or visit our website at www.simonspeakers.com.

Designed by Kyle Kabel

Manufactured in the United States of America

10 9 8 7 6 5 4 3 2 1

ISBN 978-1-4516-9838-1
ISBN 978-1-4516-6552-9 (ebook)

To Becky Timblin, my wonderful assistant.
Thanks for making the manuscript workable!
And for managing the office chaos so splendidly.

By Love Unveiled

Chapter One

Heat not a furnace for your foe so hot
That it do singe yourself.
　　　　　　　—Shakespeare, *Henry VIII*

Garett Lockwood, the Earl of Falkham, watched from the shadows as a smiling Charles II entered the richly appointed sitting room of his spacious new private chambers. No doubt His Majesty relished the trappings of royalty after spending years without. But now it was time for the king to heed his promises. Garett had waited long enough.

When he stepped forward, His Majesty started. "By God, Falkham, you have a nasty habit of appearing from out of nowhere when one least expects it."

"Which is what keeps Your Majesty's enemies guessing."

"I am glad to see you have returned," Charles said. "I wish you could have joined us in our triumphant entry into the city last year, but you made better use of your time by accomplishing the tasks I set for you."

Garett had spent the past year arranging the king's betrothal to Catherine Braganza of Portugal and then tracking down an enemy of the king in Spain. Neither was the sort of work Garett enjoyed, but given the reward promised him . . .

"Lord Chancellor Clarendon tells me you were successful in both," the king went on.

Garett lifted one brow. "Aren't I always?"

"If it suits you."

"I do only what suits my king. My king just doesn't always know what suits him."

"Indeed," Charles said dryly. "Be careful, my friend. Your king may tolerate your wit, but others will not find it quite so amusing."

"I am well aware of that, Your Majesty," Garett said in a hard voice. Ten years in exile had been more than enough to teach him that the world was a treacherous shoal to be navigated with great care.

The king sighed. "I fear I wasn't the best companion for a youth who'd just lost his family. Between my bitterness and your hatred, we bred the sort of unhealthy anger that can destroy a man if he is not careful."

"Ah, but Your Majesty's bitterness is assuaged," Garett said smoothly. "Your subjects have come to their senses at last."

"That remains to be seen. A people so fickle bears watching. Yet I believe they're truly pleased to have me on the throne again. Unlike Cromwell, I don't feed them religion with their meat."

Garett thought of all the debauchery at court and gave

a mirthless laugh. "Indeed not." When a glint in Charles's eye showed that he'd registered the rebuke, Garett changed the subject to the one that concerned him most. "Clarendon told me the Roundheads made an attempt on Your Majesty's life."

The lord chancellor had told him a great deal more than that, but Garett wouldn't be content until he heard the news from the king himself.

"Yes, by one of my attending physicians whom I thought I could trust. But to my knowledge, he is not a Roundhead."

"So you don't know who was behind the plot."

"No, but we will find out. I have had my men state that the physician was murdered while in his cell in the Tower, killed by his fellow conspirators. Clarendon hopes the rumor will confound the other assassins and provoke them into erring. Besides, we do not want his companions to silence him by killing him before we can question him. This gives us time to get the truth from him."

"Does Your Majesty believe him guilty?"

The king shrugged. "I do not know. 'Tis very odd. Until he returned to London recently, he had not been much involved with affairs of state." Charles faced Garett with a veiled expression. "In fact, he'd been living a fairly secluded life in the country, near a town you know well—Lydgate."

So Clarendon had told him the truth. "You speak of Sir Henry Winchilsea."

Eight years ago, Garett's uncle, Sir Pitney Tearle,

had sold the family estate, Falkham House, to Winchilsea. Just thinking of it still roused Garett's anger.

"'Twas a mad world in those days, Garett," Charles said placatingly. "People passed around lands as if they were so many sacks of seed."

"But those lands were sold by their rightful owners, not by usurpers," Garett snapped. "Have you considered that Winchilsea and my uncle might have conspired together to have you assassinated? They were bound by Falkham House. Perhaps this physician knew my fortunes were tied to you and thus so was the estate he'd obtained from my deceitful uncle."

Charles rubbed his chin absently. "Or perhaps Tearle and his Roundhead compatriots saw the advantages to be had in manipulating a man who would appear innocuous to everyone else. In any case, I doubt that the affair had anything to do with your return. Remember that except for your uncle and a few exiles, no one knew that you lived. And since you have continued to prefer that it be kept secret until now—"

"With good reason."

"Aye, especially given recent circumstances. But my point is that Winchilsea probably didn't know you lived."

"Unless my uncle told him."

Charles conceded the point with a nod.

"So what happens to his claim upon my property?" Garett bit out. That was the crucial question. "Your agreement with Parliament was that those lands sold during Your Majesty's exile remain with the buyers."

"Ah, but Winchilsea performed a treasonous act. I have confiscated the property, of course, and gladly return it to you. Consider it your reward for arranging my marriage to the Infanta—your lands as well as funds to improve them as you see fit."

Garett let out a breath. After all these years, he could finally go home.

But that wasn't the only thing he wanted. "What about my uncle? Will you punish him for his treachery?"

Charles strode to the window overlooking his gardens and stared out at the Cavaliers and their ladies who wandered the grounds. "I cannot. No one can prove any of your claims concerning him."

Garett bristled. "But you know bloody well—"

"Yes. Tearle paints himself a moderate, but I know more about his Roundhead companions than he realizes. He's a villain and not to be trusted."

"Then do something about him!"

The king let out an oath. "Unfortunately, there were villains on both sides in our most recent conflict, and I cannot choose to punish him without punishing them all. I have agreed to amnesty for everyone but the regicides, and that includes Tearle."

"Unless I can prove his treachery."

"Or he proves to be behind the attempt on my life." Charles sighed. "There is no proof of that, either, and until I have some, I must tread cautiously. He's powerful among Cromwell's old supporters. To cross him could mean risking the disapproval of the very subjects I wish to placate. I cannot afford to be seen as seeking vengeance upon the Roundheads."

The king leveled a hard glance on Garett. "Neither can you. You have your reward. Do not do anything foolhardy against your uncle that might jeopardize us both."

"He deserves my retribution," Garett growled. "And I won't hesitate to mete out his fair portion, given the chance."

"I speak now as your friend, not your king—I fear he will suffer less from your vengeance than you will."

Garett uttered a harsh laugh. "Has Your Majesty now become like the Puritans, crying that vengeance is the Lord's? Will my soul be condemned if I make Pitney Tearle suffer for stealing away a defenseless boy's title and inheritance?" And more, though he couldn't yet prove it.

"I believe the Almighty will understand." Charles looked upon Garett with an odd pity. "Yet now that the seed of bitterness has sprung to life within you, I wonder if you will be able to stop its vines from choking your heart."

Garett's heart had been choked long ago by betrayal and pain. And no matter what His Majesty wanted, the man responsible for that deserved to be punished. "Thank you for your advice, my liege, but after years of nurturing that seed, I can't root it out. Come what may, I mean to see the seedling fully sprung and the vines grown firm to imprison Pitney Tearle."

*　　*　　*

Weeks after her father's arrest, Miss Marianne Winchilsea, daughter to a baronet, stared sadly at the once immaculate gardens of her cherished home. How well she remembered her first sight of it, eight years ago. For a child of twelve accustomed to their cramped London town house, Falkham House had seemed a magnificent palace, with its costly glass windows and graceful gables. Yet despite its grandeur, its cheery red brick had always felt welcoming.

It had helped that the people of the nearby town of Lydgate had willingly accepted her gypsy mother. Of course, they'd been told—as had all of Father's friends—that her mother was a Spanish noble's daughter. Later, when the truth about Mother's race had slipped out, the townspeople had jealously guarded her secret, won over by her sweet disposition and her healing skills.

A lump rose in Marianne's throat as she surveyed the neglected patches of sage and lady's mantle, oregano and dragon's blood. Her parents had so loved their herb gardens. Father had even found some solace in them after Mother died.

But now he was dead, too.

She fought her ready tears, knowing they brought no comfort. How could he be dead? It made no sense. He'd been killed in a prison, where he should have been safe. Why had someone wanted him dead? For that matter, why had someone felt the need to paint him the villain and cause his arrest?

"Come, Mina, we should go," Aunt Tamara murmured at her ear, using Mother's nickname for her.

With a sigh, Marianne faced Mother's only sister.

"You agreed not to tempt fate by approaching your old home," her aunt reminded her. "Your father wasn't the only one suspected of treason, you know—there were rumors of *your* involvement."

And it still infuriated Marianne that anyone could think such a thing. Neither she nor Father had ever been anything but loyal to the Crown. "Fortunately, everyone outside of Lydgate believed your tale that I drowned myself when I heard of Father's arrest."

Thank heaven Aunt Tamara had learned of it before the soldiers had come looking for Marianne; otherwise, she'd even now be awaiting execution. No one would have listened to her protests, not with England in such chaos.

"Let's not give anyone reason to believe otherwise," her aunt said. "Return to the wagon and leave this place before you are recognized."

"No one will do so as long as I wear this." Marianne tugged at the black silk mask gentlewomen often wore while riding to protect their faces from the weather. It had been a useful tool for disguising her without drawing attention. Unfortunately, it also partially obscured her vision and was occasionally uncomfortable, but that was a small price to pay for freedom.

"Besides," she went on, "how can I discover who killed Father if I stay away from Falkham House? You heard the rumors—someone has already bought the place from the Crown, mere weeks after Father's death. I have to know if the new owner had anything to do with arranging Father's arrest and death."

That was her sole purpose these days—to figure out who'd caused Father's downfall. After Aunt Tamara had engineered her escape from London by hiding her in the gypsy camp when the soldiers had come for her, Marianne had insisted on fleeing to Lydgate, where she knew she could find refuge. The townspeople would never betray her.

Of course, Aunt Tamara hadn't approved of Marianne's plan but had gone along, knowing perfectly well that arguing with her niece was fruitless. Once in Lydgate, they'd found a spot to settle. Marianne had quickly adjusted to spending her nights in the cramped confines of the wooden wagon and her days roaming the forest in search of firewood or going to town for provisions. It hadn't taken her long to realize how hard her aunt's life with her people must have been, selling her needlecraft to gain food, using her wits to keep the wagon safe and warm, and keeping out of sight of soldiers who hated gypsies.

Aware of how little money Aunt Tamara had to spare, Marianne had begun using her skills as a healer to help them earn their keep. She'd been right about the townspeople's refusal to turn her in. If anything, they'd been pleased to have her tend their sick and act as midwife to their women.

"'Tis not too late to flee to the Continent and join my people there," Aunt Tamara said.

"I cannot. The cards are dealt, and I must play out the hand." The dark expression that crossed Aunt Tamara's face made Marianne add, with a twinkle in her eye, "But you don't have to stay."

"As if I'd hurl my niece to the wolves! Don't think to be rid of me now, poppet. Someone must keep you from darting into danger."

"True." Marianne hugged her aunt. "I'd be lost without you here."

"And don't you forget it." Aunt Tamara tugged on Marianne's arm. "So listen to me and come away before the new owner spies us."

Marianne hesitated, but her aunt was right. She would learn nothing just standing here watching the house, so she let her aunt draw her off down the road. "Does anyone know who bought the estate?"

"I have asked, but they seem reluctant to tell me." Aunt Tamara frowned. "Perhaps they still don't trust me entirely."

"They'll tell *me*." Shifting direction, Marianne headed for town.

Her aunt let out an oath. "You're supposed to stay out of Lydgate as much as possible."

"This is important," Marianne said. "I have to find out who he is. And I know just the person to tell us."

She headed straight for the apothecary shop. As they entered, Marianne threw back the hood of her cloak and began to remove her mask.

"I advise you not to do that," the owner said in a stern voice.

"But we're the only ones here, Mr. Tibbett," Marianne protested.

He softened his expression. "If the people of Lydgate are to protect you, Miss Winchilsea, you must do your part and keep your face covered when strangers are about."

She sighed. "Then you must remember to call me Mina. I'm a poor half-gypsy gentlewoman, or had you forgotten?" When his face fell, Marianne hastened to add, "Forgive me, dear friend. I do appreciate all that you and your fellows have done to keep me safe. I should never have placed you in such danger."

"Nonsense." A smile cracked his usual reserve. "It is wonderful to have such a skilled healer in our midst again."

"Don't flatter the girl," Aunt Tamara grumbled, then poked Marianne. "The mask, Mina."

With a sigh, Marianne restored her disguise.

"Now then," Mr. Tibbett said. "What might I do for you today?"

The apothecary might be a rather ponderous old Puritan given to platitudes and maxims, but he'd taught her much about medicines and herbs.

Just now, however, Marianne was most interested in his shameful tendency to gossip. "We wish to know who's the new owner of Falkham House," Marianne said baldly.

Mr. Tibbett blinked, then sighed. "So you heard about that, did you?"

"Of course. But no one will say who bought it."

"It wasn't bought . . . exactly. It was, you might say, *acquired*. The Earl of Falkham himself reclaimed his estate."

"Oh, poppet, a great noble, no less!" Aunt Tamara

said. "We should leave here before you find yourself in more trouble."

"I don't understand," Marianne said. "Pitney Tearle had no claim on it—"

"No, not Sir Pitney. The real earl, Garett Lockwood."

Lockwood? She knew that name. "You mean the man who died in the war, with his wife?"

"Not him but his son," Mr. Tibbett said. "Everyone—apparently even his uncle, Sir Pitney Tearle—thought he'd been killed with his parents. Sir Pitney was only a knight before then, but as a distant cousin, he inherited the earldom. Indeed, that's why he married the former earl's sister, because *she* was actually heir to the property through her mother if the earl died. Once all heirs to the title were believed dead and Lady Tearle was the only heir to the Falkham estate, Sir Pitney gained both the property and the title."

"But Sir Pitney sold Falkham House to my brother-in-law," Aunt Tamara said. "So by the terms under which the king was restored to the throne, this other man—the Royalist—could not reclaim his property unless . . ."

"Father died," Marianne said in a hard voice. "Or was proved a traitor. Or both."

Mr. Tibbett blinked. "Now see here, I know what you're thinking, but his lordship would never do such a thing."

"You mean arrange the arrest of my father so he could

regain Falkham House? How can you be sure? He was only a boy when he left. Who knows what his character became?"

"Ah, but he's a man of some renown now. Every day some new story surfaces of his bravery in battle, how he fought with the Duke of York under the humble name Garett Lockwood, and how he performed many heroic acts. Apparently he even stayed abroad to arrange His Majesty's marriage after the king's return. That's how he regained his lands—as a reward for his actions."

"A reward he could never have received if Father hadn't been arrested and killed," she said hotly.

Mr. Tibbett cast her a pained look. "Yes, but you must understand. Sir Pitney had no right to sell the estate, not while the heir was alive."

"Then the heir shouldn't have hidden himself off abroad," Marianne snapped.

The door opened and closed behind her, but she was too caught up in her anger to heed either that or Mr. Tibbett's warning glance.

"No one would have bought Falkham House in the first place," she continued, "if this heir had simply bothered to inform people he hadn't died in the war. It makes me wonder—"

"Ah, here's that rosemary you came for," Mr. Tibbett jumped in as he thrust a jar at her.

"Rosemary?" She slid it back at him. "What would I want with rosemary?"

"I believe," rumbled a deep masculine voice behind

her, "Mr. Tibbett is trying to keep you from wounding my feelings."

Startled, Marianne swung around, knocking off the jar of rosemary, which hit the stone floor and shattered, filling the air with the herb's pungent scent.

"Good day, my lord," Mr. Tibbett said hastily. "It's good to see you again."

"And you," the stranger said tersely.

Lord help her. This had to be the earl himself. Worse yet, she'd just insulted him, thus drawing attention to herself. A pox on her quick tongue!

What now? Apologize or stay silent? Which one would help her escape his further notice?

Thank heavens Mr. Tibbett had insisted on her continuing to wear the mask. This Royalist earl wouldn't hesitate to hand her over to the Crown, given who she was and what she and Father had been accused of.

Which he might have engineered himself.

She shivered. This man could very well be her enemy. He certainly looked daunting—tall, fiercely handsome, and nobly dressed.

Trying to gather her wits about her, she bent to pick up the shards of crockery, and her gaze went right to his jackboots of supple gray leather. As she straightened, she took in his hose of the best silk and his breeches of kerseymere. His gray woolen cape was pushed back over his shoulders, exposing his doublet and, underneath that, his shirt of fine holland.

But when she met his gaze, she realized she'd erred in keeping silent. Fed by the sight of her unusual garb, he looked suspicious. The late summer air wasn't yet chill enough for a cloak, and ladies didn't generally wear masks indoors, except to the theater.

She stole a glance at her aunt. At least Aunt Tamara's appearance shouldn't raise his suspicions too much, for despite her olive skin, she dressed like a poor gentlewoman.

Mr. Tibbett finally found his voice. "May I help you, my lord?" he asked, to draw the earl's attention from Marianne.

Lord Falkham's grim mouth smoothed surprisingly into a pleasant smile. "It's been a long time, hasn't it, Mr. Bones?"

The teasing nickname took Marianne off guard.

Apparently, it did the same for Mr. Tibbett, who hesitated before returning his lordship's smile. "It has indeed, my lord. The days when you called me Mr. Bones are so long gone I wouldn't have thought you'd remember them. In truth, I thought never to witness your return to your rightful place."

"I'm thankful *someone* in England is pleased to see me." Lord Falkham's gaze turned mocking as it flicked briefly over Marianne. "Not everyone has been so. My uncle's Roundhead friends, some of whom are still in high places, would have seen me completely disinherited if they'd thought it would profit them."

"Then God preserve us all," Mr. Tibbett said. At Lord Falkham's raised eyebrow, he added, "I assure you that we here in Lydgate would have done more to stop Sir Pitney if we'd known of his treachery. Imagine our outrage when the blackguard went so far as to sell Falkham House—"

Mr. Tibbett broke off as he apparently remembered who else was present.

The earl didn't seem to notice. "It might have cost 'the blackguard' dearly if I'd returned to find my property beyond my reach. Fortunately, matters worked out to my satisfaction."

It took every ounce of Marianne's control not to utter a harsh retort. *To his satisfaction,* indeed. Only through the death and disgrace of her father had it been so.

Mr. Tibbett hastened to smooth over the awkward moment. "In any case, I know I speak for everyone when I say how pleased we are that you own the estate once more. You'll be a good lord for Falkham House."

The earl smiled grimly, then turned unexpectedly to Marianne. "And do you agree, madam? Shall I be a 'good lord'?" When she remained silent, only too aware of the danger in engaging her enemy in conversation, his eyes darkened. "Of course not. No doubt you preferred to have Sir Henry in residence, or even Sir Pitney, instead of the rightful owner."

She kept silent, though her temper raged within her.

"We're sad to lose Sir Henry, of course," Mr. Tibbett said hastily, "but we're glad to see you've returned. I know you would have felt the loss of Falkham House keenly if Sir Henry had lived and kept ownership of the estate."

"That wouldn't have happened," the earl said with assurance.

"Why not?" Marianne asked without thinking.

Lord Falkham studied her masked visage. "I would have offered him so much money for the estate he would gladly have sold it to me."

Didn't the man know that his uncle had also attempted such a thing? Two years ago, after Lord—no, *Sir* Pitney—had become powerful among Cromwell's supporters, he'd tried to buy back the estate. When Father had refused to sell, the man had spread rumors that Marianne and her mother were witches because of their healing abilities and gypsy blood. Fortunately, Lydgate's townspeople had ignored his nonsense. But it had made Marianne wary of the duplicitous fellow.

And now she was just as wary of his nephew, especially when the man cast her a chilling smile. "Fortunately, that situation never arose. His Majesty was more than happy to restore my lands to me."

"That won't please your uncle, I daresay," Mr. Tibbett said. "He was always a grasping tyrant with grand plans for himself and a tendency to use . . . ah . . . forceful means to achieve his goals."

"I don't fear Sir Pitney," Lord Falkham bit out. "By now he must have realized he made the greatest mistake of his life when he stole my inheritance. And if my regaining Falkham House didn't prove that, I won't hesitate to give him other proofs. He'll learn his lesson, if I must teach it to him over and over."

The threat in his words sent a shudder through Marianne. She understood his dislike for Sir Pitney, but this went beyond dislike. After all, the man couldn't have known he was alive—it wasn't Sir Pitney's fault that he'd assumed the worst. Clearly, the earl was another of those arrogant nobles newly returned from exile who expected everyone to give him his due, just or not.

Still, she had to admit he seemed different from the exiles she'd known at court—more somber, somehow. His thick, ash-brown hair fell uncurled to his shoulders, in defiance of fashion, and not a trace of lace adorned his shirt or doublet. Yet no air of the Puritan clung to him, either. He had a bearing more inherently self-assured than any newly empowered Puritan.

It was that confidence and aristocratic bearing that alarmed her most of all. They could lead a man to commit all manner of crimes.

As if Aunt Tamara could hear her niece's morbid thoughts, she prodded Marianne toward the door. "We'll be leaving now, if you'll excuse us, sirs."

The earl's voice stopped them before they could escape. "Please don't leave your business unfinished on my account," he said with a cloying civility she knew was directed at her. "I'd like to hear more about my pleasurable days abroad."

Marianne stifled a groan. He clearly itched to punish her for her insults. How she'd like to spar with him, but she dared not. The last thing she needed was to draw attention to herself.

"Thank you for your consideration, milord, but we've finished our business," Aunt Tamara said, using the ingratiating manner of a practiced gypsy.

But apparently her words weren't enough for his

curst lordship. He moved forward to block their exit, placing his hand on the door handle.

"I see your companion has lost her tongue," he told Aunt Tamara, although his gaze was fixed on Marianne's masked face. "Such a pity, for I really wish to hear more of her spirited opinions."

Heat rose in Marianne's cheeks. Thank heavens for her mask.

"But if I may be so bold, I'd at least like to know your names," he continued. "I should like to begin reacquainting myself with the people of Lydgate who once served my father."

More likely, he wanted to know who'd insulted him so he could take his revenge.

"I am Tamara," her aunt said, "and this is my niece Mina. You must excuse her mask. 'Tis the smallpox, you see. She was struck by it when young, and her face is quite disfigured, milord." She shot Marianne a warning glance. "It has made her bitter and more inclined to say things she shouldn't."

Marianne glared at her aunt from beneath the mask. Trust Aunt Tamara to make her sound like a crotchety troll. And an ugly one, too.

Lord Falkham looked skeptical. "Forgive me, I didn't mean to pry."

She doubted that. He struck her as the sort of man who trusted nothing and no one.

Aunt Tamara tightened her grip on Marianne's arm. "We really must go."

For a moment Marianne feared he wouldn't let them

leave. Then he opened the door with a mocking flourish. "Then don't let me hinder you. I'm certain we'll meet again."

When they were out of earshot, Aunt Tamara muttered, "And I'm certain we won't, not if I can help it." As soon as they'd gone a good distance, she exploded. "You should have listened to me! We were nearly discovered back there. We should leave Lydgate immediately."

"I'm not leaving! It's quite possible he's the one who arranged to have Father arrested. He might even have had something to do with Father's death."

"That would mean he planted the poison so your father would be blamed. But that would have risked the king's life as well. He wouldn't have done that."

"We can't be sure of the exact circumstances. He mightn't have risked His Majesty's life but merely made it look as if Father had done so. A man with his power could do all sorts of things to ensure someone's arrest."

Aunt Tamara shuddered. "That's what frightens me. If he discovers who you are—"

Marianne laughed. "How can he? You conveniently gave me a reason to wear my mask all the time. That was brilliant of you."

"It might not keep your neck out of the hangman's noose. Especially if the earl—"

"I know. I'll have to avoid him."

"That might not be easy. He isn't the sort to let an insult pass. Be careful, poppet, that you don't find yourself caught in his trap, for he would easily devour you."

"Nonsense. He's probably already forgotten about me."

But Marianne's heart continued to pound like the heart of a bird hunted by a falcon, long after she and her aunt had passed out of sight of Lydgate.

Chapter Two

Take heed lest passion sway
Thy judgement to do aught, which else free will
Would not admit.

—John Milton, *Paradise Lost*

Weary to the bone, Marianne slipped out of the cramped cottage where she'd just served as midwife to a villager. She pulled up her hood and tied on her mask, all because of that cursed earl. Thanks to him, she didn't know when she could discard them for good.

As she headed off for the wagon, a thin stranger a bit older than her aunt emerged from the darkness at the other end of the street. When he saw her, he called out, "You, in the mask! Be you the gypsy healer they call Mina?"

She nodded. "And who are you, sir?"

"My name is William Crashaw," he said as he approached, "and I'm valet to the Earl of Falkham. You must come at once. It's a matter of great urgency. His lordship lies wounded and needs your help."

A cold chill gripped her. She didn't dare risk going

to that man's aid, even if he *wasn't* the villain who'd brought about Father's ruin. "I'm sorry, I just spent several hours birthing twins. Why don't you ask Mr. Tibbett to help you?"

"He's not at his shop," the man clipped out. "And we've no time to waste. Two men attacked my master on the road, and one stabbed him clear through the thigh. His very life is in peril."

Oh, dear. She couldn't let a man die, no matter what the risk. Besides, if he was that gravely hurt, he wouldn't be paying her much mind. "Very well. Take me to him."

But as they reached the top of the hill and she caught sight of her old home, she had second thoughts. Her mind swam with memories of coming home late at night with her mother after staying by a child's sickbed, of returning with her father from an evening's merriment at a friend's estate. This earl had possibly plotted Father's arrest, perhaps even his death. Why should she help him?

Besides, she'd never dressed a serious wound, though she'd watched Father do it hundreds of times. And this of all wounds! If she wasn't successful, she would be doubly in danger—from the king's soldiers *and* his lordship's friends.

She hesitated at the point where the road forked off toward Falkham House.

William faced her with a fierce scowl. "See here, miss, I'd send someone for Bodger if he didn't live so far away. The men at the tavern said you would be a greater help to my master. But if you can't do it, I'll take my chances with the surgeon. I can't have you make a mistake that might cost the earl his leg."

Bodger! That horrible surgeon had caused the loss of more lives than he'd saved. In any case, she still wasn't certain that the earl *had* been responsible for Father's arrest. If Lord Falkham died because of her reticence and proved to be blameless, she could never live with herself.

She steadied her nerve. "If you let Bodger cut on him, he'll be more fit for the grave than anything else. With me, he at least has a chance of survival."

Her calm voice seemed to settle William's mind. "Come on, then." He strode on. "We're wasting precious time."

In moments, they were entering Falkham House. She walked through the familiar rooms, her throat tight and raw with the pain of memory. The long hall on the second floor had been refurbished, but that was all she could observe before several booming curses rent the silence.

She raced into the master bedroom from which the sound came, only to be greeted by a sight that filled her with horror. The earl sat against the headboard of his bed with his legs stretched out in front of him and his face contorted in pain as a servant poured something onto his leg. Nearby, a kettle hung in the fireplace, and she could smell boiling oil.

She forgot the crimes she attributed to Lord Falkham, forgot the danger she risked by helping him. All she could see was a bumbling idiot using an outmoded and needlessly painful method of cleansing the wound.

"If another drop of that hits his skin," she threatened as she snatched the cup away from the old man, "I'll boil *you* in that kettle!"

"But we got to burn the poison away," the servant protested, visibly recoiling from the masked figure in black who dashed the cup to the floor.

"Out, out, before you murder him!" She pushed futilely at the stubborn old fool, sickened by the smell of scorched flesh.

"Listen to the woman," Lord Falkham ground out. "For God's sake, Will, get him out of here!"

William murmured something to the old man, and the servant left, grumbling as he went.

"I hope you haven't come to torture me more," the earl growled. "The sword wound hurts less than the old man's ministrations."

"I can well believe it." One look at his red and swollen skin made her sick. She couldn't wish such pain on even her worst enemy.

Instantly she drew an ointment from her pouch and smoothed it over the burn. He grimaced.

"Forgive me, my lord, but this should make it feel better shortly."

She turned her attention to his wound. Someone had removed his breeches, and a sheet had been draped over his groin and left leg, leaving only his right thigh exposed. An ugly laceration gaped open close to where his leg joined his hip.

"The wound is serious," she said, trying to keep her voice emotionless. He didn't need her falling apart just now. "But at least the sword went cleanly through. It doesn't seem to have severed the muscle, so it should heal well enough. Just be grateful the men didn't carry pistols."

"One of them did," Lord Falkham said through clenched teeth. "But he was a poor shot, so I was able to wrest it from him. Unfortunately, he was a better swordsman than I expected."

William spoke behind her. "And you were a better one than he expected, eh, m'lord?"

Lord Falkham's clear gray eyes clouded. "I suppose I was."

Marianne tried to ignore the ripple of horror that washed over her. After all, Mr. Tibbett had said that the earl had served as a soldier abroad. And he'd had the right to defend himself against attack.

Moving to the basin of water someone had placed nearby, she wet a clean linen cloth and began to wash the wound. The earl's tight-lipped, rigid stance told her that every touch caused him pain, but she couldn't help that. Father had believed that cleaning a wound helped it heal, so clean it she would, scrubbing away the dried blood and bits of fabric that clogged it.

"Do highwaymen often ride the roads hereabouts these days?" William asked her while watching her work.

"This is the first I've heard of," she said, concentrating on her task.

"Those were no highwaymen," the earl bit out.

William glanced at his master. "You think Tearle's behind it?"

"Of course. Aside from the fact that he hates that I've regained the manor—and the title—he fears what I could do to him if it weren't for . . ."

He trailed off to glance at her veiled face, for she'd unconsciously stopped her movements to listen.

Hastily she returned to cleansing the wound. "Have you told the constable of the attack?"

"No reason," William replied. "His lordship left both men lying in the glade with their bellies open."

"That's enough, Will!" Lord Falkham said sharply. She didn't miss the meaningful glance he gave his servant. "There's no need for the young woman to hear about such matters."

"I agree." Her stomach churned at the image William's words evoked, soldier or no soldier. "I abhor killing."

"Would you have preferred I let them murder me instead?" Lord Falkham snapped.

"Of course not, but no man's death should ever be discussed casually."

A glint of something that looked like a conscience flickered in his eyes. "I'm afraid Will and I have become far too accustomed to killing in the past few years. We saw many battles with the Duke of York."

"I can tell." Thin scars marred his skin everywhere. The Duke of York's men had served the French and then the Spanish armies, winning honor and fame. Hard to believe that the earl had been one of those.

But it did explain why he scarcely flinched as she cleansed his wound, why he seemed deadened to the outrage of being attacked near his own home. For a man as young as he appeared, he must have seen a great deal of death.

And how much of that death had he caused? She shuddered to think of the men he must have killed, even if it had been in battle.

She'd finally washed away enough blood to see what she had to work with. Thank heaven the wound looked better already. With some stitching and a healing poultice, his lordship would be moving about in a few days.

Her gaze trailed idly up his hairy thigh, and with a sudden absurd horror she realized how naked he was. A blush heated her face beneath her mask. She had worked beside Father when he'd toiled over many naked men, but this was no dirty and coarse soldier.

Even with his wound, he emanated strength, reminding her of a leashed lightning bolt, waiting to destroy anything that crossed him. Though pale from loss of blood, his thigh was thickly muscled. Her gaze moved farther up to where the sheet just missed covering the patch of hair that surrounded his—

Good Lord, what was she doing, gawking at him? Worse yet, he'd noticed, for his gaze now seemed to see right through to her embarrassing thoughts.

"Well?" he asked dryly. "Can you save it?"

For half a second, she thought he referred to something other than his leg. Then she chided herself. She was being a complete dolt about his nakedness. "Yes, but I'll need your man to fetch some things from the apothecary's shop."

"What if he's still not there?" William asked.

"The servant can give you what I need—a jar of wolfsbane ointment. And have the servant send a message to my aunt that I'll be late."

"If you just tell me where you live," William said, "I'll deliver the message myself."

"No!"

When both men shot her searching glances, she forced some nonchalance into her voice. "No need for you to trouble yourself. Just send the message. And don't . . . ah . . . mention whom I'm tending. Simply tell the servant to say I'll return soon. Aunt Tamara's accustomed to my late hours, so she'll understand."

After William left, Marianne released a sigh. Aunt Tamara would be alarmed over this. She'd repeatedly stressed the importance of Marianne's remaining unnoticed by the new earl.

"Why shouldn't Will mention that you're tending me?" Lord Falkham asked, his gray eyes keen with interest.

Trying to hide her agitation, Marianne withdrew a heavy needle and some thick black thread from her leather pouch. "Begging your pardon, my lord, but my aunt doesn't trust men of rank." That was partly true, for Father had been the only nobleman Aunt Tamara could ever stomach.

Lord Falkham surprised her by laughing. "She finds her gypsy kinsmen more trustworthy?"

"Than some of your kind, yes," Marianne retorted. "You should be able to understand that, given your anger toward your uncle."

He sobered. "Excellent point. But not all men of rank are like my uncle."

True. Mother had once hinted that a man of rank had broken Aunt Tamara's heart, which was why she scorned nobles, but it was more than that. Her aunt considered most lords to be weak, spineless fops.

Marianne glanced at Lord Falkham, whose stoic expression belied the pain he must be feeling. He certainly defied those prejudices. More was the pity, since it made her situation all the more precarious. Her plan to stay out of harm's way was rapidly falling apart.

At least he was wounded, so he couldn't come after her if she should need to flee. Yet she had the distinct impression that if he wanted to follow her, he would, wound or no.

She looked at the needle she'd just threaded. Well, after she was done here, he'd never wish to be within a mile of her again anyway. And that was for the best.

To remind herself of all that stood between them, she glanced around the room he'd appropriated for himself, which had once belonged to her parents. Her father's well-loved chairs and writing table had been replaced with new walnut furniture lacking any warmth. The earl's bloodied sword lay on the rich carpet, staining it.

He was a ruthless killer, and no doubt deserved the pain she was about to inflict on him. Yet the blood darkening the sheets beneath his leg reminded her that he was human, too, and merited her mercy.

Best get the distasteful task over with, she told herself, lifting the needle.

"I'm going to sew the wound closed so it heals better," she told him as she approached the bed. "It will hurt, I'm afraid."

"It can't hurt more than it already does. But I do hope you're skilled with a needle. I don't want my leg looking like a patched doublet come the morrow."

"Ah, but we gypsies are famed for our needlework," she said lightly to draw his attention from her actions as she eased the needle through his flesh.

"You're no gypsy," he gritted out through his pain.

His words threw her into such confusion that she stuck him.

"Damn it, woman, I'm not a pincushion!"

"Forgive me, my lord." She forced herself to remain calm. "Why do you say I'm no gypsy?"

"You speak too well, for one thing. Your aunt has a gypsy accent, but your voice is refined. Very English."

This man was far too perceptive for her peace of mind. Remembering what her aunt had once said—that the best lie was the one closest to the truth—she said, "My father was a man of rank. Only my mother was a gypsy."

The earl's eyes narrowed. "You're a nobleman's bastard? That would explain your speech, but only if you'd been raised in his household. Are you saying your father claimed you?"

She continued her stitching. "I lived in his house until his death." And she fervently wished the part about his death were no lie. "His family wouldn't accept me after that, so I went to my aunt. She has cared for me ever since."

When a flicker of sympathy crossed his face, she fought a stab of guilt. She was protecting her aunt's and her own lives. Under the circumstances, surely a small lie could be forgiven her.

"And how many years might that be? How old are you?"

"Twenty," she said. "I've been with my aunt a long time." It was true, sort of. They'd always been close.

"You've had a hard life for one so young," he said quietly.

For a moment, his words confused her. Granted, she had no parents, but she had someone to care for her. Then she remembered that he thought her disfigured by smallpox. Suddenly, she resented his misplaced pity.

"On the contrary, I've been very happy." She drew the needle through his skin. "Life is like an overgrown garden. You can spend your time cursing the weeds, or you can work to pull them out. In either case, the flowers are what matter."

Cynicism turned the lines of his mouth rigid. "Some gardens are too overgrown to save. 'Tis better to level those to the ground."

She dropped her gaze to his leg, surprised by his bitterness. "Perhaps. But then you must be sure to plant a new garden."

He shook his head. "You will have your flowers, I see."

"I suppose I sound too cheery to a man just wounded by highwaymen."

"Or too naive."

That stung. "What would you know of hardship, my lord?" she bit out as she finished stitching the wound. "Have you ever suffered in childbirth or watched children starve? You've seen death in battle, 'tis true, but you no doubt gloried in the honor of it."

She thought of the poor men and women her parents had treated. "I've seen death come to those who didn't deserve it, who only died because they were born to the wrong families. Your kind never sees that suffering. No, your kind only causes it."

His eyes darkened. "Your aunt isn't the only one who dislikes noblemen."

She turned away, confused by her own reaction. Why had she responded with such venom? She didn't dislike the nobility—her father was a baronet.

Yet she regarded the peerage differently from some. Mother had opened her eyes to the hardships of the common people, had taught her to treat them as she'd treat anyone else. That's why Father had been reluctant to be at court. Although his sympathies had always been with the Royalists, he'd been almost content under Cromwell. He'd begun to think it might not be so terrible to have a government ruled by all the people, not just a few.

Until Cromwell had become a tyrant. And now the court had returned—the idle noblemen led by a debauched king. The earl might seem different, but at heart he was like all the other Cavaliers. He saw the world through jaundiced eyes.

With angry motions, she ripped a sheet into strips for bandages, still caught up in her feelings of resentment toward him and all his ilk.

"Why do I get the feeling you wish it were me you were ripping into little bits?" he asked after a moment.

"Don't be absurd, my lord. I merely need something to bind your leg."

"You've enough bandages there to bind both legs, if I'm not mistaken."

She stopped to look down at the great pile of linen she'd torn. "I suppose I have," she said ruefully.

"Perhaps you should wound me in my other leg," he drawled. "You seem more than eager to do so."

How he could joke when his wound must hurt him terribly, she couldn't imagine. Perhaps it distracted him from the pain.

She matched his light tone. "Then I could try your old servant's remedy on the other leg, too."

"Not unless you use those bandages to tie me to the bed," he said acidly. "I shall tell him upon pain of death that he is not to try his skill at doctoring on any tenant of mine."

Just as she wondered why the man she'd just been making into a villain should concern himself with his tenants, William returned with the ointment.

"That aunt of yours was a mite troublesome," he said as he handed it to her.

That stilled Marianne's heart. "My aunt? How did you come across *her*?"

"She was at the apothecary's, carping to that poor

servant about her missing niece. I suppose she hoped to find you there."

Releasing a pent-up breath, Marianne spread the salve liberally over the earl's sewn wound.

"She gave me a tongue-lashing, she did," William went on. "Said you weren't the town's personal servant and you needed rest like everyone else. Then she scolded me for not telling her where you were. I told her you were safe. And she said I was to remember you're an innocent and not to lay a finger on you."

That last statement seemed to pique the earl's interest, for his gaze shot to Marianne's mask.

"My aunt is overly cautious." She wrapped a bandage around the earl's thigh. "Pay her no mind."

"'Tis hard to ignore a woman as sharp-tongued as your aunt." William settled himself in a chair beside the earl's bed. "Especially one so pretty."

"I thought you liked your women blond and buxom?" Lord Falkham quipped.

Marianne glared at them both. "If you gentlemen would stop discussing my aunt as if she were a tavern wench, I could instruct William on how to care for the wound."

A silence fell on the room.

"Why won't you be returning to change the dressing?" Lord Falkham asked, his face formidably dark.

Fear whispered through her. "I'm certain your servant can change your bandages quite well on his own."

The earl caught her hand as she finished tying off the bandage. "I'd rather you did it yourself."

When she tried to pull free, his hold tightened.

"Please, my lord," she said, her heart pounding, "there's no need for it. I've others to tend."

"William is unfamiliar with doctoring and might worsen the wound." But he said the words almost as an afterthought, for he'd taken a sudden keen interest in her hand.

"I'm certain he can follow my instructions."

"Perhaps." The earl snatched her other hand, which he studied several moments. Her pulse raced under the firm pad of his thumb.

At last he pinned her with a suspicious gaze. "Tell me, Mina, how did your hands escape being scarred by the pox?"

Her blood ran cold. "I don't know," she muttered, uncertain of what answer would lessen his suspicions.

"Isn't it odd your face was so badly scarred that you wear a mask, yet your hands are smooth-skinned as a babe's?" Without waiting for an answer, he slid up her sleeve to bare her lower arm. His eyes narrowed as he took in her healthy, golden skin. "You're the healer. Tell me if the pox is generally so virulent in one spot of the body and so mild in another."

"It can happen." A growing anger eclipsed her fear. How could he treat with such callousness a woman who claimed to be shy about her appearance?

"What do you think, William?" the earl asked as he resisted her attempts to yank her arm free. "Have you ever known the pox to be so discriminating?"

"Release me at once, my lord!"

He steadied a hard gaze on her. "What if I should wish to explore this strange phenomenon further?"

"Then you'll merely confirm what I thought all along—that although you have the trappings of a gentleman, you're as wicked as the rest of the king's courtiers!"

That only seemed to heighten his interest. "And what would a gypsy know of the king's courtiers?"

She cursed her slip of the tongue. "I've heard the stories like everyone else. How the court sports itself with illicit pleasures. How rogues like you climb out of one loose woman's bed only to climb into another's. Are you so jaded with beauties that you must now trouble a poor pockmarked maiden before she's scarcely finished tending your wounds?"

She wasn't certain which of her words did it, but something she said had the desired effect. Abruptly he dropped her hand, his mouth tightening into a thin line. "Ah, yes, my wounds," he said flatly. He glanced down at the neatly bound leg. "You tended them well. I had no right to embarrass you."

Her urge to box his ears only slightly diminished. "'Tis already forgot," she said with a dismissive gesture, eager to flee before he began questioning her again.

"Not by me. And I won't let your skill go unrewarded. Will, fetch my purse."

"No, please don't!" she protested, afraid to be left alone again with the earl.

William paused in the doorway, awaiting his master's command.

Lord Falkham's eyebrows lifted. "You must be paid for your services. I'm familiar enough with gypsies to know they do nothing without expecting a reward."

She ignored the insult, too anxious to get away before he questioned her scars further. "I don't take money for doctoring."

He scowled. "Surely your aunt would expect payment. I'll speak with—"

"No!"

His gaze turned curious.

She was handling this badly, but she couldn't have him talking to Aunt Tamara. "She would say the same. The healing I do is for my own satisfaction. My aunt supports us with her needlework—we need nothing more. Please, my lord, don't concern yourself with us."

His intent gaze curled apprehension around her heart. She'd erred. She should have taken the gold and been done with it even if it had meant being alone with him a few minutes. But how could she have guessed he'd be so insistent?

"As you wish," he finally said.

A sigh of relief escaped her. "Thank you. Now, my lord, I must go before my aunt becomes overly concerned."

"But you'll return to change the dressing?"

"If need be," she said evasively.

It wasn't really a lie. If he needed her, she *would* return. But he wouldn't need her. He was strong and healthy, and the wound would heal well. So when

William eventually asked about her at Mr. Tibbett's, the apothecary would tell him how to change the dressing, and the servant would be well able to take care of it himself.

Then Marianne wouldn't have to encounter the frightening earl ever again.

Chapter Three

Where guilt is, rage and courage doth abound.
—Ben Jonson, *Sejanus, His Fall*

Bess Tearle watched warily as her husband paced her bedchamber. He wore his now graying hair as all the Roundheads did, cut in a line even with his chin. But only his hair was Roundhead. From the tip of his expensive hat to his imported French stockings, he was as driven by money and a craving for advancement as the Royalists he despised. He'd been able to obtain whatever he'd wanted, for who would deny a man of his position and wealth anything?

But recently someone must have thwarted him, for these days he wore a permanent frown. Time to find out what troubled him. If she left him to brood, he would eventually take his anger out on her.

"Why haven't we moved to Falkham House?" she ventured to ask, sure that her beloved childhood home had something to do with his foul mood. "You said it was ours now, but we've been in the country for weeks and you've not made the first effort to have our belongings packed up and transported."

He grimaced. "You might as well know, since you'll learn of it eventually. I couldn't secure Falkham House as expected. 'Tis someone else's now."

That was what she'd feared. Five months pregnant, she'd been looking forward to raising her first babe there. "Who has it?"

"Your damned nephew."

Shock coursed through her. Surely he didn't mean . . . It wasn't possible! "I don't understand. I-I thought Garett died with Richard and Louise."

Pitney strode to the bedside where she sat. "It seems he escaped being killed when the army murdered your precious brother. The boy we believed was him was actually some servant. Garett made his way to Worcester and joined the king there. When Charles fled, the lad went with him. So you see, your nephew has been living in exile until recently. And now that he's returned, he's taken possession of Falkham House."

As Pitney's words sank in, hope sprang to life in her heart. "You're sure that it's him? You've seen him?"

"I didn't have to see him. The king himself is his champion now."

"But the king has been in England for over a year. Why did he say nothing about Garett being alive until now?"

Pitney turned his gaze from her. "I don't know."

She could tell from his behavior that he did know. There was more here than met the eye. "Well, at least he lives. The dear boy lives. Thank you, God, for that."

"Yes, you *would* be happy about it. Don't you care that he's stolen back the title and the estate?"

"They were always his," she said, emboldened by the knowledge that Garett was alive. She'd grown so accustomed to thinking herself bereft of family that the very fact of his existence gave her courage. "He's the rightful owner."

"Don't you understand? You are no longer a countess, and I am no longer an earl. We are *nothing* anymore." His gaze flicked down to her belly. "And our son will only inherit the title if Garett never marries or bears a son of his own. There's little chance of that, I would wager."

She looked up at the face so contorted with envy, and wished she could tell him that her son was not *his*. But she dared not. "I never cared about the title. You know that."

"But you cared about Falkham House. You told me I should get it back at all costs once I was able to. Why do you think I fought so hard to purchase it from those damned Winchilseas?"

"You shouldn't have sold it to him in the first place!" she snapped, then moderated her tone when she saw his frown. "I wanted it to belong to my family again. It matters not to me if Garett owns it as long as it belongs to a Lockwood."

"A Lockwood!" he spat. "Your damned family has caused me more grief than a hundred Royalists. Thanks to your whoreson nephew, I've lost everything!" His eyes narrowed on her. "I know what you're thinking— you're making plans to throw your lot in with him. Well, you'd best thrust that idea from your mind, madam, for it won't serve. He wants nothing to do with either of us. He'd as soon kill you as look at you."

The cold hand of fear seized her heart. "Why? He can't blame me for inheriting what he wasn't here to claim. We didn't even know he lived!"

A flash of something dark in Pitney's eyes gave her pause, especially when he turned away with a coarse oath.

"Oh, dear Lord, you *knew*? You knew he lived, and you kept it from me? From everyone?" The horror of it would surely rip her asunder. Her own nephew abandoned willfully, and she'd known none of it.

"I didn't know it at first," he said coolly. "But then letters came from Garett in France, asking me to protect his lands for him until he could return."

"You received *letters* from him? Why didn't you tell me?"

"And have you whining around the house, trying to bring him back? Cromwell himself wanted me . . . *me* . . . for his minister. But that was because of my title—he needed nobility on his side to bring the other nobles around to his cause. With that Royalist brat here I would have lost my chance, 'tis certain."

"So you left him there, alone," she said, appalled. "How did you explain to him that you didn't want him around to spoil your plans?"

Pitney gaped at her. "Explain? You don't think I told him anything, do you? I ignored his letters."

"Oh, no, surely not," she whispered.

"Don't be a silly fool. No one thought the king would

ever come back. Why should I have ruined my life for *Garett*? I'd thought for certain he'd starve in France with the other exiles if I waited long enough. After a time had passed, I didn't hear from him. I assumed he was dead." His expression hardened. "I should have known your beloved nephew would insinuate himself into the right circles so he could return to England and take it all back. I never thought the Royalists would return, never!"

"At least you were able to assuage Garett's temper by returning the house to him after you bought it from Sir Henry."

"I didn't get the chance to buy it from Sir Henry. Your nephew returned before I could manage it."

"But you said that Sir Henry—"

"I know what I *said,* damn it! Matters proved more complicated than I planned." His voice deepened. "I thought that at last the world was mine. The title, the lands—I had it all. Then that . . . that *whelp* returns, and suddenly, I have nothing."

So did she. Oh, she didn't care about the title or the prestige. But Garett and Falkham House were lost to her now. How he must have suffered with his parents dead and no one to help him!

She thought of him as he'd been at ten, shortly before her marriage. He'd been a quick-witted boy, with a confident air that had resembled her dear brother's. She'd always thought him a strong child who'd hidden his strength beneath his quips.

What might his years of abandonment have done to him? How had he survived? Despite what was more commonly believed by those who'd listened to Cromwell's tales, she'd heard that the exiles had barely kept food on the table during those years. Pitney had once boasted that even the king was destitute. So what must Garett have endured as a young exile with no money and no parents?

The weight of it all made her ill. Garett was certain to blame her as well as Pitney. How could he ever forgive her for his abandonment?

Unless . . .

Even at fourteen, Garett had known her husband well enough to see his ruthlessness. Garett would believe her when she told him she hadn't known that he lived. He would help her escape her wretched marriage. At last she could leave Pitney!

Pitney caught sight of her softened expression and closed his hands in her dark hair, twisting her head around so she was forced to stare up into his face.

"I know what you're thinking. You'd best forget going to your nephew, my dear, deceitful wife, for I'd kill you both if you deserted me. You know I could do it. And would, if matters came to such a pass."

"You wouldn't dare," she whispered, ignoring the aching in her head from where he held her hair.

"Wouldn't I?" He jerked her head back so hard that she cried out. His free hand loosed the buttons at her neck, then slipped inside to clasp her breast. Roughly he fondled it, while she fought down the bile that rose in her throat. "You belong to me, my noble wife. So if you think to take refuge with your nephew, remember I hold your life in my hands." He slid his hand down to cover the curve of her belly. "Leave me, and I will take the child from you, I swear."

A sob caught in Bess's throat. He could do it, too. Mothers had no rights when it came to children. And she couldn't give up her babe after fourteen years of trying to conceive.

She wished she could taunt him with the truth—that he'd failed at siring a child, that the father was a handsome merchant he dealt with. But she dared not. He would kill her *and* her babe.

Then he would ruin her merchant lover, the man who'd shown her the only kindness she'd seen in a long while. She hadn't told her lover about the child, for she'd known what Pitney would do if she ever fled to the merchant.

"I see that you understand me," Pitney said coldly. "Go to Garett, and I'll see him dead. And then you will have no choice but to return to me, or else leave the babe without a mother."

Her hands shook. He had her trapped. She didn't know how she could bear it, staying with him any longer. Yet bear it she must. She couldn't risk having her child raised by Pitney alone.

At her silence, his eyes sharpened with desire. "Do you promise to be obedient, then, wife?" he asked, his hand still groping inside her clothing.

She lifted her head and, with all the quiet dignity she could muster, nodded.

He released her, but only to loosen his petticoat

breeches so they fell to the floor. She could see him thickening underneath his long shirt, and she shuddered.

Forcing her off the bed and onto her knees, he pressed her head forward. "Let's see just how obedient you shall be, wife."

"Please, Pitney," she whispered as loathing filled her. How had she ever been such a fool as to marry him, thinking him daring and strong? She should have listened to Richard when her brother had said Pitney wasn't to be trusted. But she'd been blinded by Pitney's mature age, smooth words, and good looks.

She thought now of what he was asking her to do and hesitated, as she'd hesitated so many times before.

"Remember your duty, wife," he said, pulling her head toward his groin.

Her heart and mind detested him, but it mattered not, for he was stronger than she. So she proved she was obedient.

Marianne had sworn never to return to Falkham House, yet here she was with Aunt Tamara five days later, standing in the magnificent hall that stretched the length of its second floor.

She had no choice—Mr. Tibbett had said the earl was very ill. She had to determine why her stitching and poulticing hadn't worked. Despite her wariness of the man, the thought of his strong body wracked with fever troubled her.

Her aunt was regarding everything around them with unveiled suspicion. Marianne couldn't blame her. The earl had transformed the hall into a gallery of rich, dark colors and disturbing, violent images. Its paneled walls looked wholly different from when Father had owned it.

There were no quiet paintings of shepherds and sedate portraits of Winchilsea ancestors. Instead, ancient medieval tapestries depicting battles now lined the walls. Fierce men and women who all bore a marked resemblance to the earl stared out at her.

Unusual weaponry hung along one section: crossed Spanish rapiers, wicked-looking sabers, and even a jeweled scimitar. What kind of man hung such frightening accoutrements of battle on his walls?

The kind of man who wanted to remind all who entered that he wasn't to be trifled with. The earl was a hardened soldier, accustomed to blood and scarred from his many wounds.

So why hadn't he survived his sword wound better? She'd cleaned it well and sewn it shut as she'd seen Father do. The poultice she'd used had worked on weaker men many a time. His wound shouldn't have festered or caused him to have a fever.

"This is mad," Aunt Tamara muttered as they waited for William to be informed of their arrival. "I can't believe you came here again."

"William told Mr. Tibbett that the earl is very near death."

"As if I'd trust anything that rascal says." Her aunt snorted. "It's his fault you went near the earl in the first place. If not for your mask, who knows what might have happened?"

Marianne dropped her gaze, remembering his lordship's fingers encircling her wrists. She hadn't told her aunt how close she'd come to discovery that night. Could William's claim that the earl lay ill be just a trap?

The manor did seem very lively for the home of a dying man. The tuneless whistle of a footman in a distant room and the chatter of passing servant girls gave her pause. Why weren't they more concerned about their master's condition?

Perhaps they didn't know. William might be keeping it quiet to prevent them from being alarmed.

In any case, she couldn't risk ignoring the possibility that the earl *was* ill.

"Think of what could happen if the earl dies after I treated him," she pointed out. "The townspeople won't dare protect me then. And as soon as the soldiers discover that Mina and Miss Winchilsea are one and the same, I'll be arrested. Don't you see? I must help him, or I'll pay for it with my life."

Aunt Tamara's dark eyes glittered. "We could be far away by nightfall."

"I won't abandon a man to a sure death. Besides, even if we escaped, this time they'd hunt me until they found me. They only left me alone before because of your trick."

Her aunt stiffened. "Well, at least this time I'm here to protect you from that jackanapes William and his fearsome master."

An image leapt into her mind of Aunt Tamara wresting a sword from the wall to defend her niece's honor. She stifled a smile.

William entered the hall and strode toward them. Odd, but he looked much handsomer than she'd remembered. He lacked his master's intimidating build, but his wiry frame seemed imbued with a quiet determination she could respect.

"So you've come," he said in hushed tones as he approached.

His eyes wouldn't meet hers, which instantly alarmed her. "Is he dead?"

He blinked. "Oh . . . oh, no, he's well . . . I mean, he's feverish. At the moment, he's resting some, but . . ."

His voice trailed off as he noticed Aunt Tamara. "What are *you* doing here?"

"I've come to help my niece, of course."

The two stared at each other with a strange tension. The gleam that leapt into William's eyes confused Marianne until she remembered he'd met Aunt Tamara at the apothecary's shop the night the earl had been wounded.

William took Marianne's arm and pressed her forward. "Please go on to my master's chambers. You know where they are." As Aunt Tamara, too, moved forward, he stayed her with one hand. "You remain here."

Marianne halted. "Why can't she accompany me?"

"Yes, why can't I?" Aunt Tamara snapped. "Where she goes, I go, sirrah. Let me pass if you want her near your master."

William looked from one to the other. "You shan't see him," he told Aunt Tamara, stepping between her and Marianne. "Bad enough your niece might have killed him. Together you could murder him for certain. No, I'll keep you here to ensure that the girl doesn't harm him."

"Why, you barbarous rogue, you can't speak about my niece that way!"

But Marianne was more alarmed by the thought that he suspected her. "It's all right, Aunt Tamara," she called back as she headed for the master's chambers. "Remain here. What can a sick man do to me anyway?"

With her aunt's protests ringing in her ears, Marianne hurried through the vaulted passageways. Her heart pounding with dread, she pushed open the massive oak door to his bedchamber and slipped inside.

Then she froze. The bed was empty. Had they carried the earl elsewhere? She started to back out, then heard the door close behind her. Whirling around, she came face-to-face with the Earl of Falkham.

Dressed simply in an unbuttoned waistcoat, white holland shirt, and blue-black breeches, he leaned with casual ease against the door. His weight rested on his good leg, while his wounded one was bent to take the pressure off of it. His loose-fitting breeches hid the bandage around his thigh so well, however, that no one except Marianne would have guessed he was hurt. He didn't seem to be straining to hold himself up. Nor did a trace of fever flush his skin.

In short, he was the very picture of health.

"So good of you to come." His gray gaze locked on her mask, as if he could see what lay beneath. Then a smile crept over his finely chiseled features.

Relief that she was no longer in danger of having killed an earl was rapidly driven out by fiery rage. "So my aunt was right. Your 'summons' was a trick. How dare you make me fear I'd nearly killed you when all the time you were well?"

His smile broadened. "Were you worried about me?"

"I was worried your man might have me hauled off to the gaol for killing his master. What possible reason could you have for spreading such a lie? Was suffering a gypsy's touch so distasteful to you?"

He came away from the door, wincing when his weight came down on his wounded leg. "In truth, I'd thought to thank you," he said brittlely.

"By ruining my reputation . . . by spreading malicious lies and rumors so the townspeople would avoid me." He was as bad as his uncle. "What manner of thanks is that?"

His eyes darkened as he took a step toward her. "Will tried to find you, but no one seemed to know where you lived, even Mr. Tibbett. I could think of no other way to bring you here so I could express my gratitude. Tell the truth—has anyone in Lydgate really accused you of anything because of my subterfuge?"

"Not yet, but gypsies are often held suspect in this place, and your 'subterfuge' hasn't helped matters."

He frowned, reminding her of a painting she'd seen once of a vengeful devil scowling at the creator. With a shudder, she gathered her cloak more closely about her. It was dangerous to be here alone with him.

He stepped closer, still blocking her path to the door. "I apologize for any inconvenience my 'trick' may have caused. But can you blame me for wanting to thank the woman who saved my leg, for wanting to offer her, yet again, some recompense?" When she remained silent, his eyes warmed. "If you wish, you may add my latest . . . ah . . . thoughtless act to the debt I already owe you. It's a debt I'm more than eager to pay."

His words mollified her little. Her heart still beat frantically from the terror she'd felt when she'd feared being blamed for his fever. But now that her anger had cooled, her sense of caution had returned. This was no time to castigate an earl who had the power to see her arrested. She had to keep her wits about her.

"You may consider the debt paid," she said stiffly. "Seeing that you are well and that my remedies eased your pain is enough reward for me. I'd best go now, before my aunt begins to worry."

She started to move around him toward the door, but he caught her by the arm. "You can't go without allowing me to repay my debt in full."

He stood so close that she could see the spark of interest in his eyes. The attention he gave her mask sent alarm whirling through her body.

"Please unhand me, my lord," she said quietly.

He did as she asked but made no move to let her pass.

"What I did, I'd do for anyone," she went on. How she wished she'd listened to her aunt and had stayed away from Falkham House. "I've already refused your gold, so nothing else remains to be said."

"But I've something better to offer than mere coin. There's a London physician named Milburn, with a miraculous treatment for smallpox scars. He claims he can wipe them away so the skin is as soft and smooth as a babe's. I'll send you to him. 'Tis the least I can do for the woman who saved my leg, possibly my life."

She stared at him. Oh, Lord, her "horrible scars." Perhaps Aunt Tamara's explanation for her mask hadn't been so brilliant after all.

And why would he offer this? She had heard of Milburn. Her father had denounced the man as a charlatan, but some claimed to be helped by him. Milburn was most famous for treating the wealthy and always extracted large sums from his patients. Could Lord Falkham really intend to spend a fortune on Milburn's "treatment" for a mere gypsy?

She peered at him through her mask, noting how his eyes roved to her hands and then back to the silk covering her face. Could his offer simply be a trick to find out what lay beneath her disguise? Somehow she would have to refuse it without rousing his suspicions.

"Thank you for the offer, but I've learned to live with my . . . er . . . unusual appearance. If this doctor failed to help me, I'd suffer far more than I have until now."

"Ah, but think what could come of it. If his treatment

works, it might enable you to find a husband who'd care for you far better than your aunt can."

It took all her will not to move away and show her wariness of him. For he looked formidable indeed in the light that streamed through the open curtains, highlighting the broad, stern forehead and the chestnut brows drawn together in a deep frown.

"I've already said I won't accept your gift, my lord." She had to escape him, curse it! "I'm pleased you've recovered fully, but I won't be forced to endure the probing of strangers for naught when I can scarce endure the sight of my hideous face myself. My scars are too deep for any mere potion to heal."

She didn't realize how she'd erred until he lifted his hand to the hood of her cloak.

"Let me see your 'hideous face' for myself before you refuse my help," he bit out, pushing back the hood and yanking the ties of her mask loose. "If what you say is true, you may leave this house without another word."

"No!" she protested, but he was already lifting away the mask . . .

Chapter Four

No beauty she doth miss
When all her robes are on;
But beauty's self she is
When all her robes are gone.
—Anonymous madrigal

Garett hadn't been certain what he'd find when he removed the gypsy girl's mask. He'd half expected the scarred maiden she professed to be.

But the sight that now greeted him stunned him. Two warm hazel eyes widened in alarm in a face as arresting as it was unblemished. Not only had she no scars but her skin was a light golden color—not the dark olive of a gypsy, yet not the pale cream of a sheltered lady, either.

As his gaze roamed her delicate-boned face, her peach-tinged lips parted in shock. He fixed automatically on the sweet mouth, so finely drawn. He could well believe her father had been nobility. Yet he glimpsed in the stubborn set of her chin and the wild glint in her eyes that she didn't always follow a lady's rules.

Hers was a face designed by nature to intrigue, entice . . . tempt. With him it succeeded.

In the past few years, he'd thought only of his revenge and his return to England. Except for the occasional doxy for a night's pleasure, women hadn't had a place in that. But for the first time, he wanted more than only a night with a woman. Her soft words about gardens and flowers had troubled his thoughts far too much during his recovery.

He cursed his wayward thoughts. This unmasking was not about that. Yet he couldn't seem to stop staring at her.

"Are you quite done gawking at me, my lord?" she bit out.

"No," he said with perfect honesty. He turned her to face the sunlight that streamed through the multipaned window.

"You have no right . . ." she whispered as he pushed the hood completely off her head, loosing her lustrous hair from its knot and allowing it to spill free.

He caught his breath as the sun lit her face and tipped her tresses with antique gold. Lightly he trailed his fingers over one smooth cheek, marveling at the softness of her skin.

She blushed then, so prettily that his pulse leapt. Damn her for being so lovely. There was too much at stake for him to let himself be tempted by a fair face. "It seems you have no need for the physician Milburn after all."

She stiffened. "You never intended to bring me to him anyway. Your offer was merely intended to unmask me, wasn't it?"

He shrugged. "Not entirely. But your tale of disfigurement rang false. How else could I prove my suspicions? I assure you, if you'd been telling the truth and accepted my offer, I would have brought you to Milburn."

After digesting that a moment, she glanced to the door. "Well, sir, now that you've satisfied your curiosity, I wish to leave."

Did she think he'd let her go that easily? She was hiding a great deal more than just her face.

Before he released her, he must know what. "Actually, you've merely roused my interest further. You might, for example, tell me why you wear a mask in the first place."

"I don't see how that concerns you, my lord," she said, her palpable apprehension giving him pause.

She seemed poised to flee, but he didn't intend to let her slip away this time. Not without answers. "Everything concerns me. This is my domain. I don't like having two strange gypsies roaming it, especially when one hides her face and lies about the reason. It makes me wonder what mischief she is about."

"I intend no mischief." She tilted her chin up so that the light fell half across her face. "Isn't it enough that I saved your life?"

He ignored a quick stab of remorse. He had to learn the reason for her disguise, if only to ensure she wasn't one of his uncle's minions come to spy on him. Of course, if she'd worked for his uncle, why would she have cared for his wounds so skillfully?

Yet there could be other, equally sinister reasons for her disguise. After years of dealing with lies and deceit, he knew better than to trust a stranger, no matter how lovely.

"Have you committed some crime?" he probed, his tone deliberately intimidating. "Are you hiding from soldiers or the guard?"

The fear that leapt in her eyes made him wonder if he'd hit upon the truth. Then she stiffened. "No, my lord," she said, contempt lacing her words. "I'm hiding from noblemen like you who wish to devour women like me."

Her deft answer surprised him. She wasn't easily cowed, that was certain. "What makes you think I'll devour you?"

"Aren't you holding me here against my will? Haven't you tricked me into returning to your manor? That's proof enough that you intend me harm. Because of rogues like you, Aunt Tamara thought it wise to keep my face and form hidden. It was, and still is, my only protection."

His gaze strayed over her face and then her hair, which tumbled down her back like golden wheat spilling from a sheaf. "I understand why your aunt felt the need to protect you. But why do so by hiding your face?" He chose his words carefully, hoping to provoke her into revealing more. "Wouldn't it have been better to find you a protector?"

As her eyes widened, he smiled. "I see that you take my meaning. You're young and beautiful. You could easily find someone other than a nagging aunt to shield you from the world."

Her gaze turned murderous, giving him pause. She acted as if she were a well-born lady with a reputation to protect.

"Only a thoroughly wretched scoundrel could offer such a solution!"

Wretched wasn't quite the word for what her loveliness made him feel, would make any man with eyes feel. Which might have been exactly his uncle's plan. Deliberately, he let his gaze trail over her cloaked form. "Gypsies have sought noble protection for years."

She drew herself up in affronted dignity. "And that, my lord, is why so many bastards with gypsy blood roam the countryside. Not to mention gypsies with noble blood who've been thoroughly ruined because the hope of better things was dangled before their eyes, then snatched away at the last minute!"

"Is that how you consider yourself?" he asked pointedly. "Was the hope of better things dangled before you, then snatched away? You said your father was a nobleman, and judging from your coloring, you've spoken the truth. So are you a 'thoroughly ruined' gypsy?"

She paled. "I was not speaking of myself."

"So your father's 'protection' of your mother didn't ruin you," he persisted.

"I suppose not."

"But it has left you, as I pointed out before, with only an aunt and a flimsy disguise to protect you."

"The two have been enough to deter most men," she replied uneasily, turning her face away.

He leaned forward until his lips brushed her ear. "Ah, but I stripped away your feeble defenses with little effort, didn't I?"

She smelled like lavender, which took him by surprise. It was such a ladylike scent.

It provoked him to try to learn more. "Perhaps I should have offered you my protection instead of my gold a few nights ago."

Her head snapped around and she opened her mouth to retort, but before she could, the door swung open and her aunt marched in.

"I knew it!" Tamara spat as her eyes took in the scene. "I knew it was all an unscrupulous trick!"

Behind her, Will burst in, rubbing his head, which now sported a large lump. Garett scowled at them both, annoyed at having his interesting conversation with Mina cut short.

Will cast him an apologetic glance. "I didn't expect the wench to crown me with a vase, m'lord!" He tried to pull Tamara from the room, but the gypsy woman resisted.

"Unhand her this instant!" she demanded of Garett, whose fingers still gripped Mina's arm. "How dare you touch my niece! And after what she did for you, you ungrateful lecher!"

"I merely offered her a reward, woman," Garett snapped. "She hasn't had the good sense to take it. Yet."

That seemed to give Tamara pause. She glanced at her niece's stony face, then back to the earl's mocking one. "I can well imagine what sort of 'reward' you offered. But my niece is no fool—she'd never let a man's fine form and smooth words tempt her. The only reward we'll take is in gold, for the other kind tarnishes all too quickly."

"I don't want his gold, either," Mina protested as she wrenched her arm free.

Garett studied the young woman. Why was she so adamant in her refusal to take his money? She simply wasn't what he expected a gypsy girl to be.

Her aunt, however, was clearly willing to meet expectations. "We'll take the gold," she stated, ignoring her niece. "She's earned it well enough."

"She has indeed." He motioned to Will to fetch his purse.

Mina refused to meet his gaze, her cheeks pink.

In moments, Will returned. Garett removed a healthy portion of coins and thrust them into Tamara's hand. Tamara gave him a grim smile as she shoved them into a pouch hung around her waist. When William muttered something about its being too much, Tamara silenced him with a glare.

"Are you finally satisfied, my lord?" Mina asked. "You've paid me for my efforts to save your deceitful hide. Now leave me and my aunt alone. We have no use for your kind."

"Yes, you have your mask for protection, don't you?" Garett mocked.

"Just leave us be!" Mina repeated before wheeling around and sweeping from the room. Tamara cast both men a contemptuous look, then followed her niece out, slamming the door behind her.

Garett watched them go, eyes narrowing. Mina's answers hadn't satisfied him one whit. What were she and her fierce aunt doing in Lydgate? Was the mask really meant just to protect her from unwanted advances, or did she have a more sinister reason?

She speaks of flowers and gardens and chides you for killing. That's hardly the mark of someone with a sinister character.

True, but something was going on with her and her aunt. The townspeople turned mysteriously silent whenever he asked about her, and in a town like Lydgate, people never kept their opinions to themselves.

"Two fine-looking wenches," Will muttered as he stared at the closed door. "But their tongues are a mite too sharp for a man's enjoyment, eh, m'lord?"

"Indeed," Garett replied absently.

"That Tamara has a strong arm when she's wielding a vase, but I'll wager she's soft as silk when a man's got her 'neath him."

Tamara didn't interest Garett. But Mina . . . Mina had a soft mouth too tempting for words. He'd wager it was softer than silk.

Will threw his master a sly glance. "Do you mean to leave them be like they asked?"

Garett thought of Mina's evasions, her strange tale of a noble father, and her obvious familiarity with the people of Lydgate, who mysteriously pretended not to know a thing about her.

"Not a chance."

Chapter Five

To the glass your lips incline;
And I shall see by that one kiss
The water turned to wine.
                    —Robert Herrick,
            "To the Water Nymphs Drinking
                    at the Fountain"

Dawn's light washed the Falkham House garden with sudden fire, making every dew-drenched leaf and twig twinkle magically, but Marianne spared only a moment to note its beauty. Drawing her heavy cloak more tightly about her, she slipped between the shrubs and onto the weed-choked path, her breath forming misty clouds in the cool fall air.

When she found the overgrown stretch of rows, she cast a furtive glance about her, but no one stirred in this secluded part of the estate near the apple trees. This had been Mother's special medicinal garden. Here Marianne hoped to find what she needed.

She crept forward until she came upon the scarlet berries and deep purple flowers signifying black nightshade. Thank heavens they'd survived the months of neglect. Nightshade could generally be found in fields and ditches everywhere, but this was no common stock. Father had brought the specially grown variety back from France years before. Nothing else was as effective for halting spasms and healing heart troubles, both of which were common among Lydgate's elderly.

She withdrew the small spade hidden inside her cloak, then carefully dug up three plants. She'd have to replant them in a less dangerous place now that the earl was in residence.

Packing the roots with soil, she wrapped them in the wet rags she'd brought and slid them carefully into her pouch. She ought to leave now, but where else could she find so many useful medicinal plants? Mr. Tibbett used powders and dried herbs brought from London, and he didn't always carry what she required anyway. One of the townspeople had given her a little patch of land for her garden, but it would take months for seeds to take root. She was already here. Why not take what she needed while no one was about to bother her?

With her mind made up, she crept through the garden, digging up lady's mantle and woundwort, lad's love and moonwort. Fortunately, she'd brought plenty of wet rags and pouches. Some of the plants wouldn't survive, but enough would to make the beginnings of a respectable garden.

As she worked, she couldn't help thinking of the earl who slept so close by. What kind of man was he? Ever since she'd met him, she'd kept her eyes and ears open, hoping to find proof of his role in her father's arrest.

Whenever she met his servants in Lydgate, she questioned them discreetly, but they seemed to know little, having been newly hired. His men, whom she occasionally treated for minor injuries, were loyal to a fault, praising him for his just manner and prowess in battle.

He'd killed men in those battles, of course, but he'd been a soldier, so that proved naught. Was he a villain who would betray an innocent man simply to steal his property? Heaven take her, but she wanted to know very badly. Because if he hadn't had Father arrested, her attraction to him wouldn't bother her so much.

She snorted. Attraction! She was not attracted to the scoundrel. What absurdity. She wanted nothing to do with him.

So why did she thrill to the thought of how he'd looked at her in his room? Why did she shiver when she thought of his touching her cheek so delicately? And not a shiver of fear, either. That was the worst of it. More like fascination.

Attraction.

A groan escaped her. Very well, so she *was* attracted to the rogue. A little. A very little. And only because she'd had so few dealings with men.

Though her family had used to attend the occasional ball or dinner, a mere baronet with a supposed Spanish wife could never be the toast of high society. Her family had socialized little with people of rank outside of a few close friends.

Instead Father had found friends among men of science, whose mutual interest in medicine had made them oblivious to his private situation. So Marianne had grown up surrounded by men so engrossed in the fever of learning that they'd barely noticed her. Even as she'd grown older, she'd been treated by her father's friends more as a young sister than as a possible conquest.

Indeed, her mother had worried about her daughter's prospects, but Marianne hadn't cared that she might find herself husbandless. She'd always wanted to follow in her parents' footsteps; she hadn't needed a husband for that.

And after Mother had died, there had been little time for dinners and balls. Marianne had had her hands full taking care of Father's household. Once in a while one of Father's pupils had noticed her; one had even stolen a kiss. But she'd taken none of them seriously.

Now, after years of being regarded as a mind without a body, she didn't know quite how to deal with a man who seemed to see her as a body without a mind.

No, that wasn't quite it, either, for he hadn't disparaged her wit.

But he'd stared at her with such . . . hunger. Yes, that was it—like a starved man admitted to a feast for the first time in months. Coping with that look was difficult. So was resisting it.

"Stand up very slowly if you wish to live another day," a deep voice said behind her.

Her hands froze as she recognized the rumbling timbre of that voice. It was as if her very thoughts had conjured him up.

Something sharp prodded her ribs, making her

stiffen. For heaven's sake, the man was actually holding a sword to her back!

"Stand!" he commanded.

She did so, cursing her all-encompassing black cloak, which made her look like any thief in the night. "'Tis only I, the gypsy. I mean no harm, my lord."

The sword point left her ribs. She gave a sigh of relief, but the silence behind her did nothing to lessen the pounding of her heart.

"Turn around," he said tersely, and she obeyed so quickly that she nearly tripped over her cloak.

Her eyes widened as she saw his finely hewn face, implacable in the early morning light. Underneath the gray cloak draped casually about his shoulders, his clothes were in disarray, as if he'd dressed in a great hurry, but he held his sword in readiness.

His gaze fixed on her mask, which she'd worn in case a stranger came upon her, then traveled to her cloak, stained with dirt, grass, and dew. She kept her pouches of herbs hidden under her cloak, but they made a noticeable bulge, which he seemed to fix on next.

"Remove your mask and cloak," he said, his expression unchanging.

"I will not! You know who I am!"

He lifted the sword threateningly. "Remove them!"

She considered refusing again, but he had every reason to be suspicious, for she'd been trespassing in his gardens. Letting her pouches slide to the ground, she then did as he asked.

As soon as her cloak hit the ground, she became

aware of several things at once. The air was colder than she'd realized. Her hands were smeared with dirt. And though the earl had lowered his sword, he was staring at her in a way that boded trouble.

His gaze paused only a moment to take in her cheeks pinkened by the cold and her hair tied back with ribbon. Then it slid lower to linger where her chemise of cream muslin bunched over the tops of her breasts.

A slow smile lit his lips as his eyes swept down the boned bodice of her simple chocolate-brown gown to her waist, and then to her hips. She wore few petticoats these days—there was no place for them in the wagon— so her form appeared much as nature had intended it.

"Enchanting." His gaze returned to her face. "But I felt certain you would be." Then he sheathed his sword.

It took her a second to realize he'd only made her remove her cloak so he could satisfy his lustful urge to gawk at her body, but when she did, she snatched up her cloak. "You, sir, are a lecher!" she cried as she retied it about her neck.

"And what are you, my dear? A spy? A thief?" He gestured to the pouches at her feet. "Why are you skulking about in the wee hours of the morning, alarming my cook so she rouses me to confront the intruder?"

She reddened under his scrutiny. "I merely wanted some plants." She knelt to pull an innocuous one from her bag. "You see? I want to start a garden of my own, and I thought you wouldn't mind if I took a few of the ones difficult to cultivate. You have plenty, and you obviously don't use them."

Looking skeptical, he stepped close enough to bend and examine the pouches. When he found nothing but plants, he held out his hand to help her rise, which she ignored as she stood.

That seemed to annoy him. "Would it have been too much for you to humble yourself and *ask* for the plants? Think you I would have begrudged you a few herbs?"

She met his gaze boldly. "I really don't know what you might begrudge me, my lord."

He grunted, then scanned the garden. His eyes narrowed. "How did you know where to find what you needed? You couldn't have been here more than half an hour, yet you've clearly put aside a goodly supply."

The question caught her off guard. Scrambling for an answer that might pacify him, she said, "I've been here before. The former owners allowed me to take what I wished." With that half-truth, her next words came more readily. "That's why I didn't think anything about coming here now. I'm accustomed to gathering what I need when I need it."

"Is that why you came at this hour, when you thought no one would see you? I'd say that's the habit of a thief, not a guest."

"I'm no thief," she said stoutly. "The Winchilseas never called me such. And you don't care about the garden anyway, so why quibble if I take a few plants? To you they're just weeds."

His mouth thinned as he stooped to pull the nightshade from her bag. "Belladonna is not a weed."

She willed herself to remain calm. If he recognized the plant, he had to know its properties. "I use it for poultices," she said in an even voice.

"And here I thought it was to make those entrancing eyes of yours look more mysterious."

That, too, was a property of the plant—Italian ladies used it to dilate their pupils and give them a sensuous appeal. "I've no desire to look mysterious, I assure you, my lord."

He laughed grimly. "Yes, that's why you lurk about in a cloak and mask, sneak into my garden, and steal my plants, particularly the poisonous ones." When she bristled, he added, "I won't tolerate your being in this garden without my knowledge. I have enemies—"

When he broke off, fear curled around her insides. Ah, yes, his enemies, the ones who stabbed him on the highway and made him suspicious of gypsy girls. What crimes had this man committed to make him have to watch his back so fiercely?

Lord Falkham glanced at the manor. "You knew the Winchilseas?"

She swallowed. Best tread carefully with this one. "I did."

"I know little of them," he surprised her by saying. "Tell me, what manner of man was Sir Henry?"

Her desire to paint her father truthfully warred with her common sense, which cautioned her to say as little as possible. The former won out.

"He was wonderful—kind and gentle," she said, unable to hide the pleasure she took in speaking of Father.

"He cared about everyone here, rich and poor alike. I learned a great deal about doctoring from him."

A shadow passed over Lord Falkham's face. "You seem to have known him quite well. What's more, you seem to have cared for him. Perhaps you've had more experience with protectors than I first realized."

It took her a moment to realize his meaning. "For shame! How dare you imply that Sir Henry and I . . . that we . . ." She scowled. "Only a reprobate like you would think such a thing! Why, the man was old, and he loved his wife. What would he have wanted with the likes of me?"

Her response seemed to affect him, for his mood altered. His gaze, gleaming with a familiar light, raked her body. "I can easily answer that, sweetling. A man would have to be either blind or a fool not to consider your form an enticement to all manner of pleasures."

His words put her instantly on her guard. She backed around the hedge behind her until she'd put it between them. "I'd best leave now, my lord. My aunt will worry."

He stalked her at a leisurely pace. "Let her worry. You weren't too concerned about her when you came sneaking about here in the first place." He placed himself between her and her plants, though the hedge still lay between them. "Besides, you wouldn't want to leave without taking what you came for."

"I don't need them after all," she lied.

"Nonsense. You wanted them badly enough to steal them. What can I do with them now that they're uprooted? By all means, take them."

He scooped them up and laid them on the hedge. But

before she could snatch them, he vaulted the hedge with ease, landing between her and the plants.

"You still want them, don't you?" He laid one hand on the pouches behind him.

"Yes." She backed away until she came up against an apple tree, then groaned as she realized he had her trapped.

He took full advantage of that to move closer. "Then you'll have them, but for a price." His voice lowered. "One kiss. That's all. Then you may take the plants and do as you wish with them."

The quick thrill that shot through her roused her anger. She would never even consider touching the lips of this . . . this killer. Never! "Trust a rogue to ask for such a thing. How dare you?"

With an arch of his eyebrow, he stepped nearer. "What a little princess you are, with all your indignation. Remember, you trespassed in my garden. One kiss is a small price to pay for my ignoring that."

"Since when do rogues stop with one kiss? I'm not so innocent as to let you talk me into such foolishness. My aunt has warned me often enough about noblemen like you, and I plan to take her warnings to heart."

His face darkened with a dangerous quickness that made her aware of how alone they were. The servants might be about, but she and the earl were far enough away from the manor that he might harm her without anyone noticing.

"I should remind you," he snapped, "that if I wished, I could have you thrust in the gaol."

"You would do that for a few missing herbs?" she dared to taunt him. "And because I refuse to satisfy your lust? I should have expected as much from such a varlet. Well, then, call the constable. I daresay he'd rather have me free to help his wife with her sickly newborns than locked up at your whim."

She prayed he wouldn't call her bluff. Although the constable had supported the townspeople's harboring her, the man would have no choice but to act if the earl brought her to him.

But her audacity merely seemed to surprise Lord Falkham. "You would risk being sent to the gaol to avoid giving me one kiss. You're a strange gypsy indeed."

Devil take him! Must he always remind her that she acted far differently from what her role would warrant? What would a gypsy girl do? Probably use his passion to eke out some small reward for herself.

"I merely quibble over your price. These are only plants, hardly worth a kiss. Now, if you were to offer me more of an enticement . . ."

Eyes narrowed, he closed the distance between them to press his hands on either side of her and trap her against the tree. "So the gypsy princess shows her true colors."

His eyes glittered like winter sleet as they dropped to her lips. "You're right. One taste of your sweetness would be worth more than mere herbs, but the bargaining is done. You'll satisfy my 'whim,' sweetling, if you want your plants." When she eyed him warily, he softened his tone. "Come, Mina, give me my taste."

His voice washed over her like sun-warmed water, holding forth a rich promise just as enticing. Annoyed by her reaction, she plucked an apple and thrust it at him. "If you're hungry, my lord, this will serve your needs better."

"Adam may have fallen for that trick, my little Eve," he murmured, "but I am not so foolish." He pulled her body up against him, then brought his mouth down on hers.

His lips demanded a response. She pushed at his chest, but that brought her no respite from his strength. He held her anchored against him too firmly.

But just as she was feeling panic, his mouth softened and his hands stroked down to hold her waist. Gently. Far too gently. It took her off guard.

And the kiss began in earnest. He toyed with her mouth, teased it, coaxed it. Her body began to tingle with an odd anticipation. His morning whiskers abraded her skin, but she scarcely noticed, for an unfamiliar pleasure stole through her. She curved into him, her mouth clinging to his like sugar to a pastry.

Only when he had her resting limply against him did he lift his head, his eyes a tempest of emotion. "Ah, Mina," he murmured, "you're even sweeter than I expected." He kissed her nose, her cheek, the sensitive skin beneath her ear.

"My lord, please—"

"Garett." He nuzzled her neck. "With you I am not the Earl of Falkham, sweetling, but plain Garett, who just wishes to keep tasting you."

Falkham. The word rang warning bells inside her muddled head. This was her enemy! How could she allow him to touch her so intimately?

How could she derive so much enjoyment from it?

Even as his lips moved to her shoulder, sending warmth like summer's heat throughout her body, she protested, "One kiss, you said. Only one kiss."

"And you said, 'Since when do rogues stop with one kiss?'" He brushed his open mouth over her collarbone. "As it happens, you were right."

Her aunt's warnings sprang into her mind, of gypsy women seduced and abandoned by lesser nobles than the earl. And Marianne was a lady, who should know better than to let a man seduce her.

That thought acted upon her like a bracing blast of cold air. She balled up her fists and struck his chest, surprising him as he was about to lower his head to hers again.

"Would you take an unwilling maiden?" she demanded.

The passion in his eyes died as quickly as it had been born. "'Tis no unwilling maiden who trembles in my arms."

Though her body still throbbed with the feelings he'd roused in her, she would never let him know it. "I met your price. And now you demand another?"

Her matter-of-fact tone forced a scowl to his face, but at least he released her. "You talk like a fishwife discussing her wares, but that kiss was more than payment. An honest woman would admit it."

"And an honorable man would acknowledge that the bargain was met and would torment me no more with his whims."

He raked her body with a thorough glance, and wherever his gaze lighted, her skin heated. His eyes lifted at last to her lips, which she knew were swollen and red from his kiss.

So as he watched, she deliberately wiped her mouth with the back of her hand.

He stiffened. Pivoting away, he snatched up the bags of plants and thrust them at her. "Take them and get off my land."

But when she reached for them, he closed his fingers around her wrists.

"Run back to your aunt, to your poultices and patients," he ground out. "But next time I find you lurking where you shouldn't, I won't take a mere kiss for payment. Next time the stakes will be far higher."

With that, he released her. Then he gave a mocking bow, whirled on his heels, and stalked from the garden, leaving her to stand there vainly attempting to still the frenzied beating of her heart.

Chapter Six

The jury, passing on the prisoner's life,
May in the sworn twelve have a thief or two
Guiltier than him they try.
　　　　　—Shakespeare, *Measure for Measure*

Two days had passed and still Garett couldn't banish Mina from his mind. As he rode Cerberus briskly down the road bordering his fields, he cursed himself for his obsession.

But he knew what caused it. When she'd shed her cloak, she hadn't revealed her secrets, and her secrecy plagued him. One moment he believed her a perfect innocent, and the next he wondered if she worked for his uncle.

And if she did?

Then she was dangerous. She distracted him from his purpose, and that wasn't acceptable, for he meant to revenge himself on his uncle no matter what the cost. Returning to Falkham hadn't lessened that determination one whit.

His vengeance had begun with his appearance before the House of Lords to regain his lands. Although the circumstances of his exile hadn't been revealed, his sudden return had spawned rumors, which Garett and Will had fed with truths. Those rumors were even now growing to assurances, and it wouldn't be long before society would draw the right conclusions about Tearle. As suspicion of the man's duplicity spread, his uncle would soon find it difficult to show his face in public.

Then Garett could begin tightening the noose. Already he was carefully laying the groundwork. And soon, very soon—

The sound of men shouting pierced the afternoon quiet. Jerking Cerberus about, Garett spotted tendrils of smoke curling upward. Damn it all, his fields were afire! As a scream rent the air, he spurred his stallion into a run.

Oh, God, not again. Ten years hadn't dimmed his memory of that day on the road with his parents, of Will keeping him from running out of the woods where they'd gone to relieve themselves while the soldiers—

He forced the past from his mind as he galloped up to the scorched patch of field from which smoke still rose. A curse escaped him when he saw the stranger lying motionless, his shirt and doublet drenched in blood.

The two fellows shouting at each other worked for Garett. The taller one, a villager named Ashton hired to aid in the harvest, still gripped a bloody sword, which he brandished at the tenant of the fields in question.

Garett dismounted. "Stop this madness!"

Ashton jerked about, his sword at the ready, but he

blanched and dropped his weapon when he recognized his master. "Milord, I didn't realize—"

"Tell me what happened," Garett demanded, keeping a wary eye on both men.

"This villain"—Ashton gestured to the man lying prone—"tried to set fire to the fields. And he would have succeeded, too, if I'd not stabbed him before he could do his dirty work."

Garett's tenant shook an angry fist at Ashton. "You only stabbed him after I showed up to knock the torch from his hand and out of harm's way. He weren't armed. If not for y'r foolishness, I'd have taken him prisoner, and his lordship could've questioned him. 'Twould be better to know who sent the bastard to burn us out than to have a nameless dead man to bury."

Garett surveyed the scene. The torch had rolled into a patch of green grass and had clearly burned only a few moments before sputtering out.

He then searched the prone figure of the dead man. "There's no weapon."

"How was I to know that?" Ashton said. "I did what any soldier would do."

That comment gave Garett pause. "When you came in search of work, you said you were a farmer. Now you say you are a soldier. Which is it?"

Ashton paled. "I merely meant, milord, that I sought to defend myself as any soldier would."

"So you've never been a soldier."

"Nay."

Garett's gaze flew to the bloodied sword in the man's

hand and then to the man on the ground. "You're dismissed."

Ashton gaped at Garett. "But milord, why?"

"I don't countenance liars," Garett remarked. "Farmers don't carry swords, and what need have you to hide that you were once a soldier?"

For a moment Ashton's expression changed to that of a man who'd been cornered, as if someone had ripped a mask from his face. "I wasn't certain if I should say. Soldiers don't make good farmers. But if you'll keep me on, you might find it an asset to have a soldier on your side."

Garett smiled coldly. "I might indeed. But lying soldiers I have no use for."

"Your lordship would find me loyal—"

"To whom?" Garett asked grimly. "No, 'tis best for us both if you left my employ, before your 'loyalty' jeopardizes me and mine and forces me to act."

The warning in that statement made Ashton flush, but he acknowledged Garett's dismissal with a tight nod, then whirled off toward Lydgate.

The tenant farmer stared after Ashton with contempt. "Mark my words, m'lord. That one's a true villain despite his deft talk. You won't regret the loss of him."

"The true villain was the man who sent him, and that man will pay as soon as I can prove his treachery."

A low groan came from the man on the ground. Ah, so he wasn't dead, after all. As Garett knelt beside him, the man's eyes fluttered open.

"'Tis of no use," he murmured, "no use . . . no use."

Garett lifted the man's head. "What is of no use?" he

demanded, but the man's eyes had already closed again, and he'd lapsed back into unconsciousness.

"Mayhap this one will live yet," the tenant farmer remarked. "If you can wring a confession from him, you may trap his master."

Garett nodded as he surveyed the man's body, this time with a keener eye. It was impossible to tell how bad the man's wounds were beneath all the blood he'd shed. But if the man could be saved, he might reveal what he knew in exchange for a more lenient punishment.

"I know just the one to keep him alive." Garett rose. "Make him as comfortable as you can. I'll fetch the gypsy healer."

The tenant farmer nodded his head. "Aye, Mina will bring him back if there's any life still in him. She can't bear to see anyone suffer, villain or no."

As Garett mounted his horse, he thought on the farmer's words. Mina was indeed softhearted. She might not think well of his desire to keep a knave alive for the sake of hearing the man's confession. Best not to tell her what he planned if he wished to gain her help.

He rode in a frenzy back to Falkham House and beyond it into the forest. That day in the garden, he'd followed her at a distance, determined to know where she spent her nights. Now he headed there with grim purpose. She would need convincing to go with him, but her soft heart would win out in the end.

As he reached the clearing where the gypsy wagon lay, he could see no one. Their fire had a few glowing embers, but the pot dangling from a curved iron stake above it was empty. He dismounted, intending to look around. Then he heard voices raised in argument nearby. Rounding the wagon, he found Will and Tamara squared off like a bear and a dog in a bearbaiting.

"For a gypsy wench, you have mighty high ideas!" Will shouted.

Tamara's lips were reddened and her hair mussed. "And for a gentleman's servant, you have the manners of a thief! Don't you have duties elsewhere? I don't want you here."

"Apparently," Garett interjected, startling the two combatants, "Will found it more interesting attending to you than attending to his duties. Normally I wouldn't interrupt such an edifying conversation, but I have need of both of you."

Tamara's instant defensive stance didn't hide the quick flush that crossed her face. "Have you come to join your lackey in attacking me, milord?"

"Attacking! Why, you're a fine one to—" Will muttered.

"I don't attack defenseless women," Garett answered impatiently. "At the moment I have greater concerns. Where's Mina? I have need of her services."

Tamara's eyes narrowed. "I'm sure you do, milord, but she won't lend them to you."

"Listen here, woman," he said in a low voice. "A man lies dying not two miles from here. Your niece might save him. I don't have time to waste in overcoming your objections, so either tell me where she is or I'll take you off to the constable."

Tamara glared at him. "Well, then, be quick about it, for I shan't tell you a blessed—"

"I'm here!" a voice rang out from the woods. "No need to threaten her, my lord. I'll do as you wish."

Garett turned to find Mina walking into the clearing with her usual calm assurance. Twigs and dry leaves clung to her skirts, and her dark golden hair lay wind-tossed about her shoulders. Cradled in her arms were two bundles of dry branches, as if she were some goddess of autumn.

No, as if the *god* of autumn, whoever he might be, had just tumbled her in the crisp leaves. That wayward thought sent such a powerful surge of desire through Garett that it rocked him. Even Marianne's quick frown couldn't squelch that burst of wanting.

"What do you want with us?" she demanded.

He forced himself to return to the serious matters at hand. "There's been an accident. I require your services as a healer."

Will came up beside Tamara to lay a protective arm about her shoulder.

She shrugged him off. "It seems to me, milord, that you attract 'accidents.' I'm not certain it's safe for my niece to be in your company."

Mina stared Garett down, her mutinous expression mirroring her aunt's.

"I'm inclined to agree with you," Garett said to Tamara, "but that doesn't change anything." His eyes didn't move from Mina's face. "Feel free to accompany your niece, but I still need her to come with me."

Tamara stepped forward, but Will grabbed her arm, and when she tried to wrench free, he caught her more firmly about the waist.

Mina threw down the branches. "If you'll call your dog off," she snapped, "I'll consider doing as you ask."

Garett nodded to Will, who released Tamara.

"Come, then," Garett told Mina. He walked toward his horse, but when Mina didn't follow, he pivoted to fix her with a hard stare.

She wasn't so easily intimidated. "Is this a command or a request, my lord?"

"Which will make you come freely?" he asked, a trifle impatiently.

Her eyes locked with his, a strangely endearing fierceness in their depths. "A request." She clearly didn't intend to move until they settled the point.

"Madam, would you come with me now while the man still breathes?" When she hesitated, he added, more tersely, "Please?"

She gave a regal nod. "I'll fetch my medicines." Then she pivoted and walked gracefully to the wagon.

The moment Mina was inside, Tamara strode up to Garett with eyes flashing. "If you seek to seduce her this way, you toy with the wrong maiden."

"Don't be absurd, woman. What need have I to seduce a gypsy?"

Tamara lifted an eyebrow. "Mayhap I've used the wrong word. Mayhap you have something other than seduction in mind."

"Damn it, woman, I don't—"

"We gypsies are known for our soothsaying," she broke in. "Shall I tell you your future?" When he frowned, she added, "If you should force your will on my niece, I can do little to stop you, but be warned. That girl is pure sweetness—her innocence is a balm to those bitter at heart such as you. If you're not careful, you'll begin to crave that balm. And when you come to that pass, be sure you have her heart well in hand, or 'tis you will suffer for it, not she."

"Don't worry," he bit out. "Your niece is comely, I'll warrant you, but I've never forced a woman. Nor do I intend to begin doing so now."

She scrutinized him, and when he didn't turn away from her stare, she relaxed. "Then we'll deal well together, for she'll never go willingly to your bed."

He stifled a smile. Apparently she didn't know about her niece's foray into his garden . . . and his arms. Mina might have her pride and her strange, noble-bred pruderies, but she'd been wild, sweet passion in his embrace.

And she'd be so again. He'd make sure of that.

Hours later, Marianne and the earl rode toward the gypsy wagon as the moon's silvery light trickled through the trees. Numb from exhaustion, she shifted in Garett's uncomfortable saddle, too tired to worry that half her body rested against his. Her every muscle ached, and she longed for the relief of her pallet, hard though it was.

Never had she worked so fiercely to save one patient.

But then, never had she seen so terrible a wound. When she and the earl had arrived at the clearing where the man had lain, she'd nearly despaired. Belly wounds were the worst. She'd feared he would die, even though his scars had marked him as an old soldier accustomed to wounds.

The man had been blessedly unconscious, but his tenacious heart had clung to life. Only his faint pulse had kept her from giving him up for dead. Then she'd had little time to wonder about the scorched ground or to question why anyone would plunge a sword into a laborer's belly. Instead, she'd gone right to work.

Under her direction, Garett and a tenant farmer had moved the man into a carriage William had fetched from the manor. Then Marianne had sat with him through the slow, tortuous route over the rutted road to Falkham House. Another hour had been spent moving him into a chamber, which had proved, ironically enough, to be her old bedroom. Then she'd called for water to be boiled, herbs to be mixed and steeped, and linen bandages to be prepared.

Bathing the man had taken most of her will, for his wounds had sickened her. Yet she couldn't have given up when he'd fought so hard to live. Determined that his fight wouldn't come to naught, she'd stayed beside him, bathing his wounds, forcing broth and medicinal concoctions between his feverish lips, and trying to stanch his bleeding. When at last Garett had taken her from the chamber, ordering her to return to the wagon for some much-needed sleep, she'd argued with him. In the end, of course, he'd prevailed.

Now she was glad he'd insisted. Her body felt as if someone had beaten it with a sack of potatoes. Her eyes were scratchy, and her lids slid down of their own volition, lulled by the rocking gait of the horse.

Garett settled her more closely against him. His warmth was too enticing to resist. Even when his arm tightened about her waist and he rested his chin against her head, she couldn't summon up the energy to fight him.

"If I didn't do so earlier, I must thank you for what you've done for me this day," his husky voice murmured.

"'Twas not done for you but for that poor, wretched man. I'm not even certain he'll live."

"You nearly killed yourself tending his wounds. 'Twas more than he deserved."

She bristled. "He may not have great estates and fine friends in London, but he enjoys the starling's song and the smells of autumn as much as you. So he deserves to live as much as you."

Garett stiffened. "You misunderstand me. I don't begrudge any man, poor or rich, the right to live. As a soldier, I've taken it away from too many not to realize how precious it is. Besides, there are villains among the rich and saints among the poor; a man's worth shouldn't be measured by the coin in his purse. But no one can know the true state of another man's soul, nor the true extent of his capacity for villainy."

True. Oh, what was she to think of this strange earl? He voiced the same sentiments as Father, and he *had* worked beside her to save a man of no consequence. It didn't fit the image of hardened killer she'd formed of him when she'd first heard of his arrival.

And his concern for *her* puzzled her exceedingly. Often throughout the day he'd demanded she take a short rest, and his manner had often been so gentle with her, so kind. . . .

She sighed. Much as she hated to admit it, she sometimes even found him appealing. Her body certainly did. Even now, in her exhaustion, it thrummed with an awareness of his. His sinewy arm rested across her belly, his hand gripping the side of her waist. He and she seemed to glide through the forest on a dream, the moonlight changing the trees into fairy creatures guarding their way.

As if to take advantage of the mystical night, Garett began to caress her ribs. She started at that, but his hand only grew bolder, slipping up until his thumb rested underneath her breast. Although the back of his thumb barely pressed the bottom, it seared her. She shifted to put distance between them, but he only settled her more tightly against him.

Then he lowered his head to nuzzle her bare neck below her coil of hair.

She swallowed. "What are you doing, my lord?"

"I think you know." He pressed a kiss behind her ear, making every inch of her body tingle. "You have such soft skin, sweetling. I can't resist tasting it."

And she couldn't resist letting him. His lips seemed to soothe the tired tendons and taut skin of her neck.

Under his ministrations, she tilted her head back until it rested on his shoulder.

Taking that as an invitation, he reined in the horse and shifted her until she lay back in his arms. Then his mouth was on hers.

At the first touch of his kiss, she froze. But his tongue slid along the crevice of her lips, begging entry, and the jolt of heat it sent through her made her gasp. His mouth devoured hers, his kiss exerting a force too powerful for her inflamed senses to reckon with.

Somehow he'd done it again, she thought dimly. He'd swept her inhibitions away with his infernally dark kisses. She fought to regain her power over her own body . . . until his tongue darted into her mouth, heralding the surge of pleasure that then stole through her.

His lips claimed every part of her face. They felt warm, so very warm against the skin that lay exposed to the chill night air. Like Galatea, the statue whom Pygmalion's devotion had brought to life from the cold, hard stone, she awakened under his kiss.

"What a creature of passion you are," he drew back to murmur wonderingly, as if he'd read her thoughts. Gently he planted a kiss against her tightly wound coil of hair. "I long to see what secrets your sweet form holds for me."

"No secrets . . ." she murmured as he nibbled her earlobe, sending a strange new heat radiating upward from her belly. "Please . . . please . . ." She trailed off, not certain what she was begging for.

"I'd bid you return with me to Falkham House this

instant if I didn't know how tired you are. Tonight it would be sheer cruelty to take you to bed." He slid his hand over her cinched waist, resting it just beneath her breasts and making her blood roar in her ears. "Then again . . ." he muttered, lowering his lips to hers.

Take you to bed. The words echoed in her mind, striking the alarm. She thrust her fists against him, determined to show him she wouldn't be going anywhere with him this night.

When he tore his lips from hers, his eyes questioning, she whispered in a voice fraught with fear, "Please, my lord . . ."

For a moment he tensed, his hands gripping her waist. His gaze played over her anxious face. Then with a groan, he brushed his fingers over her swollen lips. "I know. As tired as you are, I have no right to press you. We'd best end this dallying before I find myself doing what I'd regret on the morrow."

Reluctantly, he settled her body back as it had been before he'd started kissing her, although his arm seemed to hold her more intimately than before. Then he took up the reins and set the horse in motion again.

As they rode on, her cheeks flamed. How thoroughly mortifying! He'd only stopped out of concern for her weary state. He'd taken her behavior for an invitation, and rightly so. Oh, how could she have come to this pass?

She fought to clear her befuddled brain. Her tiredness had so weakened her will that she'd allowed him flagrant liberties, and now he thought her a wanton.

This was what came of dreaming of fairies in the night. It made a woman forget the central baseness of all men. But this was no fairyland and Garett no fairy prince. He might even be a murderer, and she had better not forget that.

When they reached the gypsy wagon, Garett dismounted, then caught her at the waist and lowered her to the ground. She tried to slip by him, but his hands tightened on her waist, holding her trapped between him and the horse.

"What? No kiss for the night, my gypsy princess?" he rasped. "Are you angry that I put a temporary end to our pleasures?"

She glared at him. "I'm angry that in my weariness I didn't make my true emotions known to you."

"So I merely imagined you soft and willing in my arms. A trick of the moonlight perhaps." His voice lowered. "Or the trick of a gypsy who's peeved she didn't get her way."

"Peeved! I'm not peeved. I'm infuriated! You play games with me, and somehow force my will out of my very head! 'Tis maddening! You make me forget that you . . . you . . ."

Heaven help her, she'd said too much.

The moonlight glinted off his eyes eerily, giving him the appearance of an avenging gray-eyed angel as his gaze bored into hers. His hands closed on her upper arms. "Yes? What do I make you forget about me, Mina?"

That you're a villain.

No, she couldn't say that. "That we're too different."

"For what?"

"For anything!" She stumbled on. "You regard me as an amusement, someone to toy with in the country. I want naught of that."

Only after his fingers relaxed on her arms did she realize how hard he'd been gripping her. "And if I tell you that isn't what I want?"

She arched one eyebrow. "I'd call you a liar."

"And perhaps you'd be right." His glittering gaze played over her face. "Or perhaps not. I've never wanted a woman as much as I want you. This very instant. So much that tomorrow I'll wonder how I ever tore myself away."

His words set her emotions into turmoil again. "But I don't want you!"

"Don't you?" He caressed her cheek, then trailed one finger down to tip up her chin. His lips brushed hers so lightly that she found herself disappointed and wanting more. Unconsciously, she swayed against him, so that he caught her about the waist and deepened the kiss, taking her mouth with such fervor that her very bones turned to jelly.

When he drew back, his eyes shone with triumph. "You don't fool me, Mina. You may say you don't want me, but your desire shimmers inside you like a lantern-encased flame I can see and dimly feel, but not yet touch." His sudden fierce smile sent a delicious shiver down her spine. "I'm a patient man. I can wait for you to break the glass and join my fire with yours. Just don't make me wait too long or the blaze may consume us both."

Abruptly he released her, leaving her with her heart pounding and her knees knocking. He'd taken the weariness right out of her and replaced it with confused yearning. What was she to say when he proved all her protests false?

She had to escape him!

Quickly she slipped from between him and the horse, hurrying to the wagon as if her life depended on it.

"Good night, little coward," he called after her, his soft chuckle mocking her.

She hastened into the wagon without an answer. Then she stood several moments just inside the door, holding her breath in case he decided to stay and tempt her more. When at last she heard the tramping of his horse through the forest, she let out a heavy sigh.

"Did he harm you?" came a question out of the darkness, startling her.

"Nay," Marianne managed to choke out.

A long silence ensued. "But he kissed you, didn't he?"

Marianne blushed, thankful her aunt couldn't see in the dark. "Why think you so?"

"I heard his horse approach some time ago. The two of you were doing *something* all this time, and it wasn't talking."

Marianne groped her way to her pallet in the hidden cupboard at the back of the wagon. "I'm tired, Aunt Tamara," she murmured as she began to undress.

"He's handsome, poppet, I'll grant you that. But don't let his manly looks sway you. Remember, in his eyes you're naught but a poor gypsy girl. He isn't honorable like your father. He's filled with anger, hate, and a keen urge for revenge. If once he captures your affection, he will be as wormwood to your sweet wine, turning it bitter."

With the taste of the earl's kiss still fresh on her lips, that warning unsettled Marianne. "Don't you think it might happen the other way? Not that I would ever fall prey to such a man's snares, but still, might I not turn his bitter heart sweet?"

Her aunt's cynical snort cut through her. "It takes a strong love to turn wormwood water into wine. I don't think this nobleman has that in him."

Marianne didn't answer as she slid onto her pallet and underneath the coverlet. But a small, persistent voice within her whispered that wine wasn't made overnight, and gypsies couldn't always see the future.

Chapter Seven

Revenge is a kind of wild justice,
which the more man's nature runs to,
the more ought law to weed it out.
—Francis Bacon, "Of Revenge"

The next day Marianne found it difficult to concentrate on her patient. She hadn't wished to return to Falkham House so soon, but her conscience hadn't allowed her to abandon the wounded man ensconced in her old bedchamber.

To her immense relief, the earl made only a brief appearance in the sickroom early in the morning. Once he determined the patient was still unconscious, he left the doctoring to her, telling her he'd return later.

Sometime around midmorning, Marianne was bathing the wounded man when his eyes fluttered open and he murmured a few words.

She leaned over him in excitement. "What is it? Would you like something? Water, perhaps?"

His eyes closed again, but relief pulsed through her. At least he was partly conscious. She finished bathing him and tried to make him more comfortable. Then she left him resting to search for the earl.

As she descended the stairs, the sound of arguing wafted up to her from the entranceway.

"I told you before," William was saying. "His lordship won't see you and m'lady. You must leave."

Marianne descended farther, curious to see who could make William behave so abominably.

"I don't care what he wishes," came the harsh reply. "We shall not leave until I see him, so you'd best tell his lordship we await his pleasure."

Marianne crept silently down the stairs, stopping short a few steps from the bottom at the point where she could just see into the hall.

First she spotted a lady dressed richly in a satin morning gown with fur-trimmed overskirts. The woman looked so sad as she twisted a silk kerchief in her hand that Marianne pitied her.

That pity only deepened when the woman's husband came forward to snatch the kerchief, muttering something under his breath that made his wife blanch. He was dressed in elaborate and foppish finery, with a great deal of rich lace showing at the edges of his boot hose and at his cuffs.

And when he turned, Marianne stiffened. Sir Pitney! How could he be here at Falkham? Oh, Lord, and he could identify her, too!

She forced herself to relax and think logically. It was highly unlikely that Sir Pitney would recognize her unless he looked closely. She'd seen him only a couple of times, when she'd been a gangly and awkward fifteen-year-old. Besides, he wouldn't expect her to be alive, for he must have heard of her supposed suicide.

Still, she kept well out of sight as she backed up the stairs. Then she heard footsteps from beyond the hall and realized Garett had come himself to evict his uncle. Though she knew she should flee, she couldn't tear herself away from the confrontation to come.

To Marianne's surprise, the woman spoke first. "A good morning to you, Garett."

"And to you, Aunt Bess. If I had known it was *you* who had arrived, I would have come to greet you sooner."

Marianne crept back down the stairs until she could just see around the door leading into the hall. Standing in the shadows, she watched with unabated curiosity.

Lady Tearle stared at her nephew while he smiled at her. Then Sir Pitney moved up to clasp his wife roughly about the waist. "We've come to tell you the news. Your aunt is with child. We were certain you'd wish to know of it."

When Lady Tearle's blush confirmed Sir Pitney's words, Garett gave her a half smile. "I'm pleased to hear of it." He pointedly addressed only her.

"I'm so glad to see you after all these years," she said softly, and pulled away from her husband. Sir Pitney let her go, but kept a watchful eye on her as she held out her hands to Garett.

He lifted them to his lips to kiss. Clearly the gesture affected her, for when he released her, she wiped her eyes. "You've grown so tall," she said with forced lightness. "I can scarcely believe it's you. And you seem . . . more quiet than you were as a boy."

Garett's gaze swung to Sir Pitney. "I have my years in France to thank for that."

Her husband glowered, but she paled and began, "I think you should know that—"

Sir Pitney cut her off, stepping forward to clasp her arm. "Can't you see that the earl is a very busy man, my love? We mustn't take up too much of his time with talk of our private affairs."

Something in Sir Pitney's tone made Marianne shudder. Garett clearly noted it as well, for his brow knit in a dark frown.

"Go on back to the carriage now, Bess," Sir Pitney said with more force. "I'll be there shortly. Your nephew and I have matters to discuss."

Lady Bess nodded fearfully and turned away, but before she could leave, Garett stepped forward to block her path. "You're looking well, Aunt Bess," he said solicitously. "I hope you feel as well as you look. If you should find yourself in need of my help—"

"I take care of what is my own," Sir Pitney cut in.

Lady Bess blinked, then fled as Garett watched, his eyes narrowing.

As soon as she was gone, he turned on his uncle. "I'd best not hear you've been mistreating her. She and you may have abandoned me to the wolves in Europe, but she at least is my blood, and I won't have one of my blood abused, no matter how poor her choice in husbands."

Abandoned him? And what wolves did he mean?

"You whoreson bastard!" Sir Pitney cried. "You ride into England on His Majesty's coattails, wrest from me the estates I worked hard to improve, and then have the audacity to command me in how to care for my wife!"

Garett laughed scornfully. "How exactly did you improve my estates? By letting the tenants starve while you took their earnings to pay the taxes and finance your grand schemes for power? By abusing the townspeople in every neighboring village until the Falkham title became a hated one?" He strode up to tower over his uncle. "The only place spared your 'improvements' was this house and Lydgate. Then you had the audacity to sell *my* house to strangers, forcing me to fight for its return. 'Tis no wonder that Cromwell died. Counselors of your ilk would be enough to send anyone to his grave."

"I poured money into these lands—"

"And took most of what you poured in back out again," Garett said coldly. "You stole more than enough from me, so if you're here to ask for money—"

"I merely came to tell you of the coming babe!"

Garett snorted.

A sneer crossed Sir Pitney's face. "And to remind you that if you should die without an heir, my son—and it will be a son—will inherit."

Garett's face darkened then, making Marianne shudder. She'd seen that black look before. She was glad someone else was the recipient of it.

"'Twould be very convenient for you if I should die without an heir, wouldn't it, Uncle? It might even be as convenient as certain other deaths were for you."

Sir Pitney's eyes narrowed. "What other deaths? What are you implying?"

Garett paused, and the rigid set of his jaw showed that he struggled to control himself. "You know exactly what I'm implying. But it takes more than a couple of bumbling highwaymen to bring me to ground, so perhaps you should rethink your plans. You may not find them very easy to carry out."

At the mention of the highwaymen, Sir Pitney paled.

Garett's slow smile was mirrored on Marianne's face, for she enjoyed seeing Sir Pitney discomfited after what he'd done.

"Yes, Uncle," Garett taunted him with smug satisfaction. "I knew it was you who set them after me. Just as I knew you sent a man to burn my fields. But your little ploys aren't working. Your hired 'highwaymen' lie dead in the potter's field, and I dismissed the spy you'd hired from the village."

"What spy?" Pitney said, looking distinctly uncomfortable. "You're mad, nephew. All this talk of 'highwaymen' and 'spies.' You can't prove any of it!"

Bitterness so transformed Garett's expression that Marianne could hardly believe him the same man who'd kissed her so tenderly the night before.

"I can't prove it yet, but I will soon. For you see, the man whom you sent to burn my fields, perhaps even my estate, was captured alive. Your spy tried to kill him, to keep him from talking, but was unsuccessful. So your lackey lies even now within these walls."

As Marianne gasped, he bent close to his uncle. "His wounds are being well tended, I assure you. Once he's well enough to talk . . . well, who knows what things a man might reveal if given the right persuasion? He might even reveal enough to hang the one who hired him."

Marianne backed into the shadows, her stomach churning sickly. Dimly she saw Sir Pitney glower at Garett and witnessed Garett's triumphant stare, but most of her thoughts were reserved for her own personal distress.

The earl was all she'd feared and more! 'Twas his thirst for vengeance that had sent him to request her services, not any good deed. Come to think of it, he'd never said one word of concern for the wounded man except to express his desire that the fellow live.

And for what? Merely so Garett could torture the truth from him? Could the earl truly be the kind of monster who saved a man's life only to take it again?

"You haven't won yet, nephew!" Sir Pitney growled. "I won't see you lay claim to all I've striven for!"

Garett's harsh laugh was like a knife twisting in Marianne's heart, reminding her of her aunt's words the night before. Aunt Tamara was right, she thought despairingly. Bitter water would always be bitter.

"Listen to me and listen well," Garett told his uncle in an ominous tone. "In London, when I appeared before the Parliament, I kept my anger in check because of His Majesty's determination to keep peace in England.

But in my own land, where none would fault me for having you drawn and quartered, I find it difficult to endure your presence. So I suggest you return to your powerful friends in London before I decide to test your fencing abilities."

Sir Pitney backed away from the malice on his nephew's face, clearly convinced Garett would act as he said. Once Garett saw his uncle was truly cowed, he turned to leave the room.

Sir Pitney's voice stopped him. "You're as arrogant as your damned father. Yet even he was brought low in the end. Remember this whenever you think you're safe in your manor—men are easily bought in these times. Even women have their prices. Don't be too sure you've rid yourself of all the enemies in your house."

Sir Pitney's words pushed Garett beyond the limits even of rage. "I could rid myself now of all my enemies," he ground out, reaching for the dagger he always kept at his side.

Marianne's heart stopped, but Garett's gesture evidently alarmed Sir Pitney enough to convince him to flee, for he slipped out the front door, leaving Garett shaking with fury.

"I'll see you hanged yet, Uncle!" Garett cried into the empty room.

And Marianne, at least, was convinced he really would.

She released her pent-up breath in a long, audible sigh. Then she went still as the sound echoed in the stairwell and off the stone stairs.

To her horror, Garett's head snapped around, and he strode to where she stood in the shadows. "Why are you skulking about down here?" he snarled.

His tone reminded her of what he planned for his prisoner. "'Twas you who brought me here to serve your despicable ends. And now I'm being shown what a beast you truly are!"

His eyes bored into her. "How long have you been spying on me?"

"You dare to accuse me, when you've been toying with my life and that of a poor wounded man? Spying! As if I'd deliberately seek to learn how thoroughly you've played me for a fool!"

A shadow crossed his face. "Don't speak of what you don't understand, Mina," he clipped out. "You shouldn't have been eavesdropping."

That really inflamed her temper. "I didn't intend to, but I'm glad I did. Now that I know what you intend, I shall . . . shall put an end to your contemptible plans!"

She didn't know how, but somehow she'd move the soldier out of the earl's clutches. Whirling around, she started up the stairs.

He hurried up to clasp her arm. "Don't behave foolishly. What do you think you could do now? Could you, one woman, move the man out of my house without my knowledge? None of my servants would help you. And your only other choice is to let him die to 'save' him from me. You would never do it. Whatever else you may be or might have been, you don't have the heart to let any man perish if you can help him."

Marianne's hand clenched the banister as she acknowledged the truth of his statements. Devil take him, but as usual, he held all the reins.

Still, she refused to be part of his vengeance. Possibly he'd already made her father part of it. She'd have nothing further to do with his hatred for Sir Pitney and his obsession with Falkham House.

That was the third choice, one he hadn't mentioned.

Silently she moved back down the two or three steps she'd climbed, refusing to look at him. He released her arm then, and she kept walking, her eyes fixed on the oak door of the manor house as if it were her only salvation.

She would leave and not come back. Perhaps she'd even leave Lydgate. Somehow she'd find a way to determine if he'd played a part in her father's arrest. And if he had, she'd find a way to make him pay for it.

Later. But not now, not while the memory of his conversation with Pitney was fresh in her mind, mocking her for being a fool.

She heard his heavy steps behind her, but she didn't stop.

"Mina, you can't leave now. The man may die without you."

She paused, praying for the strength to ignore his words.

"If he dies, his last hours will be painful," Garett went on. "You could ease his pain."

Curse the man for playing on her soft heart. She

whirled around to glare at him. "If he lives, you'll torture him, and that pain would be greater than any pain he suffers in death. I can't stand by and watch it!"

He gaped at her. Then as comprehension dawned, his expression darkened. "What kind of heathen do you take me for? Am I to hang him by his thumbnails until he tells the truth? My God, I've seen enough hacked and bloody limbs in war without wishing to see a man tortured at my own command!"

She watched him warily. His expression of horror made her want to believe him, but she knew better than to trust him. "You told Sir Pitney there were ways to persuade a man to reveal all. I'm not so naive I didn't know what you meant!"

"I didn't mean I'd put him on the rack, for God's sake. I am not the devil you would paint me!" His fierce glower belied him, making him appear the very monarch of hell.

He advanced a few steps, and she backed away instinctively. "I don't believe you. What else could you have meant?"

"Merely that I intend to imprison him until he tells me what I wish to know. A man whose loyalties are bought will only endure a dungeon for so long before he decides betraying his employer is the most prudent course."

She surveyed him disbelievingly. "You would merely imprison him?"

"If he lives, 'tis all I intend."

If he lives . . . "Even to put him in a dungeon is

cruel when he's newly recovered," she pointed out lamely.

"The man strove to burn my fields," Garett growled. "Men could have been killed. Be careful, Mina, that your pity isn't misplaced. The man's a villain, after all."

He might have a point. But would he really only imprison the man? If so, she couldn't leave yet, for the wounded man would certainly die if she abandoned him.

As if the earl sensed her thoughts, he edged closer. "On my honor, I shall not perform any barbarous tortures on the man. If you wish, you can stay in the dungeon with him to make sure I don't. I swear you can trust to my honor in this."

Her head shot around at his seemingly sincere words. "Honor is but a paper sword when a dishonorable man wields it."

His lips thinned. "If you were a man, we'd duel at dawn over those words."

She paled but didn't take back the insult.

At her silence, his eyes glittered. "I needn't prove my trustworthiness to a gypsy. My past speaks for my honor. So does yours. You lied to me . . . you skulked about my gardens . . . you listened to my private conversations . . . Where is your honor?"

"I only tried to protect myself—"

"From what? I don't even know that. I know nothing about your past, since both you and the townspeople avoid my questions."

She swallowed hard. So far he hadn't pried too

deeply into her past. If he ever did . . . if her refusal to accommodate him in this matter made him seek harder for answers about her, she could be in serious trouble. Still, it galled her to be a party to his plans, even if the wounded man deserved imprisonment.

He stepped closer, sensing her hesitation. "Why is it so hard for you to accept what I wish to do to this man? As a gypsy, surely you've seen harsher punishments for criminals."

Weighing her words, she avoided his intense scrutiny. "Remember, my lord, I was raised a lady. I have a lady's principles even though my blood isn't pure."

"Then uphold those principles and do what you know is best for your patient. 'Tis only your pride that's wounded now. But that man will die without you. Believe me, pride is a paltry thing next to a man's life."

She met his piercing gaze squarely. "If pride is so paltry, why won't you abandon it and forget all your plans for vengeance? Only your pride suffered when your uncle took your lands and title. Didn't you live well in France those years you were in exile? Why not forget the past? You have everything you want now. What purpose is to be served in tormenting more people?"

When his eyes locked with hers, they were like two shards of ice. "You know nothing, nothing at all." Stiffening his shoulders, he added through gritted teeth, "I want you to stay and tend the man. You know what I need of you, and you have the ability to give it. And I know your aunt at least won't say no to the money I'll offer for your skills. But be warned that no matter your choice, I won't alter my plans for him a whit. So stay or go—'tis your decision."

With that flat statement, he turned on his heels and strode toward the stairs, leaving her to make an impossible choice.

Chapter Eight

There's a divinity that shapes our ends,
Rough-hew them how we will.
—Shakespeare, *Hamlet*

Garett frowned into the fire, then glanced at the soldier. The man had lain quiet for several hours in the incongruously lacy bedroom that had once clearly belonged to a lady of the house. Garett doubted the man would live much longer.

Then Garett's gaze roamed to the figure who sat curled up in a stiff-backed chair. In the end Mina had stayed. Not that he'd given her much choice. He'd known she could be convinced. But now he took no joy in the knowledge.

She'd seen to it he felt like a monster for what he was doing. Who was she—a gypsy wench without a penny to her name—to lecture him on honor and responsibility? God only knew what she'd done to survive in the last few years, she and her devious aunt.

Her head drooped forward so her tangle of curls fell in soft waves over her shoulders, past where her lace-edged chemise peeked above her boned bodice, then cascaded down the front of her azure dress. What a pretty picture she made, her legs tucked up under her as if she were an innocent child.

But the delectable lips were not a child's, nor the shapely calf exposed to his view where her plain muslin skirts had hiked up. It was enough to make a monk sit up and take notice. No wonder her accusations had driven him frenzied with anger. He couldn't bear to have that delicious creature think him such a beast.

He jerked his gaze away. How had he come to this pass, to let a beautiful woman toy with his resolve? What she thought of him was of no consequence. No one else would fault him for imprisoning a man who'd tried to destroy his tenants' livelihoods.

Nor would anyone else criticize him for wanting his revenge against Tearle. His frown deepened. If she only knew . . .

But how could she? He himself had only suspicions and no proof.

He thought back to those first painful days in France. Only after a long while had he adjusted himself to the thought that he'd never see his mother's kindly face again or trade witticisms with his father. Most wrenching of all had been not knowing why they'd been killed. He'd almost welcomed the hardships of France, because they'd distracted him from his grief and confusion.

And there *had* been hardships. The king's friendship had helped them little, since Charles, too, had been destitute and eventually forced to leave France. Without family or funds, Garett, a boy of fourteen, and his equally bereft servant had done whatever backbreaking, dirty work the French had seen fit to give them.

That had given him plenty of time to think about his uncle. As Tearle had continued to ignore Garett's letters, Garett's suspicions had grown until he'd been certain that his uncle had been planning to steal his inheritance. That he might have done unspeakable things to manage it.

With that certainty had come caution, particularly when a man had arrived from England seeking to kill Garett. That's when Garett, convinced his uncle had wanted him dead, had stopped using his title, even his given name. He and Will had faded into the group of exiles until such time as they'd been able to fight back. They'd just been two more nameless English fellows without a home.

In the meantime, he'd nursed within his breast a hatred for his uncle bordering on madness. And once he'd been old enough to convince the Duke of York to let him and Will serve in his mercenary army . . .

Those years he wanted to forget altogether. Only his raging hatred for Tearle had seen him through the wretched, bloody battles fought not for love or country but for money, always money. He'd thought of Tearle every time he'd watched a man flogged for disobedience or a soldier friend hacked to death. Then he'd forced himself to hone his skill with the sword to a fine art so that one day he could plunge it through his deceitful uncle's chest.

And now? In Garett's more bitter moments, he

wanted to forget all caution and murder his uncle. He could do it easily enough, without much risk.

But death was too good for the bastard. He wished to see Tearle's treachery clearly revealed to the men Tearle considered his friends—the Roundheads who'd given him power and the merchants who'd given him money for his ventures. Garett wanted Tearle so discredited, so universally vilified that he'd be forced into exile as Garett had been. Exile would be a much more fitting punishment to a man who thrived on power.

Still, today it had taken all his self-control not to thrust his dagger through Tearle's heart. Only Aunt Bess's presence had given him the strength to resist that urge, though oddly it had also fired his desire for revenge.

Aunt Bess. He remembered her as a laughing young woman who'd teased him about his insolent tongue. He'd secretly worshipped her, never dreaming what her husband would later do to him. Now he felt certain she didn't realize the full truth about Tearle. Garett couldn't believe she'd have stayed with the man if she'd known.

Then again, perhaps she was happy to be carrying a child. The prospect of children seemed to make most women happy.

Yet she hadn't seemed particularly happy.

Garett looked at Mina. Would she feel joy at the prospect of children?

He snorted. He was a fool even to be thinking such things. Only his gypsy princess tempted him to abandon his purpose. Well, he couldn't allow her to do so. His plans might very well rest upon the soldier's confessing all about Tearle.

As if Mina sensed Garett's dark thoughts, she stirred, her eyes slowly opening. She seemed disoriented as she looked about the room. Then her gaze rested on Garett, and she frowned, uncurling her legs and sitting up in the chair.

"Is he any better?" she asked as she rubbed her eyes.

"Not that I can tell, but he seems no worse, either."

With a weary sigh, she rose and walked to the bed. She bent over to rest her hand on the soldier's forehead, unknowingly presenting Garett with an enticing picture of her derriere. He couldn't help smiling at the sight, and she turned just in time to catch him at it.

"What are you so pleased about?" she grumbled.

"Nothing you'd approve of."

With a shrug, she checked the soldier's bandages. She looked concerned as she glanced at Garett. "He may die despite my efforts. He hasn't stirred since we brought him here."

"I know. And then we can add another death to Tearle's account. As you no doubt heard this morning, it was Tearle's spy who gutted your patient. Tearle's the villain in this, not I or my men."

Looking troubled, she picked up her bag of medicines and went to sit by the fire. "Perhaps you weren't at fault this time, but you've killed before, haven't you?"

He stared at her. "Yes. That's what soldiers do."

She pondered that a moment. "So you killed men only while you were a soldier?"

Garett thought of the highwaymen and the men he'd killed defending himself during his short term as the king's spy in Spain. "Mostly."

She paled. Her eyes dropped to her hands, where she toyed with the pouch of herbs that never left her side. "Why haven't you killed your uncle if you hate him so much?"

"I have my reasons," Garett said stiffly, displeased with the direction the conversation was taking. "But rest assured his time will come."

Her gaze darted to his face, and he suddenly hated that he couldn't tell her more. He couldn't bear how she looked at him, as if he were some beast. "Mina, I'm a law-abiding man. I wouldn't kill in cold blood unless someone tried to kill me."

Her expression shifted to one of confusion. "You wouldn't kill for other reasons? To defend a cause, for example, or . . . or perhaps to ensure you could keep something you felt rightfully belonged to you?"

"By my troth, I don't know," he said irritably, wondering why she was delving into such deep subjects all of a sudden. "I suppose it would depend. Would I fight for my lands if some foreign army sought to take them? Of course."

She leaned forward, her eyes burning into his. "What about if someone else sought to take them? Like . . . like Sir Pitney. Would you have killed Sir Pitney to get Falkham House back . . . if . . . if he'd owned it?"

"I didn't need to kill anyone to get it, so why even ask the question? Why do you care what I did to get it back?"

"I'm just trying to understand you," she said unconvincingly.

Garett would certainly have pursued that line of conversation further if the soldier hadn't groaned and begun to toss about in bed, mumbling to himself.

Instantly, both Garett and Mina were at his side. "Easy, man," Garett muttered as the soldier tore at the bedclothes. Mina pulled the counterpane back over his body. His eyes opened slowly, but they had a feverish cast.

At first he didn't seem to notice either Garett or Mina. He struggled to leave the bed, but Mina forced him to lie back down. "Hush, now," she said. "You'll open up those wounds and make them worse."

The man thrashed even harder. But as she continued speaking softly to him, pressing him back on the bed with gentle hands, he calmed down. When at last she'd settled him against the pillows, he fixed his gaze on her with a strange intentness. Then he began to shake his head and murmur, "No, no."

"What is it?" Mina asked.

The soldier dropped his head back onto the pillow and covered his face. "It can't be. You're dead!"

Clearly the man was delirious. Garett shot Mina a questioning glance, but she shrugged as if she didn't know quite what to make of it, either. She continued tucking the man's sheets around him, ignoring his words.

"Don't talk," she soothed him. "'Tis not good for you to talk."

The soldier dropped his hands from his face and stared at her, his eyes a bright, feverish blue. "I know you're dead."

"Nay." She took his hand. "Can't you feel my fingers? I'm quite alive."

He shook his head violently, then began to cough. "No, you're not. But 'tis all right."

"Shh, shh," she murmured.

"Mayhap you're an angel now." He pinned her with his fever-ridden gaze, then nodded painfully. " 'Twould be good for me. Good to have an angel nearby if I die."

Mina did resemble an angel, with her soft hair glowing in the lamplight. No wonder the soldier thought he was already halfway into heaven.

"You're not dying," she assured the soldier.

The soldier's face softened, and his voice grew wistful. "You're an angel. 'Tis fitting. Always knew you were a good girl."

It was odd how the soldier seemed so certain he knew Mina. Just who did he think she was?

The soldier struggled to rise. "Never believed the wicked things Tearle said of you. All lies, it was. Nasty lies about your mother, too . . . old lecher." He groaned, then shifted in the bed. "Always wanting her body though she was a gypsy."

Suddenly Garett wasn't so certain the man was delirious. When Mina blanched, Garett's blood ran cold. She regarded him hastily, fear in her eyes, then dropped her gaze.

"You were sent as a vision to me. Your father—" The solder paused to cough again.

Mina's hands shook. "You don't know what you're saying," she countered. "Now, hush, before you hurt yourself!"

Her tone didn't intimidate the soldier, for he fixed pain-filled eyes on her. "Can see why Tearle wanted you and your mother . . . even if you are dead."

"I'm not dead at all." Her lips thinned as she caught sight of the blood seeping through the bandages. "Now see what your foolishness has done? You've hurt yourself. Lie still, and let me give you something to help you sleep."

Wanting to hear what else the soldier had to say, Garett darted forward to stop her, but the sight of the man's wounds made him hesitate. She was right—the man had to be kept still. So Garett watched grimly as Mina forced her special opium-laced cinnamon tea between the soldier's lips.

As she continued her ministrations, he couldn't ignore the cold suspicion gripping his heart. What had Tearle said? *Even women have their prices.*

Then there had been all her questions about whom he would or wouldn't kill. Why did that interest her? Clearly, the soldier had known her. And Tearle had known Mina's mother, the gypsy, but how? He hadn't lived in Falkham House since long before Mina had claimed to have come to Lydgate. The soldier had even hinted that Tearle and Mina—

No, he couldn't believe it.

He watched Mina remove the soldier's bindings with shaky fingers. The soldier had mentioned things she'd done. Had she done them with Tearle or against Tearle? Garett wished to God he'd questioned the man before Mina had hurried to sedate him. Why was it that the one thing the soldier had revealed was something he didn't want to hear?

But he couldn't just dismiss it as delirious ravings. Too many bits of truth were mingled with the madness, and she'd clearly wanted them squelched. He had to find out more. If she was somehow connected to Tearle, she could be more dangerous than he'd realized. If Garett was to force a confession from his uncle, he couldn't have Mina telling the man about Garett's every move.

He clenched his fist so tightly that his nails bit into his palm. She wouldn't look at him. Clearly she hid something. What was it? He had to know! Whatever it cost him, he'd find out what she was . . . *who* she was. Somehow he'd get it out of her.

For once, he'd make the duplicitous Mina tell him the truth.

Chapter Nine

On a huge hill,
Cragged and steep, Truth stands, and he that will
Reach her, about must, and about must go.
—John Donne, "Satire 3"

As Marianne washed the blood from the soldier's reopened wounds under Garett's watchful eye, she cursed herself for a fool. She should have been prepared for the possibility that Sir Pitney's spy might recognize her.

When Sir Pitney had been trying to force her father into selling Falkham House, his men had been everywhere, spreading their lies that her mother was a witch. Any man who'd worked for Pitney in the last few years was certain to have known about that ridiculous maneuver of his.

Pitney had underestimated the townspeople's loyalty to her parents. And their intense dislike for him. During his short tenure as owner of Falkham House he'd been hard and cruel, unconcerned about his tenants or their needs. So of course his accusations of witchcraft had fallen on deaf ears.

Yet now, two years after he'd spread his lies, he was finally going to succeed in ruining her life. The soldier's words had to have raised questions in Garett's mind about her identity.

At least the man hadn't revealed her family name. But he'd revealed that she was supposed to be dead.

A chill shook her. How might Garett interpret *that*? If he guessed . . .

She fought panic as she bound the soldier's wounds with fresh bandages. Oh, why couldn't the soldier have chosen to rave while Garett was out of the room? With her heart pounding, she snatched a glimpse of Garett's face, then dropped her eyes as she saw him watching her, his expression unreadable.

Hoping to escape his questions, she lifted the soiled bandages and headed for the door.

"Leave them," Garett ordered.

She stifled a groan. "I must wash them or—"

"Later," Garett clipped out. "Now you're coming with me. We must talk."

She could insist on staying with the soldier. No, that would only prolong her torment. Better to have his inquisition done with.

Still, as Garett ushered her into his chambers, her heart beat a staccato rhythm that wouldn't be quelled. What could she tell Garett about her family without revealing too much?

Garett motioned for her to take a chair, but she remained standing, not wanting to give him any advantage. After all, at the moment the advantages were all his.

He seemed to know it. His lowering stare pinned her where she stood, making her stomach roil.

"Had you hoped he wouldn't awaken?" he asked.

She blinked. "What do you mean?"

"The soldier. If he'd died, your little secret would have died with him."

Garett's imperious tone reminded her of Father's, when he'd been trying to elicit a confession of her petty misdeeds. She stared at the scowling earl, forcing herself not to be intimidated. She was no longer a child, easily cowed. "What little secret?" she asked evenly.

The set of Garett's jaw revealed his displeasure. "He knows you. And Tearle knows you. Surely you see what I must make of that?"

The vague question was designed to bring confessions tumbling from her lips. Well, she wasn't such a ninny. "Make of it what you wish, my lord, but your fabrications aren't necessarily truth."

That answer clearly tried his patience. "Deuce take it, Mina, how does a minion of Tearle's—or even Tearle himself—know you and your parents so well?"

She strove for nonchalance. "If I knew, I'd tell you, but I have no idea."

With a bleak frown, he ran his fingers through his hair. "I am not one of your patients, I'll have you know. That soldier may lie down and hush when you croon to him, but I demand answers! Do you work for Tearle? Did he send you here to finish what the highwaymen began?"

She gaped at him. He couldn't actually think— He

couldn't possibly have the audacity, the overweening nerve to believe—

"Answer me!" he bellowed.

"I could have killed you ten times over, my lord, if I'd so chosen!" She strode boldly up to him as her temper rose. "I could have slipped enough laudanum in your wine to send you forever into sleep or put mustard and hedge garlic into your wounds until you screamed for me to stop the burning. I did none of that." She planted her hands on her hips. "Think back to that night. Why, it wounded me even to cause you a moment of pain! Surely you saw that?"

A muscle pulsed in Garett's clenched jaw. "You saved me because you had to. There were too many witnesses. If you'd killed me, your own freedom would have been forfeit, for the constable would have come for you first."

"And since then? We were alone in the garden, alone in the forest . . . don't you think I could have thrust a knife through your heart if I'd wanted? But I didn't. And after how you touched me and we . . ." She choked back her hurt. "How could you even think I'd try to kill you, especially for some vile scoundrel like Sir Pitney?"

Though a guilty flush filled his cheeks, his eyes narrowed when she mentioned his uncle. "So you do know Tearle."

Oh, heavens. She shouldn't have mentioned him.

She felt like Ulysses trying to steer a course between Scylla and Charybdis. She couldn't deny the soldier's words, but neither could she tell the truth or let Garett continue in his erroneous idea that she worked for his uncle. So how could she allay his suspicions? Would the gypsy girl she pretended to be have known Sir Pitney? That didn't seem right somehow . . . and yet—

"I'm waiting for an answer," Garett snapped.

"Yes," she blurted out. "I know Sir Pitney."

Garett's eyes turned a flinty, cold gray. "How? *Why?*"

Marianne cast desperately about for some half-truth that might keep Garett from guessing too much about her, but nothing came to mind.

"Were you his mistress?"

Marianne's startled expression was perfectly genuine. "That's repulsive! He's as old as . . . as Sir Henry, and I've already told you I wasn't *his* mistress. Why must you always think such nasty things about me?"

"Gypsy women sometimes have protectors, as I've pointed out before. And an old protector is as good as a young one, if not better, for he has more money."

"For the last time, I've never had a protector! And if I chose one, it wouldn't be your uncle."

"Why not?" Garett persisted. "He has wealth enough and good connections. What objection do you have to him?"

"Faith, but you're as bad as a constable with your questions!" She whirled to put her back to him. Him and his infernal suspicions. What could she say that wouldn't reveal her identity?

"Answer me, Mina."

She hesitated, but nothing came to mind except the truth. "Sir Pitney knew my father. And my mother."

"And?"

"He knew enough about Mother's relationship to my father to ruin him."

"So did he ruin your father?" Garett was implacable.

A solution to her dilemma leapt into her mind. "I'm not going to tell you such a thing. I have no reason to believe that you'll keep quiet about my father's indiscretions if you guess who he was."

"By your own admission, your father's family abandoned you," he stated baldly, stepping forward until he towered over her. When she started to move back, he caught her by her wrists. "Why protect a family who never acknowledged you?"

A tear slipped out to roll down her face, then another and another. The charade was suddenly too much for her. She hated playing this role, hated not being able to shout to the world that her father was a good, honest man. But she dared not tell the truth, for her life and her aunt's life might be forfeit if she did.

Her tears, however, seemed to touch some human feeling buried deep within Garett. He gazed at her, then muttered a low curse and released her wrists, only to draw her into his arms.

Relieved that the inquisition seemed to be over, she let him hold her as her tears fell unbridled, soaking his linen shirt.

"Damn you, Mina," he murmured against her hair. "You're a liar who steals into my soul to torment me when I'm least prepared."

"I've never done you harm," she whispered achingly. "Why must you always suspect me of such despicable acts?"

The low groan that escaped his lips pierced her. Abruptly he released her, turning away to stride to the fireplace. He stood staring into its depths, a dark silhouette against the leaping flames. "Because you came to me cloaked in black cloth and lies. Because you have gypsy blood." He paused, and she could see the muscles in his back tighten. "Because you know my treacherous uncle."

"Not in the way you think."

He shot her a fierce glance. "And because you're the first woman to touch my heart since my mother was murdered ten years ago. That's what worries me most."

She stilled, her breath drying up in her throat. She hadn't wanted to touch his heart. Or be so terribly glad of it.

So why did she want to comfort him? Why did his expression, a mix of self-reproach and desire, send a heady rush of excitement through her veins, mingled with a bittersweet longing?

"What shall I do with you, sweetling?" He glanced beyond her to the door that led into the chamber where the soldier lay. "If you work for Tearle, I dare not let you go. Until you tell me who you are and why I should believe your claims of innocence, I must have you where I can keep an eye on you."

She tensed. "What do you mean?"

"You'll have to be my . . . ah . . . guest here . . . until

such time as you tell me the truth about your past. Until you can prove Tearle didn't send you to pry into my affairs and search for a weakness through which to strike at me."

"Guest? *Guest?*" Her voice rose with her temper. "You mean 'prisoner'! You can't do that to a—" She stopped just short of saying "lady."

"To a gypsy?" His eyes narrowed on her. When she dropped her gaze, he caught her by the chin to force her head up. "All you need do is tell the truth. And don't give me any of your tales, for I can tell when you're lying. You must tell me it all, or I swear I'll keep you here until you do."

"You're a devil and a blackguard!"

"You're not the first person to say so," he replied coolly. "But you're the only person who's lied to me without repercussion. I intend to rectify that. I want the truth. Now."

She jerked free of his grip to back away from him. "If I give you the truth, my lord, it could cost me a great deal. I won't risk it."

"You won't tell me," he said in disbelief.

"No more than I've already said. I've never been nor will ever be a spy or mistress or anything for Sir Pitney. You can trust my word on that."

His lips thinned. "I cannot. The last time I trusted someone, he stole my title, my lands, and everything I held dear." His eyes darkened to winter sleet. "I've lost the habit of trusting people."

Marianne tried another approach. "If you keep me here, my aunt will report you to the constable."

He snorted. "The constable has known my family all his life. He'll not countenance the foolish claims of a gypsy wench like your aunt."

Oh, Lord, he really meant to do this. "You'd keep me here against my will? What kind of man does such a despicable thing?"

"One who's tired of being lied to. Come now, if you fear Tearle, I'll be your protector, no matter what you tell me, even if you say that Tearle used his knowledge of your father to force you into his service or something equally sordid. Just tell me the truth."

She gazed at him a long moment. How she wanted to unburden herself to someone! But him? She didn't dare. Even if he'd had naught to do with Father's arrest, he was still a king's man. He wouldn't harbor a woman said to be an accomplice to an attempt at regicide, no matter how much he desired her.

"I have nothing to say," she whispered.

Her answer leached the warmth from his eyes. He lifted his hand nearly to her cheek before dropping it. "Then I hope time loosens your tongue. Otherwise, you and I shall spend a long, silent winter together."

Chapter Ten

The brain may devise laws for the blood,
but a hot temper leaps o'er a cold decree.
—Shakespeare, *The Merchant of Venice*

Will stood outside the gypsy wagon and glanced around him, frowning. He felt distinctly uncomfortable, although the early morning was milder than usual for fall and not a cloud marred the blue sky. With great reluctance, he raised his hand to tap at the doors, but they opened before he could touch them.

Tamara stood in the entrance, her face taut with anxiety. "Where is she?"

She put her hands on her hips, and the action thrust her ample bosom forward. Will fought the urge to stare at her breasts. Given that the simple loose blouse and heavy skirt she generally wore were tousled, she had probably just come from her bed. Her hair, a soft cloud of sable curls, fell to her shoulders in wild abandon, and the sight of it drove every thought from his head.

Keep your mind on the business at hand and off Tamara's sweet curves. 'Twill be bad enough when she hears—

"Well?"

"She's still at the manor."

Tamara swore, then marched past him down the crude wooden steps that Will himself had built for the wagon in an attempt to soften her toward him.

"Where are you going?" he cried, hurrying after her.

"To rescue my niece from your demon master."

He clasped her arm, forcing her to stop, and she pinned him with the kind of threatening glare he was getting used to seeing from her.

So he let go of her. "He won't let her come back with you," he stated baldly. There. It was out. Garett's pretty little healer was staying in the manor no matter what her thoroughly appealing aunt had to say about it.

"What do you mean?"

"He— She— Oh, a pox on't, he thinks Mina is one of Tearle's spies. He won't let her go until he's sure of her loyalties."

Shock lined Tamara's face. Then she looked as if she might faint.

Will's heart sped up. Damn, but she was taking it badly. He'd promised the little miss he'd tell her aunt what had happened—that much he could do without being disloyal to his master. He'd expected Tamara to be furious, to launch into one of her tirades. This deathly pale he hadn't expected.

"He hasn't harmed her," Will said, putting his arm around her. "You needn't worry about that."

She lifted her eyes to his, their deep brown suddenly so dark with anxiety that a pang shot through him. In that moment, she looked young and oddly vulnerable.

"Aye, but he will," she said solemnly. "Especially when he learns—"

"Learns what?" Will asked, his eyes narrowing.

Tamara's expression grew shuttered. "That she's a virgin. 'Tis like uncloaking the falcon to put her so near his grasp."

"My master is no ogre."

"Still, he wants to take her innocence. Haven't you seen how his eyes drink her up whenever he's about? And she, innocent that she is, can no more resist his pull than he can hers. She's like the falconer's lure to him. He means to have her. And now he's found the way to keep her under his spell."

Will drew her closer, encouraged when she didn't thrust him away. "Have some faith in your niece. When I left, that 'innocent' was giving him the roughest side of her tongue. She wouldn't even let him eat his breakfast in peace! She's much like you, she is. She'll not give him an easy time of it."

Tamara shook her dark head, clearly unconvinced. "So many other things are part of this, things you don't know." She tipped up her chin. "Your master's not for her. God knows what he might do now that she's in his care."

"Come, love, it's not so bad as all that." Wrapping his arms around her, he pressed her head against his chest. "Besides, if you're right and he means to . . . er . . . win her affection, what of it? Consider us. You've chipped away at my heart since the day I saw you. Perhaps 'tis the same between them."

When Tamara's body stilled, Will thought he'd touched her heart at last. But when she turned toward him and he glimpsed her scoffing expression, he realized with a sinking heart he'd been too hasty.

Impatiently she disentangled his arms from about her waist. "You're as bad as he is, speaking your sweet words." She frowned at him. "Chip away at your heart indeed! You have no heart, or you'd not let him treat her so. Don't try to placate me. I shan't let you two devils ruin us."

Normally Will was a patient man, but since he'd begun wooing the thorny Tamara, he'd discovered a great capacity for impatience. He couldn't shake off her barbed words as he had before.

"What's there to ruin?" he muttered. "You're gypsies. 'Tis not as if you've lived like nuns."

The instant he saw Tamara's reaction, he realized he'd erred. Normally she blustered and fumed, mostly for show. But now an emotion akin to hatred flashed in her dark eyes, stunning him.

"I didn't mean it, Tamara!" he blurted out.

But as he reached for her, she slapped his hand away. "Don't you ever touch me again, William Crashaw. If you do, I promise I'll cut all the sensitive parts of your body into bits!" Then she stalked off toward Falkham House.

Will had no choice but to follow her, ruing his words. Somehow he had to convince her not to engage his master in battle. Tamara might be sturdy and brave, but she was no match for his lordship. Will couldn't bear to watch her lose all in a fight she couldn't win. Because then there was no telling how she'd react. She might even refuse to let him near her anymore.

Well, he didn't intend to let that happen. If he had to annoy his master, so be it, but he wouldn't let Tamara walk away from him. Not yet.

A few hours later, when the earl entered his study, Marianne slipped into the Falkham House library. It was dim and stuffy, but Garett had left it intact, thank heaven. Then again, that made sense—Father had done little to alter it, so it must be much as it had been when Garett was a boy.

She scanned the shelves, looking for John Gerard's *Herbal*. If she remembered right, Gerard had an excellent explanation of the properties of an herbal mixture she wanted to try on the wounded soldier.

But another book, its binding intricately embroidered, caught her eye. Her breath stuck in her throat as she drew it out. She opened the volume to read "A Pleasant Conceited Comedie Called Loves labors lost. As it was presented before her Highnes this last Christmas. Newly corrected and augmented By W. Shakespere."

She paused to savor the familiar title. When the Winchilseas had first moved into Falkham House, she'd read the play often. It had once been her favorite. Its light wit had never ceased to lift her spirits when she'd felt gloomy.

But that wasn't the only reason it had fascinated her. With trembling fingers she turned the page and found the faded inscription: "To my son Garett. Continue to greet the world with a light heart even when it seems bleak, and you will never lack for strength. With love, Mother."

Marianne's heart lurched. Until she'd seen the book, she'd forgotten about those lines. Now the memories flooded back. As a girl, she'd wondered about the boy named Garett. His mother's words had been so much like something her own mother might have said that Marianne had adopted the inscription as if it had been meant for her.

But it had been meant for a child who'd lost his mother at a much younger age than she. How strange that those early days of dreaming about the unknown boy Garett, whom she'd gently been told had died in the war, had come to this.

In the imagination of her youth, he'd been a charming, happy lad who'd loved Shakespeare as much as she. That Garett had been mischievous, of course, but good at heart, eager to aid the sick and poor. She'd invented conversations with him about books, about Lydgate . . . about life itself. It had made the story of his death seem even more tragic.

In later years, she'd found other books to read, and the boy Garett had receded into the depths of memory. Until now.

Blindly she stared at the ironic inscription. She'd never imagined another kind of Garett—an aloof man who couldn't trust and didn't seem to know how to have a light heart. Last night, when she'd asked him whom he'd killed and for what reasons, she'd learned more about his pain than anything.

She couldn't imagine the Garett she now knew ever reading or enjoying the play she held. But had his mother known a different Garett? Just how much *had* the war ripped from him?

So lost was she in her ruminations she didn't hear the door of the library open. Too late she felt the presence of someone else and closed the book, only to have it snatched from her hand.

Whirling around, she found Garett staring at it with torment in his eyes. Then his gaze grew shuttered. He glanced from the book to her face.

She felt absurdly like a child caught with her finger in the Sunday pudding, and that angered her. The house and library might now be his, but they'd once been hers.

Wordlessly he opened the book to find the inscription. As he read it, his expression softened. Then he snapped the book shut and lifted a probing gaze to her face.

"How—" he began, then paused. "*Why* did you have this book just now?"

Of course he would ask her that. And what could she tell him? The truth. "I was looking for books about herbs."

"Laying aside the fact that you were reading, a pursuit I didn't imagine was common to gypsies, this book says nothing about herbs."

"I like Shakespeare."

"That, too, seems an odd interest for a gypsy."

"Yes, and I'm glad I pursued it today." She plunged on, determined to move him to another train of thought. "Or I wouldn't have seen that inscription. I never thought of you as having a mother. Tell me, my lord, what was she like?"

A shadow crossed his face. "Why do you wish to know?"

"It would help me understand how the boy with a 'light heart' could grow into the man who'll stop at nothing for his petty vengeance."

Garett stared at her, his face devoid of expression, his eyes two smoldering coals. "In time, my light heart served me ill. Mother was wrong. Only pain makes you strong. And the anger that pain brings."

The matter-of-fact words struck her hard. She'd hoped to appeal to the part of him that had once found something to be lighthearted about. How foolish of her to think she could touch the softer parts of him. He had no softer parts.

Yet she couldn't forget the inscription. "Your mother seemed to have great hopes for you. No doubt *she* would have thought such anger beneath you."

"No doubt." His face hardened as he tossed the book atop the shelf. "I don't want to talk about my mother; I want to talk about you. Why this sudden concern for my feelings and my future?"

"That should be obvious. Your feelings and future now have a profound influence on mine, whether I like it or no."

"So you think you can doctor my anger like you do a disease, and then I'll set you free? I'm sorry, sweetling, but the cure for my illness won't come from your hands." His voice turned fierce. "Nothing will suffice for me except that Tearle be given justice. Even your telling me the truth won't alter that; it will merely give me more weapons with which to fight him."

A lump formed in her throat. "It won't give you any weapons, for I've nothing to confess that could help you destroy Sir Pitney."

He searched her face. "Yes, but do you have things to confess to *him* that might destroy *me*?"

"What on earth would that be? You've done nothing illegal or even immoral in my presence." Her eyes narrowed. "Except for holding me prisoner against my will."

"You have a choice, a very simple one. Tell me all I wish to know, and you needn't stay one more minute."

"The choice is untenable," she said in a stiff voice.

He surprised her then by chuckling. "Why is it that whenever the choice concerns me, you find it 'untenable'? For a gypsy, you're amazingly particular. You won't take my gold, nor my protection, nor even my trust. In fact, there seems to be only one thing you will take from me."

"What is that?" The words were out before she could stop them.

At the bold, searing glance he shot her, a slow heat coursed through her body. She blushed. He took only one step toward her, but it put him agonizingly close.

"This," he murmured. Then he bent his head to hers.

The moment their lips touched, she backed away, but he caught her about the waist, pressing his lean, hard body intimately against her as his mouth, soft and inviting, enveloped hers.

He didn't force himself on her. That might have made everything easier. No, he coaxed and teased, tracing the seam of her closed lips with his tongue until she felt weak with longing.

She pulled her hands up between their bodies, intending to press him away, but he grasped one hand in his and brought it back around until he held it captive behind her back. Then he did the same with the other, until both sets rested on the swell of her bottom.

Why wasn't she screaming her outrage? He held her against her will!

Or did he? She had a sneaking suspicion that if she fought him, he would let her go. Trouble was, she had no desire to fight. The hands laced through hers were so warm that she couldn't think past the sensations they startled within her. When his thumbs began to caress the backs of each, a trembling began in her nether regions that she could neither understand nor deny.

Then mercilessly he renewed his assault on her lips. As he tantalized her with kisses, a profound pleasure such as she'd never experienced seeped through her, enriching her blood with a glorious, tingling heat. Desperately, she fought the pleasure, fought the temptation to surrender her mouth totally to his.

"Open to me, my gypsy princess," he murmured against her lips, his breath a hot caress. "Let me taste more of your sweet sorcery."

The asking undid her. Like a morning glory opening its petals to the sun, she allowed him to plunge his tongue deeply inside her mouth.

After that, sanity left her. His hands released hers, but she slid her arms about his waist of her own accord. He pressed her back against the bookshelves, and she did nothing except strain eagerly against him.

He groaned as he felt her compliance. His hands cupped her derriere, pulling her against the full length of his hard body. His mouth made forays to other parts of her, to her closed eyelids, her suddenly sensitive ear, her bared neck.

Then, while still bombarding her senses with kisses, he moved one hand up to cover her breast. She felt it even through her boned bodice, and the shock of it in such a private place dampened her ardor.

Heavens, what was she doing? She was behaving like a wanton!

She tore her lips from his. "Don't," she whispered, wrapping her fingers around his wrist in an attempt to pull his hand away.

His hand moved . . . but only to the knot of her linen scarf so he could work it loose. "Just this once, sweetling, don't play the lady with me. I prefer the enchanting gypsy."

With a hard swallow, she watched as he pushed the loose ends of the scarf aside, baring the swell of her breasts above the low square neckline of her bodice and chemise. He raked his gaze boldly over the curves revealed to him.

Her cheeks heated. "I can only be what I am, my lord." Snatching the ends of the scarf, she attempted to tie them back.

He brushed her hands aside, silencing her protests so effectively with a kiss that she didn't at first notice his fingers slip behind her back to tug at the laces of her gown. Only when she felt the bodice loosen did she realize just what liberties he was taking with her. Then his hands reached up to slide the top of her gown and loose chemise off her shoulders and downward.

Before she could bring her dazed mind around to the task of protesting his insolence, he captured her hand and pressed it hard against his chest. He wore no coat or waistcoat, only a thin holland shirt. Through the material, underneath her palm, she felt the rapid beating of his heart.

His gaze, like silvershine, pierced her. "What you are," he said in a low, gravelly voice, "is the first woman to make my heart race in some time. Like it or not, you're too tempting by half. And I'm not the sort of man who resists temptation."

Then he kissed her again with a near-savage eagerness that banished all thought from her mind. His tongue swept her mouth until she felt weak as a newborn kitten. Faint moans of delight sounded in her throat.

Had those come from her? Oh, but she knew in her heart that they had.

His hand slipped up again to cup one fully naked breast. At the shocking intimacy of it, she went still as stone. "This isn't right, my lord," she protested, though she did nothing to dislodge his hand. What he was doing felt so astonishingly good. Heaven help her.

"You've called me rogue often enough," he said wickedly as he teased her nipple with the rough pad of his thumb. "Surely you wish me to live up to the name."

"Perhaps you should . . . live up to another of your names," she stammered as a traitorous intoxication stole through her. "The name of gentleman, perhaps."

"You don't think me much of a gentleman," he retorted as he caressed her breast. "So you can hardly expect me to behave like one."

A shudder of pure pleasure escaped her, and his eyes gleamed. She scarcely cared. Her control was slipping. His hand cooled her warm flesh, and the sensation that shot through her as he kneaded her breast beneath his palm was like the first relief from summer that a fall wind affords.

When she swayed against him, he let out a ragged breath. "Oh God, you could send a man into madness." Then he lowered his lips to hers again, brushing soft kisses first on her mouth, then her neck, and then down the sensitive flesh above her breasts until he found the crest he sought and seized it in his mouth.

As his tongue flicked over her nipple, she buried her fingers in his wavy hair, holding his head closer to feel more of the exquisite sensations he was provoking. All care for what he might be was temporarily forgotten. Gone were any maidenly objections, any sense of how a lady should behave. She only knew that his caresses and kisses dazed her. She felt sweet and burning and wild all at once, like the gypsy she was supposed to be.

She should stop this! But as his hand slipped up to caress her other breast and a deep yearning crept through her, forcing her to the brink of oblivion, she could not, or, rather, *would* not stop him. That vague realization brought with it a teasing feeling of anticipation, which overwhelmed any vestiges of her inborn prudery that might have controlled her actions.

His mouth left her breast. His eyes locked with hers as he parted her legs with his thigh, then set his foot on a low shelf behind her in such a way that she ended up astride his knee. She ought to protest, but a strange urge to wrap her legs around his thigh and hold on tight assailed her.

When she gave in to it, he rewarded her with a long, lingering kiss. He worked his knee up and down, rocking her atop it, and the feelings that shot through her were so . . . Oh, heavens, she'd never felt so eager and hot and . . . and excited! What was he doing to her?

Between her legs, she was all damp and aching. And he seemed to know it, too, for he resumed sucking her breast with more urgency, making everything more intense—the heat, the ache . . . the pleasure.

Only after he had her gasping and shimmying atop his thigh like some wanton did he bring his foot to the floor so she slid enticingly down his hard thigh to stand on her own two feet again.

"This way, sweetling," he said urgently, lacing his fingers through hers and leading her to the thick fur rug that lay by the hearth in the midst of the spacious library. In a state of dazed need, she let him guide her.

He knelt and pulled her down beside him, then began with great impatience to undo the ties of his shirt. She watched spellbound as inch after inch of dark, hairy chest revealed itself. Good Lord, but he was thickly muscled. She wanted to touch him, to run her fingers over every part.

His hands had just moved to his breeches, eliciting a shocked gasp from her, when a knock at the door sounded. He stilled his movements. She blushed and he frowned. Neither said a word. At their continued silence, the knock sounded again.

His frown deepened. "I'll be with you presently," he barked out and reached once again for Marianne.

"My lord, it won't wait," urged a voice Marianne recognized as William's.

"If you value your life, it will," Garett growled, his fingers moving swiftly to the ties of Marianne's skirt.

But for Marianne, that knock was a sign from God, reminding her that this wasn't right. "No," she whispered, pushing Garett's hands away.

"My lord, I really must speak with you," William urged beyond the door, though Marianne could tell he spoke with great trepidation.

With an oath, Garett stood. "Don't move," he commanded her in a low voice, then strode for the door.

She fumbled with her gown, desperately trying to

cover herself before Garett reached the door. But as he neared it she heard another voice that made her increase her efforts with something akin to panic. Her aunt's.

"I told you to wait downstairs," William snapped.

"I wanted to see him now, not a century from now," Aunt Tamara retorted.

Before Garett could even reach for the door handle, the door burst open and Aunt Tamara marched into the room.

"Milord, I've come to protest that—" She stopped short at the sight of Marianne kneeling in the midst of the rug, her scarf lost who knew where, her gown loose about her waist and barely covering her, and one hand held guiltily to her throat.

Shame washed hotly over Marianne. She glanced at Garett to see if he, too, felt embarrassed beyond all countenance, but his face was expressionless, though a muscle worked in his jaw.

"What's she doing here, Will?" Garett's gaze coldly assessed Aunt Tamara. The calm in his voice and his unashamed manner told Marianne volumes. He was a nobleman for whom dalliances with maidens of lower class weren't unusual. For him, their encounter had been a mere trifle, nothing to destroy his self-assurance.

But damn it, she wasn't a tavern wench whom he could tumble at will! A lump of anger formed in her throat as she rose from the rug.

Aunt Tamara remained shocked into silence until she recognized the hurt in Marianne's expression. Then

Aunt Tamara turned on the earl, her entire body quivering with rage.

"Will told me some barbarous story about your suspicions. You claim my niece is a spy for this Tearle creature, is that it? You say that's why you must keep her here." She flashed a disparaging glance William's way. "A pox on that! I see your true intentions. That foolish tale was but a ruse to keep me from her while you took your pleasure!"

Aunt Tamara glared at Garett, daring him to deny her accusations.

Swiftly, William stepped forward, placing his hand on her arm. "I wouldn't lie to you, Tamara. I didn't dream—"

She pushed his hand away. "I told you this would come of it. I told you he'd ruin her."

It was Marianne's turn to be alarmed. Not for a moment did she wish her aunt to believe she'd given herself completely to Garett. "Nothing happened," Marianne asserted, moving a few steps toward her aunt. "He didn't . . . I mean . . ."

"What your niece is so eloquently trying to say," Garett bit out, "is that you interfered before I could 'ravish' her."

"But something did happen," Aunt Tamara said, gesturing to the rug.

"Perhaps," Garett conceded. "Your niece is old enough to choose a lover if she wishes."

Marianne glared at him. How dare he imply that she would take him for a lover! If he hadn't been so . . . so . . .

seductive she would never have so much as let him touch her.

She opened her mouth to retort, but he went on, oblivious to her anger. "I warn you, Tamara. What happens between me and Mina is no longer your affair. Until she—or you—tells me who she is and why my uncle knew her and her parents, I intend to keep her here. She's made her bed and now she must lie in it. And there's not a damned thing you can do about it."

Aunt Tamara gaped at him, but her incredulity and outrage were nothing to Marianne's.

With coldness seeping through her bones, Marianne spoke in the most distant, ladylike voice she could muster. "I didn't choose you for a lover, my lord, so disabuse yourself of that notion. I certainly didn't choose to be your prisoner, nor to be accosted and mauled simply because I was here. You are the one who's made my bed, which is why I won't lie in it."

His eyes narrowed on her as she stood there, every limb quivering with anger.

"Mauled you, did he?" Aunt Tamara broke in. "Well, it won't happen again. Come, Mina." She turned to the door. "This time we're leaving Lydgate, and the sooner the better, I say."

Garett stepped forward to place himself between Aunt Tamara and Marianne. "You may leave whenever you wish, Tamara," he said with quiet authority, "but your niece stays here."

Marianne glanced at her aunt, whose fury was palpable.

"You're a runagate, milord, despite your great title," she snapped. "But you shan't have your way. Not this time, by my faith. I'll go to the constable first. I'll tell him what you intend to do. I'll trumpet your crimes about the town until—"

"You won't do any such thing," Marianne said sharply. The last thing either of them needed was to involve the constable. If pressed, he wouldn't dare take their side against the earl. He might even decide it was safer to reveal Marianne's identity than risk Aunt Tamara's forcing the issue.

Aunt Tamara looked at her niece in surprise. "Don't you want him to release you?"

"Of course. But gypsies aren't generally loved in Lydgate," she said pointedly, hoping her aunt would realize how dangerous it was to threaten Garett. Although the townspeople had given Marianne safe harbor, they might not be so eager to champion her if it meant incurring the earl's wrath.

When comprehension showed in her aunt's eyes, Marianne felt a measure of relief. "The constable won't listen to a gypsy. He might even expel you if you feels you're a troublemaker. We wouldn't want that, would we?"

"No, love, you wouldn't," William interjected, obviously alarmed by the turn the conversation was taking.

"Let her go to the constable, Will," Garett remarked. "Let her see how much good it does. Then again, perhaps I should go—"

"No!" Marianne cried. At Garett's grim smile, she flashed her aunt a warning glance. "No one's going to the constable, especially not you, Aunt Tamara."

Aunt Tamara's mouth snapped shut, but her expression showed she didn't like being made to listen to reason. "I can't permit him to force himself on you."

"He didn't." A slow blush suffused Marianne's face. "You can trust me on that." She couldn't let her aunt believe a lie, or Aunt Tamara would challenge the earl until she forced him to act. Marianne didn't even want to consider what Garett might do then.

Aunt Tamara, never one to submit graciously to circumstances, muttered, "I don't like it."

"Neither do I. But if his lordship"—Marianne laced the word with sarcasm as she cast a glance his way—"if his lordship can refrain from his lascivious attentions, I suppose you and I can endure this arrangement until I demonstrate I am no more a lackey of Sir Pitney's than is William."

Garett stood there with his arms folded across his half-bared chest, his eyes boring into Marianne's. His cold half smile made it clear his anger hadn't entirely waned. "I'm more than willing to do whatever Mina wishes." He let his eyes rest for a brief moment on her bodice, which hung shamelessly low.

Marianne jerked her gaze from his. Curse the man. He was remembering the wanton way she'd returned his "lascivious attentions."

"I'd rather you did as *I* wish and not as my niece wishes," Aunt Tamara said, showing she, too, lacked confidence that Marianne could resist Garett's attempts at seduction.

"Your niece can take care of herself," Marianne snapped. "Don't worry. His lordship may think confining me will intimidate me into confessing imaginary crimes, but time will prove my innocence. If he insists on keeping me here, I'm willing to give him that time."

And without losing my virtue, she told herself firmly. She would prove Aunt Tamara and Garett wrong about her ability to protect it.

Next time he attempted to seduce her, he would find it not nearly so easy. After today, she wouldn't be so gullible and foolish as to let him touch her.

"Then we're agreed?" William said tactfully, keeping a cautious eye on both his master and the two women.

The stony silence in the room was his only answer.

Chapter Eleven

Stone walls do not a prison make,
Nor iron bars a cage;
Minds innocent and quiet take
That for an hermitage.
— Richard Lovelace,
"To Althea from Prison"

Two weeks later, Marianne sat shaded by an apple tree in the garden, her slippered feet tucked beneath her and her muslin skirts spread out on the grass. The volume of *Love's Labors Lost* lay open in her lap. Idly she glanced at the burly man who stood a few feet away, pretending not to guard her. Garett certainly knew how to choose his lackeys. This one had served with the earl in Spain and was completely loyal to his master. She flashed him a smile, but he ignored her.

With a sigh, she closed her book. Reading Shakespeare's play merely depressed her. Why hadn't she ever noticed its somber notes before? As a character said morosely in the play's final scene, "Our wooing doth not end like an old play: Jack hath not Gill."

That was certainly true. In the time since Garett had

taken her prisoner, she'd expected more attempts at seduction, but he'd become nothing but her jailor since that day in the library.

Meanwhile, the wounded soldier had died despite her attempts to save him. He'd done it without saying another word, which was both a blessing and a curse. Although he hadn't revealed her identity, he also hadn't exonerated her of being Sir Pitney's spy. It made her despair.

His death seemed to have affected Garett, too, who'd become even more distant. At times he ignored her. At other times, his grim manner and intense scrutiny of her disturbed her deeply.

She stared forlornly across the garden. These days Garett was utterly single-minded, obsessed with his purpose. When he did speak to her, it was to tell her, oddly enough, about improvements to the estate or to ask her opinion in some matter of housekeeping. He kept the conversation polite and innocuous. But the ever-present Sir Pitney lay between them.

And every day began with the one question she wouldn't answer: "Who are you really?" She wanted to retort with the same question, for she truly didn't know who he was, either. Was he a calculating manipulator who'd betrayed her father and cost him his life? Was he a heartless, debauched Royalist who'd cavorted with the king in France? Or was he the winsome boy of her youthful imagination?

One thing she knew for certain. He turned her body into a raging inferno of emotion whenever he gave her his dark, penetrating stare. Even now, the memory of his stirring kisses made her tremble all over and an unfamiliar ache start up in her breasts where he'd caressed her. She didn't understand it. Nothing had prepared her for such a violence of feeling.

Her mother had once tried to describe the pleasures to be found with a man. But she'd spoken in such vague generalities that Marianne hadn't been able to relate any of the descriptions to her own experience.

Thanks to her study of medical books and her experience with healing, Marianne knew, of course, what a man and a woman did together in the privacy of their chambers. But she'd never given the act much thought, for it had sounded messy and shameful and somehow odd.

She gave it a great deal of thought these days. All the time. Day and night. She often found herself wondering what it would be like to have Garett's body cover hers, to feel his magical hands touching her private places, to have his demanding lips move lower to . . .

"Fie!" she said aloud. She'd vowed not to let him seduce her, yet here she was, doing the seducing for him! How could her mind have such trouble remembering who he was whenever her body started remembering how he'd touched her?

Not that she didn't have enough reminders of the role he might have played in her father's imprisonment. Aunt Tamara reminded her often enough during the daily visits Garett allowed them.

Yet somehow everything Marianne believed true

when she was away from Garett disappeared when she was with him. He could be cold, but she'd never seen him violent or deceptive. To his tenants and servants, he was an authoritative but understanding master. Even to the soldier, he'd shown glimmers of compassion, especially in the man's dying hours, when Garett had fetched a minister for him.

Still, how could she trust him when she knew the depths of his hatred for Sir Pitney? There was no way of telling how far he might have gone to regain Falkham House and thus thwart his uncle.

She shook her head. This endless dithering would get her nowhere. She wasn't going to sit in the sunshine on such a beautiful day and let him control her thoughts. Bad enough that at present he seemed to control her future.

So she rose, dusted off her skirts, and headed back toward the house with the volume of Shakespeare tucked under her arm.

Then she heard horse's hooves approaching. She swung around, expecting to see Garett. Instead, an unfamiliar man on horseback pulled up short in front of her.

He was clearly a Cavalier, but one of a more outrageous stamp than Garett. He dressed boldly, with lace cuffs, a profusion of looped ribbons, and a flowing silk cravat tied about his neck. His doublet was of a rich, royal blue brocade, and his flowing white shirt of the finest linen. Golden curls grew past his shoulders in unabashedly shining glory.

Despite his fashionable appearance, however, there was no mistaking he was Garett's friend, for he had the same arrogant stance.

"What have we here?" With a sly grin, he doffed his plumed hat, exposing more of his gold mane, then dismounted and handed the reins to the groom who ran from the stables.

Seeing him up close, she realized he was like Garett in yet another way—he towered over her, his broad shoulders filling out his doublet.

His gaze traveled brazenly over her. "As usual, Falkham has excellent taste. Tell me, nymph, what forest did he find you in?"

She groaned. Why did all these Cavaliers have to be so terribly wicked? He was worse than Garett, if that was possible.

"Probably the same forest where he lost you. 'Tis an odd thing about forests—they're excellent for slipping away from ill-mannered friends," she shot back, annoyed at the way he assessed her attributes as if she were a horse for sale.

He chuckled. "Quick-witted, too, I see."

"Yes, and I have all my teeth," she said tartly.

"Devil take me, now I've insulted you." Stepping forward, he snatched her hand up to kiss. "I never meant to offend such a divine creature."

A low voice answered from behind her, "Be careful, Hampden. This 'divine creature' is a gypsy. She might just cast the evil eye on you if you keep annoying her."

Garett strode up to stand at her side, startling her.

He was frowning, but his easy manner toward the other gentleman told her that Hampden was a friend.

Hampden straightened with a look of genuine pleasure. "I can well believe she's a gypsy." He winked at Marianne. "She's already put a spell on me." When Garett's expression turned threatening, Hampden grinned. "And on you as well, it appears."

Garett's open displeasure delighted Marianne. She was so pleased to see Hampden elicit some emotion from Garett that she couldn't resist teasing him herself.

"Oh, sir," she protested to Hampden, "surely you know Lord Falkham can't be bewitched. Not the unflustered, infallible earl. Women have no effect on him at all, particularly women of my sort."

"What sort is that?" Hampden asked, eyes twinkling as Garett glowered.

"The sort who don't jump at his every command." She sighed theatrically. "Alas, I'm too strong-minded for his tastes. He prefers a woman he can intimidate, and I'm afraid I don't suit."

A mocking smile touched Garett's lips. "Mina's not being quite fair, Hampden. 'Tis not strong-mindedness I dislike but deliberate defiance."

When Marianne frowned, Hampden clasped her around the waist and pulled her outrageously close. "Well, I like a little defiance myself. Meek women are tedious. Give me a saucy wench any day."

Marianne was just beginning to regret having encouraged Hampden when Garett stepped forward to disengage his friend's arm from around her waist.

"I'm afraid you'll have to find your own saucy wench," he growled as he rested his arm casually across her shoulders. "This one is under my protection."

"So that's the lay of the land, is it?" Hampden said.

Marianne bristled, tiring of their game and angry that Garett implied she was his mistress. "That's *not* the lay of the land, and Lord Falkham knows it. I wouldn't be here if I had a choice." With a sniff, she pulled away from Garett and stalked to the house, ignoring them as they followed close behind her.

"'Tis good to see you again, Falkham," Hampden said. "And in such good company, too."

"I'm not nearly so glad to see you," Garett replied dryly. "You've only been here a few minutes and already 'my company' is ready to slit my throat. Your throat, too, I might add."

Hampden chuckled. "That face and figure alone are lethal enough to slay a man. What would she need with a knife?"

Marianne whirled to survey the two men, who seemed to be laughing at her. "If you gentlemen are quite through discussing my person, you might consider another topic for conversation. One that's not quite so rude."

A wicked grin crossed Hampden's face. "I can't help it, pigeon. You're such a refreshing change from women at court. Most of them simper and smirk and never let you know what they're really thinking. Only the king's mistresses exhibit your . . . er . . . strong-mindedness."

"Mr. Hampden!" How dare he compare her to the

king's mistresses? Oh, if only she could tell him just how wrong he was about her character!

"I meant it as a compliment," he said sincerely, shocking her even more.

"Mr. Hampden, if you're going to—"

"Lord Hampden, to be precise," Garett put in. "I suppose I should have introduced you properly. Mina, this is my dear friend, Colin Jeffreys, the Marquess of Hampden, who served out part of his exile with me in France."

She glanced from Garett to Hampden disbelievingly. "Another one? Just what I need—*two* wretched noblemen tormenting me!" She rolled her eyes heavenward, and the men laughed. Then she pivoted and headed back for the garden.

"Where are you going?" Garett called out.

"Where I don't have to put up with arrogant lords!" Both men chuckled.

"We'll see you at dinner, then?" Hampden shouted, but she didn't answer.

Garett watched her go, unable to tear his gaze from the sway of her hips. Two weeks, and he still couldn't think for wanting her. It vexed him exceedingly. How could he desire her so badly when she might very well be Tearle's spy?

That reminded him . . . He looked around for the guard. Only when he spotted his man standing alert at the edge of the garden did he relax.

"My God, Falkham, where did you find her?" Hampden asked when she'd passed out of sight.

"You might say she found me." Garett turned back toward the house.

Hampden followed. "Is she really a gypsy? I can scarcely believe it. For all her sauciness, she's as graceful as any lady."

Garett smiled grimly. That was precisely the problem. Mina had this inexplicable ability to turn the most sordid task—like sewing up a man's wounds—into a polite encounter at a royal dinner. She had a true lady's approach to life. If anything unsavory came her way, she turned it aside before it besmirched her.

After that day in the library, he'd been prepared for anything. Although she hadn't instigated their kiss in the library, she hadn't fought it either, and once he'd got past her token protests, she'd been downright eager.

Until her aunt had discovered them. Then Mina had attempted to use his actions to gain her release.

After that, he'd expected her to try deliberate seduction, perhaps as a way of getting him to set her free. Instead she'd confounded his expectations—she'd done nothing the least bit scandalous.

That day in the library, he'd thought she was enamored of him. In fact, he'd counted on it in his attempt to gain the truth from her. He'd tried coldness, and he'd tried barbed questions. He'd been unrelenting in his inquisitions, but it had gained him nothing. Not only had she kept silent but she hadn't even seemed affected by his distant air. That irritated him most of all.

"Is she?" Hampden repeated, bringing Garett out of his thoughts.

"Is she what?"

"You know. A gypsy."

"Yes. Partly, that is. She's a nobleman's bastard."

"That would explain why she's here under your protection."

Garett debated whether to tell his friend the truth. Perhaps he should. Hampden might know something that could help uncover Mina's true identity. And her relationship to Sir Pitney.

"Actually she's here because I suspect she works for my uncle," he said baldly.

"The hell you say! That pretty thing? She has a sharp tongue, I'll admit, but she doesn't strike me as Tearle's preference. He likes his women soft and weak." Hampden frowned. "From what I hear, he particularly enjoys seeing them cower. Your Mina doesn't seem to cower before anyone."

"I know," Garett admitted. "But it's possible he knows something about her and is using it to force her into doing his bidding."

"If you say so. But I can't see it."

"Well, she didn't come to you claiming she was scarred by smallpox and so had to hide her face beneath a mask. Nor did you witness her being recognized by Tearle's henchman before he died. Nor have you seen—"

"Enough. I take your point." Hampden rubbed his chin. "Perhaps you're right, but I still can't believe it. Her eyes are those of an innocent." He grinned. "A devastatingly attractive innocent, I might add."

Garett gritted his teeth. "You can't have her, Hampden. Regardless of what I suspect she is, she's still under my protection."

Hampden cocked one eyebrow. "Ah, but is that all she's been under? I mean, if you haven't bedded her—"

"Don't even think it," Garett growled, suddenly annoyed by Hampden's insinuations.

"I can't help but think it, since it bothers you so." Hampden laughed. "I'm glad I came to visit. I've been here only a few minutes, and already I'm having the time of my life."

Garett gave his friend a long, steady look. "I think, Hampden, this is one time I won't be sorry to see you leave."

"You may be right," Hampden said without a trace of remorse.

Marianne nervously smoothed the simple muslin of the best gown she had at present. Her others had been left behind in London, not that she'd have dared to wear them anyway. What she wouldn't give to appear at dinner in one of her silk and velvet gowns, especially since she was to dine with two men who already thought the worst of her character.

She sighed. A gown wouldn't change their minds about that.

This gown was perfectly serviceable and attractive, even if it wasn't fine enough for consorting with an earl and a marquess. Aunt Tamara had made the gown especially for her when they'd first come to Lydgate, so it exactly fit her petite figure, accentuating her slender waist and delicate build. Though the only lace adorning it was that of her chemise, the edges of which peeked above the low neckline, the amber yellow fabric seemed to pick up the gold in her hair, which she'd carefully dressed in artful curls.

Still, the gown wasn't satin, nor did it have an embroidered stomacher. Oh, well. She had to make the best of what she had. She'd suggested that she not come to dinner at all, but Garett had said he didn't want Hampden to think he was deliberately hiding her away.

Hampden. Oh, dear. The mere thought of matching wits with him and Garett all evening started butterflies in her stomach. So as soon as she entered the dining room, she looked for the one man who wouldn't make her nervous. William.

Over the past two weeks, William had become something of a friend. She knew why—his attentions to her aunt were obvious—but she didn't mind. At least he didn't suspect her of being in Sir Pitney's employ.

Only after William smiled at her did she venture a glance at Garett and his friend, though she almost wished she hadn't. The two of them stood near the fireplace, talking animatedly. They didn't notice her enter, giving her time to observe them. To her chagrin, they were both dressed to impress.

Hampden she noticed first because of his richly curled blond hair and burgundy doublet. His breeches were burgundy as well, though his stockings were a modest black. They were the only modest thing on his person—the wide lace collar of his snowy shirt, the embroidered waistcoat, the profusion of ribbon loops on his breeches all bespoke a man of consequence. Yet his broad chest and sculpted calves weren't those of a mere man of fashion. Indeed, they reminded her of . . .

She turned her gaze to Garett and sucked in her breath. Oh, Lord, did he always have to cut such a handsome figure? As usual, his clothing was modest—dove-gray breeches, black silk stockings, and a black doublet with the cuffs of his dove-gray waistcoat emerging from beneath. Not an inch of lace adorned his collar.

Nor was his glorious hair curled like Hampden's. Instead, its wanton waves and roughly hewn edges made him look like a highwayman. She never ceased to feel a thrill of danger when she saw his unfashionable hair.

As if he felt her eyes upon him, Garett turned. His gaze swept down her bodice to her tightly cinched waist, and he frowned, cutting her more deeply than words could have. No doubt he disapproved of her simple dress.

She hesitated, suddenly embarrassed to be dressed so poorly, but Hampden saw her and his eyes brightened. "Ah, Falkham. If I'd known what you hid out here in the country, I'd have come to visit sooner."

Garett's frown deepened. "Why haven't you worn that dress before, Mina?"

Her feelings even more wounded now, she lifted her chin to smile at Hampden. "I saved it for a special occasion. But I see now I . . . I couldn't hope to dress properly for a dinner such as this. So if you'll excuse me . . ."

Abruptly she left the room, a hard lump lodged in her throat. And she'd thought she looked beautiful! How could she have forgotten how richly the nobility dressed for dinner? Had she really been playing the gypsy so long that she no longer knew what to wear to a simple dinner in the country?

She hadn't even reached the stairs before Garett came after her. "God, Mina, I didn't mean—"

"It doesn't matter, Garett. You have your dinner with Lord Hampden. I'll be fine."

"No, you don't understand." For the first time since she'd met him, Garett looked truly ill at ease. "There's nothing wrong with what you're wearing, except that it's . . . it's . . ."

"Too common?"

His eyes dropped meaningfully to her bodice. "Too provocative." At her frown, he added hastily, "I know it's what all the ladies wear. By their standards it's not even daring, but damn it, I can't stand having Hampden see you looking so ravishing."

The way he avoided her gaze said that he told the truth. Garett was *jealous*? And of Hampden, no less. She didn't know whether to be thrilled or furious.

"Come back to dinner, sweetling," he murmured. "Please. I wouldn't have you miss dinner just because I . . . I made a foolish blunder."

Two surprises in one night, she thought, blessing Hampden for having come to visit. Garett was jealous *and* he'd admitted to a blunder. Well, the least she could do was show him she appreciated his truthfulness.

"Fine," she said with a regal air.

He relaxed and, with a cordiality she seldom saw, escorted her back into the room.

Hampden waited for them, looking amused. After Garett seated her and the two men sat, Hampden said, "I'm glad my surly friend here convinced you to return. Dinner would have been dreadfully dull with only the old bear there for company."

Marianne glanced at Garett, who struggled to keep his face expressionless. Lifting her glass of wine, she fell in with Hampden's teasing. "Lord Falkham's not so awful. But if you want scintillating dinner conversation, don't ask him about his estate improvements. Not unless talk about crops interests you."

Garett lifted one eyebrow. "I'm sure Mina would prefer to talk about her father."

Why couldn't he ever let up? She forced back a sharp retort, sipping her wine to give her time to think. "Actually, my lord, I'm far more interested in how you and Lord Hampden met."

There. A safe topic. The two men could reminisce, and she wouldn't have to worry about parrying Garett's verbal thrusts in front of a stranger.

Hampden gleefully took up the gauntlet. "We met in a stable. You'd never know it now to look at him, pigeon, but our friend Falkham was once a stable boy."

She eyed him uncertainly. "You're not serious."

"Very much so. He and I both were stable boys. In

France. We worked for a dreadful old count who enjoyed having two English lords in his employ."

Garett, a stable boy in France? "Why?"

"Why did we work for the count, or why were we in France?" Hampden asked.

"Why were you stable boys?"

"Oh. Couldn't do much else. When we first arrived, Falkham was only fourteen, and I sixteen. We weren't the only English nobility there, you must realize, and not a soul wanted us."

"But what about the king?" Marianne asked. "Surely he championed you. Surely he helped his countrymen."

Hampden smiled mirthlessly. "Ask Falkham about the king."

Marianne's gaze flew to Garett.

Garett drank some wine. "The king was as destitute as we were. He could scarcely keep food on his own table, much less help us fill our bellies."

"But they told us—"

"Cromwell and his men?" Bitterness crept into Garett's voice. "What else were they to say? The Roundheads preferred to let the English think that their king lived richly in France, when in truth, he went from acquaintance to acquaintance, gathering what help he could, always trying to find someone to help him finance another uprising. His Majesty gave us his friendship, but he could give us little more."

"When the king left France, Garett joined the Duke of York's army," Hampden put in.

"Yes." Garett turned somber again.

Marianne suddenly wished the conversation hadn't gone this direction.

Hampden wouldn't let him sour the evening, however. "It wasn't all bad in France. Remember Warwick, Falkham?"

Garett's eyes lost their faraway look. "How could I forget? He stank of burned wool whenever it rained."

"Still does, from what I hear." Hampden turned his gaze to Marianne. "Warwick's coat caught fire one day. We put it out, but the edges were still charred. Warwick had as little money as the rest of us, so he cut off the charred parts and continued to wear the coat."

Hampden chuckled, but Marianne couldn't join him. She found the story more sad than funny.

"Don't worry, the man didn't suffer during the winter," Garett said, correctly guessing the source of her concern. "He kept as warm as any of us. If anything, we were the ones to suffer from smelling his smoky coat. We used to say, 'Where there's smoke, there's Warwick.'"

Hampden joined Garett's laughter, and after a moment, so did Marianne.

"There was little enough to laugh about in those days," Hampden said, sobering. "The count and Garett's uncle saw to that."

"Sir Pitney?" she asked. But Sir Pitney had been in England, unaware of Garett's existence.

Hampden cast Garett a penetrating glance. "You didn't tell her about the letters, about the man Tearle sent to kill you?"

Garett shrugged. "I'm sure she knows."

"How could I?" She turned to Hampden. "Sir Pitney knew that Garett lived?"

The marquess grew grim. "Perhaps not at first, for apparently a servant boy accompanying Garett's parents and killed with them was mistaken for Garett and buried as the Falkham heir. It's the only reason Garett escaped death himself."

"You were *there*?" she asked Garett. "But . . . but . . ."

"Why do you think the soldiers assumed I was dead?" His expression was tormented. "My parents were taking me with them to Worcester. We stopped for a rest, and Will, Father's valet, took me into the woods so I could relieve myself. We heard the shouts and ran back, but they were already lying gutted . . ."

His voice had grown choked, so Hampden jumped in. "Will dragged him, struggling, back into the woods. It saved both their lives. Cromwell's men left no one breathing, not even the footman who wore Garett's old clothes." Hampden's voice hardened. "That's why everyone believed Garett dead. But his uncle found out otherwise eventually. Garett sent him four or five letters with proof of his identity. Sir Pitney ignored them."

She was already reeling from the horrifying picture Hampden had painted of a young Garett watching his parents die, but this— "That's appalling!"

"Not as appalling as what happened later." Hampden cast Garett a furtive glance. "One day a man came looking for Garett, with a sword in hand and a thirst for blood. Fortunately, he found me instead, and I was armed and more than able to defend myself." He smiled. "I'm afraid Sir Pitney's man didn't return to England."

At Garett's now determinedly aloof air, Hampden quipped, "And the count complained because I'd dirtied his floors."

Marianne felt all at sea. Why hadn't Garett told her all this? No, she knew why. His stubborn pride made him think he shouldn't have to explain himself to anyone.

"Tell me about this count," Marianne urged. It suddenly seemed important to learn the whole truth of why Garett had returned from exile an embittered man.

"Ah . . . the count," Garett said, breaking a slice of toast in half with a loud snap.

"The count was the only man to truly make me hate the French," Hampden said. "I'm sure Falkham agrees, since he tormented Falkham more than he did me. He hated Falkham. Used to call him 'le petit diable.'"

Marianne could easily understand how Garett might have gained that nickname. "At least he enabled the two of you to fend for yourselves. Without him, you said you might not have found work."

"I'm not sure that would have been so awful." Garett sipped some wine. "We might have been better off begging in the streets of Paris."

Hampden chuckled. "True. After the beatings the old man gave us, 'twas a miracle we lived to manhood."

Having suddenly lost her appetite, Marianne put

down the spoon she'd been about to lift to her lips. "Beatings?"

"Actually," Hampden said, "mine weren't as bad as Falkham's."

Garett cast her a gleaming glance. "That's because the count knew Hampden provided his best source for court news in the city. Hampden always talked the man out of beating him by offering to tell him some juicy bit about his enemies no one else knew."

Hampden smiled. "Ah, yes. I bribed him with gossip. I almost forgot. Of course, it helped I was sleeping with his enemies' wives." He shrugged. "At the time, it seemed a better way to get funds than working in the stables."

Marianne's face turned a brilliant red as she stared down at her soup.

It was Garett's turn to chuckle. "So that's how you got your 'tales.' I used to envy you that ability to find out all of the Paris court's secrets. Now that I know—"

"You wish you'd been old enough to get a few of your own?" Hampden finished helpfully.

Garett gave him a mock threatening look. "I wish I'd put you onto the count's wife. Then you might have lightened the load for both of us."

"That sour-faced old—" Hampden broke off, as if he suddenly realized a lady was in the room. "Ah, but she hated you as much as her husband. Neither of them could stand your ridiculous pride. They thought to teach the barbarian Englishman a lesson. They loved your being a penniless nobleman. But it infuriated them you never broke under their beatings."

Marianne's throat constricted at the thought of a fourteen-year-old Garett being beaten. She couldn't help asking the next question. "Were . . . were the beatings terrible?"

Garett shot Hampden a warning glance as he said, "No."

Hampden raised both eyebrows. "I take it you haven't shown her your back, or she'd know that was a lie."

"It's time we moved to more suitable topics of conversation," Garett stated flatly, his eyes fixed on Marianne, who felt sicker by the minute.

Hampden shrugged, then launched into a witty description of the latest news from the English court. But Marianne no longer listened. Images of Garett being beaten flashed before her eyes, killing her peace.

She began to understand why he hated his uncle. Sir Pitney could have spared Garett those hard years, but he'd knowingly let his nephew remain penniless in France while he'd plundered the boy's estates.

What had Garett said? "Only pain makes you strong." Now she knew what had happened to the lighthearted boy his mother had spoken of. That boy had been killed, first by his parents' brutal deaths and then by his uncle's betrayal.

She glanced at Garett as he questioned Hampden idly about the court. It was a miracle he'd withstood it at all. Then there'd been his years as a soldier, which he refused even to talk about. No wonder he distrusted her.

Her thoughts were interrupted by a familiar name on Hampden's lips. "Winchilsea's death set the town buzzing," he said as he cut a piece of meat. "No one really believed the man to be guilty until he was killed."

"You think he was innocent?" Garett asked, his expression oddly shuttered. "From what I'd heard, the poisoned medication stayed in his possession from the moment he left his home. Clarendon believes he might have been working with the Roundheads, and I'm inclined to agree. It's just the sort of thing they'd do."

"Who really knows? But I'm not convinced. Still, I'm one of only a few who've given him the benefit of a doubt. After he died, the gossips immediately tried and convicted the old man, since no one remained to prove him innocent. His daughter—"

"Daughter?" Garett's eyes narrowed on her. "I didn't know Winchilsea had a daughter."

Cold fear gripped her heart, but she forced a measure of calm into her expression. "They say she killed herself after she heard of his arrest."

"That's right," Hampden said as Garett continued to stare thoughtfully at her. "Threw herself into the Thames. Some even think she might have been involved in the poisoning."

"Tell me, what was this daughter like?" Garett asked coolly.

Hampden sat back to wipe his mouth with his napkin. "Something of a recluse and quite plain, from what I was told. I gathered she didn't like people."

For once, she was glad that the court gossip was as patently false and cruel as usual. "Actually, Miss Winchilsea was painfully shy."

"You knew her?" Garett asked, his gaze boring into her.

"Of course. I told you I knew her parents."

"Why didn't you mention her before?"

She made a dismissive gesture. "I didn't know her well. She kept to her rooms, spoke to no one, and rarely interfered with my life. I'm not surprised she drowned herself. She was the type to faint at the sight of blood. I can well imagine how horrified she must have been to hear about her father's arrest."

Hampden snorted. "'Twas a silly thing to do. I could never see you, madam, throwing yourself into the Thames at such news. I wager it would never even enter your mind to do so."

"Not Mina," Garett said wryly.

She glanced at him, relieved when she noted no trace of suspicion in his expression. Between Hampden's half-truths from court and her own fabrications, she'd kept him from guessing the truth, thank God. Yet how long could that last?

Hampden began to speak of the king's newest mistress as Garett made outrageous quips about what Hampden said. Marianne listened, her anxiety growing. It confirmed what she'd already gathered—both men knew His Majesty very well.

Now more than ever she had to keep her identity secret. Garett clearly believed her father guilty and could easily believe the rumors about her involvement. If he ever learned who she was, he'd be quick to turn her over to the king. So no matter what the cost, that was one secret she had to keep from him.

Chapter Twelve

Trifles light as air
Are to the jealous confirmations strong
As proofs of holy writ.

—Shakespeare, *Othello*

Four days later, Garett accompanied Hampden out the entrance to Falkham House, more pleased than he dared admit that his friend was leaving.

"Where's your beautiful 'prisoner'?" Hampden asked. "Didn't she wish to see me off?"

"Mina's been out all night, caring for a tenant's wife who's in childbirth," Garett said as the groom walked Hampden's horse up.

The wicked grin that crossed Hampden's face irritated Garett enormously. "That's a soft heart for you. Such a pity she couldn't be here. I was so looking forward to snatching a parting kiss."

Only with the greatest effort did Garett keep his face expressionless. "Then thank God she's not here. It saves me the trouble of protecting her from your ill manners."

"'Tis not my manners that bother you, and well you

know it. You hate she's taken a liking to me. And I to her."

Damn him. "You take a liking to every woman who crosses your path."

"Perhaps. But your little pigeon intrigues me more than most."

Even knowing that Hampden was baiting him, Garett struggled not to lift the marquess forcibly onto his horse and send him off to London with a good kick in the arse.

Hampden apparently interpreted Garett's somber silence correctly. "How couldn't I be intrigued by the woman who's managed to raise your ire . . . and your possessiveness. Never thought to see you act that way. 'Til now, you've been too busy with your plans for vengeance to take serious interest in any woman."

Garett had reached his limit. "If you're waiting for an explanation of my behavior, you might as well hie yourself off to London. How serious I am about Mina is none of your bloody affair."

At Hampden's broad grin, Garett realized just how truly obsessed with Mina he sounded. He gave Hampden a self-mocking smile. "Besides, you think making me jealous will torment me, but it won't work."

"Why not?"

"First, I know you flirt with her only to annoy me and not because you truly feel for her."

Hampden suddenly grew serious. "And second?"

Garett's eyes searched his friend's face. When he found there only genuine interest, he decided to tell the truth. "As much as your overtures to her may irritate me, they're only a pinprick compared to the torment I endure every day she's here without my being able to touch her."

Hampden shook his head. "You're a fool not to have made her yours the moment you laid eyes on her. As for your first reason—you misread me, Garett. If I thought I had a genuine chance of stealing her affections, you can be certain I'd attempt it."

"You've never fought me for a woman before."

"True. And I probably never will. Unless you decide to toss away Mina's heart. Then, dear friend, I'll be more than glad to step in and comfort her."

That image disconcerted Garett. He glanced away. "You assume she has a heart, and that she'd offer it to me."

Hampden mounted his horse and took up the reins, then stared down at Garett, his laughing green eyes solemn for once. "Oh, she has a woman's heart, that's certain. If you weren't so determined to delve into her 'deep, dark past,' you'd realize it. As for whether she'd offer it to you—that remains to be seen. I imagine that if you continue to persecute her, she won't. That would be a great loss for you, Falkham." He gave a half smile. "And a gain for me."

Without another word, Hampden turned the horse and prodded it into a trot. He didn't even glance back as he rode away.

Garett felt an odd relief. He'd lied to Hampden about jealousy not affecting him. Hampden's overtures to Mina had cut like a knife.

Especially given her response. During Hampden's stay, Mina had met the marquess's wicked sallies with teasing rebuffs that had bordered on flirtation. It had driven Garett mad, no matter how much he'd told himself it had all been harmless. Despite his words to the contrary, Hampden was loyal to his friends and had recognized that Garett wouldn't like his toying with Mina.

Garett wasn't so certain of Mina, however. With Hampden, she became a sparkling, delightful creature, her cares temporarily forgotten. She extended that cheeriness to Garett occasionally, but only because Hampden was there and drew it out of her. Garett hated that. Damn it, but he wanted to be the one to make her eyes shine.

He turned back to the manor, furious that he was letting it matter so much to him. Of course he wanted her. That was understandable. Her sweet form and daring spirit would entice any man. But his desire for her mustn't become more than that. If he allowed her to wheedle her way into his emotions, she'd take advantage of it.

For God's sake, she might even have ties to his damned uncle!

He suddenly saw her in his mind's eye, standing with her hair unbound, explaining to Hampden the difference between a toadstool and an edible mushroom. Her expression of pure delight in her subject had given him pause. She didn't act like a calculating spy.

Abruptly, Garett wheeled away from the house and

strode for the stables. He was tired of not knowing who she was. His questions and gruff manner hadn't intimidated her, hadn't wounded her as he'd hoped they would, making her throw herself into his arms and confess all.

Instead they had thrown her into the arms of Hampden.

Time to change tactics.

Garett saddled and mounted Cerberus. Mina had responded to his kisses before. She'd do so again. Somehow he'd seduce her into telling him her true identity.

He snorted. Seduce her into telling her secrets. What an absurdity! He couldn't touch the damned woman and keep his wits about him, much less maneuver her into telling him anything of substance.

He rode off toward the tenant's home where Mina had gone. No, he didn't want to seduce her for anything more than the most basic reason, that he desired her. That was certainly reason enough.

As he neared the tenant's house, he heard the soft, mewling cries of a newborn. Good, soon she'd be ready to return with him.

He dismounted, his gaze going to the guard he'd placed on her. "The babe has come?"

"Aye." The guard was a man of few words.

Garett joined him beneath an oak, watching the entrance to the wattle-and-daub cottage. "How long ago?" Mina had left Falkham House shortly after dinner the night before.

"No more than an hour."

So she'd only just finished. She was sure to be exhausted. He leaned against the oak, training his gaze on the door.

He hadn't waited long when Mina stepped out to stand on the threshold. With a weary sigh, she brushed several damp tendrils of hair from her face. She rubbed her arms and shoulders as her gaze went to the guard. Then she spotted Garett.

"Is the babe well?" he asked.

She gave a rueful smile. "Just like a man, he was stubborn even during his birthing. I had to work a bit to coax him from the womb."

"And the mother? Did she survive?"

Surprise flickered across her face. "Better than expected, under the circumstances."

"Good. Her husband's a fine man. He'll need her to care for the child when he tends his fields."

"I imagine that he'll need her for other things as well," she said dryly. "Believe it or not, some men depend on their wives for more than just raising their children."

"True. Inasmuch as this is their second child in as many years, I suspect her husband won't give her long before he depends on her for . . . ah . . . more important duties."

Mina's cheeks pinkened considerably. Then she tilted up her chin as if to say she was far too dignified to respond to his comments. But when he chuckled, she didn't quite succeed in keeping a smile from curving up her mouth.

The tenant whose wife had just given birth stepped out of the doorway, capturing Mina's attention. He didn't seem to notice Garett standing in the shadows of the oak.

"I'm coming," Mina told the man and started to go back into the cottage.

"Nay," the tenant protested. "Time for you to go 'ome and get y'r rest. You done enough already. Me wife's sister will take care of her right and proper now that you did the 'ard part." He grabbed Mina's hands. "'Tis a beautiful babe, and we're mightily beholden to you for it. Y'r mother'd be right proud of you, she would, if she was alive to see it."

Garett narrowed his gaze on Mina. She blanched, then jerked her head ever so slightly in Garett's direction. Following her movement, the tenant looked over and started when he saw Garett standing there.

The man dropped Mina's hands. "P'raps I'd best go back and see 'ow me wife is comin' along," he muttered as his face turned almost purple. Quickly he walked back into the cottage, nearly tripping over the threshold in his attempt to get himself out of sight.

A long silence ensued, during which Mina avoided Garett's gaze. "I-I'd best look in on her myself," she murmured and turned back to the cottage.

"No," Garett ordered, pushing himself away from the tree. "You're exhausted. Anyone can see that. You should return with me to the manor."

"I'm not—"

"You heard the man. They don't need you here any longer." He strode quickly to her side.

She gazed up at him as if trying to determine what he thought of the tenant's words. When Garett merely matched her stare, she turned her face away, her shoulders stiffening.

"Whatever questions you have," she said with quiet dignity, "you might as well ask now."

Garett cocked his head in the direction of the guard, who stood under the oak. Mina sighed, then let Garett lead her to his horse. He swung her up into the saddle, mounting behind her.

As they moved off, he could feel the rigidity in her body as she attempted to hold herself apart from him.

"Well?" she asked when they were a good distance from the cottage.

Though broaching the subject was bold of her, the anxious note in her voice betrayed her fear. Good, he thought coldly. It was time she realized how serious he was about discovering her identity.

"It's an odd circumstance, don't you think, that everyone seems to know your mother?" he asked.

"No, not at all. We gypsies are like mice. We creep into everyone's barns at one time or another."

He lowered his head until his mouth was beside her ear. "'Creep' is a good choice of words, Mina. Now tell me exactly when you and your mother first 'crept' into Lydgate. You implied that you only came here after she and your father died."

She jerked her head forward, away from his lips. She remained silent, but he could see her hands clench the pommel.

"Your refusal to tell me what I wish to know tires me," he clipped out. "Until now I've kept this between you and me and your aunt. That has gained me naught. Perhaps it's time I called upon the good citizens of Lydgate."

"Wh-what for?" she stammered, her shoulders not quite so erect.

"Clearly they know more than they've led me to believe. I doubt they'll be as reluctant to spill the truth when the neighboring earl brings pressure to bear on them."

She twisted in the saddle to gaze back at him with alarm in her eyes. "Why must you involve them? They don't know anything of use to you. Don't you think they'd have told you if they had?"

He halted the horse and dropped the reins to close his hands on her shoulders. "No, I don't. I've seen how they are with you. They're so grateful for your medicines and healing that they'd not deliberately cause you harm."

She wriggled free of his grip, then lifted her leg over the horse's head and slid to the ground. With a fierce expression, she began walking toward the manor. He rode beside her, watching as she trod the road with deliberation.

"If they know nothing," he asked as he kept pace beside her, "why do you fear their involvement?"

"I don't fear it! But I know you quite well by now, my lord. You'll pound them with questions they can't answer. And when they don't tell you what you wish to hear, you'll torment them until they say something—anything—to placate the angry earl. Who can say what a people beset with fear will blather?"

The sheer logic of her argument raised his ire to even greater heights. "What do you think I wish to hear?"

She stopped to stare up at him, hurt in her eyes. "That I'm truly the despicable, devious gypsy you believe me to be. That I'm a spy for your uncle." Now she was crying, fat tears rolling down her pale cheeks. "If your suspicions are confirmed, then you can finally say that no one in this world can be trusted. Then you can make your dark plans, fashion your dear tortures for your uncle, and no longer worry that perhaps—just perhaps—you are wrong!"

She wheeled away from him and the horse, ducking her head to hide her tears as she strode off as quickly as her skirts would allow.

He leapt from the horse and was beside her in a few strides. Grabbing her arm, he tugged her about to face him. It took all his will not to let the pitiful sight of her reddened eyes and damp cheeks affect him.

"Can you really think I want to be proven right?" he demanded, his anger riding him hard. "I assure you I don't. I want nothing more than to lose myself in your tempting arms. But I can't. Not without knowing the truth. I don't have it in me to trust quite that much."

"I know. And even though I know why, I can't bear it." She gave him a beseeching glance. "Why not just release me? Send William to escort me and my aunt to the Channel. We'll leave England—'twas what my aunt wished to do in the first place. You'll never have to see us again. You can have your battles with your uncle without once fearing I'll somehow betray you to him."

Garett lifted his hand to brush away her tears, fighting to eke out words past the lump forming in his throat. "I can't do that, either, sweetling." He trailed his fingers down her face, over the smooth curves of her neck to where her hair tumbled over the scarf of her bodice. Abruptly he dropped his hand.

Then he groaned and snatched her about the waist, pulling her roughly against him. "I can't let you go without knowing it all . . . without knowing you completely."

"That will never be," she whispered.

"The hell it won't." Driven by anger and need, he cupped her head in his hands and kissed her with all the fierce fervor he'd suppressed for two weeks and more.

She tried to twist away from him. When that didn't work, she brought her hands up to push against his chest, but he merely clutched her closer, kissed her more hungrily.

Grasping her soft bottom, he lifted her against him so he could feel her softness against his hardening loins. She gasped, and he deepened the kiss, his tongue entwining with hers. Her hands stopped pressing against his chest, then crept upward to clasp his neck.

Only then did he take his lips from hers. He rained gentle kisses over her face, tasting the salt of her tears.

She moaned. "You . . . you can't simply kiss it all away."

He pulled back to caress her cheek and wind a long lock of her dark golden hair around one finger. "True enough. But while I kiss you, I can forget it's there."

"I can't," she said, a tear trailing from her eye.

"My God, don't cry anymore, sweetling." Her tears made something clutch at his heart. He caught the lone tear on his thumb, then sucked it off as he fixed his gaze on her. "Your sorrow can be banished as easily as that. Just tell me what I wish to know."

"That would truly begin my sorrow."

Burying his fingers in her hair, he forced her head against his chest. "Nay. You underestimate my desire for you. I have the power and wealth to give you whatever you wish—a house of your own, rich gowns, enough gold to make you content for a lifetime. And if it's fear that keeps you silent, I can shield you from whomever you fear . . . especially Tearle. Just trust me."

She threw back her head, her umber eyes as wild and tormented as those of a hunted fox. "Trust you? The only one I fear is you!"

Then with a sob, she thrust him away, lifting her skirts and running toward the manor.

He started to follow her, then stopped himself. Her parting words hammered themselves into his brain. She feared him.

He'd known she disliked his being a nobleman and disapproved of his obsession with vengeance. And he'd realized early on that she'd do almost anything to keep him from knowing her secrets.

But truly fear him? That he hadn't known. Until now.

Slowly his disbelief turned to anger and then fury. He had never hurt her. He'd imprisoned her, true, but with silken bonds. She'd slept in a soft bed between clean sheets and eaten the best food she'd probably tasted in her life. He'd never forced her to join him in his bed—some men would have.

Yet she fought his touch as if he were some scarred beast. Why? Because he was nobility? Or was there some other mystery in her past that made her dart from him?

He clenched his fist so tightly that his fingernails dug into his palms. She feared him, did she? A little gypsy who'd probably run from soldiers and constables all her life feared him—the one man who hadn't tormented her in any way except to desire her.

Well, then. Perhaps it was time he gave her something to fear.

"A pox on you, old fool!" Pitney Tearle shouted at the moneylender who sat with stony countenance behind the lacquered desk. Pitney stared at the man's treasures, crammed into every inch of the tiny room, and the sight increased his fury. "How dare you refuse my business? How dare you, a . . . a heretic!"

The moneylender's eyes were cold. He didn't flinch but met Pitney's gaze squarely. "I no longer lend to Christians," he replied with a shrug. "One minute they claim usury is a sin, and the next they want to reap its rewards."

Pitney sneered. "It's Papists who hate usury, not good, solid Englishmen. I hate Papists and all they believe in, so you've nothing to fear from me on that score."

The old man crossed his arms over his chest. "'Tis all the same to me. Christian dogs. I'll have no part of it anymore."

Pitney threw himself at the man, grasping him by his doublet to lift him off his chair. "You've lent to me before, and you'll lend to me again. You still lend to Christians every day, old man. Don't you deny it! I know of three 'Christians' at least that you regularly lend money to."

The dark eyes that stared back at him showed no fear. "I lend to whomever I choose. I choose not to lend to you."

Pitney dropped the man in the chair with a curse. Should he try another tack? Intimidation clearly wasn't working. And he needed money badly. The fortune he'd gained in stealing Garett's lands was running out. Pitney had spent part of the last of it helping his friends with their fruitless attempts to regain a footing in the new government. The rest had been given over to a cause equally unsuccessful—trying to eliminate his nephew.

If only he could rid himself of Garett, then he truly would inherit the Falkham estates. Never again would he be at the mercy of moneylenders. He scowled at the old Jew. This was the fifth moneylender or merchant he'd tried. No one wanted to lend him money—Jew or Gentile alike.

"Why won't you lend to me?" He pinned the man with a baleful glare.

Everyone else evaded the question. But this one smiled. "You're a poor risk. 'Tis unlikely I'll see any return on my money."

Rage filled Pitney at the man's audacity. "I've always paid you back before. You've made a great deal of money off me, you fool."

"That was before," the man replied smugly.

Pitney planted both fists on the desk and leaned down to stare into the moneylender's face. "I'm a friend of Cromwell's son. I know half the merchants in this city, and every one of them will attest to my reliability."

"Aye? Then where are your fine friends? They don't want you now that they know how you got your money. No one loves a thief—even one in fine clothes."

Dread gripped Pitney. What stories had the man heard about him? Until now Pitney had been careful to cover his tracks in his more unsavory endeavors. No one who couldn't be trusted had been left behind to tell tales. Even with his treachery toward Garett, he'd been cautious. He'd burned the letters Garett had sent. He'd made very public the funeral of the boy who'd taken Garett's place in death. When Garett had returned, Pitney had pretended to be as surprised as any.

Had all his caution been for naught? He rounded the moneylender's desk to thrust his fist in the man's face. "What do you mean, calling me a thief?"

"You'd be surprised how easily rumor runs its merry dance through our fair city. Everyone knows about you, Sir Pitney." The man's eyes sparkled with malice.

"When you were having my fellow Jews burned for witches, no one dared cross you, especially not someone like me, with a family to feed. But now even your friends know your treachery to your own nephew. And they know he won't let it pass. So no one fears you. Including me."

Pitney cuffed the man viciously, but the old man merely winced and rubbed his jaw. Then he continued to level that accusing stare on Pitney.

"Strike me if you like," he grumbled. "But except for the paltry power in your fist, you've no other strength now. Your power is gone. Your nephew has seen to that. And I'll die under your fists before I lend you one more pence."

"Damn you and all of them!" Pitney whirled on his heels to leave.

He found his way down the rickety stairs with difficulty, his knees shaking with his anger. He *had to* eliminate his nephew's threat to him. Though the king's championing of Garett had struck him with dread, until now Pitney had been certain he could salvage his reputation in the eyes of the court. He'd groveled before the king he despised, hoping to counteract the effects of Garett's tales.

But the rumors accompanying Garett hadn't been so easily squelched. The exiles had spoken of Garett's sufferings. That pompous rake Hampden had insinuated that Pitney had tried to have Garett murdered in France. That had sent the merchants fleeing, suddenly loath to do business with him.

He knew Garett couldn't prove a thing, but that was the worst of it. Garett didn't have to. Innuendo and rumor did it all. And if Garett ever suspected . . .

Pitney ground his teeth together. Garett had to be rendered ineffective. Or wiped off the face of the earth.

Chapter Thirteen

Loyalty is still the same,
Whether it win or lose the game;
True as a dial to the sun,
Although it be not shined upon.
—Samuel Butler, *Hudibras*

After hours passed, during which Marianne saw nothing of Garett, William showed up to bring her into town. As soon as he led her into Lydgate's finest inn, she began to fret. Garett was making good on his promise to involve the townspeople in his search for the truth.

And he'd commanded that she come unmasked. It made her feel undressed. She hadn't appeared publicly in town without her disguise in weeks.

Quickly she scanned the ale room for some sign of Garett. When she saw nothing of him, she shivered.

"You mustn't let the master worry you, miss," William whispered as he led her toward a chair near the hearth. "It's just that he don't know what to do with you. You and your aunt being so closemouthed and all . . . well, that bothers him."

What an understatement. "Where is he?" she whispered back as William beckoned her to sit.

William cocked his head upward. "We're to wait 'til they send a message down for us to go up."

She groaned. The town council used one of the inn's upper rooms for their meetings. Garett had obviously called them in.

A pox on him! How she wished she hadn't become embroiled with him. If she'd only acted more meekly the first time they'd met . . . if she'd just been more careful when she'd treated his wounds . . . if—

This serves no purpose.

Instead, she should prepare for what was to come and decide how to act.

Telling the truth—that she was Sir Henry's daughter— was one choice. But Garett, with his loyalty to the king, would follow his duty and give her over to the soldiers. Aside from the danger to her—the possibility that she might hang for her involvement in the supposed plot to kill the king—the truth would endanger others as well: her aunt, Mr. Tibbett, any townspeople who'd knowingly aided her. Given the choice, the council might prefer to have her keep her secret rather than risk being accused of treason for harboring her. At least if they said nothing, Garett could never really prove they knew all along who she was.

Of course, she might be trusting too much to their loyalty. They might just reveal her secret to the earl the moment they saw her face. They might claim her mask had kept them from knowing the truth.

No, they'd never betray her so easily. Nor could she betray them by telling all at the first sign of trouble. Her only safe recourse was to keep silent and hope everything worked out.

Shifting uncomfortably in the hard chair, she glanced around the room. The guarded looks occasionally thrown her way by the other patrons of the inn were, for the most part, kind and encouraging. She took some comfort from that.

Then she caught a stranger gazing at her as if he knew her. But how could he? She would have remembered the sly coldness in his manner. He nodded at her with blatant insolence, and a chill swept through her.

She leaned over to William. "Who is that man wearing the sword?"

William followed the direction of her gaze, then grew wary. "'Tis Ashton. M'lord believes he's Tearle's man. He's the villain who stabbed that soldier attempting to burn the fields."

Good Lord. She'd often wondered who'd been responsible. Garett hadn't lied—it had been another of Tearle's men. "Why does the earl let him roam freely about Lydgate?"

"Oh, Ashton serves his uses. You can be sure he only reports to Tearle what m'lord wishes him to report, though the cursed bastard don't know it."

When Marianne looked at William questioningly, he dropped his gaze.

A sudden suspicion twisted her insides. "That's why

he's here—to see me and tell Sir Pitney your master has caught me!"

"Nay!" William clasped her hand. "I'm sure m'lord has nothing to do with his being here. The bastard's a curious devil, and most probably heard about the council's being called. He's here to see what the whole thing's about, that's all."

Marianne couldn't quite believe him. It wouldn't surprise her if Garett's intentions were to send another of his oblique, vindictive messages to Sir Pitney.

Her stomach churned. Regardless of what Garett intended, if Ashton had recognized her, the results would be the same. Either he would immediately tell the earl her identity or he'd pass his knowledge on to Sir Pitney. Who knew what Sir Pitney might do with it?

She cast a furtive glance Ashton's way again, but this time his head hung low over his mug of ale.

Please, God, she prayed. *Don't let him have recognized me.*

After a few minutes, he stood and left the inn. She didn't know whether to be glad or terrified. William watched him go with a scowl, which only distressed her more.

Stop it! she told herself. *You have enough to worry about at the moment.*

Then her thoughts turned to a new source of concern—whether Garett had played any part in Father's arrest. That no longer made much sense to her. Garett was the king's man—she knew that for certain now. He would only have planted the poison if he'd been certain he could keep His Majesty from taking it and couldn't be caught.

Would he plan such an elaborate plot—and risk his future with the king—just to regain his lands? Garett did seem obsessed with Falkham House, and he did seem to resent Father for having bought the estate. But his hatred of Sir Pitney overrode all of those. Garett would more likely have plotted his uncle's ruin than Father's, for Sir Pitney was the one truly at fault for his exile.

What's more, her heart told her Garett couldn't have done it. The same man who'd expressed concern for his tenants' well-being, who'd shown compassion to the soldier who'd burned his fields and who'd treated her with courtesy most of the time couldn't also have ruined her father.

Then who? Sir Pitney was a possibility, since he, too, had wanted Falkham House. He, too, had hated Father. Still, would he have done such a thing, knowing that his nephew had returned with a stronger claim to the estate?

The innkeeper descended the stairs to approach her and William. Avoiding her eyes, he bent to mutter something in William's ear.

William nodded and stood. "We go now," he said, offering her his hand. She took it and rose on shaky legs.

But as she passed through the room toward the stairs, she realized everyone watched her, waiting anxiously for her to give some sign that she was in control, that their futures were safe in her hands. As she climbed the stairs, she forced an expression of calm assurance to her face. She had to show the people of Lydgate that they could count on her to manage the earl.

The first thing Marianne saw when she was led into the room where the council met was Garett standing at one end of a long table. His eyes were trained not on her but on the men who watched her enter. Clearly, Garett hadn't told them what the meeting was for, because they looked first surprised, then alarmed.

Mr. Tibbett grew red, as he always did in an uncomfortable situation. And the mayor, whose foppish mannerisms were the joke of the town, began to smooth the lace trim of his petticoat breeches repeatedly. She felt their anxiety so acutely that it was difficult to keep from bolting out of the inn and taking her chances that Garett wouldn't find her.

Then Garett leveled a fierce gaze on her, clearly seeking to pierce her defenses and frighten her into blurting out whatever he wished to hear. She matched his gaze with a scathing one of her own. Devil take him, she'd show him that no matter his tactics, she wouldn't be intimidated.

Mr. Tibbett broke the silence. "My lord, if you could tell us what this is about . . ."

Garett turned his eyes from Marianne to Mr. Tibbett. "As you know, I've taken an interest in Lydgate from the time I returned to Falkham House and reclaimed my inheritance. After all, my tenants come to your town for their goods, their amusements . . . their ale."

One of the men laughed nervously.

"I believe I've been careful to look to your needs as well," he went on. "But now it is I who need your help."

"How's that, my lord?" asked the mayor, his hands now nearly frenzied in their nervous movements.

"You all know Mina," Garett said, gesturing toward her. "You may not . . . ah . . . recognize her without her mask, but you know her all the same. From what I understand, she's taken care of many of you and your children."

Murmurs of assent filled the room.

"Although she's a gypsy, I realize she's been a great help to this town. But it has come to my attention, gentlemen, that she isn't what she appears to be. She has admitted to me that she has noble blood, something you may not have realized."

Marianne saw the look of alarm in the men's faces. Quickly she asked, "Must you proclaim my bastardy to the world, my lord? I fail to see how that suits your purpose."

The men at first seemed confused by her statement but then quickly realized what she must have told Garett. Some of them relaxed.

Garett shot her such a quelling glance that she caught her breath. "In any case, her past isn't typical of a gypsy. Recently, it's also come to my attention that she has connections to my uncle." His gaze left her to sweep the men in the room. "You all know that my uncle stole my lands when I was in exile. But you may not realize that since I've returned, he's also sent men to burn my fields and even to kill me."

Angry mutters could be heard throughout the room,

and Marianne's pulse quickened. Their anger wasn't for her, but it alarmed her to realize that Garett knew just how to manipulate the council members to gain their sympathies.

"So you see why I must be cautious in my dealings with strangers, particularly ones who know my uncle well," Garett continued. "That's why I've come to you. I know you've trusted Mina to cure your ailments, and I don't doubt your trust is warranted. But I also know she's hiding something. I must wonder what it is and why she won't tell me how she knows my uncle."

Mr. Tibbett darted a glance at Mina, his face suddenly ashen. "My lord, I'm sure her connection to Sir Pitney is of little consequence. As for what she is hiding . . . well, if I may be so bold, gypsies are often reticent about their pasts. They . . . they lead rather sordid lives, after all."

Garett eyed him skeptically. "How then can all of you so trust one of them? Don't you question her motives in healing your ills? Haven't you wondered why she takes no coin for it?"

Marianne groaned. All her stupid mistakes were coming back to haunt her.

The mayor leaned forward. "Ah, but she does take our coin, my lord." Then he hesitated, as if uncertain whether he'd said the right thing. "I mean, 'tis worth it to give her a bit of gold for all the good she does."

Garett's eyes sought hers, cold and gleaming. "'Tis only my coin you refuse, then?"

She swallowed but didn't answer.

"My lord, I do not think you should worry for us,"

Mr. Tibbett put in hastily. "We've dealt with gypsies before. Some are undoubtedly scoundrels, but we will vouch for Mina and her aunt's trustworthiness. They've never harmed any of us."

Garett's stormy gaze shifted to include the entire council. "Tell me this, then. Why did she lie about the reason for her mask?"

The mayor settled back in his chair. "Who knows? Women are funny about such matters. Perhaps she's shy."

Despite her fear, Marianne bit back a smile. Trust to Lydgate's eccentric mayor to come up with such an absurd reason.

Another man spoke up. "Mayhap she didn't want us to think she was a whor—a disreputable woman. Mayhap she feared we'd take her for one if she . . . she displayed her attractions openly. You understand." The man flashed Marianne a sheepish look, as if to say it was the best excuse he could come up with at the moment. She gave him a quick smile.

Garett caught it and clenched his fists at his sides. "You all seem eager to overlook Mina's odd habits. But you've still not sufficiently explained her connection to my uncle."

Mr. Tibbett drew himself up. "My lord, you mustn't be concerned on that account. Sir Pitney is our enemy if he is yours. I have no doubt whatsoever that Mina stands with us in this."

"Of course I do," she staunchly declared. "I detest Sir Pitney."

"Why?" Garett leaned down to plant his fists on the table. "Tell me, gentlemen, why should she care? She's a gypsy. She has no reason to side with me against my uncle. She owns no lands nor owes me any loyalty. So why would my uncle be Mina's enemy? What has he done to her to make her hate him?"

The men looked nonplussed. The silence in the room was oppressive.

"I told you already," Marianne said hastily. "He knew enough about my father's relationship to my mother to ruin him."

"Time for you to be silent, Mina," Garett commanded without looking at her. He didn't have to. His harsh expression would silence anyone.

He let his gaze rest on every man at the table, each of whom looked more uncomfortable by the moment.

"When did Mina first come to Lydgate?" he asked, the shift in his questioning temporarily unsettling them all.

As the men glanced at each other uncertainly, Mina bit back the impulse to answer for them. *Please, God, let them be wise in this and not say anything that contradicts what I told him.*

After a long silence, the mayor answered, "I-I really don't remember, my lord. One day we just . . . realized she lived nearby, that's all."

Garett's expression would have frozen a hot bath. He turned to Mr. Tibbett. "Is that your answer, too, Mr. Bones?"

Mr. Tibbett turned several shades of red. He was

clearly torn between his allegiance to Garett and his loyalty to Mina. After hesitating a moment, he dropped his eyes to the table and nodded.

Garett's gaze was chilling. "Did any of you know her father?" he went on relentlessly. "How about her mother?"

An uneasy quiet reigned. That only enraged Garett further.

"You, my Lord Mayor," he said pointedly. The mayor shifted in his seat. "Have you nothing to tell me about Mina's true identity that will assure me she's to be trusted?"

The mayor looked as if he was going to faint at any moment. "My lord," he practically squeaked, "she once threatened to thrash your uncle."

Marianne had a hysterical urge to laugh. She'd almost forgotten the taunt she'd thrown Sir Pitney's way the day he'd come to her father with his final offer, after having sought to destroy her parents' reputations.

Garett wasn't amused, however. He slammed one fist on the table. "Have you any idea whom you're dealing with, gentlemen?"

Their cringes gave him his answer.

"Damn it to hell, what hold has she over all of you? How can this one girl make you risk so much to protect her?"

Marianne's stomach sank at his words. Oh, Lord, what had she brought upon them all?

Mr. Tibbett rose with a solemn expression. "My lord, we wouldn't have you angry with us. Do we fear you? Indeed we do. We know our town wouldn't survive without your tenants, our tradesmen couldn't thrive without your patronage, and even our church would founder without your charity."

He glanced at Marianne, and his expression softened. "But we trust you to be just, as your father was before you. Mina has done you no harm—"

"Yet," Garett interjected.

Mr. Tibbett swallowed. "Nor will she ever. I would stake my life and reputation on that. She fears all noblemen these days and thus believes she has good reason to fear you. But surely you cannot fault her for her caution, nor find in it signs of deceit."

Garett's gaze shot to Marianne. "Only the guilty have anything to fear."

"Or the unjustly accused," Mr. Tibbett said. "In any case, she has proven herself worthy of our trust. Would you have us repay her kindness by betraying her secrets?"

When Garett turned his black frown on Mr. Tibbett, Marianne could bear it no longer. "My lord, I'm the only one who should bear the brunt of your anger. If you think me a criminal, then charge me with a crime and hand me over to the constable. If I'm to be imprisoned, at least let it be by a true jailor."

At that, Garett let out a low curse. "You know I don't want you imprisoned. But I'd welcome your trust. Clearly you're hiding from someone or something. I don't care who or what it is, even if it's my uncle. I can't protect you if I don't know what I'm protecting you from. And I can't trust you if you won't trust me. So why not tell me the truth and make it easier on all of us?"

Oh, how much she wanted to. How nice it would be to trust him. Yet she couldn't. He was still the king's man. Would he protect her from the king? Would he protect her aunt and the people of Lydgate as well?

She dropped her gaze. She couldn't rely on him. It was too risky. "My lord, I've nothing more to say."

An ominous silence filled the room. Garett finally bit out, "Gentlemen, if I might have a word alone with Mina?"

There was a furious scraping of chair legs as the men hurried to leave the room. Mr. Tibbett paused near her, but at the stony glare Garett shot him, he clearly thought better of trying to speak to her and left.

For several moments after the room emptied, Garett simply stood in silence at the opposite end of the table. Her heart hammered to the beat of her fear, making her want nothing more than to flee. When at last she ventured a glance at Garett, he was staring at her as if she were some exotic creature in the marketplace.

"I'm impressed." The bitter irony underlying his words cut her. "I thought I was the only one, but now I see you've bewitched an entire town. How do you manage it?"

She could only stare at his harsh face.

His gaze flicked over her as he rested his hip on the table. "My mother once told me that the mark of a true noble lay in his ability to command the loyalty and respect of those beneath him." He paused. "If I hadn't met your gypsy aunt and seen with my own eyes the wagon you live in, I'd swear you were as much a lady as I am a lord."

"They are simply grateful for my doctoring."

"Nay. They care deeply for you. What's more, you care deeply enough for them to trust them with your life. Tell me, sweetling, why can you entrust your secrets to Lydgate's fool of a mayor and not to me?"

Was that really hurt she heard in his voice? "He earned my trust, my lord. They all did."

He rose and came toward her. She backed away, but he caught her around the waist.

As he cupped her chin, his eyes bored into hers. "What must I do then to earn your trust, my gypsy princess?"

His unmistakably wounded gaze disturbed her deeply, tempting her to tell him all, even when she mustn't. "You could set me free."

Disappointment clouded his features. He seemed to struggle with himself before his expression grew shuttered. "Ask of me anything but that. I can't set you free, even to gain your trust."

His flat tone sparked her anger. "Why not? You heard the council. I'm no friend of Sir Pitney's. You've no reason to keep me, no reason to suspect me so. I have done no wrong!"

He stared at her, frighteningly implacable. "Then why won't you tell me the truth about your past?"

He had her there. As long as she could give him no proof of her true character, she couldn't escape him if he chose not to release her. She pushed herself away from him, the acrid taste of defeat choking her.

"William!" Garett shouted, his eyes following her every movement.

The door opened and William thrust his head in the room. "M'lord?"

"Take her back to Falkham House," Garett growled.

She stood frozen, her heart sinking as she heard the words that sealed her doom.

"Won't you be coming with us?" William asked.

"Not yet," Garett bit out, flashing Marianne a bitter glance. "I still have a few people to talk to in Lydgate."

If he'd hoped to frighten her by that veiled threat, he didn't succeed, for the one thing she'd learned from the council meeting was that no one in Lydgate would betray her. She moved mechanically toward the door.

Then he stepped forward to stop her. "I warn you now. I'll learn the truth if I have to question every man and woman in Lydgate. So it does you no good to fight me. It just prolongs your torment."

"I'm afraid I have no choice. I can't say more than I've said. Thus I'll learn to endure the torment and to hope that in time you come to your senses."

Firmly she removed his hand from her arm. Then, without a backward glance, she accompanied William from the room.

Will stole a glance at the little gypsy. She sat her horse like a fine queen, but the sorrow in her face told him that her meeting with his master and the council hadn't gone well at all.

What a shame that he couldn't do more to help her. But what? Mina was as closemouthed as her fetching aunt. Without knowing their secrets, he couldn't advise them of how best to deal with his master.

The secrets didn't bother Will as they did the earl. Will wasn't bedeviled by the past like his master. He didn't care what life Tamara had led before. All he knew was he wanted to swing her up in his arms and kiss her every time he saw her. What was it the bloody woman did to him, anyway? After all, she was older than he. A man of his youth could have a number of women. Why go to a hostile wench with a good five years on him?

But her lips were no less pleasurable for it . . . when he could get her to still her barbed tongue. Even her bold manner didn't bother him. He'd die before telling her, but he enjoyed their squabbles. He liked finding ways to stun her into silence so he could snatch a moment's sweetness from her.

He sighed. This time he'd have to work hard to get back in her good graces. When she saw how unhappy the earl had made her niece—

Will glanced again at Mina. Poor girl. The master had been a mite harsh on her, and all because he wouldn't be practical like Will and admit he just wanted the lass in his bed. The earl ought to have bedded her the moment he'd laid eyes on her and put to rest all his doubts. Why, anybody could see she wasn't a criminal.

As Will watched her, tears escaped from beneath her

lashes, and he felt it like a punch in the gut. "Don't cry now, miss. 'Twill be all right in time."

"He'll never let me go," she said mournfully.

About that she was probably right. The master's heart was entwined with hers, though he wouldn't admit it.

"What shall I do, Will? I can't bear this much longer without going mad."

"Don't say that. What would your aunt say if she heard you talking such foolery?"

Mina stared down at the reins. "What will she say when she hears about today?"

Will started to retort, but something in the faraway gaze of her eyes arrested him. She appeared to ponder some idea. Suddenly, she straightened in the saddle and her face brightened. "Will, would you do me a great favor?"

"If I can," he replied, watching the play of emotions on her face with keen interest.

"Would you let me visit Aunt Tamara before we go on to Falkham House?"

He should have known she'd want something like that. He couldn't blame her, for she deserved some matronly comforting right now.

Still . . . "Come now, miss, you shouldn't ask it of me. I doubt the master would want it."

"But he needn't know," she persisted. "We could just stay a little while. Please, Will. I need to . . . to talk to her."

The break in her voice made him feel awful. He shifted nervously in the saddle and looked ahead to

Falkham House, a short distance away. He well understood her unhappiness. And the earl had already been allowing her to visit Tamara as long as Will or the guard accompanied her. How was this any different?

He stole a glance at her, and pity welled up within him. The girl was so small and weary. Her cheeks were streaked with tears. What would Tamara say if she found out he'd denied her beloved niece such a simple request?

And why deny her? What could it hurt?

"All right," he muttered, "but let's be quick about it. I don't want the master coming back to find us gone."

She glanced away. "That would be wretched, wouldn't it?" She spurred her horse down the road and into the forest, and he followed her. In a short time they pulled up outside the gypsy wagon.

"Come in with me," she told him brightly as she strode up the steps. "I know you want to see her, too."

He shrugged, but his steps quickened as he followed her into the wagon. Once inside, they found Tamara sitting on her pallet, working with her needle. She looked up as they entered, and her face lit with pleasure as she saw her niece. Then she caught sight of Will, and her eyes gleamed with a different emotion.

His heart caught in his throat.

"I talked him into bringing me for a visit." Mina took a seat on a nearby stool, then gestured companionably to the other, so Will sat down as well.

Tamara's gaze shifted to Mina, and her face darkened. "Has anything happened, poppet?"

"A great deal. But before I tell you, I'd like some tea." She smiled at Will. "I'm sure our guest would like some, too."

Will returned the smile. "Actually I wouldn't mind a bit of something to warm me." He flashed Tamara a wicked grin.

Tamara scowled at him, then stood and planted her hands on her hips. "The tea can come later. What happened?"

Will watched as Mina stared steadily at her aunt. "Please, Aunt Tamara," she said in an oddly strained voice. "I can't talk when I'm parched. Make us some of your cinnamon tea. I do so love it. It's been a long while since I had any."

"My cinnamon tea?" Tamara said, a perplexed expression on her face. Suddenly, her face cleared. She flashed Will a searching look. "Ah, yes, my tea. All right then, if you insist on having tea first, that's what we'll do."

Her abrupt acquiescence surprised, then peeved, Will. Why was it she never hopped to do what *he* asked?

She rummaged in a corner of the wagon, then returned with a pot and some packets of leaves and sticks, along with a jar of honey. Dazzling Will with a brilliant smile, she prepared the pot, carefully measuring out various leaves. For a moment, he wondered what all the fuss about the tea was.

Then Tamara passed him on her way out of the wagon to the fire. The sway of her hips absorbed his thoughts, and he didn't think about the cinnamon tea anymore.

Chapter Fourteen

Though those that are betrayed
Do feel the treason sharply, yet the traitor
Stands in worse case of woe.
—Shakespeare, *Cymbeline*

Is he still asleep?" Marianne pulled on the reins as Aunt Tamara pushed through the wagon's curtains and climbed up onto the seat beside her.

"He's coming around, I'm afraid. I wasn't sure how much opium he could tolerate without tasting it in the tea."

"I suppose we should have left him there."

"Then when he awakened, he would have sought out his lordship. The man would have been on our trail immediately. With us in a mule-drawn wagon, Falkham and his great horse would have found us in a few hours' time. This way we at least have Will under our control."

Marianne was skeptical about that, as skeptical as she was about Aunt Tamara's reasons for bringing William with them. "Now we have a man to protect us," she quipped as she adjusted the mask she'd returned to wearing.

Aunt Tamara merely grunted.

Marianne trained her eyes on the road ahead and wondered how many miles were between them and Garett now. "A pity William couldn't have slept longer. He won't be happy when he finds out—"

"Tamara, you damned witch!" came a bellow from inside the wagon.

Aunt Tamara grinned. "I think he's found out."

"Untie me this minute!" William shouted. "Or I swear when you do, I'll beat that sweet bottom of yours 'til you wish you'd never laid eyes on me!"

As Marianne bit back a smile, Aunt Tamara cried into the wagon, "You're staying put 'til we're safe away, damn you! So hush your shouting before I stuff your mouth with a handkerchief."

A tense silence reigned for a long while after that. It made Marianne uneasy, especially since she felt guilty over how she'd tricked William. But she'd had no choice. Garett would have kept pressing the matter until they'd all ended up in the gaol. She couldn't just let him lead her like a lamb to the slaughter, could she?

Aunt Tamara had been right—trying to find out who'd framed Father had been fruitless. Marianne had simply risked the lives and futures of several people. Well, no more. If they could keep William tied up another day or two, he'd have to go so far to fetch Garett that the two men would never catch up to them before they reached the Channel, and once in France, she and Aunt Tamara would be free of Garett forever.

She sighed. That's what she wanted. Truly.

Yet the memory of his mouth on hers, his hands caressing her, threatened to swamp her with regret. Fiercely, she reminded herself of how he'd looked in the upper room of the inn, his face clouded over with anger and determination, and his eyes the color of gray ice. *That* Garett was the man she was fleeing, not the Garett who'd showered her with sweet kisses.

Suddenly a crash behind her rocked the wagon.

"Fie on him," Aunt Tamara snapped as Marianne tried to control the startled mules.

The wagon swayed dangerously, and Aunt Tamara shifted her position. Abruptly an arm snaked through the curtains to snatch her off the seat and into the wagon's dim confines. Marianne halted the mules, then thrust her head through the curtains.

William sat cross-legged on the wagon floor with Aunt Tamara's bottom settled in his lap. The rest of her flailed around the two wiry arms gripping her waist. Although she kicked and struggled furiously, William had the upper hand.

How had he escaped his bonds? And what was she to do about it? As strong as she and Aunt Tamara were, they could never subdue William long enough to tie him up again.

"Let me go, you brute!" Aunt Tamara beat on his arms with her fists, but it did her no good.

William merely glared at Marianne. "What did you two sly wenches do to make me sleep?"

Marianne swallowed. She had to convince him not

to take her back to Lydgate. "It was harmless, William, really. Aunt Tamara put opium in your tea, that's all."

"You should have slept longer," Aunt Tamara bit out, giving up the fight. "But fractious man that you are, you couldn't be reasonable. How did you get loose?"

William shifted Aunt Tamara on his lap as if she were a sack of meal. "I was a soldier once, remember?" He thrust one leg out, and for the first time Marianne noticed the knife handle that peeked above the edge of his boot.

Aunt Tamara saw it, too, and reached for it, but he jerked her back against him. "Not so fast, my blood-thirsty wench. I can well imagine what you'd do to me with *that*. I don't like being trussed up, so I'll just hold on to it for a bit. And you."

That sent Aunt Tamara into a frenzy of struggle.

He swore under his breath. "Be still. You ain't going nowhere yet."

"Please let her go," Marianne said. "She can't harm you now."

"I'll be the judge of that. So tell me—where do you suppose you're off to?"

"France," Aunt Tamara answered. "Mina and I shall put as many miles between us and that demon master of yours as possible."

"Was I going with you?"

"Aye," Marianne answered. "At least as far as the Channel. Then it's your choice—return to Garett or stay with us."

Aunt Tamara snorted. "There's no choice for him— he's not staying with us after we reach the Channel."

William dropped his head to plant a quick kiss on Aunt Tamara's head, and she turned a brilliant shade of red. "You wouldn't want to lose me now, would you, love?" he murmured with a grin. "I could be useful to you both. You've need of a man to take care of things."

"Then you'll go with us?" Marianne asked.

William's grin faded. "Nay. I must return to my master. And you at least must return with me."

Since William had slackened his hold on Aunt Tamara, she chose that moment to jab her elbow into his stomach.

Though he grunted, he tightened his arms around her waist. "By my troth! Don't you ever sit docile like a woman ought?"

"I'll not be docile if you carry my niece off."

"Besides," Marianne put in, thinking quickly, "you can't make us go back. There's two of us to your one. You could return alone, but by the time you arrive, Garett will have decided you willingly helped us escape. He won't be likely to take you back in his employ."

William scowled. "You've thought this all out, haven't you? Trying to ruin my life after all I've done for you."

"Done for her?" Aunt Tamara fairly screeched. "You helped him keep her captive, or have you forgotten?"

William eyed them both keenly. "Well, 'tis really of no consequence. Garett will find us before we even reach the Channel."

Marianne ignored a quick spurt of apprehension. "He's hours behind us. And he stayed in town to question people. He may not even have returned to Falkham House yet."

Oh, Lord, she dearly hoped that was the case. William's loud guffaw told her that he didn't think it was.

"The master could no more stay away from you than a wolf can stay away from a doe," William said dryly. "He'll be on our trail already, I warrant you. And I wouldn't want to be in your shoes when he catches up to us."

Aunt Tamara twisted to gaze up at him. "And how will he know which way we've gone, Sir Know-It-All? We could have taken a hundred different roads."

William shrugged. "'Twasn't but three months past that the master tracked a man through Spain and caught up with him a week after the villain fled to Portugal. His lordship did that on a mission for the king. And he won't give this any less attention. He'll find us, and there's naught you can do about it."

Much as she wanted to scoff at William's words, dread stole over Marianne. Then something else he'd said caught her attention. Three months past. Three months past her father hadn't yet been accused of trying to kill the king.

"William, when did your master return to England?" she asked.

The servant eyed her with suspicion. "Why do you wish to know?"

"I can't tell you," she said, "but it's important. Please. What harm is there in telling me?"

He scowled, then sighed. "Suppose you're right. Wait a bit and let me think . . . well, when we left Spain in search of his quarry, we didn't return. We crossed the Channel from Portugal. A rocky crossing it was—"

"When did you return?" Marianne broke in. She had to know if Garett had been in England when Father had been arrested.

"I believe 'twas late July. Two days after my birthday." He grinned broadly. "I told m'lord that seeing England again was the best of birthday gifts."

Marianne let out a breath. Garett hadn't even been in the country when the poison had been found in Father's medications. He hadn't needed to be there to have treachery done, yet it seemed unlikely he would have been plotting from afar to have Father arrested, while chasing after some man in Spain.

Aunt Tamara's voice jolted her from her thoughts. "Enough chatter, poppet. Drive on and be quick about it. We need to gain more time on the earl."

With a nod, Marianne closed the curtain and started the team moving. All this time she'd assumed that Garett had returned to England with the king and the other exiles. She'd assumed that his revenge had taken so long for him to bring to pass because regaining his lands from his uncle had taken time.

But if he hadn't returned to England until after Father's arrest, he couldn't have been involved in Father's death.

A weight lifted from her chest, leaving her almost giddy with relief. She tried to tell herself it was because she couldn't have endured thinking she'd allowed such a villain to take liberties with her. But the truth ran deeper. She didn't want Garett to be a villain. She wanted him to be a man she could respect, could care for.

She sighed as she coaxed the mules into a brisker pace. Even if he was, it changed nothing. She still had much to fear from him.

He said he desired her, but he desired Mina, the mysterious gypsy girl, not Marianne, the suspect lady. Learning who she was would, at best, deepen his suspicions concerning his uncle and at worst force him to turn her and her aunt over to the soldiers. A man who embarked on missions for the king wouldn't allow the daughter of a suspected traitor to go free.

She swallowed hard, fear gripping her. He musn't find them. He mustn't!

Oh, why was she worrying? Regardless of what William said, Garett couldn't work miracles. After all, he might not even have followed them. After their confrontation that day, he might be glad to be rid of her.

Throughout the afternoon, she clung to that hope. By the time the sun had set, her hope rose more. There'd been no sign of Garett. What's more, the moon was full, so they could keep going for a while yet.

If only she weren't so tired.

She thrust her head through the curtains to ask her aunt to take her place on the perch, only to find Aunt Tamara and William both asleep on the pallet. William's arms cradled her, and Aunt Tamara wore a soft smile as her body curved into his. They looked so blissful in their sleep. How could she wake them?

The mules plodded on. The wagon passed through a village with a couple of brightly lit inns. The smell of roast beef wafted from one of them, making Marianne's mouth water. She would give anything for a hot meal instead of their cold provisions right now. And only think how wonderful it would be to sit by a warm fire and sleep in a soft bed.

But she dared not stop with Garett possibly in pursuit.

After reluctantly leaving the village behind, she pulled her cloak more tightly about her. For a while, the cold wind seeping beneath the wool kept her awake, but soon even that didn't stave off sleep. If she could just lay her head on a pillow for a few minutes . . .

When she awoke with a jerk, she realized she'd been dozing. But for how long? Her mask had slipped down over her nose. As she jerked it into place, she glanced around. The mules had drawn the wagon off into a meadow and were busily munching grass, and the moon was far higher than before.

Devil take it. She must have been asleep a few hours. Thank Providence she'd awakened while it was still night.

Then she realized what had awakened her—the sound of hooves rumbling in the distance. She seized the reins in a panic. It couldn't be Garett, since the sound came from ahead of them, but still, the noise made it clear that more than one horse was approaching.

A pox on't, who would be riding the road at night?

Stories of highwaymen flashed through her mind, and she opened the curtains to call into the wagon, "Someone approaches!" but William and Aunt Tamara merely grunted in their sleep.

Frantically she tugged at the reins to urge the mules back onto the road. They wouldn't budge from their grazing, curse them! Leaping down from the perch, she yanked on the reins in desperation, but the mules were as exhausted and hungry as she, loath to leave the pleasant meadow at the side of the road.

Then the horsemen rounded the curve, and her heart sank. Nine well-armed soldiers rode wearily toward them. She said a silent prayer. Perhaps they would ride on without noticing the wagon. The last thing she needed was soldiers engaging in their favorite pastime of persecuting gypsies.

But her prayer went unheeded. The moonlight clearly outlined the wagon, catching the eye of the soldier who rode at the head of the band.

"Look here!" he called to his fellows. "'Tis a gypsy's wagon. Just what we need to keep us in the captain's good graces when we tell 'im we lost that thief. If we bring 'im some vagabonds, he might go easy on us."

Fading into the shadows beside the wagon, Marianne held her breath.

"Come on, Harry," another soldier cried. "I ain't up for anything but a good bed and a mug of ale."

Unfortunately, Aunt Tamara chose that moment to thrust her head out the curtains. "What is it?"

"Hush!" Marianne whispered, but it was too late.

The soldier sighted Aunt Tamara's hair silhouetted against the wagon's pale curtain.

"Oho!" the soldiers' leader shouted, pulling his horse off the road. "'Tis a gypsy *wench* we have this time."

"Will!" Aunt Tamara cried as the soldiers rode into the meadow.

But William was already out the back doors, knife in hand. The soldiers laughed when they saw his puny weapon and thin frame. Three leapt from their horses to rush him, but he fought fiercely, his wiry strength taking them by surprise. He sliced open the arm of one man, who yelped and fell back, but another jumped down to join the fray, and the lot of them finally managed to disarm him. Then two soldiers held him while one slammed his fist into William's stomach.

"Leave him be!" Aunt Tamara leapt down from the wagon to run blindly into the crowd of soldiers. One caught her easily about the waist.

"Harry, you found us a good wench," he shouted, his hands lifting to cup Aunt Tamara's ample breasts.

William strained helplessly against his captors with a strangled cry, which turned into a groan as a soldier hit him again and again.

Marianne's vision clouded with fury. Whipping her cloak about her, she stepped forth from the darkness. "Release her!" she cried.

The men paused to stare at her. At first her cloak and mask seemed to disconcert them.

"She's got the smallpox," Aunt Tamara told them quickly, accustomed to thinking on her feet.

"The smallpox, eh?" The man named Harry sneered at them. "Show us the pox, and we'll leave you be!"

God rot him. What should she do?

As she hesitated, Harry darted forward to grab her arm. Before she could slap him with her free hand, he jerked her around and up against him so hard that it knocked the breath out of her.

His fingers clawed at the mask as she fought him. Then it was gone and the hood of her cloak pulled back, setting her hair free.

"Well, lads?" Harry asked as he dragged her struggling form before the other men and yanked loose her cloak so it fell around her feet.

Someone released a low whistle. "Faith, Harry, 'tis a bonny one ye've got there!"

"Isn't she, though?"

His arm wrapped about her waist, and he slid a knife beneath her laces. In moments her dress came apart at the back. As the other soldiers cheered him on, he snatched away the scarf at her breasts, pushed down her stiff bodice, and squeezed one breast so hard that she cried out in pain.

It was too much to bear. Marianne kicked at him, grimly pleased when her heel hit some part of Harry's anatomy.

But it wasn't enough. With a curse, Harry threw her facedown on the ground and sat atop her, jerking her arms back painfully.

"Little lying witch, aren't you?" he growled. "The pox indeed! Well, then, gypsy witch, let's see 'ow long you last the night with us. Perhaps we can teach you and your friend the right way to please a man."

Marianne groaned, certain she was to be crushed beneath Harry's weight long before he could defile her. As she struggled for breath, another soldier shouted, "Harry! Someone's coming!"

Wonderful. Now there would be another assailant to add to their torment.

"So?" Harry said. "He'll go on when 'e sees it's well-armed soldiers."

Marianne tried to scream, praying that whoever approached would come to their aid, but Harry forced her head down into the grass, muffling any sound.

Then above the thundering of blood in her ears, she heard hooves thundering on the road. When the sound abruptly stopped, she found herself hoping . . .

"What are you men doing?" a harsh voice rang out from behind her.

Garett. Thank heaven, it was Garett!

Then a chill swept through her—there were nine men to his one.

"It's none of your business, I'm thinkin'," Harry cried.

This time Garett's voice was much nearer. "Get off her! Now!"

"Who do you think you—"

Abruptly, Harry's weight left her, and she looked up to see Garett suspending the soldier aloft with only one hand clenched around the man's neck.

Harry struggled fruitlessly for breath. As Garett lifted

him higher, the soldier's face turned purple. Only when he was clawing at Garett's hand did Garett toss him to the ground. Harry lay there choking and gasping as Garett turned his back on him.

While the others stared, awestruck, Garett knelt beside Marianne and turned her onto her side. His gaze swiftly took in her partly bared breasts and slashed laces, and rage glittered in his eyes. He stood and helped her to her feet, then laid her cloak gently about her shoulders.

But there was nothing gentle in his expression as he turned to face the soldiers, keeping a protective arm about her waist. "Who's your captain?"

A soldier laughed nervously. "If you think he'll care that we had a little fun with some gypsies—"

"He'd care if he heard you assaulted friends of the Earl of Falkham."

"Earls don't traffic with no gypsies," one man called out.

By this time William had found his voice. Struggling against the arms that held him, he cried, "He *is* the earl, you damned fools. And I wouldn't anger m'lord unduly. I'm just his valet, but she"—he nodded toward Marianne—"she's his runaway mistress."

Though the revelation seemed to give the men pause, it wasn't enough to keep them from closing in.

Garett thrust Marianne aside and unsheathed his sword. "Think before you act. If I'm not the earl, you've lost nothing but a night's enjoyment. If I am, you'll seal your fate by attacking me."

The men hesitated. Then Marianne saw Harry rise from the ground behind Garett. "Garett!" she screamed as she pointed at Harry.

Garett wheeled just in time to deflect the blade that Harry drove up at him. Harry thrust again, but this time, Garett not only parried the thrust but also forced the sword from Harry's hand.

Then he pressed the tip of his own blade against Harry's throat. "What say you, Mina?" he asked coldly. "Shall I kill him or give him over to his captain?"

"I beg you, m'lord," Harry croaked, "I didn't know she was y'r mistress."

Hastily Marianne laid her hand on his tensed arm. "Please don't kill him on my account."

His muscles tightened under her hand. "Why not?"

"I don't want his blood on my head."

Garett clenched his jaw, and she feared he might actually ignore her and act on the threat anyway.

Then he lowered the blade. "Who's your captain, damn you?"

Harry let out a long breath. "Merrivale," he squeaked, his eyes still locked on Garett's sword.

"He'll hear from me, I assure you," Garett snapped, "and I'll make certain you receive a flogging for what you've done this day." He turned to the other soldiers. "As for you lot, be glad my mistress can't bear the sight of blood. Leave now, before I change my mind."

Harry scurried to his horse. The men holding William released him abruptly, and he fell to one knee. Aunt Tamara's captor thrust her aside. Then the soldiers hurried after their leader, clearly not eager to take their chances with the earl after having witnessed his skill with the sword.

Aunt Tamara rushed to William's side, cursing the soldiers as she ran her hands over his body, searching for broken bones. Rigid as a statue, Garett watched the men leave. Only after they were out of sight did he sheathe his sword and turn to Marianne.

"They didn't . . ." he began as he pulled aside her cloak to survey her again, this time more carefully.

His expression of concern and raw pain made her pulse quicken. "Nay." She suffered his gaze a moment in silence before drawing her cloak back into place. "I have you to thank for that, my lord."

In the moonlight, his eyes seemed like two dark jewels burning their brilliance into her flesh. "Yes." Then his face grew shuttered. "We'll discuss that later."

He glanced over to where Aunt Tamara sat fussing over William, who grumbled about her ministrations. "How is he?"

"No broken bones," Aunt Tamara said. "He'll live."

"Good." Garett turned to William. "There's a village a few miles from here. Do you think you and Tamara can make it there on your own?"

"Aye, m'lord," William answered.

"I'll go on ahead with Mina and see to the inn." He tossed a pouch to William. "Here's gold if you need it."

"Leave Mina here, milord," Aunt Tamara said. "I can tend her as well as you."

Garett snorted. "Aye, and spirit her off. You

convinced my man once to help her escape. I won't give you the chance to do it again."

Guilt stabbed Marianne. "Garett," she said softly, "William didn't leave with us of his own accord."

Garett turned his fierce gaze on her. "Oh?"

"We . . . we . . ." She faltered, unable to bear how he awaited her answer, as if once again she was going to prove his suspicions right.

"We drugged him," Aunt Tamara said without compunction. "'Twas the only way to get her from you. Then once he awakened we were so far away he saw no point in going back."

"Damn you, wench, you know that isn't true," William protested.

"William did feel certain that you'd find us," Marianne admitted, ignoring her aunt's scowl.

"It helped that he kept throwing things out of the wagon to show me the way," Garett said dryly.

"What?" Aunt Tamara whirled on William. "You wretched traitor! I ought to—"

"Now, Tamara," William said, "'twas a good thing he caught up to us, wouldn't you say?"

She only glared at him.

Garett shot William a sympathetic glance. "Come along as quickly as you can. As this night has attested, the roads aren't safe for gypsies."

"Don't worry, m'lord," William said. "We'll leave the wagon here and take the mules. No one will bother us then."

As Aunt Tamara argued that plan with William,

Garett lifted Mina in his arms and strode for his horse. She clung to his neck, too exhausted from the night's events even to protest when he set her upon his saddle, then climbed up behind her. He pulled her back to rest against his hard frame as he started the horse toward the road.

"You might as well catch a little sleep now while you can," he murmured. "Because later on you and I shall have a very long talk."

And somehow she suspected that she wouldn't much like what he had to say.

Chapter Fifteen

Melting joys about her move,
　　Killing pleasures, wounding blisses.
She can dress her eyes in love,
　　And her lips can arm with kisses.
Angels listen when she speaks;
　　She's my delight, all mankind's wonder;
But my jealous heart would break
　　Should we live one day asunder.

　　　　—John Wilmot, Earl of Rochester, "A Song"

Marianne clutched her cloak to her chest as she sat staring blindly into a newly started fire. She was still drowsy. Lulled by Cerberus's slow gait and Garett's arms about her, she'd dozed nearly all the way back to the inn, and Garett had let her.

Then he'd led her into the inn and up to this room, where he was now discussing the terms of the night's stay with the innkeeper. She caught snatches of conversation about "two others to follow" and "breakfast sent up early." But all she could think of, as she came fully awake, was how close she'd come to being ravished.

As a sheltered noblewoman, she'd never before fallen

prey to such brutal treatment. True, she and Father had sometimes treated the wounds of those who had. But Father had prohibited her from assisting him in situations where women had been cruelly abused. Nor had she ever seen anyone beaten before her very eyes as the soldiers had beaten William.

She couldn't banish the images from her mind. No wonder Aunt Tamara had always been so protective. No wonder Garett thought she needed a protector. The memory of that soldier's hands mauling her breasts . . .

A shudder wracked her. It bore no comparison to the love play between her and Garett that day in Falkham House's library.

She darted a glance at him. Even as weary as he must be, he stood tall and strong and startlingly handsome as he spoke to the innkeeper. He'd risked his life for her. He'd been dreadfully outnumbered, and there'd been one moment when she'd even feared the worst, but he'd prevailed.

Perhaps she ought to consider accepting his offer of protection. Her life lay before her, an endless stretch of battles with men like those soldiers. It would be so much easier just to let Garett have what he wanted in exchange for living in his care, and be done with it.

Now that she knew Garett hadn't been involved in Father's arrest, she could rest easy in his arms.

She sighed. Nay, she'd never be able to do that. It went against everything she'd been taught about the importance of marriage vows. Father had risked much to make his union with her mother a holy one. He'd married a gypsy precisely because he'd loved and re-spected her too much to have her in any other way. That sort of mutual affection was what Marianne wanted for herself.

And she would never have it with Garett, who de-sired only to take her to his bed. While she could never succumb to him without succumbing body and soul, he would not see it in the same light. So if she gave in to him, eventually her pain would be far greater than if she left him behind, particularly once he discovered who she really was. Now more than ever she had to find a way to flee him or lose her soul in the process.

As Garett walked out with the innkeeper, leaving her there, she realized, rather belatedly, that the room was meant for them both. That set her pulse pounding . . . with alarm *and* anticipation. Did he mean to leave her no choice? Would he take her like that soldier?

She swallowed. No, she couldn't believe it. But he intended something, probably seduction. And if she wasn't careful . . .

Swiftly she rose to scan the room. Perhaps she could still escape him.

What a foolish thought. Hadn't she just learned how difficult it was for a woman to traverse England safely without protection? Besides, Garett stood just outside the door. She could hear his low but compelling voice still speaking to the innkeeper in the tiny hall.

She paced back and forth, watching the shadow of her body that the firelight cast on the opposite wall. The dark figure almost seemed to dance, mocking her.

She could allow herself to *be* that figure, let herself sink into—

Abruptly she jerked her gaze back to the fire. She was not going to be such a creature! She would not let herself be tempted by Garett, no matter how glad she was to see him or how convincing an argument he made for her giving in to him.

The door opened, startling her. He was here. Alone.

He closed the door with careful movements, then shot the bolt behind him, the ominous click grating on her ears. Oddly enough she didn't fear him. He would never hurt her.

She feared herself. And what he might want of her . . . what she actually might be willing to give.

When he sat down to remove his boots, she asked, "Are we sharing this room?"

A shadow crossed his face. "You give me no choice. I can't risk your trying another foolish escape." His voice shook as he tossed his boots aside and rose. "Next time, you might not be so lucky as you were tonight."

An awkward silence ensued, during which he surveyed her, seeming to note every grass stain and tear in her cloak from where the soldiers had roughly handled her. A muscle throbbed in his jaw, making her shiver.

"I should have killed them," he said in a guttural voice. "I should have killed every one of the damn bastards."

The vehemence in his voice startled her. "There were too many. You'd have been killed instead if you'd attempted it."

"Would it have mattered to you?" The words seemed wrenched from him. His eyes locked on hers as he stepped closer, taking off his coat and flinging it across the other chair by the hearth. "You didn't care what your leaving might do to me. Why concern yourself about whether I live or die?"

As if realizing how much he'd revealed, he averted his face from her to stare bleakly into the fire.

Her heart leapt into her throat. What *had* her leaving done to him? "I would never want you to lose your life, my lord. Surely you know that by now. And despite what you may think, I'm grateful that you—"

"I don't want your gratitude!" he shouted, whirling on her with such a fierce visage that she jumped. When he saw her reaction, he forced some semblance of calm into his voice. "There's only one way you can show me your thanks."

She stiffened.

"'Tis not what you think," he added as he saw her expression, "although God knows I want that, too. What I ask of you now you owe me, for the hours I've spent in torment this day, wondering what danger you might be in. And then to find you in the very danger I'd imagined—"

His muttered curse flooded her with guilt. A pox on him, she had nothing to feel guilty about!

"I want your vow." He gave a short, harsh laugh. "I don't suppose it means much to a gypsy, but you once said you had a lady's principles. Well, then, I want the lady in you to swear you'll never take a chance like that

again. Swear to me you won't leave Falkham House unless I'm with you."

A long breath escaped her. Of course he would ask
that. But how could she grant it? Escaping had to be her
ultimate goal, for if she stayed—

"Swear it, Mina!" He advanced so close that she
could see the grim determination in his face.

Steadily she met his gaze. "I can't."

His hands clenched at his sides. "You'd rather risk
rape or worse from a band of dirty, wretched soldiers
than live with me?"

"You know I wouldn't." A sob caught in her throat.
Under different circumstances . . .

Ah, but the circumstances hadn't changed. She was
still a fugitive, and he was still the king's man.

Right now, however, he didn't look like the king's
man. He looked younger, more vulnerable. "You do
understand what would have happened tonight if I
hadn't come?" he choked out.

Before she could answer, he reached up to yank at
the ties of her cloak. They came loose, sending her cloak
pooling about her feet. Her loosened bodice barely covered the crests of her breasts. In the firelight, the bruises
on the upper swells were readily apparent.

His eyes filled with a desperate anger as he saw the
dark contusions. Lightly he touched one. "This is only
a sample of what they might have done to you. Yet you
don't care."

"Of course I care! Don't you think I wish I could
travel as I pleased without having such men paw me and

treat me cruelly simply because I'm a gypsy? I care, my lord, a great deal more than you'd ever understand."

"Then let me protect you." His fierce gaze bored into her. "Give yourself willingly into my safekeeping. Swear to me you won't leave. Swear it!"

"And if I do? You will try to seduce me."

The firelight lit his face with an unholy light as he searched her features. "Would that be so very awful?"

No. That was the trouble. "I do not want to be forced to—"

"Forced!" he snapped. "I'm not some grubby soldier who'd throw you down in the field and grind you into the dirt. I've no need of such barbarities." He reached up to cup her cheek. "And you have no real desire to fight me. Only your stubbornness keeps you tilting at windmills—a foolish sport."

"You're no windmill," she countered. And if she gave in to him now, she would be lost. She had to get away before that happened. Slowly she backed toward the door.

He followed her. "Ah, but you're certainly Don Quixote, since your urge to fight is misplaced. What are you fighting to keep? Nothing save a distrust for men of rank that keeps you from acknowledging a few truths."

"Such as?" Could she make it to the door and free the bolt before he could reach her?

"You want me."

That statement certainly got her attention. "Nay," she murmured. "Never."

"Your lips said otherwise the last time I tasted of them."

How she wished she could deny it. But she couldn't. It was true.

"What's more, there's no reason in hell for you not to have me."

She sidled past the chair and saw his coat lying over it. "You're a conceited lout if you think I'd willingly give myself to you."

Scooping up his coat, she threw it at him, then darted for the door. She heard him swear, but she dared not look back as her hand nimbly slid the bolt open. Then she was opening the door.

But before she could even slip through, the door slammed shut with the force of a weight that also pressed her body against the flimsy structure.

"I can't believe after what happened tonight, you'd try it again," Garett hissed in her ear. He turned her to face him, trapping her against the door by pressing his hands on either side of her shoulders. "By God, I'll make sure that was your last attempt."

"Garett—"

"If you won't give me your vow, then I must bind you to me some other way." And with that he took her mouth in a plundering, rough kiss.

Angry, she bucked against him, driving her fists into his chest as she wrenched her lips from his. He let her pummel him, even while his strong legs parted to clamp her limbs between his. When she wouldn't give him her mouth, he buried his face in her neck, lightly nipping the sensitive skin.

He covered her body so completely with his own that

she felt like a flower encased in ever-hardening clay, destined to be imprisoned forever.

Then his lips sank lower to the swell of her breast, and he deliberately kissed a bruise left by the soldiers. "I'd never hurt you so, sweetling," he murmured as he raised his head.

The glittering passion in his gaze mesmerized her. "You're hurting me now," she choked out in one last attempt to fight his desires. And hers.

"Where?" When she stared at him blankly, he added, "Here?" He pressed his fingertips against her throat where his lips had been moments before.

She felt powerless to speak. Worse yet, she could feel her pulse beat with heightened pace under his fingers.

So could he, for his gaze grew more fiery. "Perhaps here," he said, sliding his palm down until it barely rested over the breast he'd just kissed. It also rested over her heart.

Yes. That was where she hurt.

It was the last coherent thought he allowed her. Then his mouth slid over hers once again, with less insistence and more heat. It startled into life a slowly burgeoning desire.

His lips invaded; hers welcomed the conquering foe. His body clamored at the gates; hers gave up the keys to the city.

Need swamped her. It was as if every part of her body demanded she acknowledge how intensely he made her feel. The scrape of his whiskered face against her cheek started one rush of sensation. Then came the tantalizing dance of his tongue inside her mouth, teasing her into responding, into pressing her breasts against the rigid wall of his chest.

He pulled away only enough to lift her in his arms. "Tonight, sweetling, you'll give me at least one of your secrets."

Would she? She began to fear that she would.

After he set her down beside the bed and stood there unashamedly shedding his doublet and waistcoat, she opened her mouth to protest, but her words died in her throat as he pulled his shirt over his head, baring his upper torso.

Oh, good Lord. She'd seen men's bared chests before, those of Father's patients. But none like this.

Broad shoulders gave way to a well-knit, muscled chest sprinkled liberally with dark brown hair. That hair led her eyes downward, following the rough-edged line it made down his belly, then lower to where a bulge showed in his breeches.

She sucked her breath in sharply and jerked her gaze away. What was she thinking, to be gawking at him? She ought to be—

"Oh no, sweetling," he murmured as he caught her to him. "No regrets. This moment became inevitable the night I first felt your gentle touch as you bound my wounds."

She tried to deny the thrill racing through her at his words, but when he plundered her mouth in another of his long, dizzying kisses that stole her breath, she could no longer.

One part of her felt him slide her bodice past her shoulders. Another heard him curse as he fumbled with the ties of her skirt. Yet another saw the two pieces of her gown swish down to cover her feet like doves coming to roost.

But her heart only heard, felt, and saw the driving passion that rode him as his hands skimmed down her ribs to rest on her hips. Perhaps he really did care. He *had* come for her, had risked his life for her.

And she wanted him. That much she had to admit.

Especially when his gaze trailed down to rest on the full swells nearly completely revealed above the neckline of her chemise, and then darkened hungrily. Every feminine instinct within her preened to have him admire her body so.

As he drew the loose neckline down and began to rub his palm in ever-widening circles over one breast, a shuddering sigh escaped her. It felt so good, so very delicious. Where was the shame she ought to feel? Why was she consumed instead by this rapidly rising pleasure, this sensual longing that danced just ahead of her like the Pied Piper charming the children into danger?

She averted her eyes from his devouring gaze, then gasped as he dropped to one knee so his mouth could caress her breast. Oh, heavens. It was even better than last time, now that she'd witnessed herself the difference between tender caresses and cruel abuse.

This, she reveled in. Her head fell back at the sheer wanton warmth, and she buried her hands in his dark mane, clasping him tighter to her. That provoked him into greater eagerness until he was pleasuring each of her breasts with teeth and tongue and lips so deliciously that her knees wobbled. But he held her in place, his arms wrapped about her waist.

Had she lost all semblance of sanity to give her body up so easily to his?

Yes. But it was a sweet insanity. His hands and mouth seemed to know no boundaries. They teased, caressed, and provoked her until she swayed against him, wanting more, needing everything he might offer.

Only then did he rise to peel her chemise from her, leaving her naked before him. Stark desire illuminated his face, and she gloried in the awe in his face as he raked her bare body hungrily.

It wasn't right for him to see her thus. Only her husband should be allowed to gaze upon her without her clothes. Yet she wanted no other man to see her thus. None but Garett.

"Your body is a holy place, a cathedral," he whispered as his eyes swept back to meet hers.

"Is it?" Her voice caught. She had to break the spell he cast on her. She had to! "Then why do you wish to profane it?"

A wicked half smile played over his face. "Not profane. Worship. Let me worship at the altar, sweetling, lest I be banished to hell."

"I can't save you from damnation." Desperate now to resist her own desires, she wielded the one weapon that might stop him from seducing her. "If you take me now, you may forget the past for a time, but at the slightest mention of your uncle, you'll turn against me."

The muscles of his jaw tensed, but he didn't release her. Instead, he jerked her against him so she could feel the bulge in his breeches. "Nay, I can't, even if you prove as treacherous as he."

His mouth caught hers again, ravaging with a wanton abandon that drove her need even more into the open. She fought the urge to lose control, fought it and lost. Hardly aware of what she did, she clutched him to her, her hands roaming down to cup his trim, hard buttocks through his breeches. With what was half-moan, half-growl, he pressed her backward until she fell across the bed. In a trice, he'd stripped off his breeches and fallen atop her, his body trapping hers beneath his. His knee parted her legs, and she tensed as she realized the moment was near.

She felt a tear escape, more out of anger with herself for her inability to resist him than out of any pain.

Garett's face darkened at the sight. He caressed her cheek, rubbing away the wet spot as he stared into her face. "For once, don't lie to me, Mina. Tell me I haven't mistaken you. Tell me you desire me as I do you."

How she wished she could proclaim him wrong. If she did, she knew he'd leave her and not touch her again. But she couldn't bear having him think she regarded his attentions as she did those of the soldiers. Every part of her rebelled against lying about how he made her feel.

Still, to admit the shameful truth, that her body

warmed and tingled wherever his skin met hers, was hard. She dropped her gaze. "I don't know what I want."

His soft chuckle held a hint of relief. "Yes, you do. You're merely too proud and stubborn to admit it."

That brought out the rebellious streak in her. "Fine. Then I *don't* want—" she began, but he muffled her answer with his lips.

He explored her mouth with a leisurely thoroughness that had her blushing even while she wanted more. But though his lips merely enticed, his hands enflamed, moving over her naked form like those of a sculptor memorizing every curve and dip and line.

When he lifted his mouth from hers, shifting so he lay propped on one elbow beside her, she stared at him in confusion, incapable of speech. All she knew was she wanted to taste his lips again. With a boldness that came from who knew where, she drew his head down to her, but he resisted.

"There's more of you I would taste." He kissed her hair, her brow, her cheeks. When his tongue darted into her ear with startling intimacy, she moaned.

Then his hand inched down her belly to rest on the soft curls hiding her most private place. She stiffened.

He halted his hand. "You act like a complete innocent."

"That's because I *am* a complete innocent," she admitted, her gaze locking with his.

For some moments he searched her face. Then a smile tipped up his mouth. "I should have known you were by the way Tamara protected you. Fool that I was, I thought she only disapproved of me. But any man would have raised her defenses, wouldn't he have?"

Marianne nodded. Would he release her now that he realized she was a virgin?

"Then I'm to be your first." His eyes gleamed with some dark pleasure that sent a delicious shiver coursing through her.

"Yes. Unless you—"

He took her lips again, but she scarcely responded, because all her senses were taken up by the realization that his fingers were parting her womanly folds.

"Oh, God, sweetling," he whispered, "you're warm, so very warm . . ."

Before she knew it, his fingers were working an incredible magic within her. She tried to ignore the pleasure that stole through the portals of her body, but how could she? The desire he brought to life within her was as deep as the sea and just as timeless. Only moments passed before she found herself arching up against his hand, searching for some elusive feeling that seemed to hover just beyond her reach.

"Garett . . . oh please . . . oh, Garett . . ."

With a dark smile, he increased the tempo of his motions until she was moaning and writhing beneath his hand, seeking the satisfaction that eluded her.

Then he settled himself between her legs and something else replaced his fingers within her. He sheathed himself so quickly in her that the sudden fullness startled her. Yet he paused at the barrier marking her innocence.

"Hold on, dear heart." With his eyes gleaming down at her, he braced his hands on either side of her shoulders. "Hold on to me, for I shan't ever let you go now. After tonight, there will be no secrets between us."

She wished she could believe him. No secrets. How wonderful it would be to cast aside her uncomfortable role, to bare her soul to Garett as he'd bared her body. But in her heart, she feared it could not be.

Well, if she couldn't tell him everything, at least she could give him this. So she blotted all secrets from her mind, all save the secret of his wonderful body melded to hers.

The initial pain, which she'd known to expect, still took her aback. But after he paused a moment so she could adjust, he fell into a slow and steady rhythm that had her gasping and shimmying beneath him.

His body danced with hers until she and he were one glorious blur of sensation. She clutched him closely as she met him thrust for thrust, savoring the feel of him within her.

He brought her sensual gifts she'd never dreamed existed. All was whispers and thunder together, passion and strength and sweet excess. Her head fell back as her body was rocked by tremors, then jolts, then quakes of pleasure.

Suddenly he strained with a burst of strength against her, and she felt his warmth flow into her. Then the tension left his body, and he fell atop her.

Spent and satiated, she curved her body around his, loath to let him go. After a few moments, he shifted to her side, but he kept one leg and arm thrown familiarly over her body. Propping himself up on one hand, he let the other trail down the contours of her belly.

A sudden shyness assailed her, and she ducked her head against his shoulder.

"Come now, my gypsy princess, don't hide that pretty face of yours. You might lie to me at times, but I can always trust your eyes to reveal what you're really thinking. Let me see your eyes."

He tipped her face up to his. She couldn't help but meet his gaze, for she, too, hoped for some sign that their joining had meant more to him than just a moment's enjoyment.

What she saw was a raw desire so fierce it masked any other emotion. A sultry heat spread over her body again at the blatant invitation his eyes offered.

His lips curved in a soft smile. "Say it, sweetling. Tell me you found as much pleasure in our coupling as I. Tell me you wanted me. You might as well admit it, for I shan't let you have a moment's rest until you do."

The sensual things he was already doing again to her body with his hand made it difficult to think, much less answer him with any modicum of dignity. "It was . . . interesting," she murmured, unwilling to feed his arrogance more than that. Then she gasped when his hand darted between her legs.

"And?"

"And . . . and pleasant," she admitted breathlessly as he played on her as expertly as a musician played a flute.

"And?"

Her head fell back and her eyelids sank shut. He was making it difficult for her to think. "Please, Garett . . ."

He chuckled softly. "Say it, sweetling."

At that moment she would have said anything he wanted. "I want you," she whispered. "I want you . . . I want you . . ."

With a low growl he slid over to cover her body with his once more. "Then you shall have me," he murmured before showing her yet again what having was all about.

Chapter Sixteen

Truth is child of Time.
—John Ford,
The Broken Heart

The day was half gone when Garett awoke to find himself buried by a tangle of shapely limbs and worn bed coverings. Thick locks of honeyed hair tickled his bare chest and covered the face of the one whose body pressed against his.

Mina. After weeks of unquenchable desire for her, he finally had her in his arms and in his bed. And to his surprise, he found her aunt had been right. One taste of her had merely whetted his appetite.

Lightly he stroked her hair from her face, marveling at its silky texture. How she could sleep with her body draped over his was beyond him. Yet he'd managed to sleep as well. Even in her sleep she entranced him.

Unconscious of the influence her bare form already exerted on his body, she lay with a sweet artlessness in her expression that touched some tender part within him, a part he'd thought long ago dead.

His gaze trailed down to the bloodstained linen

tumbled about her legs. Then he shut out the sight, letting his head fall limply back against the pillow. She'd been such an innocent. He'd never dreamed a woman with a past like hers could come to a man's bed so unsullied.

If he'd guessed the truth before, would it have made a difference?

He thought not. His hunger for her had been irrational from the beginning. He wouldn't have been able to wish it away simply by telling himself she was a virgin.

He gazed again at the gentle curves of her face. What he wanted most to do was awaken her with soft kisses, to press her back against the pillows and . . . His loins tightened almost painfully at the thought.

No, he told himself with deep regret. She needed time to rest. He'd shown her little enough mercy the night before. She'd enjoyed it, even if she'd found it difficult to admit it. He'd delighted in arousing her in spite of that, until she couldn't help but return his desire.

But she'd surprised him. It hadn't taken her long to realize that the same trick worked on him, as he'd discovered the first time he'd tried to go to sleep. Never had he seen a woman find such enjoyment in lovemaking. Never had he been given such a gift.

He stared at her wistfully. Much as he wanted to, he couldn't lie abed all day watching her sleep. He needed to see how William and Tamara fared.

Carefully he slid from underneath her sleeping form. Unfortunately, he wasn't careful enough. She mumbled some unintelligible phrase, then turned toward where he lay poised and ready to leave the bed as soon as she settled. But her eyes opened and she caught sight of him.

"Garett! What are you . . ."

She trailed off as her gaze slid down his bare chest and belly to where his desire was making itself known yet again. It was all he could do to keep from grinning at her expression of complete mortification. Her eyes widened further, her mouth formed a small O, and then she turned several shades of crimson.

"Oh, heavens," she whispered. "I don't suppose I dreamed it."

He laughed. "Not unless we had the same dream."

"I can't believe I . . . Aunt Tamara is going to murder me!" She hid her blushing face in the covers.

"Nay. I'll wager it won't be you she'll murder."

Her head snapped up at his dry remark. She gave him a look of earnest appeal. "Then we shan't tell her."

A twinge of uneasiness went through Garett. "Keeping it from her will be difficult once you're established at Falkham House as my mistress."

The color drained from her cheeks as she sat up to drag the bed clothing about her naked form. "I cannot be your mistress."

"You already are," he replied evenly, his unease growing at her response.

She clutched the linens to her like a shield. "Last night . . . Garett, it should never have happened. It mustn't happen again."

When she rose from the bed, he caught her and

pulled her back down, not just to keep her from fleeing him once more but also to have a reason to touch her.

"Listen, sweetling, we can't undo it even if we wished to. Why fight this tie between us? There's nothing left to keep us apart now, no reason not to find our pleasure where we may."

Her eyes flashed. "No reason except my future. I plan to marry one day. If I stay with you as your mistress, no man will ever have me."

He didn't like the turn this conversation was taking. "Your loss of innocence wouldn't stop any man who had eyes from marrying you. But this talk of husbands is fruitless. As my mistress, you don't require a husband."

"I don't require a lover, either. Nor do I want one."

His grim smile masked the hurt her words gave him. "Then you deny you found enjoyment in our lovemaking."

With a blush, she stared down at her hands.

Her silence encouraged him. "You see? You cannot deny that you want me. And God knows I want you. Can't you accept that for what it is?"

When she lifted her eyes to him, they shimmered with unshed tears. "'Tis not enough."

"It's more than what you had before."

"You don't understand. You'll never understand."

He leaned forward to brush a kiss over her hair. "I want you with me. That's all I care about."

"That's not true. Have you forgotten you don't trust me? That you think I'm in some terrible conspiracy with your uncle?"

He hadn't forgotten. He'd hoped—nay, believed—she would tell him the truth now that they'd made love. "It's you who doesn't trust me. I've already told you that your secrets are safe with me. No matter what you tell me, I'll protect you. Now that I've bound you to me as a man binds himself to his mistress, you can surely tell me about your past."

For a long time she stared at him, as if debating something. Then she wrenched her gaze from his. Staring down at the stained bed linens, she asked, "What is the worth of a man's bond to his mistress?"

When a low curse erupted from his lips, she met his angry gaze. "I didn't say that quite right. But when you speak of such a bond, what do you mean?"

He dropped his hands from her. "That I'll be your protector."

"You'll protect my life with yours?"

He struggled to control his growing anger. "Didn't I do so last night?"

A haunted look briefly crossed her face. "Yes, but I require more than that."

"Money," he said, a bit surprised that she would be so mercenary. "That I'm more than willing to give. You'll never want for anything."

"Until you tire of me."

He tried to draw her into his arms, but she wouldn't allow it. A coldness crept through his veins. "I assure you, sweetling, I shan't tire of you for a long time."

She twisted the linens in her hands. "Men tire of women, my lord. 'Tis not unusual."

"Men tire of common women. You are anything but common."

A ghost of a smile flitted across her face. "In any case, it's not money that concerns me. I get along quite well with my skills as a healer. But this 'bond' you speak of must require other promises on your part. Would this bond force you to side with me against . . . against those I see as my enemies?"

"Of course," he clipped out, tiring of what began to sound like an odd rendition of marital vows.

"Even if they were your own friends? Would you take my part against your friends?"

That stopped him briefly. If for some unforeseen reason he had to choose between Hampden and Mina, whom would he choose?

The choice would be hard, but in the end he knew he wouldn't choose Hampden. "Yes. Against my own friends, though I don't see why that would be necessary."

"You'd stand for me against your blood kin? Against your country?" She paused, her eyes lit with a strange light. "Against your king?"

A part of him recognized that somewhere in her questions lay the key to the riddle of who she was. But another part was angered by what was tantamount to her conditions for being his mistress. The insult to his pride prevailed.

"If you wish me to swear complete loyalty to you for all eternity, Mina," he replied coldly, "you'll have to place some faith in me first. You ask a great deal and offer very little. I still don't know why you've hidden your identity from me when every bloody man, woman, and child in Lydgate seems to know your past. Nor do I know how you and my uncle are acquainted with each other. I'll make no promises until you tell me something. Anything."

She stared away from him into the fire that was now only ashes. He could feel her arms stiffen under his hands. "I'm afraid, Garett," she said softly.

He caught her hands in his. "Afraid of me?" he asked, almost dreading the answer.

"Yes . . . no . . . I don't know."

Her confusion twisted something within him. He drew her to him, and this time she didn't resist. She laid her head against his chest as if seeking reassurance in the beat of his heart. Then her arms stole about his waist, and she clasped him to her.

At least she could cling to him for comfort. He brushed a kiss across the tangled waves of her hair. "You've nothing to fear from me, sweetling. Surely last night proved that. I couldn't harm you if my life depended on it."

She was silent a long time. Then she lifted her face to his. "Last night only proved you want me. But sometimes wanting isn't enough."

"Then let my word, my honor, be enough. I'll protect you, Mina, no matter what you tell me. I swear it on whatever god or holy book you find sacred."

For a moment, she looked as if she might say something. Then she lowered her head once more to press it against his chest. "Give me time to think."

He sighed. Yet he had to grant her request. She was like a wild deer that had to be coaxed into trusting before it would finally allow a human near.

"As you wish," he murmured soothingly against her hair.

She relaxed in his embrace. For a long time they stayed with arms entwined as he stroked her hair. Then he began to be aware of the softness of her body, the press of her breasts against his chest, the woman scent of her filling his senses. Suddenly he needed to know that her giving of herself the night before had been more than a moment's whim.

Cupping her chin, he raised her head until her lips were inches from his. "I'll give you whatever time you need, but I'll be damned if I let you spend it just thinking."

Her eyes dropped to his mouth and her lips parted, giving him the invitation he sought. So when he bent his head toward her, she didn't argue the point.

Pitney glared at the thick ledgers stacked atop his fashionable walnut desk, then toppled them over, wishing he could make them disappear. His expenditures mounted daily. Unfortunately, his income did not. His friends wanted repayment for his loans, his enemies were taking away his power, and his bankers refused to lend him any more money.

He still had some lands and his small estate. But what good was it when the tenants seemed to feel no inclination to toil in their fields? They openly defied him, and when he tried to exert his power over them, they sullenly worked for a few days, then disappeared to a local alehouse to drink their troubles away.

Pitney thought of Garett's well-tended lands and gritted his teeth. All this was that bastard's doing. Damn those soldiers who'd mistaken a footboy for Garett and had killed the wrong person along with Garett's parents.

With head pounding, Pitney called for a servant. The stooped woman who answered his summons came in hesitantly with head bowed. Pitney sneered at the trembling woman. At least he was still master of his own house.

"Fetch my wife! And try to move faster than the slug that you are." He took a perverse pleasure at the way the woman's face reddened. He almost hoped she would respond to the insult, for Pitney badly wished to tear into someone.

But the woman controlled herself, backing carefully from the room. Pitney frowned. He'd take his fury out on his wife instead.

Lately, however, that had been more difficult to do. He couldn't beat her—he didn't want to risk the life of his unborn child. All he could do was threaten. And his threats seemed to fall on deaf ears. It was as if she'd found another hope to sustain her, one that gave her immunity to his venom.

Garett. She still hoped her nephew would "rescue" her. Well, Pitney would make sure that never happened. It gave him one more reason to kill Garett.

A knock at his study door made him smile. The servant had been quick indeed. But it wasn't his wife who burst through the door. It was Ashton, his eyes bright and eager.

Ashton made a sketchy bow before announcing breathlessly, "I have important news, sir."

"Of Falkham?"

"Of Falkham. And another who interests you." Ashton smiled conspiratorially as he knocked the dust from his clothes. "Your nephew has a companion now—Winchilsea's daughter."

Pitney gaped at Ashton. "Miss Winchilsea?" When the man nodded, he growled, "It can't be. You were mistaken. That chit is dead."

"Nay. The soldiers who were sent to the gypsy camp for her must have lied. She's alive. I saw her myself, and I promise you I'd never mistake that pretty face. She's in Lydgate, living at Falkham House."

Pitney sat back in his chair. So the beautiful Miss Winchilsea was still alive, was she? His cock hardened as he remembered her sweetness and youth. She had her mother's bewitching, wild look about her. Just the kind of woman he enjoyed.

Except she'd been insolent, far too insolent for a girl. He'd wanted badly to press her down into submission. He'd even contemplated offering to make her his mistress once her father was safely locked away.

That, too, Garett had taken from him. Worse yet, Garett had her now. Miss Winchilsea and his nephew. A potentially dangerous combination. If she guessed who was really behind her father's arrest and told Garett . . .

"Did Falkham know who she was?" Pitney asked.

"I don't think so. The villagers talked of her as Mina, although you know they all knew her. When I saw her last, his man was taking her before the town council. I overheard someone say Falkham was suspicious of her and wanted to know who she was."

Pitney leaned forward, ideas taking shape in his brain. "Who does he think she is?"

"A gypsy healer. Before Falkham kept her at Falkham House, she stayed in a wagon with a gypsy woman."

Pitney laughed. "I suppose she won't tell him who she is for fear he'll turn her over to the king's men. Excellent! Quite a comeuppance for the aloof little bitch, don't you think? To be forced to live as her mother ought to have—a Romany slut servicing a nobleman. Her mother had no right to wed a pure-blood Englishman. And now Miss Winchilsea is paying for it. Ah . . . there is some justice in this world."

Ashton shifted on his feet. "But sir, what if he finds out who she is? What if she protests her father's innocence? If she knows that you—"

"Quiet!" Pitney ordered, nodding toward the open door. Anyone might come along to hear them. He lowered his voice. "We'll have to act before he does. But I need time to think of a way to have her discovered with Falkham. Even the king's favorite subject will have difficulty explaining why he's harboring a traitor."

Ashton's face brightened. "Aye. 'Tis brilliant. You could discredit him before the king."

Pitney frowned. "Perhaps. Trouble is, she hasn't been found guilty of anything yet. But if perchance I brought soldiers to capture him and if perchance he resisted . . ." He grinned broadly. "Well, there are all sorts of possibilities, aren't there?"

Ashton patted his rapier. "Aye, sir, that there are."

"I might even find a way to dispose of Miss Winchilsea before she stumbles onto something that might prove that her father was wrongfully accused and murdered."

Ashton flashed him a knowing leer. "Before you do, you ought to sample what Falkham's been sampling. Lord, but she's a fine piece of work."

"And a dangerous one," Pitney retorted. "Don't forget that."

"What could she tell? She has no idea of my involvement. I was nowhere in sight when the medications were knocked over and the king's dogs swallowed the poison. What—"

A sound from the doorway made both Pitney and Ashton turn. There stood Bess, terror shining in her face. She whirled to run, but her pregnant state made it difficult for her to move quickly.

Pitney bellowed, "Come back here, Bess!" as Ashton dashed out after her. In seconds, Ashton led her struggling back into the study.

"Shut the door!" Pitney commanded, and Ashton kicked it shut.

Bess stared at him, hatred and disgust in every line of her face. Pitney rose from his chair, wondering how much she'd heard.

"How long have you been standing there?" he demanded.

She tilted her chin up, though her lips quivered. "Only a few moments."

"Don't lie to me. You know what happens when I catch you in a lie." He opened a drawer in his desk and withdrew a riding crop. The blood drained from her features as he slapped it into his palm. "How long, Bess? What did you hear?"

"N-nothing." But her eyes remained transfixed on the crop.

He slammed it on the table, making her jump. "Did you hear us talking about poison?"

She dropped her gaze.

He rounded the table and lifted the crop.

"Yes!" she cried, holding her hands up in front of her face. "Yes."

"Leave us, Ashton," Pitney muttered, and his man obeyed.

As soon as Ashton was gone, she babbled, "I don't understand what you've done, but I promise I won't say a word to anyone."

"Don't play the fool. You know quite well someone tried to poison the king, and the poison was only discovered because some fool knocked it over and His Majesty's dogs lapped it up."

"You planted the poison? I know you always hated

His Majesty, but plot against the king? That's insanity! How could you be so wicked?"

"'Twas neither wicked nor insane. When power is at stake, great men must be daring. Our king is rapidly undoing everything the Roundheads sought to build. I couldn't let that happen. Come now, surely you didn't think that milksop Winchilsea was behind the poisoning?"

Her expression altered to one of pure shock. "You truly are mad," she whispered, backing away from him.

How dare she see his brilliance as insanity? Stupid woman! "Was it mad to choose Winchilsea to carry the poison so that if it were discovered, he'd be the one to suffer? Was it mad to get you your precious Falkham House back?" He smiled diabolically. "That was my intent, you know. Sir Henry was doomed once the poison was discovered. And with him gone, I could have bought Falkham House from the Crown. So you see, I did it for you, my dear."

Her eyes blazed her outrage. "You will not blame this crime on me!"

Pitney strode around her till he stood behind her. "That's precisely what I'll do. If you breathe a word of this, I'll make certain you're found as guilty as I, sweet wife." He trailed the crop over her back, feeling a surge of pleasure when she trembled. "Keep in mind what I might do to you. I can bribe the maid to swear you confessed your crime to her. Ashton would fabricate tales about you if I requested it. So you had a part in my crime and didn't even know it."

She whirled on him, her eyes tinged with horror. "You would betray your own wife?"

"Only if she betrays me." This time he lifted the crop to the gauzy scarf tucked in her bodice. He flicked the crop beneath it, pulling it loose to bare the tops of her full breasts. Then he traced a design over her white flesh with the tip.

Her face reddened, and she knocked the crop away. "Garett won't let this crime pass. He'll find you out, and then what will you do? Already he's made your name a mockery at court and among the gentry. You can't stop him."

Cold anger turned his blood to ice. He brought the crop heavily down on the desk, his anger growing when she didn't so much as jump.

He tossed the crop away in disgust, then jerked her against him. "If you say a word to Garett, I'll kill you and make certain you suffer in the dying. Don't think you can stop it by having me arrested. I still have men who owe me, who'll do my bidding no matter what." She struggled, but he laughed hollowly. "Don't think I won't do it, Bess. You'd best keep your pretty mouth shut."

He pulled her hand down to feel his swollen breeches. "Be glad that even in your bloated state, I can still feel this for you. That and the babe and your ties to the nobility are the only things keeping you alive. If you ever lose them . . ." He twisted her wrist suddenly, making her cry out.

"I won't say anything," she whispered. "I won't."

"Good girl." He stared into the face that bore some slight resemblance to the man he hated. Anger and a desire to punish swelled within him like an infected boil that required lancing.

He dropped her wrists and began to undo the buttons of his breeches. He couldn't take his anger out on the one who truly deserved it. But at least there was someone he could punish.

Chapter Seventeen

A mighty pain to love it is,
And 'tis a pain that pain to miss;
But of all pains, the greatest pain
It is to love, but love in vain.
—Abraham Cowley, "Gold"

Y ou haven't told him yet, have you?" Aunt Tamara
asked, stooping beside her niece, who knelt in the
Falkham House garden pulling up weeds.

"Nay." Marianne kept her head bent over the plants,
unwilling to let her aunt see her chagrin.

"It's been a week already since he rescued us. Hasn't
that been long enough? You should tell him."

Shading her face from the sun, Marianne scanned her
aunt's expression. "How can I?"

Aunt Tamara plopped down in the piles of dirt
strewn with wilting thistle and ragwort. She looked ex-
asperated. "Any fool can see that the man's besotted.
Now that you're certain he didn't betray your father,
why not tell him who you are? Perhaps he can help you
discover who *did* commit the crime. You've little reason
to keep your secret now. What do you fear?"

"You know what I fear."

Aunt Tamara idly pulled up a weed. "I think I can read a man correctly, poppet. There's no way on earth that man will send you to be hanged."

Marianne twisted the long stalk of a ragwort, jerking it out of the ground without caring whether the root came with it. She wished she could be as certain as her aunt was about how Garett would react upon learning the truth.

"He's bedded you, hasn't he?" Aunt Tamara remarked with her characteristic bluntness. "Well, then, time he knew what he got himself into. I'm thinking he ought to do right by you. And he's more likely to do it if he knows you're of his kind."

Tossing down the weed, Marianne rose to stride away from Aunt Tamara.

Her aunt simply jumped up and followed her. "He *has* bedded you, hasn't he? I can't believe the two of you spent all that time in the inn just chattering."

Marianne stopped to glare at her aunt. For once in her life she wished the woman weren't so forthright. But she should have known Aunt Tamara would ask about it the first time they were alone together. Until now, either William or Garett had been with them whenever they'd met.

Affecting an air of nonchalance, Marianne stared her down. "I haven't asked what you and William did that night. How dare you ask what passed between Garett and me?"

"Don't get impudent with me, girl. For all my faults, I'm still the only guardian you have."

The rebuke stung. The thought of what her aunt had sacrificed to come with her to Lydgate made Marianne frown.

Aunt Tamara's expression softened. "Besides, you can't just go on this way forever."

Her gentle tone broke Marianne's reserve. A hot tear slipped down her cheek, and she brushed it away, heedless of the smudge of dirt she left on her face.

Aunt Tamara licked the tip of her thumb, then rubbed at the smudge. "Come now, don't cry. 'Tis unlike you to cry."

"I don't know what to do," Marianne admitted.

"Tell him the truth."

"And if I do? He knows I've lied to him in the past. What's to make him believe me this time? He might cast me aside in disgust or"—a lump formed in her throat so thick she could hardly speak through it—"or relinquish me to the king's men in anger. He's capable of going to great lengths to revenge himself when he feels slighted. I've seen that with his uncle."

Aunt Tamara snorted. "As if you could compare yourself to Tearle. What have you done to the earl to make him wish revenge on you? Told him a few lies? 'Tis hardly the same."

Marianne stared off at Falkham House, her heart wrenching as she thought of Garett's tenderness in the past week. At night, he took her with such sweetness that it made her ache to tell him everything. If she weren't so afraid of how he'd react . . .

That first morning she'd awakened in his bed he'd

made her no promises. And she couldn't blame him, either. He'd been right—how could he promise her anything when she told him nothing? Yet it would kill her if he abandoned her now, when she'd finally come to realize a most painful truth.

"You love him, don't you?" Aunt Tamara asked.

Marianne wanted to deny it, but she couldn't. "Does love make you a coward? Does it make you cautious, afraid to gamble all on the chance that your lover cares for you when he's not even whispered one word of love?"

Aunt Tamara enfolded Marianne in a warm embrace. "Love makes you vulnerable, poppet. If anyone knows that, 'tis I."

Something in her aunt's words made Marianne draw back to stare at her.

"Will has asked me to marry him," Aunt Tamara said quietly.

Pleasure for her aunt warred with bitterness over the contrast to her own situation. "That's wonderful," she managed. But she did mean it. If ever someone deserved happiness, it was Aunt Tamara.

"I told him I'd consider it. But I've half a mind to refuse him."

"Why? He loves you—any fool can see that."

"Perhaps. But how could I marry him? A gypsy wife would keep him from doing what he really wants." At Marianne's raised eyebrow, she said ruefully, "The rogue wants to own an inn. Damn fool. He's even got some money set away for it. He thinks I'd be a fine innkeeper's wife. Me—who's more like to be tossed in the gaol than asked for a pint of ale."

"You could pretend to be Spanish, as Mother did."

"I like what I am," Aunt Tamara said, a stubborn set to her chin. "I don't want to pretend to be another." Her face softened, making her look so very young. "Still, it tempts me."

"Then tell him yes."

When her aunt looked at her with concern, Marianne suddenly realized the real reason Aunt Tamara hesitated to grab this chance for happiness. "If you're worried for me, don't be. Just give me a few more days. I'll find the pluck to tell his lordship the truth. I promise."

Aunt Tamara relaxed, then squeezed Marianne's arm. "'Tis best. You'll see." Then she looked beyond where they stood, and her mouth twisted into a wry smile. "Speak of the devil . . ."

Marianne glanced over to where Garett crossed the well-groomed lawn toward them, and her heart flipped over in her chest.

"'Tis time I return to the wagon anyway," Aunt Tamara murmured, giving Marianne's arm another reassuring squeeze before she swept off across the garden.

With a tightness in her belly, Marianne watched Garett approach. He looked every inch the lord of the manor, for he'd just come from town and had yet to discard his plumed hat and imposing cape. It made her blood leap.

Cursing herself for ten kinds of a fool, she studied his face, trying to read his expression.

"You must return to the house," he ordered as soon as he was near enough to be heard. "We've scarcely enough time as it is for all the preparations."

"Preparations?" she asked, acutely conscious of how grimy and mussed she must look.

A hint of amusement crossed his face as he took in her dreadful state. "My guess is it'll take you a bit longer than I'd expected to make yourself presentable."

With a sniff, she walked past him toward the house. "What is it I'm making myself presentable for?"

As Garett strode alongside her, he thrust a letter into her hand. "See for yourself." Then, without giving her time to read it, he muttered, "Damn Hampden and his games. One day I swear I'll pay him back for all his tricks."

Between the letter and Garett's grumblings, Marianne pieced together that Hampden was bringing a group of six ladies and five gentlemen with him from court that evening. He wrote that Garett had been too long without company and needed to be reminded of his obligations to society.

Hampden further stated that he expected a good dinner and entertainment. "And," the letter had said, "make certain your pigeon is there when I arrive. I wish to give her a proper greeting this time."

"What does he mean by 'a proper greeting'?" Marianne asked.

Garett grimaced. "Never mind. But suffice it to say he's most certainly already on his way. He sent me enough notice to prepare for him, but not enough to send him a refusal. Wretched varlet. I ought to abandon the house tonight and see how well he likes arriving here to no dinner and no entertainment."

"But you won't, will you?" Marianne said with a twinkle in her eye.

Garett snorted. "No. I'll play the host as he bids. And you, my dear, will play hostess."

Marianne gaped at him. "But . . . but I can't!"

"Why not? I assure you none of them will care. I'll tell them you're my widowed second cousin come to visit or some such nonsense, and everything will be respectable. You've told me many times that you were raised as a lady. I'm certain you can comport yourself as such for one evening."

She searched his face, wondering if this was a deliberate trap of some sort. He returned her scrutiny without apparent guile until she lowered her eyes.

What was she to do? She couldn't be seen at dinner by a group of nobility from court. It would be madness! One of the guests might have known her or her father. It was far too risky.

"I can't be your hostess, Garett," she persisted. "I wouldn't feel comfortable." That was certainly an understatement.

His gaze turned suspicious. "Is there something you fear?"

"Aye," she said, forcing a smile. "That I'll make a fool of myself."

"You, who stood before an entire town council and challenged me? I doubt that. So what frightens you?"

What could she answer? If she protested too strongly, he might guess the truth.

"You see? You've nothing to fear." The determined set of his mouth warned her nothing would change his mind.

Then she had a flash of inspiration. "I don't have an appropriate gown."

Garett's smile surprised her. "I've already had Lydgate's dressmaker preparing a number of gowns for you. As soon as I received Hampden's letter, I sent a messenger to town to make certain one would be ready for tonight."

A quick surge of pleasure flooded her. He'd gone to such trouble for *her*?

Then she sobered. Now she was trapped, as surely as a bear at a bearbaiting. She'd simply have to hope she didn't know Hampden's friends. During her days in London, she hadn't moved in society circles very much.

Still, there was always a chance . . . "Have you any idea whom Hampden is bringing?"

"I imagine it's the usual group of exiles whom we both knew in France."

She relaxed. She'd known none of those people personally.

At any rate, she had no choice, so she might as well make the best of it.

As the glittering crowd swirled about the great hall making small talk, Marianne sat near the fire with a false smile on her lips and a glass of wine in her hand. Her family hadn't used this room much, deeming it far too grand for their tastes, but it suited Garett and Hampden and their friends. All were dressed in rich attire, the gentlemen as beribboned as the ladies. They lounged on the aging oak chairs with an ease she could never feel among their company.

She didn't belong here. Not anymore, if she ever had.

At least she hadn't recognized any of Hampden's friends. And though she'd stood anxiously as Hampden had introduced her, none had apparently recognized her, either.

"Falkham tells me that your husband died recently. I'm so sorry for your loss, Mrs. Pidgen," said a masculine voice with a hint of mockery.

Marianne twisted to find Hampden leaning on the back of her chair.

"Hush," she whispered, though she was very glad to see a familiar face. "He thought that the role of widowed cousin might preserve my tattered reputation, so be a good boy and play along."

"Yes, but Mrs. Pidgen? Good God."

"It's your fault." She gazed up at him with a teasing smile. "You did tell him to make sure that his pigeon was here. He was just trying to oblige you."

He snorted. "Was the name your idea or his?"

"His, believe it or not." Occasionally, the lighthearted Garett she imagined in her youth surfaced. It just wasn't often enough. "He couldn't very well call me Mina, or people might guess—" She broke off with a blush.

His eyes darkened a fraction. "That you're his mistress?"

She glared at him. "That's ungentlemanly of you, Hampden."

"But true, I imagine." When she stiffened, he added in a gentler tone, "Don't be angry. I couldn't help but notice that the two of you are different together this time. More, shall we say, comfortable. But 'tis nothing to be ashamed of."

He patted her shoulder and moved away, leaving her tense and annoyed. She glanced down at the sparkling red satin of her new gown. Hampden was wrong. It *was* something to be ashamed of. She was Garett's kept woman. No matter how she tried to deny it to herself and to him, that's what it was. He dressed her, he fed her, and he provided for her in every way.

She turned her gaze to where Garett stood, casually bracing a hand against the wall as he spoke with a stunning woman who wore the most outrageously low-cut gown Marianne had ever seen. Her name was Lady Swansdowne, and her widowhood was real, not that she behaved any differently for it from how Marianne did. Apparently Lady Swansdowne had inherited an immense fortune she enjoyed flaunting. One of the men had said she was considered the most eligible woman in London. Clearly she was also the most beautiful.

As Marianne watched the woman flirt expertly with Garett, tears stung her eyes. She blinked them back. Garett was paying the woman no more attention than any of his other guests, but Marianne still felt desolate.

She couldn't be to him what that woman was—a potential wife. Not as long as she remained in her guise as gypsy.

Yet if she dropped her guise, she might lose him altogether. Her fingers closed on the arm of the chair. She couldn't go on this way. She'd go mad. No, she had to tell him everything soon and take her chances. It was the only way to determine if he truly cared for her. Even life in prison would be preferable to the torment she'd experienced lately, to the feelings of doubt assailing her.

A servant approached Garett and whispered in his ear. Garett nodded, then, with a few words and a bow to Lady Swansdowne, approached Marianne. She forced herself to smile, to ignore her pangs of jealousy.

"You're the loveliest one here." Taking her hand, he turned it over to press his lips to her wrist. When her pulse quickened, a wolfish grin curved up his mouth. "Later, sweetling, I'll show you just how lovely I think you are. But for now, we must go in to dinner."

She allowed him to help her to her feet, but her knees felt weak.

Later. And much later she'd tell him the truth. But after she did, would he still want to "show her" how he felt about her?

Dinner proved singularly painful. Garett sat at the head of the table and Marianne at the foot. Never had she felt such a gulf between them. Although he often smiled at her, she could do little more than acknowledge it with a tight smile of her own. When should she tell him the truth? And how? Was there any way to do it without making him hate her?

Hampden sat beside her, but not even his witticisms could keep her mind from playing over and over that dreaded future discussion.

Then the present conversation trickled through her reverie.

"Oh, surely, Hampden, they must have learned something by now," a young man named Lord Wycliff was saying. "Someone obviously killed the man. Winchilsea didn't stab himself. They have to have some suspects. After all, whoever did it might be His Majesty's enemy and must be routed."

The other conversations stopped as all eyes went to Hampden. Even Garett seemed interested.

She fought to keep her face expressionless. Mechanically she ate some venison pasty without tasting it.

"All I know is it was a conspiracy," Hampden responded coolly.

Lord Wycliff snorted. "Everyone knows that. What's happened to your famous penchant for gossip? Don't you have anything more interesting than that?"

Hampden sighed. "His Majesty is closemouthed on the subject. I've tried to weasel information out of Clarendon, but he's wary of everybody."

"And rightly so," another man said and began to tell a humorous story about Clarendon. Marianne offered a silent prayer that the conversation had shifted.

Then a soft voice came from Hampden's other side. "I know some news about Winchilsea."

The venison pasty stuck in Marianne's throat.

"What could you possibly know?" Lord Wycliff asked with a sneer.

The girl's voice rose higher. "I found out from Elizabeth Mountbatten that Sir Henry's dead wife was a gypsy."

Panic gripped Marianne. She fought the impulse to glance at Garett. Perhaps he hadn't heard. Perhaps he wouldn't make the connection if he had.

Spurred on by a chorus of excited questions, the girl who'd imparted her bit of gossip with hesitation went on. "He actually married her. Can you believe it? A baronet married to a gypsy."

Lady Swansdowne leaned over the table with a wicked glint in her eye. "That might explain why their daughter was so unusual."

"Unusual?"

Marianne stiffened. Garett had asked the question. She couldn't help it—she looked at him. Her heart sank. His eyes were trained on her, glimmers of suspicion already evident. She didn't look away. She couldn't. His gaze seemed to hold her there.

"Why, Miss Winchilsea was a perfect pedant," Lady Swansdowne continued. "She studied constantly. 'Tis said she even prepared her father's medicines. I suppose she learned all that from her mother." Her voice fell to a conspiratorial whisper. "She probably prepared the poison meant for His Majesty."

"It's hard to believe any noblewoman would do such a thing," Hampden said, "but I suppose it's possible.

Perhaps he was even innocent, and his daughter committed the crime. If so, 'tis no wonder she killed herself."

Lady Swansdowne added spitefully, "I wouldn't be surprised at all if she had done it. You know how gypsies are with their potions and poultices. I'm sure they know all manner of poisons."

Only when Hampden clasped her hand under the table did Marianne realize how badly she'd been shaking. Had Hampden guessed the truth, or was he merely being kind to a gypsy who was bound to be offended by the woman's talk? Marianne didn't care. She squeezed his hand, grateful for the gesture.

Meanwhile, Garett seemed oblivious to anyone but her. She tried to ignore the chant storming through her mind: *He knows, he knows, he knows.* She couldn't bear it if he found out from a chance bit of false gossip.

Someone spoke to him. He answered without taking his eyes from Marianne.

She tore hers away from his now piercing gaze. Picking up her fork, she had to order her body to do the simplest things—lower the fork, spear a piece of roast pheasant, lift the fork again.

"What did this Miss Winchilsea look like?" Garett asked, his tone deceptively casual. "Perhaps she was a pedant because she couldn't be anything else."

The chant in Marianne's brain grew louder.

"I'm sure she was as plain and dark as a crow," Lady Swansdowne remarked, appearing to tire of the whole conversation.

Lord Wycliff laughed. "You never even saw the woman, Clarisse. How on earth could you know what she looked like?"

"An acquaintance of mine knew her fairly well," came a bored voice from down the table.

Marianne darted a glance at the slightly built man who'd spoken, wishing she could just silence him with a look. But he wasn't even gazing at her.

He was flashing a taunting smile Lady Swansdowne's way. "He was one of those . . . oh, you know, terribly earnest students who think to learn all the mysteries of life from books. Told me he was her father's pupil. Even claimed to have stolen a kiss from her. You'll be happy to hear, Clarisse, that he also claimed she was quite a beauty and not the tiniest bit dark at all."

The fork dropped from Marianne's hand, clattering loudly on the pewter plate. "Excuse me," she murmured, reaching for her glass of wine. She took a large gulp. Never had she dreamed her one innocent kiss would come back to haunt her like this.

"Sad then that she killed herself," Hampden said beside her. "I wouldn't have minded meeting such an intriguing creature."

Marianne tried to tell by Hampden's tone whether he'd guessed the truth, but he didn't seem to realize the irony in his words.

Had Garett? Was it possible Garett could have heard everything and not have guessed the truth? She doubted it, yet her heart clung to the hope that he hadn't pieced together the facts.

As the meal went on and the conversation drifted to other matters, she clutched that shred of hope in desperation. If he had guessed the truth, then the time had at last come for her to test the "bond" he claimed was between them, and she wasn't ready. Not yet.

She forced herself to look at him. She could read nothing in his expression. Determined to pretend nothing was amiss, she smiled at him. He nodded briefly, and her heart sank.

He knew.

Don't assume the worst or you'll slip and say something you shouldn't. It's possible he didn't guess at all.

She schooled herself to act normally, to trade witty remarks with Hampden as always. Although eating was difficult with her stomach roiling and her heart racing, she lifted the fork over and over to her lips with mechanical precision.

Lord Wycliff suddenly stood. "I wish to drink a health," he announced.

Everyone grew silent.

Marianne bit back an oath. The drinking of healths was popular among both the nobility and the common folk, but once it began, the dinner would drag on endlessly until every man had pledged a multitude of healths.

Lord Wycliff began:

> Five times I drink the health
> Of Helen, my heart's desire.
> Each of the five can only hint
> At the depths of my love's fire.

Despite her tumultuous emotions, Lord Wycliff's crude rhyme made Marianne smile. She watched as he drank his full glass, then repeated the rhyme and drained a fresh glass four more times.

She'd heard of this custom, popular on the Continent. Men drank healths to the women they loved, even to their mistresses, according to the number of letters in the woman's name. Often the women were absent, as was the case with Lord Wycliff's love. As she saw Lord Wycliff's face grow flushed from his wine, Marianne found herself wondering what Helen was like.

Then Hampden stood, and she gazed up at him in surprise. Ruefully he winked, then began his own pledge:

> Seven is the number of perfection,
> As perfect as my lady Tabitha,
> And though she may scorn my passion,
> I'll drink her health as is the fashion.

When Hampden sat down after drinking his seven healths, he leaned over to Marianne and whispered, "Not much of a poet, am I?"

"You're better than Lord Wycliff. But tell me, who is Tabitha?"

"My latest love, though she's been playing coy with me. I thought I'd press my case. She's not here, but her brother is sitting next to Lady Swansdowne, and he'll be certain to tell her if I don't drink her health." He grinned. "At least her long name gives me an excuse to get thoroughly foxed."

Marianne laughed, but the laugh died as Garett stood. The room fell silent again, but she felt certain everyone could hear the loud beating of her heart.

He gave her a brief glance, then lifted his silver chalice.

> Fair is the lady I speak of,
> Her walk and her speech so sublime.
> But she veils her person with false words,
> Now for us is the unveiling time.

Marianne scarcely noticed the whispers that rose around her concerning Garett's odd pledge. She sat with her breath held as Garett drank the health, then refilled his glass. Her blood quickened every time he drained it, then refilled it. She counted the number of healths, her heart leaping into her throat when he passed four and went to five.

The Earl of Falkham wasn't drinking to the gypsy girl Mina or even the false widow Mrs. Pidgen. He was drinking to Miss Marianne Winchilsea.

Numbly she witnessed him give the eighth health. For the first time since he'd begun, he fixed his eyes on her face, and the cold fury there made her mouth go dry.

Then he drained the glass and sat down.

Marianne was aware of several things at once. Hampden whispered something soothing in her ear that made her realize he hadn't guessed why Garett had drunk the eight healths. Lady Swansdowne sat back in her chair with a smug smile, apparently convinced that the eight were for the letters of her name—Clarisse.

And Marianne's shred of hope that Garett hadn't guessed the truth disintegrated in her hands.

Others were talking around her, but the clamor in the room did nothing to banish the silence in her heart. She'd taken her chance. And judging from Garett's now grim expression, she'd lost.

Not caring who noted the sudden paleness of her face or the trembling of her hands, she stood shakily to her feet.

"Forgive me," she choked out. "I'm afraid I feel suddenly unwell."

Then she fled the room.

Chapter Eighteen

Women, like flames, have a destroying power,
Ne'er to be quenched till they themselves devour.
                    —William Congreve, *The Double-Dealer*

Garett rose. His hands gripped the table so tightly that his knuckles whitened. "I beg your pardon, but I must see to my ill hostess."

As he strode from the room, he ignored the murmurs rising up behind him. He wanted only one thing—to corner his deceitful mistress and determine the full extent of her lies.

He was halfway up the stairs when Hampden called to him. He paused to fix the marquess with a stony glare.

Hampden marched up the steps, his expression filled with righteous anger. "Just leave her be, for God's sake. What did you expect her to do? Sit meekly by as you pledged the health of another woman?"

"You mean, after all that talk you didn't even guess at the truth? God, you must be nearly as besotted with her as I."

Hampden stared at Garett as if he'd gone mad. "What are you babbling about?"

Garett wasn't about to explain the situation to Hampden until he knew everything. "Don't worry. Mina knew exactly to whom I drank my healths. Something else has her upset—something that is none of your concern."

Turning his back on Hampden, Garett continued up the stairs. In moments he was at the door to the bed-chamber Mina had occupied since the day he'd forced her to remain at Falkham House. Without knocking, he threw open the door.

Mina stood beside the bed, stuffing her meager clothes into a canvas sack. For a moment he paused to watch her, unable to reconcile the vision of loveliness before him with the criminal she was believed to be. Could that innocent face and those gentle, caring hands belong to a murderess?

No! every part of him cried out.

Still, she had lied to him. So he steeled himself against the soft feelings that threatened to overcome his resolve. Stepping into the room, he slammed the door.

She jumped, then continued her packing with grim purpose.

"Going somewhere, Miss Winchilsea?" he snarled.

She stiffened but refused to look at him. Wordlessly she turned for the bureau, where she drew forth her bag of herbs and liniments, which she put in the sack along with her clothes.

The way she ignored him maddened him. He stepped forward to grip her wrist. "Stop that packing this instant! You're not going anywhere!"

She met his gaze with a look of utter desolation that

made his heart twist. "Am I not? Either you'll give me over to the King's Guard or you'll cast me out. But I'm certainly going somewhere."

He stood there thunderstruck. He'd been prepared for defiance, even resentment. He'd expected her to try to defend herself and convince him she wasn't guilty.

He hadn't been prepared for this sad acquiescence. It clawed at him, making him irrationally angry with himself for tormenting her.

"What makes you think I'll do either?" he asked, unable to keep the tone of bitter reproach out of his voice.

Tears started in her eyes, which she brushed away with the back of one hand. "What other choices have you? You've pledged your loyalty to the king, and I'm His Majesty's proclaimed enemy. If you allow me to slip away, you can claim I escaped and thus not lose any honor. If you give me to the soldiers, you've done your duty. But you can't harbor me. That I understand only too fully."

Her sadness struck him profoundly. One part of him ached to reassure her, to tell her he'd protect her with his very life. The other part reminded him that she'd lied to him from the very beginning. She'd played on his sympathies until he'd been a puppet dancing to her tune. Well, no more.

"Did you commit the crime you're accused of?" he asked, more forcibly than he'd intended. The question had eaten at him all evening. "Did you indeed prepare the poison found in your father's medicines?"

She went rigid. Eyes ablaze, she whirled on him.

"You need to ask? Oh, but of course you do. I've forgotten what a treacherous woman I am in your eyes."

"Mina—"

"Don't call me that, my lord," she hissed. "'Twas a nickname given to me in love by my mother. It stands for my middle name, Lumina." She gave a bitter laugh. "You'd love the irony of it. In the language of my mother's people, it means 'light.' Once you spoke it with what I thought was affection. Now I see I was misled. March me off to the hangman, then, if that's what you wish. But remember it's Miss Winchilsea you're sending to die. Mina died the day she foolishly gave her future into your keeping."

"Damn you!" he cried, clasping her by the shoulders. "I've risked my life for you. The least you can do is give me the truth!"

At those words, all the fight seemed to drain from her. She went limp in his hands. With a soft cry, she pulled away, going to stand by the window.

For several long moments, she remained silent. When at last she began to speak, it was in a toneless, flat voice that Garett scarcely recognized as hers. "I suppose you do deserve the truth. Well, then, I didn't put poison in my father's medicines. I'm certain he didn't, either, for my father was never a traitor."

"So how did it get there?"

"Someone clearly planted it, realizing he'd be blamed, but I don't know who hated my father that much. He had no enemies. Yet someone wanted to ruin him forever." A sob caught in her throat. "And then kill him."

For a fleeting moment, Garett considered telling her that her father was alive. Then he thought better of it. For one thing, Garett couldn't be certain her father still lived. For another, the king suspected that her father was part of some conspiracy. If that was the case, then she might be part of the same plot and shouldn't be trusted with the crucial knowledge that her father was alive.

"You say someone else planted the poison," he told her. "But by all accounts, you gave the medicines directly into your father's keeping, and they never left his sight."

She shuddered. "I've heard what they say. It's true that I gave them to him as soon as I'd prepared them. But what happened after that, I don't know. I wasn't with him after he left the house. Perhaps he laid the pouches down somewhere or someone switched them." She leveled a defiant gaze on him. "But when they left my hands, they were pure. I swear it."

Faced with her determined air, Garett was hard-pressed to believe she lied. God, how he hoped she told the truth. If so, he would leave no stone unturned until he proved her and her father innocent.

Then he reminded himself of all the times she'd lied in the past. Could he trust her? And there were so many nagging questions she still hadn't answered. "Why did you return here, of all places? Why not flee England altogether?"

She gave a shaky sigh. "I had thought—actually had hoped—that if I stayed in England, I could find the man who'd painted my father a villain. That hope proved fruitless."

She fell silent. Garett thought back to the first two times he'd encountered her. So many things he'd wondered about made perfect sense now . . . her disguise . . . her fear of being brought to the constable . . . her ladylike demeanor. Only one thing still perplexed him.

"You feared me when you first met me. I suppose it was because you knew I was the king's man. So why didn't you flee when you had the chance? Why continue to put yourself in danger?"

She hesitated before speaking. At last she stammered, "I'd rather not . . . answer that . . . my lord."

He strode up to grip her shoulders. Her eyes were dry now, but they held a trace of fear—fear of him—that rekindled all his anger.

Shamelessly he used her fear against her. "You have no choice but to answer," he said with cold formality. "I'm the only thing standing between you and a dank, dark prison. So I suggest you tell me what I wish to know."

For a moment, revolt flared in her eyes. Then she mastered her emotions. "As I said before, I wanted to find the man responsible for my father's arrest. I couldn't leave until I did."

Her evasive manner made him persistent. "If you had no idea who the man was, why stay here? Why not look for him in London?"

Her gaze remained steady and calm even though he could feel her tremble. "Think, my lord. Who stood to benefit from my father's demise? Who would be unable to realize all his dreams as long as my father remained at Falkham House? Who?"

A chill gripped him with such force that he felt turned to ice. "You thought that *I* had planted the poison?"

"I thought you had caused his arrest and somehow arranged to have him implicated in a crime. I wasn't certain who'd killed him. But you must admit you were the only one with reason to want him out of the way."

He thrust her away with a curse. "You thought me such a monster?" As her suspicions sliced through him, he gritted his teeth against the pain. "When did you stop believing me capable of it? Did you believe it when I made love to you? Did you actually lie in my arms believing I murdered your father?"

"No!" Tears welled in her eyes. "By then I knew you couldn't have been responsible."

That was something. It would have destroyed him to think that their nights together had been a sham—that she'd pretended to enjoy them when all the while she'd hated him.

"I wanted to tell you all," she went on, "especially once I realized . . . I had planned to tell you soon. But I was afraid of what you'd do with the truth."

"When did I ever cause you to fear me?" he bit out. "How many times did I promise I'd protect you no matter what?"

"You didn't know what you promised. I couldn't rely on such promises."

Her answer wounded him, for he'd meant every word and had thought that he'd convinced her to trust him at least a little.

In his pain, he remembered another subject about which she'd been evasive. "What of your relationship to my uncle? How does he know you so well?"

"He tried to buy Falkham House back from Father. He tried all manner of villainies to force Father to sell to him, including spreading rumors about me and Mother. But Father refused to sell. I couldn't tell you before because I couldn't let you know my father had owned Falkham House. That should be obvious."

Her answer made sense, but he couldn't accept it entirely. Other conversations now filtered into his memory, conversations with the king about the attempted assassination. "Why did my uncle stop trying to force your father to sell?"

She shook her head, clearly bewildered by all his questions. "I don't know. Perhaps he realized Father was going to stand firm."

"Or perhaps there was another reason entirely. Did you know the king suspects my uncle of having been involved with the poisoning attempt?"

She stared at him oddly. "I wondered once if he could have done it. But knowing you were returning to claim your estates, why would he have wanted to help you regain Falkham House?"

"He didn't know," Garett responded. "He didn't know for certain that I lived until the day I actually arrived in London."

Her face darkened. "Then he could really have been the one who—"

"Yes," Garett interrupted. "He hates the king. He truly would want to see him dead."

She grasped his arm. "So Father was innocent! Sir Pitney did it all, then had Father murdered in his cell!"

Knowing that her father hadn't been murdered, Garett couldn't entirely accept her version. And there was the problem that Sir Henry had never let the medicines out of his sight, according to all witnesses. Besides, why would his uncle take such elaborate measures to rid himself of Sir Henry? Why not simply kill him?

"There's another explanation," he remarked coldly. "My uncle and your father could have worked out an arrangement that both found satisfying. Perhaps your father agreed to do Tearle's dirty work in exchange for my uncle's agreeing to give up any hope of repurchasing Falkham House."

Garett didn't entirely believe the theory he proposed, but once he'd spoken it aloud, he realized how plausible it was. Tearle had always been a likely suspect. And Falkham House was the clearest link between the two men.

"You cannot think such a thing!" she cried. "Father would never commit such a villainous crime! Never!"

"Perhaps he feared what Tearle might do if he continued to resist selling Falkham House. He might even have feared for you and wished to save you from Tearle's dark clutches. He might have done it for you, Mina. 'Tis possible."

She threw herself at him, beating her fists against his chest. "Don't say such things! They're lies, they're all lies!"

The vehemence of her reaction made him feel like the worst runagate alive. He caught her wrists, dragging her body up against his. "Listen to me," he said as he tried to restrain her. "If your father loved you as much as you clearly love him, he might have done all manner of things to save you."

She shook her head. "Not my father. He wouldn't have committed treason. He would have found another way." Frustration and anger knit her brow. "If you believe him guilty, you must believe me guilty as well, for I ground every powder and mixed every liniment he ever used. My mother and I, not my father, had the knowledge of medicines . . . and of poisons."

He stared blindly past her, feeling bombarded with information. He could sort out the truth eventually. But in the meantime, she was here before him, twisting his insides with every trembling glance and wordless plea.

He wanted to believe her. God, how he wanted to believe her.

Then he thought of his uncle, who he now felt certain was behind the assassination attempt. Tearle was just the type of man to manipulate someone like Sir Henry.

More cold suspicion washed over him. Tearle was also the type to use a woman to do his dirty work.

Garett dug his fingers into Mina's wrists, wanting to trust her and uncertain if he should.

Her body stiffened, as if she could sense his distrust. "Garett," she said, her expression turning bleak. "What shall you do with me now?"

What a question. How could he decide such a thing? It meant choosing between her and his honor. His head throbbed from the choice.

How he wished he could turn back time. She should have remained the gypsy girl, the woman he could have kept as his mistress forever. Perhaps she'd been right when she'd told him not to ask who she was.

He forced himself not to think of that. It did no good to speculate about what he should have done, what she could have been. Now he must face the truth and make choices.

But first—

"We go to London tomorrow," he announced. Only there could he find out the truth. A few possibilities remained to be explored, and he would explore them all before he decided anything.

"What will we do there?" she asked in a tremulous voice.

He surveyed her ashen face. He knew what she feared, and he hated witnessing her pain. But at the moment he felt incapable of reassuring her, for he didn't himself know what might happen once they reached London. In his own private hell, some part of him also wondered if her fear might bring forth the truth. Then he hated himself for thinking it.

"Tell me what you're going to do!" she demanded, her voice rising.

"I don't know." He tried to ignore the sight of her on the brink of tears. How he wished he could wrench loose the hold she seemed to have on him, for it took all his will to resist the urge to protect her at all costs. "At the moment, Mina, I don't know a bloody thing. But London's an excellent place to get some answers, so we're going there as soon as everything is ready."

"London no longer holds any answers for me. So all the answers must be for you. Tell me, Garett, what exactly do you hope to find there? Do you really think you can ferret out the truth when so much time has passed and His Majesty himself has apparently not determined for certain that my father was guilty? What will you do that he hasn't?"

Her chin came up as his gaze passed over her face. She seemed resolved to stand up to him, as if only by doing so could she preserve her dignity. For a moment, desire pounded through his blood, making him wonder that she could still make him want her so very much.

"Devil take it, I told you I don't know!" He had to get as far away from her right now as he could, before he made a fool of himself and forgot what she'd done. "You'd best hope I find something that vindicates you, since you're presently in bad need of my help. Though God only knows what there is to find."

With that he released her wrists to thrust her away from him. For several seconds she gazed at him with pain in her eyes. Then without a word she squared her shoulders and turned away to resume her packing.

"We leave early, Mina," he said with finality, "and

you *will* be going with me." With that he turned on his heel and strode from the room, slamming the door behind him.

 "You might've told me," was the first thing Will said when Tamara opened the wagon door to his insistent knocking.

"Told you what?" she asked as she dragged her fingers through her hair.

The gesture seemed to inflame Will, for he grabbed her and kissed her hard before pulling back. "Well, to begin with, you might've told me your niece is a damned baronet's daughter, and that she's in a fair amount of trouble with the king and his guard."

Tamara gave Will a more considered look. "So his lordship knows the truth now, does he?"

"How do you think I found out?" Will fairly shouted. "He's acting like a bloody madman. Lord Hampden and his guests were packed off without so much as a fare-thee-well. Now he's barking commands at the servants to prepare his horses for a trip and stalking the hall with a look of murder in his eye."

"Oh, my God," she whispered, her heart faltering. "Where's Mina?"

"Don't worry, as near as I can determine he hasn't touched her. Poor girl's in her room. Alone."

"You mentioned a trip . . ."

Will frowned. "Aye. He plans to set off for London tomorrow with her."

"The devil you say! Is he truly that cruel? Would he see her hanged for something she hasn't done?" Tamara shook her head. "She told me she feared what he'd do if he knew. But I didn't listen to her. I urged her to tell him."

"She didn't. I suspect that's why he's so enraged, though he won't admit it. He found out by accident. Some guest of Lord Hampden said enough about Miss Winchilsea to let his lordship put it all together."

A chill passed through Tamara. She could easily see how that would infuriate the man.

"Damn, but I wish you'd told me this!" Will went on. "I might have helped you break it to him more gently."

Tamara gave him a critical appraisal, pleased to see he was sincere. Then she kissed him soundly. "You've said you love me, Will. 'Tis time to prove you mean what you say. Get her out of that man's clutches, whatever it takes!"

Will cast her a cold glance. "So my love is to be used as a bargaining tool? I must earn my lady's favor with noble deeds? I'm no knight, love. I'm just a poor, scarred servant looking for a bit of happiness. I won't buy your love, for it won't mean a whit if you don't give it to me."

She ought to be angry, but she wasn't. A fierce joy washed over her to witness the depths of his good character. She'd played with enough men to know how easy it was to twist their wills to hers. And when she'd done so, she'd felt a secret loathing for their loss of pride. It was why she'd never remained with a one of them.

But no matter what game she played, Will remained his same, steady self. Though she might at the moment wish he weren't so strong, she also reveled in his strength. It would be a boon to them in the coming hard weeks.

"Very well," she said softly. "I won't ask it of you as a test of your love. I'll ask it of you as a friend. You have my love whether you do it or no. But Will, I still ask, please do this one thing for me."

With a sigh, Will pulled her to him. "I can't take her from him even if it was possible. The man's half in love with her already. If she leaves him again, he'll hunt her down once more."

"Or worse yet, he'll have the soldiers do it."

"Nay! I know he wouldn't betray her. He's angry now is all. Give him time to get used to the idea of who she is. Then all will be well. You'll see."

She gazed up at him with narrowed eyes. "I'll not see her hurt, do you understand? She's all the family I have left, and I won't lose her because some man is letting his ballocks rule his brain."

Will stiffened. "She has played his mistress, and that has clouded his judgment. But he'll be fair with her. I'll see to that. I'm going to London to serve his lordship, so I'll keep an eye out for her."

She flashed him a brilliant smile. "And if you think he means to give her over to the soldiers?"

"He won't."

"So you say. Still . . ."

Will stared at her a long moment before taking her

hands in his and kissing them. "If I think your niece is in any danger, I swear, upon the love I have for you, I'll protect her."

"Even against your master."

Will looked grim. "Even against his lordship."

She threw her arms about his neck with a little cry. He stood there stunned, then wrapped his arms around her.

"Thank you," she whispered against his shirt.

"Anything for you, my love."

She drew back from him, her eyes shining. "When you come back, William Crashaw, I'll be here waiting."

"To be my wife?"

She gave him a little half smile. "To be whatever you wish me to be."

He let out a rueful laugh. "I doubt that, for you always were intractable. I don't expect you to change because I've granted you this favor."

"'Tis a good thing. I'm looking forward to many years of being your intractable wife."

"And I'm looking forward to many years of this," he murmured as he drew her to him and sealed her mouth with his.

So am I, Tamara thought as she surrendered her body to him. *So am I.*

Chapter Nineteen

How can I live without thee; how forgo
Thy sweet converse, and love so dearly joined,
To live again in these wild woods forlorn?
—John Milton, *Paradise Lost*

Marianne's horse stepped into a rut, jolting her out of her half-drowsy state. Through the slits in her mask, she looked for Garett, relieved when she saw him riding slightly ahead and to the right of her.

For once she was grateful to be in disguise. Her cloak and mask kept the cold autumn wind from chapping her face and whipping about her body, and they shielded her from the eyes of men. All men, including Garett. It left her free to watch him without fearing he might see the emotions written on her face.

Surprisingly enough, wearing her mask and cloak again had been his idea. She derived some small comfort from his apparent reluctance to have her identity discovered while they traveled. Didn't that say something about what he intended?

Yet she felt certain of nothing anymore, not even his feelings. He'd spoken to her little since they'd risen.

He'd spent most of that time preparing for the trip and sending a messenger ahead to alert the London household of their arrival. Obviously he planned to stay in London a while. Did that bode well or ill for her?

Shortly after noon they'd left Falkham House. Despite their slow pace, Garett had mostly ignored her, which wounded her deeply. And when he did glance at her, his eyes held such a wealth of pain and anger—and grim determination—that she was almost glad he avoided speaking to her. It was as if any soft emotion he'd felt for her had vanished entirely.

She shivered. That did *not* bode well for her.

William called out to Garett from where he came behind, driving the cart that carried their trunks. "Shall we stop in Maywood, m'lord? 'Tis near evening. We won't be like to find a more suitable town before London."

"I'd thought we'd go on," Garett bit out. "It's only a few hours more."

Marianne kept silent, although her heart felt twisted into a million painful knots. Soon she would know what Garett intended to do with her. The question was, could she endure whatever it was?

"Begging your pardon, m'lord," William persisted, "but it's unsafe on the roads at night with all the footpads and runagates these days. And we've the miss with us."

Garett remained silent, but a muscle worked in his jaw. Marianne wondered if he was remembering the last time she'd traveled.

"She might like a rest and some food before we reach

London," William continued. "The house will be in an uproar once we arrive."

Garett glanced at Marianne. "Would you like to stop for the evening?" He spoke with such cold formality that she shuddered.

She nodded stiffly. She would *not* let him see how much his behavior upset her. She did have *some* pride, after all.

"Very well," he murmured, then barked an order to his men.

Marianne stopped twisting the reins as the pressure on her heart eased somewhat. At least he cared enough to ask how she felt, even if he did it with the barest of civility.

When they arrived in Maywood half an hour later, they stopped at an inn William professed to know well— the Black Swan. They'd scarcely come to a halt in the inn yard before servants scurried out to help them dismount and to attend to the horses.

Numbly Marianne watched the activity—and Garett. This time was so different from the last time she'd approached an inn with him. Then he'd been angry but not cold. Now he behaved as solicitously as then, but it wasn't the same. What had happened to the fiercely protective Garett? Had he retreated from her so completely that he no longer even cared what the morrow brought?

Trying to keep herself as remote from him as he was from her, she allowed him to lead her into the inn. But when he began to discuss the arrangements with the innkeeper, she realized to her chagrin that he intended for them to share a room as husband and wife despite the tension between them and his apparent reluctance to speak to her.

As soon as the innkeeper stepped aside to talk to his wife, she stood on tiptoe to whisper in Garett's ear, "What are you doing? We can't . . . I can't . . ."

"Tonight, Miss Winchilsea," he clipped out, "you will have to accept my company. I cannot chance your attempting an escape."

She flinched, as much from his formal tone as from his reasoning. "You have my word I won't try such a thing. Please, Garett—"

"It's out of the question." He stared straight ahead, but she thought his expression softened. "You'd be in danger in a room alone without a man's protection."

Had she just imagined it, or had his tone been more than cordial? She had no time to determine for sure before the innkeeper was urging them to follow him.

Soon they were settled in a spacious room, the best in the house. Once they were alone, Garett sat down on the edge of the large four-poster bed to remove his mud-caked boots.

With a sigh, Marianne untied her mask and cloak. She threw the cloak across a chair, but she kept the mask in her hand, staring at it sadly. "I used to hate this disguise. Yet here I am wearing it again."

He paused to fix her with an unflinching stare. "It's fitting for a woman with so many secrets."

His gaze seemed to cut through to her very soul as

she stood there, her blood thrumming in her veins. "I have no more secrets from you now."

His eyes darkened, and he looked as if he was about to reply. Then a knock at the door broke the spell.

When he answered, a servant entered with the meal he'd requested. Both he and Marianne stood silent, watching the servant place several dishes and a flagon of ale on the table. After the servant left, Garett sat down before the table. But Marianne couldn't keep still just now, so she wandered over to the window.

"Come away from there and eat something," Garett commanded, his sharp tone reminding her that her face could be seen by anyone watching from the yard. With a shiver, she backed away.

She glanced at the feast he'd ordered: boiled leg of mutton and roast pigeon, boiled peas and freshly baked bread. There were even apples roasted with cinnamon for dessert. Her stomach growled.

But her hunger was as nothing compared to her emotional turmoil. She doubted she could eat a bite without having it come back up, so she made no move to join him.

"You've eaten scarcely anything all day," he persisted, his voice oddly husky. "And little to nothing last night."

So he'd noticed. Somewhere in her deadened state, she was surprised and a little reassured that he had. "I was preoccupied."

His harsh laugh grated. "Indeed," he remarked with heavy sarcasm.

Suddenly she could bear no more. She faced him, twisting the mask in her hands. "Answer me one thing, Garett. If I had told you the truth when you'd first asked, what would you have done? Would you have turned me over to the King's Guard?"

For a moment, his composure cracked to reveal raw anguish. But he quickly masked it. "I'm not even certain what I'm going to do with you now. How can I know what I would have done then?"

That answer wasn't the least satisfactory. "I wish you'd just make a decision and stop tormenting me. I no longer care what you do with me. Send me to prison, send me to hang, but tell me what you intend or I'll surely go mad."

Pushing back from the table, he rose. "Have you no idea how difficult this is for me? I have a duty to my king and my country."

"So you'll give me over to them without a qualm."

"No, damn it!" He strode toward her. "But neither can I just pretend it never happened. If you hadn't been entangled with my uncle—"

"Entangled?" Her temper flared. "I wasn't 'entangled' with your uncle, unless that's what you call his lust for my mother."

"He's suspected of being behind the plot."

"He sought to ruin my father!" She stared him down. "And that's how he set out to do it."

"How could he slip poison into your father's medications without either your or your father's help?"

"I don't know! But any fool can see I'm telling the

truth. If I were part of a conspiracy, why would I have remained in England after it was all over?"

"To avenge your father. You've already admitted that much. Perhaps you thought my uncle—"

"Your uncle." She shot him a contemptuous glance. "You seem far more concerned with my feelings about your uncle than with my supposed involvement in a heinous crime. Why is that? What is it about your uncle that would make you turn against me solely because I might have some tie to him?"

When his face darkened, she went on, no longer caring if she angered him. "Yes, he stole your birthright. But you regained it, didn't you? Why has he so obsessed you that you would see me punished for his crimes?"

Eyes blazing, he approached her. "I don't want to see you punished. But for him I want justice."

She clasped his doublet with both hands. "Why? Why is it so important to you?"

He glared at her, his implacable expression making her despair. "He killed my parents."

She gazed up at him in numb shock. "I thought the soldiers—"

"Yes, it was Cromwell's men who actually did the dirty deed." His voice hardened. "But they were sent there by my uncle."

Oh, Lord, if that was at the heart of his vengeance, then how would she ever reach him? "You know this for certain?"

He pushed her hands from him and whirled away. "I can't prove it, if that's what you mean. But only he knew they traveled in disguise. Only he knew the route they took and when they departed. He didn't do the deed with his own hands, but he ordered it done. More and more I'm certain of it."

Oh, her poor dear love. No wonder he was so bitter. No wonder he didn't know what to do with her. If the root of his pain lay in this terrible thing, if he believed she and his uncle had conspired together, then how could he have any pity for her?

Except that she'd had nothing to do with his uncle's machinations. Somehow she had to make him realize it. Otherwise, she'd be lost, for without his belief in her, she saw no reason to go on.

Hang him, she wouldn't let him do this to them! He might not trust her, but some part of him recognized her for what she was, the part of him that wasn't obsessed with his vengeance. She must appeal to that part if she was to save her soul. And his.

"Now you see why I can leave no stone unturned in bringing him to justice." He faced her, his eyes haunted. "I can't let him continue to live unscathed and commit further crimes with impunity. He must be punished."

"And he shall. I know you'll find a way to prove his guilt. But you can't prove it using me, for I know nothing. If I could tell you anything that would lead to his arrest, I would. Can't you at least believe that?"

He closed his eyes, his expression a twisted mask of uncertainty. "I don't know, Mina," he ground out. "You've so bewitched me I don't know what to think or feel anymore."

She could see the intensity of his struggle. Yet she had to weight the balance on her side if she was to gain his trust. And his love. More than anything she'd ever desired, she wanted his love. The fates that had decreed him to be the Earl of Falkham were not going to deprive her of that.

She stepped close enough to lay her hand on his arm. When his eyes flew open, his gaze almost feverish, she took a carving knife from the table. As his gaze followed her every movement, she pressed the knife's point to his neck.

"If I'm truly the villainess you claim, there's nothing to stop me from driving this blade into your throat. And why wouldn't I? You're taking me to be hanged anyway. What's one more death?"

He merely stared at her without a hint of fear.

"You see, you don't believe me. If you thought yourself in danger, you'd at least attempt to wrest the knife from me. But you don't because you trust me not to harm you." Her voice broke, but she forced herself to continue. "You just don't know you do."

Abruptly she turned the knife so it pressed against her own neck where the pulse beat, and before he could move, she pricked the skin enough to draw blood.

With a harsh curse, he grabbed her wrist, twisting it just enough to force her to release the knife, which fell in a clatter on the floor. Then he clutched her to him so tightly that she had to fight for breath.

"You can't even bear to see me hurt myself," she whispered against his doublet. "How will you bear to see strangers hang me?"

"No one will hang you," he declared in a voice thick with emotion. "I won't allow it."

She fought back tears. "If you give me to the King's Guard, you may not have a choice."

"That's enough!" Clasping her head in his hands, he forced it up until their eyes met. "There will be no prison. There will be no hanging. You've proved well enough that I can't bear to have them take you."

Her heart beat triple time as she searched his face. Had she won the fight or just delayed the battle? "What about your vows to the king, to your country?"

"False vows, all, if they make me act against my character." He gazed at her, his expression anguished. "I can't watch you suffer. I hope to God that you're as innocent as you say. But if you're not . . . my pride will simply have to endure a bruising, for I can't betray you, even if I'm a fool for not doing so."

Relief flooded her. But she still worried. He was a man of honor—he wouldn't forsake his duties easily, and she didn't know if she had the right to ask him to do so. "I wouldn't have you be a fool, my lord." She covered his hands where they still framed her face. "If you still don't believe me, I'd have you act however you feel is wise."

"Enough," he choked out. "I tire of this talk of what I will or won't do. And wisdom? I lost all wisdom the day I set eyes on your cloaked form. I should have ordered you gone from Lydgate then."

"Why didn't you?" she asked, her throat thick with suppressed longing.

His eyes darkened with an emotion she'd not thought to see again. Desire. Then his gaze dropped to her lips. He slid his thumb over her lips, slowly, tenderly. "For the same reason I can't let you go now."

Then his mouth was on hers, firm and warm and searching. She gave herself up to his kiss, relieved he could still feel desire for her, if nothing else.

And oh, what desire did he feel. He clasped her to him as if fearing she'd disappear. As his mouth ravaged hers, his hands roamed her body freely. Nor did she stop their wandering. It was enough for her that despite all he feared, he wanted her.

She pressed her body against his, her heart filled with so much love that she had to show it. He'd taught her how, and now she took what she'd been taught, mastered it, and gave it back to him threefold. She clasped him about the waist, opened her mouth to the onslaught of his demanding kisses, and thrust her hips against his. They stood entwined that way, kissing and caressing each other, for several intense moments.

Then he groaned deep within his throat and tore his lips from hers. "Damn you, Mina," he murmured, his eyes bright with the force of his hunger. "I thought I'd numbed my heart years ago in France. But you'd awaken a heart beneath the breast of Death himself."

"You awakened mine." She stroked his cheek. "'Tis only fair I should stir yours."

Her words made him flinch, and he closed his eyes as if to shut her out.

"You won't thrust me from your mind as easily as

that," she vowed, then reached behind her to clasp one of his hands. She pressed it to her breast so he could feel her heart racing, as once before he'd had her feel his.

His eyes flew open and he stared at her, raw passion lending an almost holy glow to his face. "I want you past all reason," he rasped. "I don't know who you really are, but I want you all the same."

Her fingers tightened painfully on his hand. "You do know who I am. I'm Mina, the gypsy girl who saved your life. And I'm also Miss Marianne Winchilsea, who wouldn't tell you the truth for fear of losing your affection. Both of us are the same woman. Both of us want you, too."

And to show him she meant it, she flattened her body against his, her arms encircling his waist, her cheek pressed against his chest. His heart beat wildly, giving her some hope that he cared for her beyond just desiring her body.

"Ah, Mina, you're tearing me in two," he murmured, burying his fingers in her hair. He planted a kiss on the top of her head, then released her and strode to the door.

Opening it, he fixed her with an impassioned gaze. "Now's your chance. You can leave if you wish. I won't stop you."

She gaped at him. Did he think she'd offered herself to him in an attempt to have him free her? She gave a shaky little laugh. "Where would I go? All the soldiers in England would hunt for me if I left."

"You don't understand. I won't keep you here against your will any longer. You can walk out this inn and disappear. You'll be safe forever from the soldiers, for none of them knows yet that you live."

After what he'd just said, how could he be casting her aside? "Do you really want me to leave? I-I thought you cared for me."

"Damn it, Mina! I don't know what might come of this trip to London." His voice turned bitter. "You could be seen and recognized by someone. Tearle could try to rid himself of you." His eyes turned to shards of ice. "Or I could discover things about you that would— Never mind. You're better off away from me, I tell you. At least you'd be alive! I can give you money and whatever else you—"

"I'm not leaving!" She walked over to wrench the door from his grip and slam it shut. "I'm staying with you to the bitter end, Garett, even if it means I'm damned forever."

Either he found a way to trust her, or he cast her aside. But his decision had to be based on what he wanted and not what he thought best for her.

For a moment, she thought he would argue. Instead he lost the haunted look he'd worn all evening. "Then we'll be damned together," he growled, pulling her roughly up against his hard body. "For I'll never let you go now. Never."

Giving her no chance to answer, he captured her mouth in a long, drugging kiss. She didn't resist; she wanted him so much that she could scarcely contain her yearning.

His breath mingled with hers, and it was as if he gave

life to her. Every inch of her skin trembled with anticipation—her blood sang at his touch. A sweet tension
built in her, endowing her with strength while it filled
her with such urgency that she was soon tearing at the
buttons of his doublet.

He felt the urgency, too, she knew. His caresses were
less than gentle, and she reveled in the roughness. His
hands cupped her bottom, pressing her hard against the
growing thickness in his breeches. She gasped at the
sudden intimacy, and he buried his face in her neck with
a groan.

"You're so soft," he said huskily against her ear.
"Sometimes I forget how soft. I don't mean to hurt you,
sweetling."

She drew his body back against hers. "You haven't
hurt me." *Not physically.* And she would learn to live
with the other kind of pain. But for now, she'd have him
in body at least.

Stretching up to kiss his neck, she felt his muscles
tighten beneath her lips. Timidly she slid the tip of her
tongue into his ear. At that delicate caress, his control
broke. With a growl, he lifted her in his arms and strode
toward the bed.

Then all was a flurry of leather, linen, and lace as he
removed her boots and every stitch of her clothing, his
gaze growing bolder with each swath of skin he
revealed.

Although he'd seen her naked now several times, she
still felt embarrassed to have her body so blatantly ob-
served. But when she snatched up a sheet to cover

herself, he murmured, "Don't," and brushed it away. So she knelt on the bed in silence. His eyes locked with hers as he removed his own clothing. With an almost painful longing, she watched him unveil himself. She ought to look away, but she didn't want to miss seeing every part of him, for it might be her last time.

In the dusky light filling the room, his body seemed dusted with gold, for the sprigs of chestnut hair that covered him caught the sun's dying rays. He reminded her of a mighty oak—solid and unyielding in its majesty.

And while she watched with unabashed pleasure, his gaze trailed over the whole of her bared body. He climbed onto the bed in front of her, then reached out almost reverently to skim the back of his hand lightly down from the hollow of her neck to the ripe fullness of her breasts. There he paused to tease one nipple, which thrust itself boldly against his finger.

Flashing her a dark smile that made her breath stutter, he moved lower, down her belly to her hips and then to her thighs. He stroked her from her hips to her knees. Then he ran his hands up the insides of her thighs, caressing the sensitive inner skin until she thought her legs would turn to water.

A delicious shiver shook her, for everywhere he touched her she tingled. But when his hand moved higher between her legs, and he buried one finger in her honeyed warmth, she could stand no more. She swayed against him and clutched at his shoulders, wanting only to feel his body melting into hers.

With a groan, he caught her against him and kissed her deeply, even while his other hand continued to work its magic. As he brought her higher and higher to realms of fulfillment she'd never reached before, she arched against him, making low moans in her throat.

He tore his lips from hers. "That's it, my gypsy princess. Show me your true mettle."

Then he pressed her down against the sheets and entered her in one glorious thrust. As he drove himself inside her, he fixed his glittering gaze on her face. "Have I removed your disguise . . . once and for all?" he asked as his breathing grew labored. "Have I . . . truly captured . . . the elusive Mina?"

"Yes," she whispered, meeting his thrusts with abandon. "I'm yours. Yes, yes . . ."

The words became a chant that kept time with her rapidly beating heart and his quickening plunges. Soon she was swept up in the pattern of the dance, in the grafting of his body to hers so they became one limb, one branch, one tree pulsing with life. Then they were at the height of the dance, and he filled her with his seed with a cry of triumph.

Afterward they lay spent and panting, their arms and legs entwined. It took several moments for Marianne's heart to slow its frantic pace. Garett's hands still would not cease their roaming, although now his caresses were gentle reminders of what they'd just shared. His tenderness made a lump form in her throat, and she fought back her tears, knowing he wouldn't understand them.

Garett propped himself up on one elbow to stare

down at her, his face aglow. He toyed with a lock of her hair as she gazed up at him and wondered what was to become of them now.

"I hope you've not made a tragic mistake in staying with me, sweetling," he murmured, his face turning somber.

"Hush," she whispered, wanting not to lose the beauty of the moment. "Let's not speak of the morrow 'til it comes." When he started to retort, she placed a hand over his mouth. "I'm hungry, Garett," she said lightly, desperate to erase the worry from his brow. "I'd like to eat now."

He gave her one last searching glance, then pulled her hand away from his lips and planted a soft kiss in the palm. "As you wish. We'll eat. And we'll leave the morrow until tomorrow."

A reprieve. That's what he was allowing, and she snatched it gladly.

She started to rise from the bed, but he pressed her back down. "Stay here," he told her with a sudden gleam in his eye. Then he left the bed to go to the table.

She watched as he filled two wooden platters with food, then returned to the bed. He seemed totally oblivious to his nakedness, but she couldn't help but stare at his brawny chest, lean waist, and well-knit thighs. When he climbed back onto the bed, carefully balancing the platters, he caught her staring at him and gave her a wolfish grin that made her blush.

He set the platters down between them.

"What are you doing?" she asked.

With a grin, he broke off a piece of bread spread lavishly with butter and brought it to her mouth. Her heart giving a tiny flutter, she ate it from his hand.

His fingers brushed her lips, and she shivered in delight. Such an intimate thing, to be fed by someone. She'd never been so reckless as to eat her meal in bed. But as Garett offered her another piece of bread, his eyes burning when she took it on her tongue, she found she enjoyed this new way of eating.

In moments she was reciprocating, feeding him bits of pigeon that she'd torn from the tiny bones. Her fingers never left his mouth without his licking, sucking, or kissing them, and as soon as she discovered what a pleasure that was, she gave his the same tribute. When taken from his hands, the food tasted like manna—even the peas, each one placed on the tongue with care, became fruits of the gods.

Crumbs soon littered the bed. Their meal became a game to see who could feed the other in the most enticing manner, as they both, by silent agreement, sought to forget what lay before them in London. He laughed when she offered him bread held between her teeth, which she wouldn't release until he took it also between his. Their playful tug of war ended when the bread softened in both of their mouths and broke, prompting yet another kiss.

After they had eaten their fill of pigeon, mutton, bread, and peas, he lifted a slice of baked apple, dripping with juice. A wicked glint in his eye, he offered her a taste. She took it in her mouth, and the spiced juice dripped down onto her breast. Before she could wipe it away, he bent his head to suck it from her skin. Then his mouth seized her nipple, teasing it until she moaned deep in her throat.

Drawing back, he stared down at the bed, littered with crumbs and dishes, and smiled. He shifted her over so he could slide the top sheet from beneath her. Then he climbed off the bed and lifted the sheet by its four corners, bundling platters, bones, and all up in it. Striding to the corner of the room, he tossed the bundle down.

As he strode back to the bed, his intentions fully apparent by the jutting tilt of his staff, she managed to tease, "But Garett, I'm still hungry."

He climbed into bed. "I know, love." His eyes lit with desire as he pressed her down against the pillows. "But you won't be for long."

Chapter Twenty

The course of true love never did run smooth.
—William Shakespeare,
A Midsummer Night's Dream

The sun had reached its zenith when the travelers at last halted before Garett's London house. Marianne stared at the imposing structure, reminded of how powerful Garett had become since he'd regained his lands. Now he held her life and future in his hands.

Unable to slow the frantic beat of her heart, she watched him dismount. Despite their blissful evening together, she still felt uncertain of what he intended for her. With the morning had come a terrible foreboding to wrap its icy arms about them both. Silently they'd dressed. He'd seemed preoccupied. Only the brief kiss he'd given her just before they'd left their room had sustained her through their somber journey.

That, and the memory of last night's passion.

She'd shamelessly used his desire as a weapon to force him into recognizing she meant more to him than he'd admit, and she thought she'd been successful. But he hadn't spoken of what he meant to do once they reached London, and his continuing silence throughout the morning made her fear that he didn't yet entirely trust her.

Now he helped her dismount, his gaze resting briefly on her masked face before he accompanied her into the house. Fifteen well-dressed servants stood at attention inside the door, their smiling faces disguising any concerns they had about the hardship put upon them by their master's surprise visit. Unfortunately, fifteen pairs of eyes also followed her with curiosity.

When Garett introduced her as his guest Mina and made no explanation for her mask, Marianne was surprised. But he was right to be circumspect. No need to make the servants a party to shielding a criminal. As long as they didn't know who she was, they couldn't be held at fault for keeping silent about her presence. He made it clear she wasn't to be discussed beyond the confines of his house. The servants seemed to accept that command as if it were common for him to ask it.

Once Garett had sent the servants about their duties unloading the carts, he took Marianne and William aside.

"I have some matters to attend to that may take me well into the evening," he told William. "While I'm gone, make certain no one enters this house. No one, not even tradesmen or friends of the servants."

"Yes, m'lord," William said.

"And make whatever preparations are necessary for us to travel to France."

"France!" William and Marianne exclaimed in unison.

Garett's countenance grew stony. "Just do as I say," he told William, then dismissed him with a curt nod.

As William left, Garett turned toward the door, but Marianne laid her hand on his arm. "Why are we going to France?"

The muscles of his arm tensed beneath her hand, and he refused to meet her gaze. "We may not be. I don't know yet. Everything depends on what I discover this afternoon. But if matters don't go well—" He frowned. "It would be best if you didn't remain in England."

A knot grew in the pit of her stomach. "And you? You would go with me?"

His brooding gaze shifted to her. "Of course. Someone must protect you."

She gaped at him. "You would stay there with me?"

"Until it was safe for us to return—*both* of us."

"But what about Falkham House and your lands?"

"What about them?"

She wasn't fooled by his forced nonchalance. She knew how much he loved his land and wanted to make Falkham House a place of glory again. "You would leave them behind for me?" she asked thickly, emotion choking her.

His eyes glittered. At that moment he seemed almost to hate her for the hold she had on him. She felt as if she held a falcon by one leg and it was clawing and fighting to be free of her, all the while realizing it couldn't be.

"I can think of no other way to keep you from being

hanged or imprisoned," he said with a sudden aloofness that chilled her blood. "If you remain in England, someone is bound to reveal your presence eventually. Then they'll come for you."

"I can't allow—"

"Let it be!" He clasped her shoulders and gazed down at her. "I couldn't endure seeing you taken, do you hear?" he added, a raw thread of pain in his tone. "Nor could I prevent it. So we won't risk it."

"You could send William with me. Aunt Tamara could be here in one day. Then we three could travel and you could stay—"

"No!" His fingers dug into her shoulders. "I told you last night I'd never let you go. I meant it."

"But such a sacrifice—"

He silenced her words with a quick, hard kiss, born as much of fury as affection. Then he stared down at her with eyes clear and distant. "Speak of it no more. I will have agents to tend my estates. In time perhaps—" He broke off. "It doesn't matter. It may be the only way to keep you safe."

She wanted to tell him she loved him, to spill out her emotions for him like jewels and somehow make his sacrifice easier. But if she told him how she felt, he would feel even more of a need to sacrifice. If he chose to take her from England, it had to be because of what *he* felt, not what she felt. Yet he'd said they might not leave. What did he plan to do?

"Where are you going now?" she asked, a sudden worry making her frown.

He looked uncomfortable, and his gaze shifted from hers.

She clutched at his arm. "Garett! What are you going to do?"

He lifted her hand from his arm, squeezing her fingers briefly before releasing them. "Just remember, don't open the door to anyone," he murmured. Then he was gone.

For a long time after he left, she stared at the closed door. "I love you, Garett." And some day she prayed she'd have the chance to say it to his face.

Then with an aching heart, she curled up in a chair to wait.

Garett stood in the foyer of the king's sitting room, nervously watching the door. Never had he come to the king for such an important favor. Never before had he so feared being refused.

That was what came of caring for a woman. For the first time in his life, he felt true heart-pounding fear, and not for himself, either. The thought of Mina—Miss Winchilsea—being taken by the soldiers made his blood run cold. He didn't know how she'd managed it, but she'd crept into his soul and made a nest there. He couldn't seem to oust her.

He didn't even want to anymore. That was the worst of it.

"His Majesty will see Lord Falkham now," the Gentleman of the Bedchamber entered the room to announce.

Garett straightened, his pulse suddenly racing in a manner uncharacteristic of him. He forced himself to assume the air of a man of leisure. This was just like any other encounter in which he wanted to elicit information without revealing what he knew. Except this time, his opponent was the king.

With measured steps, he followed the Gentleman of the Bedchamber into the sitting room. Charles was at the window, watching his latest mistress play tennis with three other ladies in the gardens below. He turned as soon as Garett entered and flashed him a warm smile.

"Your Majesty," Garett said with a bow.

"So you've come out of hiding, have you?"

Garett looked at Charles blankly.

The king chuckled. "I wondered why Falkham House held such an appeal for you that you wouldn't even occasionally grant us your presence. Then Hampden informed me you'd locked yourself away at the old manor with a new mistress. That explained a great deal."

Garett couldn't halt the brief frown that crossed his features. "What else did Hampden tell you about my mistress?"

Charles seemed pleased he'd managed to disconcert his friend. "That she's exotic—a gypsy or some such thing—and that she has a quick tongue. He says she's quite a beauty." He smiled as he added, "And that you guard her jealously."

Garett hardly heard that last phrase. So Hampden hadn't told the king anything about Garett's earlier suspicions of Mina. That was something at least.

"Hampden ought to keep his observations to himself once in a while," Garett said, easily falling into the part Hampden had unwittingly given him.

"Come now, Falkham, you ought to bring her to court. Let us all have a look at her. Or is that why you're here?"

Garett met Charles's questioning gaze with a steady stare. "No, Your Majesty. This time I've come to ask a favor. It concerns someone who interests us both."

Charles strode back to the window and looked out with a frown. "Your uncle."

"Yes."

A worried expression crossed the king's face. "I don't know what more I could do about him. You've done quite well on your own. His reputation is in a shambles, he's badly in debt, and he's lost many of his powerful friends. No one dares champion him against you."

Garett's grim smile acknowledged the king's words. "There's still the matter of his involvement in the attempt on your life."

"Yes, there is that, isn't there?" Charles narrowed his gaze speculatively.

Careful, man, here's the tricky part. "Have you wrung a confession from that physician? Has he implicated my uncle?"

With a sigh, Charles shook his head. "He insists he's innocent. But they haven't used torture yet—I'm loath to allow such barbaric methods for a man of rank."

Garett hid the relief that washed through him. Mina's father still lived and was apparently unharmed. Until

Garett had heard it from the king himself, he couldn't be certain of it. "But you're convinced he's guilty."

"I don't know. I've always had this instinct that he speaks the truth. Still, everyone else believes him guilty. Or else his daughter."

"Daughter?" Garett asked, playing dumb.

"He had a daughter who prepared his medicines."

"And what of her?"

A look of scathing contempt crossed the king's face. "A silly twit, evidently, though I would never have guessed it when I first met her. The news of his arrest so alarmed her she threw herself into the Thames and drowned."

"Silly twit, indeed." Garett fought to keep relief from showing on his face. Thank God no one yet suspected Marianne was alive. "Do you think she had a part in putting the poison in his remedies?"

"'Tis possible, I suppose. It's very odd, though. Sir Henry insists she gave them immediately into his keeping and they never left his hands. He could have lied about it, or even blamed it on her now that she's dead, but he hasn't. He just seems bewildered by the whole matter. Of course, I suppose she could have planted the poison herself, then killed herself when she realized she was to be discovered. Who knows? But I can't believe she planned alone to kill me."

"That seems doubtful indeed," Garett agreed with a calm in his voice that he didn't feel. He wondered what the king would think if he knew the truth about Marianne's supposed death.

"But what favor do you wish me to grant?"

Garett met the king's stare with the most innocuous one he could muster. "I wish to question the prisoner myself."

Frank surprise showed on Charles's face. "Why?"

"Remember, Your Majesty, what services I performed for you in the past. I was quite adept at gleaning information from unwilling participants."

The king's face clouded. "Yes, you were. I always wondered about your methods."

"I assure you I never did anything unsavory."

Charles studied him a moment. "No, I don't suppose you did. You manage to intimidate a person just by turning that scowl of yours on them."

Garett bit back a smile. "Except for Your Majesty, of course."

"Of course," Charles remarked dryly.

"If you'll permit me to question this Sir Henry, perhaps I can be more successful at dragging a confession from him."

"Or an admission that your uncle was his fellow conspirator," Charles said with a lift of his eyebrow.

"Yes."

Charles rubbed his chin. "I believe if anyone could do it, you could," he murmured, half to himself.

Garett schooled his features into nonchalance as he awaited the king's answer.

After a long pause, Charles shrugged. "Well, then. I suppose it cannot hurt to have you attempt it."

Garett felt the tension leave his limbs. "Thank you, Your Majesty."

He remained standing in respectful silence while the king called in his Gentleman of the Bedchamber and commanded that Garett be brought to the Tower to visit the prisoner. When the men came who were to accompany Garett, he took his leave of the king, wondering how long it would be before he saw His Majesty again. Then he thrust that thought from his head and followed the men out of Whitehall.

Throughout the long ride across London, Garett focused on the more difficult task at hand—speaking with Sir Henry. When they reached the imposing group of towers, a sudden cold fear assailed Garett—the same fear that had eaten at him from the time he'd discovered who Mina really was.

The chilly corridors were more forbidding than he remembered. The snorting and roars of wild beasts filtered through the halls, because part of the Tower was still used to exhibit wild animals—bears, lions, and all manner of exotic beasts brought from England's many colonies. Hearing the noises darkened Garett's mood considerably. No matter what he discovered, no matter what she'd done, he'd never allow his gypsy princess to be forced to lie in this place. Never!

Then they were at Sir Henry's cell. The turnkey opened the door, and Garett entered. At least the room was spacious and well provisioned. Then he caught sight of the prisoner, who stood with his back to Garett, staring out the window at the sun glinting off the Thames.

Garett could tell the man had once been well

proportioned, for his clothes hung loosely on him. Now he was thin to the point of being gaunt. His hair was completely white, yet he wasn't stooped with age. He stood quite proudly in his worn doublet and breeches.

Garett motioned to the turnkey and guards to step outside the cell. They obeyed, the turnkey closing the door behind Garett.

"Sir Henry?" Garett asked.

The man turned, and Garett had to force himself not to react, for his hazel eyes were those of his daughter.

They now filled with a hostile defensiveness Garett recognized all too well. "So they've sent another to torment me, have they?" Sir Henry muttered. "And a good strong young soldier by the look of you. Have they decided 'tis time to use more forceful methods of persuasion?"

Garett was still recovering from the shock of being faced by a man so like the woman he cared for. "Nay," he choked out, unable to stop staring at the man.

Sir Henry grew more testy. "Well, sir, may I at least know the name of my tormentor?"

"Garett Lockwood."

Sir Henry frowned, seeming to search his mind for where he'd heard the name before.

"The Earl of Falkham," Garett added.

Sir Henry's gaze shot up to rest on Garett's face. He scrutinized him with a keen eye. "Sir Pitney's nephew. I've heard of you from the gossip among my jailors. You're the one who's put Sir Pitney to rout, so they say."

"Yes."

"Good for you. I always hated that ne'er-do-well."

Garett remained silent, pondering that statement.

"You've been given my house, haven't you?" Sir Henry asked with a certain challenging bluntness.

Garett's eyes narrowed. "'Twas my house from the beginning. I'm the legal heir. The house should never have been sold to you."

"That may be. But we thought you were dead." Sir Henry shrugged. "In any case, it matters little. If by some miracle my innocence is proven, you're welcome to the estate. I prefer my quiet house here in London. Falkham House was the joy of my wife and daughter." The man's expression altered, stark pain shining in his eyes. "It was to be my daughter's legacy. But with her dead, I see little point in fighting for it."

Garett moved closer to the older man and took his arm, leading him away from the door. "Suppose I were to tell you that your daughter isn't dead."

Sir Henry's face betrayed nothing, but his eyes lit for the merest instant. Then he frowned. "Is this a new form of torment, my lord? Tantalize me with hope, then dash my hopes against the rocks? If so, it will not suffice. I know she's dead. They told me that the first day I was arrested."

"Ah, but did they tell you how she died? By drowning herself in the Thames? Now ask yourself, would Mina ever do something so foolish as to kill herself?"

Sir Henry snorted and shook his head. "I know, I know, I couldn't believe it myself. Mina would never—"

He broke off, then dug his fingers into Garett's arm. "How do you know my daughter's nickname?"

"Her aunt Tamara calls her that." Garett met the gaze of his lover's father. "It stands for Lumina, her middle name. Your wife, the gypsy, gave it to her. It suits her well. With that golden hair and gentle smile, she is like a light."

Sir Henry's face turned ashen. He jerked away from Garett, moving to sit on his narrow, hard bed in stunned silence. He closed his eyes, then opened them again to fix Garett with a disbelieving stare. "Is my daughter truly alive then?"

"Aye. The tale of her drowning was a ruse your wife's sister used to help Mina escape London and the King's Guard."

Sir Henry studied Garett with an intense gaze. "And how did you come to know of her?"

Now came the difficult part. "She returned to Lydgate, and I took her prisoner." He said it coldly, deliberately failing to mention how much time had passed before he'd discovered who she was.

Sir Henry buried his face in his hands. "Then she is a prisoner of the king now as well."

"Nay."

Sir Henry's head shot up. "She isn't in the Tower, imprisoned as I am?"

Here was where Garett had to school himself to be hard, to refrain from showing any emotion. "Not yet. The king still believes her dead. So her life—and her freedom—are in my hands. You have the power to give them both back to her. I'll arrange for her to flee to France, and I'll make certain she's left there with sufficient money, if only you'll tell the truth about the attempt on the king's life. Tell me who your fellow conspirators are, and I'll set her free."

Sir Henry stiffened, his face reflecting his pain, and Garett felt a stab of guilt. Irrationally he wanted to assure the man he could never hurt Marianne. But this was his last chance to learn the truth. Garett had to use the only thing the poor old man would respond to.

"Is she unharmed?" the man asked in a faltering voice.

Guilt gripped Garett anew, a different guilt this time. "Yes. She's been well provided for and treated with the courtesy befitting her station." He prayed God didn't strike him dead for that lie.

Sir Henry released a long-drawn breath. "She's well," he whispered, half to himself.

Garett stepped closer. "She'll continue to be well as long as you tell me the truth. Who planned your attempt on His Majesty's life? Who prepared the poisons? Was it my uncle?"

Sir Henry stood, rather unsteadily, then met Garett's piercing stare with great dignity. "You, my lord, are a reprehensible snake. I knew your father briefly. He would have cringed to witness his son use such low methods."

That statement struck Garett to the heart, for he knew Sir Henry spoke the truth. And though he could justify his actions to himself, saying he couldn't protect Mina without knowing the whole truth, he sought that knowledge for partially selfish reasons. Because he wished once and for all to have proof he could trust her.

Suddenly his manipulation of Mina's father seemed too unsavory to bear. What's more, it was pointless. No matter what his methods revealed, he could never believe in his heart that Mina had conspired with his uncle against the king, even if Sir Henry claimed she'd made the poisons herself. Her innocence, her kind heart, cried out against such a deed. She truly was a light in the darkness that had so long shrouded his soul. How could he question the purity of that light when it shone before him with every sweet smile?

In that moment, Garett knew he could never believe wrong of her.

Sir Henry seemed oblivious to Garett's turmoil. "My lord, I wish to God I could accept the terms of your nasty bargain, for then I could save my daughter. But I can only beg you to find some mercy in that cold heart of yours. Even to save her life, I can't tell you who made the attempt on the king's life, for I don't know. 'Twas not I."

His sincerity filled Garett with even more guilt. Garett turned to hide his turmoil. How could he ever have doubted her innocence? He'd been ten kinds of a fool for not recognizing that the love she offered could only have come from an innocent heart. If he'd listened to his own heart more, he might have seen it sooner and saved them both countless days of pain.

"My lord?" Sir Henry asked in alarm at Garett's continued silence. "What will you do now?"

Garett faced the father of the woman he loved. "Whatever I can to prove your innocence, of course. And Mina's."

Sir Henry's mouth thinned into a line, showing his blatant distrust of Garett. "Why would you strive to prove our innocence?"

Garett said the only thing he could think of. The truth. "Because I love your daughter, sir."

There. The truth was out for all the world to hear, and Garett didn't care what the world thought of it.

Apparently Sir Henry had a great deal to think of it. Amazement soon gave way to speculation. Then he assumed a stance not much different from the one Garett's father had used when Garett as a child had committed some grievous wrong. He stood with his bony arms crossed, his jaw firm, and his narrowing eyes intended to intimidate.

"Just how long have you kept my daughter prisoner, my lord?"

For the first time since his childhood, Garett felt true shame. He didn't regret what he'd done, but he also couldn't help but recognize how Mina's father would regard it. He swallowed, suddenly wondering what on earth he could tell an irate father. He could lie, but eventually Sir Henry would learn the truth if Garett was successful in proving Sir Henry's innocence. Still, telling the truth presented another set of unique problems.

"How long?" Sir Henry demanded again.

Garett looked up into unsmiling eyes and chose his words carefully. "Long enough to come to know her," was all he said.

But it was enough. Sir Henry's hands clenched into bony fists. "Has she been a prisoner in your house all these many weeks?"

"Nay. I didn't discover her identity until quite recently." That much was true, although what he implied was misleading.

Sir Henry's face relaxed a trifle.

"Her aunt was with her," Garett added, hoping to mollify Sir Henry.

"If you've hurt her or—"

"She's happy and well, I assure you, sir."

Sir Henry snorted. "I'll be the judge of that. And if I find you've compromised her, I'll expect the wrong to be righted immediately."

Garett suddenly resented being treated like a callow youth. Temper flaring, he took a step toward Sir Henry. "I love your daughter, sir. By my honor, I wouldn't wish to see her suffer."

Sir Henry appeared to be assessing him. After a long scrutiny, he nodded. "Well, then. Have you some plan for keeping her from going to prison for a crime she had no part in?"

Garett felt a surge of relief that he was to be spared any more probing questions about his relationship with Mina. "Not yet. We must first determine who really did commit the crime, and how they managed to involve the two of you. Mina seems to think my uncle may have done it to regain Falkham House."

" 'Tis possible." Sir Henry frowned. "Sir Pitney sold it to me for a pittance because he needed funds. Later, when I'd improved it, he apparently decided he had the money to buy it back. But I never wanted to resell it."

"So perhaps he thought to force you out by painting you a traitor."

Sir Henry paced the room, his hands behind his back. "It was the way he liked to work. When he was trying to compel me to sell the estates back to him, he spread filthy rumors about my wife and my daughter, seeking to discredit me among my neighbors."

Mina had said much the same thing. With a surge of self-loathing, Garett suddenly realized what the soldier's strange words about Pitney and Mina had meant. How could he have believed Mina capable of having a relationship with his treacherous uncle? No wonder she hadn't wanted to trust Garett with her secrets.

Somehow he'd atone for the way he'd distrusted her. He'd find out who was really behind the attempt on the king's life, no matter what it took. And then he'd spend the remainder of his life making it up to her.

"If my uncle truly is the culprit, let's consider how he might have planned the crime. What about the medicines themselves? How could poison have been added to them?"

Sir Henry shook his head. "I cannot say. I spend every waking moment thinking about it, but to the best of my memory, that pouch never left my hands."

"Your medications weren't in bottles?"

"No. I'm terribly clumsy. I've broken many a bottle, so I find it more useful to carry my remedies in small pouches."

Garett pondered that a moment. "And you're certain the pouch was in your possession at all times?"

"I'd swear to it. Every time I went to court, Mina rose early in the morning to prepare my powders and fill two or three pouches with them. Then I placed them beneath my belt, where they remained until I administered the treatment."

An image suddenly flashed into Garett's mind, a brief memory of a childhood trick he'd played on his uncle, whom he'd disliked even then.

Garett's mouth went dry as he leveled his gaze on Sir Henry. "The pouches you used. Were they special ones? Did you buy them somewhere, or were they made at home?"

Sir Henry flashed Garett a quizzical look. "I used the same ones over and over for the king. Mina always wanted them to be fitting for royalty, so she'd made them specially of white satin and embroidered them with furbelows and the like. Why?"

White satin. Garett began to scowl. "I think I know how the poisoning might have been managed." Swiftly he explained what he thought.

"Aye, aye," Sir Henry said, his expression filling with horror as he, too, saw how that could work. "So very easy to be a villain, eh?"

Garett nodded. And so very hard to prove the villainy. But surely someone would remember—

"What will you do now?" Sir Henry asked.

Garett laid his hand on his sword hilt. "Somewhere there is another who can fill in the pieces. It will take time to gain more knowledge, but perhaps I can use what I know to persuade the king to refrain from questioning you until I've done my own questioning."

"All that's well and good, but while you're seeking the king's enemies, what becomes of my daughter?"

Garett's face softened as he thought of Mina. She would be his now, forever. He would see to it.

Then he remembered she believed her father to be dead. A dark frown marred his brow. When she learned how much of the truth he'd kept from her, she wouldn't be happy, that was certain.

Sir Henry's concerned voice broke into his thoughts. "What about my daughter, my lord?"

Garett wiped the frown from his face. She might not be happy, but he'd convince her to forgive him. He had to. "I'll make sure she's kept safe, sir—you've my word of honor on that. And when it's all over, with your permission I'll take her to wife."

On that, he'd brook no argument.

Chapter Twenty-one

Let secret villainy from hence be warned;
Howe'er in private mischiefs are conceived,
Torture and shame attend their open birth . . .
—William Congreve, *The Double-Dealer*

Marianne anxiously paced the hall off the entrance to Garett's London house. Garett had been gone but a few hours, yet she could hardly endure the waiting. Her mind kept returning to their last conversation.

He was offering to sacrifice a great deal for her. One part of her rejoiced to know it, for it proved he cared more for her than he'd admit. But another part wanted to refuse the sacrifice. If indeed they fled to France, what would they do there? Could Garett truly be happy knowing he'd left behind everything he'd striven for? It wasn't likely.

He'd said naught of love or marriage. Clearly he intended them to live as husband and wife but not to speak the necessary vows. She hugged herself tightly, tears in her eyes. Could she continue with him in such a manner? She didn't think so. Her heart was given to him, but could she trust him not to break it?

Yet he'd said he'd never let her go. Wasn't that a vow in itself?

Such questions plagued her until a pounding at the heavy oak door brought her out of her thoughts. She stood motionless, uncertain what to do. Another bout of pounding began, and she broke out in a cold sweat.

The noise brought William, who stepped into the hall and gestured to her to be silent. The noise also drew other servants. They stared at the door uneasily.

Then a voice bellowed, "Open this door immediately in the name of His Majesty the King!"

Marianne paled, drawing her cloak more closely about her and steadying her mask. Conscious of the servants' alarm, she nodded toward the door, indicating that William should open it. William frowned, but he motioned her into an alcove as he strode forward. She watched from the shadows as he opened the massive door a crack and asked what was the matter.

Before he could stop them or Marianne could flee, men were forcing their way inside. They had frightening faces of fierce aspect, their doublets greasy and dirty. By comparison, the soldiers who then followed with reluctance appeared to be almost gentlemen.

Then another man entered, whose aging countenance did nothing to soothe Marianne's fears. Sir Pitney Tearle. What was he doing here? Had he learned of her presence, or did he simply wish to harm his nephew?

She froze in the shadows.

"Where's your master?" Sir Pitney demanded of William.

"He's not here. And what mean you, bringing your lackeys here to soil m'lord's house?" William gestured to the men who were tracking mud and dirt across the stone floor.

Another man, whose uniform clearly showed him to be the soldiers' captain, fixed William with a grim stare. "Listen here, you're speaking of the King's Guard, so you'd best keep a civil tongue about you. My men and I don't wish to be here. But the gentleman there has made claims we can't ignore. He says your master harbors a criminal—a woman who might have made an attempt on His Majesty's life."

One of the more timid maids gasped, then went ashen as several pairs of eyes turned her way.

"Don't just stand there," Sir Pitney told the captain, gesturing to the trembling maid and the other servants. "Question them all before the woman has a chance to escape. If he's in London, then she's got to be with him. Why don't you start by questioning that skittish one?" He pointed to the maid who'd gasped.

The maid began to weep. "I-I don't know about no criminals, sir, truly I don't!"

Sir Pitney had just stepped forward to clasp the maid's arm when Marianne could bear it no more. She left the shadows and strode into the hallway.

"What is this all about?" she demanded of the captain of the guard.

Her masked face and noble bearing seemed to give

him pause. He gazed at her with frank suspicion. "And who might you be?"

"I am, shall we say, a friend of his lordship," she replied evenly, hoping that the captain would assume she was Garett's mistress, perhaps even a married woman who wouldn't want her visage known. "He isn't here at the moment, and I was just preparing to leave myself. Perhaps you could return later?"

Sir Pitney's eyes narrowed, and he smiled smugly as if he knew exactly her game. But the captain seemed to assume what she implied, for he shifted from foot to foot in discomfort. "I'm sorry, madam, but I—"

"You fool!" Sir Pitney sputtered when he realized the captain wasn't going to act. "It could be her—Winchilsea's spawn!"

The captain flushed. "Madam, I'm afraid the gentleman here thinks you might be the one we seek. I shall have to ask you to remove your mask."

"Really, Captain, this is terribly embarrassing—"

"Don't I know it. But I must ask it of you all the same." He stood there, his manner polite, but his eyes watching her.

For all his seeming bumbling, the captain was no fool. She'd have little chance of convincing him to release her. And one look at the hatred burning in Sir Pitney's eyes told her he'd never agree to let her pass even if the captain did.

"As you wish." She undid the ties that held her mask. The fighting was over. At least Garett wouldn't have to sacrifice his lands for her.

When she removed the mask, Sir Pitney stared at her with satisfaction.

"You see," he told the captain, who she felt certain still didn't know who she was. "'Tis the little gypsy witch herself."

The captain moved forward. "I'm afraid I must ask you to come with me."

Sir Pitney stepped into the captain's path, blocking it. "Nay, not without Lord Falkham. He's the traitor in this, for he's been protecting her."

Marianne's heart raced. Oh, God, so that was his plan—to use her to entrap Garett. His spy, that man Ashton, who'd seen her in Lydgate when Garett had brought her before the council, must have told Sir Pitney about her. Perhaps he'd even followed them to London. Sir Pitney had taken it from there.

"Nay," she told the captain. "Lord Falkham doesn't know who I am. He took me for his mistress, but I never told him my true identity, for I feared he'd relinquish me to the soldiers if he knew."

Sir Pitney laughed harshly. "You work hard to shield your lover, don't you? Such a shame you won't succeed. We'll just wait here until he returns, and see what story he gives, eh, Captain?"

The captain looked uncomfortable, but it was apparent he knew where his duties lay. Lord Falkham had been caught harboring a woman accused of treason, and thus must be questioned. "We'll wait," the captain said gruffly.

At his signal, his men took up a post by the door

while Sir Pitney's men moved to the back of the house in search of other entrances.

Sir Pitney sidled up to Marianne, a leer on his face. He pushed her hood off her head, then skimmed his hand over her hair. When she slapped his hand away, he caught her wrist, squeezing it painfully.

"A pity you went to him instead of me, gypsy brat. I might have protected you from the soldiers far better," he hissed, his face looming over hers.

His eyes fastened on her lips, and he smiled. Then he lifted his other hand to her neck, closing his fingers loosely about it. "Such a lovely neck. A shame to see it stretched by the noose. Of course, perhaps that needn't happen. I still have some influence, and with Garett out of the way, my power will rise again. I could persuade His Majesty to release you into my hands."

With utter contempt blazing in her face, she spat at him.

His gaze hardened as he wiped the spittle from his chin. Then he lifted his hand. "For that, you gypsy bitch, I'll—"

"Strike her and you forfeit your life!" a voice rang out.

Every head turned. Standing in the doorway was Garett, his sword already drawn and his expression one of unmitigated rage. Heedless of the soldiers who drew their weapons, he strode into the room toward where Sir Pitney stood, still gripping Marianne's wrist.

"Unhand her this instant!" Garett commanded.

Sir Pitney obeyed, but only to draw his own sword.

"Gentlemen!" the captain bellowed and put himself

between them. "I came to take a prisoner, not to see the shedding of blood. Sheathe your weapons before I have my men arrest you both!"

Marianne held her breath as the two enemies watched each other warily, neither moving to do as commanded.

"Gentlemen!" the captain repeated.

Sir Pitney was the first to relent, for he had the most to lose by not complying. He clearly believed Garett was to be arrested.

Once Sir Pitney's sword was sheathed, Garett turned to Marianne with a burning look in his eyes. "Did he harm you?"

"Nay." She cast him a gaze that pleaded with him not to force matters.

He slid his sword back into its scabbard.

"My lord, I've something to tell you," Marianne hastened to add before Garett could reveal anything to further ruin his position. "I'm afraid these gentlemen believe me guilty of a crime. I've told them you don't know who I really am, but—"

"Silence!" Sir Pitney shouted. "The man may speak for himself of what he did and didn't know."

Marianne glanced to the captain in silent appeal, but he merely turned his hard gaze on Garett. "My lord, I must ask you to tell me what you know of this woman."

Marianne begged Garett with her eyes to save himself.

Garett turned to face the captain. "This is Miss Marianne Winchilsea, daughter of Sir Henry. I have been aiding her for the last several weeks because I believe her to be innocent of wrong. To my knowledge, no one has accused her of any crime. Thus there is no reason for you to arrest her."

Marianne stood stunned. For her, he was risking his reputation, his lands, his very life! She wanted to stop him, but she didn't know how.

Sir Pitney's face grew mottled with rage. "She's a traitor. She only escaped being accused because she was believed dead!"

The captain watched both men with interest.

"I say she's blameless, as was her father," Garett retorted.

"Then who committed the crime?" Sir Pitney asked. "No one carried his medicines but he—everyone said so. And she prepared his medicines. Nay, he was guilty, and so is she. You can't prove otherwise!"

"Ah, but I can," Garett remarked coolly.

Marianne gasped.

Sir Pitney's eyes narrowed. "How?"

Garett turned to the captain. "This discussion must be continued in the presence of those with the power to determine a judgment. His Majesty should hear what I have to say. I won't speak further until you bring me and Miss Winchilsea before him."

Marianne sucked in her breath. What game was Garett playing? Had he really discovered something while he'd been gone, or was he bluffing, hoping he could prevail upon His Majesty to release them both simply by virtue of his friendship with the king? Her pulse raced as a desperate hope rose within her.

The captain seemed uncertain what to do, and Sir Pitney took advantage. "Don't be a fool, man." Sir Pitney dropped his hand to the hilt of his sword. "If you bring this lunatic before His Majesty with these ridiculous ravings, the king will have your head for it. Cast them both in the Tower. Then His Majesty may question them at his leisure."

"You'd like that, wouldn't you?" Garett retorted. "Of course, before we'd spent one day there, you'd make certain we were murdered."

"You wretched—" Sir Pitney caught himself as he felt the captain's eyes on him.

The captain turned a questioning gaze to Garett. "My lord, you realize I don't have to grant your request."

Garett smiled coldly. "I know. But if you don't, I'll fight you and your men when you try to take us prisoner. I won't win, of course, but I'll die trying. And how will you explain that to the king? He may not easily accept your tale that I fought because I was guilty. The king knows me well, and he's never had reason to doubt my loyalty, whereas Sir Pitney's loyalty has been doubted time and again."

"You damnable liar!" Sir Pitney sputtered.

"Quiet!" the captain said irritably. "All right then, I'll take you to Whitehall. Then we'll see if His Majesty grants you an audience."

Some of Marianne's tension fled. Garett knew something he wasn't saying. She was sure of it.

At the captain's command, two soldiers flanked her, and two moved to flank Garett.

"One other thing," Garett said. "You must bind us both—Miss Winchilsea and I."

The captain looked offended. "My lord, I trust you and my lady not to—"

"Aye," Garett broke in. "But my uncle doesn't. I wouldn't like to find my throat cut simply because I stumbled in the street and he took it for an escape."

Marianne glanced at Sir Pitney and felt a sickening lurch when she saw his face whiten to an unearthly pale. Clearly Garett had guessed exactly what Sir Pitney planned. Sir Pitney had made a potentially fatal mistake, and he knew it.

"Captain," Sir Pitney interjected, "perhaps Lord Falkham will feel more comfortable if I don't accompany you at all. I have done my part in the king's service. I need not be there to accuse them, for their crime speaks for itself."

Garett laughed harshly. "Afraid, dear Uncle, of what I might have to say before the king? Afraid it might concern you?"

The captain shot Sir Pitney an assessing glance. "Sir, you must come with us. You must also explain how you knew of the lady's presence here."

For a moment, Marianne thought Sir Pitney would protest. Then he drew himself up in forced bravado. "If you insist."

The captain motioned to a guard, who clapped manacles around her wrists. Numbly, Marianne watched as Garett whispered something to the captain. The captain gave Garett an assessing glance, then murmured a command to another guard, who nodded and left the house.

Then a soldier stepped forward to manacle Garett. Garett's eyes never left her face. His expression seemed to say, *Trust me.*

She wanted to, but she'd never been so afraid. She'd found her love in the midst of hardship. How could she bear to lose him so soon after finding him? He gave her a reassuring smile, and she smiled back, forcing all the love she felt for him into her expression.

His eyes burned suddenly as his lips formed words. She thought he said "I love you," but she wasn't certain. It could also have been "I want you."

Then they led the two of them out to the street as hope grew within her heart.

Marianne shivered while waiting with Garett to be led into the audience room of King Charles II. She could just see inside it, and hear how it echoed with the sounds of booted feet tramping the marble floors. The king himself sat in an oaken chair, tapping his bejeweled fingers impatiently on the arm of his chair. When Sir Pitney Tearle strode in ahead of them, as if he came to court every day, the king's eyes narrowed. Then the captain of the guard brought her and Garett in.

The king noticed Garett first, frowning as he apparently spotted the manacles. Then he saw her and looked noticeably startled.

"Miss Winchilsea?" he inquired, half-rising from his chair.

She managed a low curtsy despite the manacles, and he jumped to his feet.

"Take those manacles off the lady!" he commanded the captain. "And off Lord Falkham, too." When the manacles were removed, the king asked, "What is the meaning of this? I was only told some muddled tale about Falkham harboring criminals and wishing an audience."

Sir Pitney seemed loath to speak in the presence of the king. Flashing him a scathing glance, Garett stepped forward.

"Your Majesty," he said as he rubbed his chafed wrists, "I see you know Miss Winchilsea."

The king nodded. "My guard informed me months ago she was dead." His eyes flicked briefly over the captain, who colored.

"As you can see, she is not," Garett continued. "I found her at my estates some weeks ago, pretending to be a gypsy healer."

Charles sat down, an odd expression on his face. Then his eyebrows quirked upward. "Ah, so this is the gypsy mistress I've heard so much about from Hampden?"

It was Marianne's turn to color. Hampden and his quick tongue! If she ever came out of this alive, she'd make certain he suffered for his gossip.

"Yes," Garett responded, his voice a tinge harder. "Only recently did I discover who she really was. Now it seems my uncle wishes to have me condemned for protecting a traitor."

"Your Majesty," Sir Pitney hastened to put in. "The woman clearly aided her father in the recent attempt on your life. Everyone knows—"

"Miss Winchilsea," the king said, "I'm sure you realize the grave position you're in. Have you anything to say in your defense?"

She swallowed, but bravely met the king's gaze. "My father was not a traitor, and neither am I, Your Majesty. I can't explain how the poison came to be in my medicines, but upon my honor, I didn't put it there."

Charles leveled his gaze on Garett. "Is this why you came to me this morning with a request to question my prisoner?"

Garett nodded. "I think you'll be interested in hearing the results. Before we left my house to come here, I took the liberty of asking the captain to have your prisoner brought here so we might better unravel this tangle."

Marianne glanced up at Garett in confusion. Silently he took her hand in his and squeezed it, though he avoided her gaze.

"Bring him in, then," the king ordered.

Behind them, the double doors opened, and Marianne turned to see who was entering. A middle-aged man accompanied by two guards walked in. Marianne's mouth dropped open, and her knees turned to jelly.

"Father?" Her voice rose as he spotted her and smiled. "Father!"

She'd been told he was dead! Yet clearly he stood before her, gaunt and tired, but in good spirits. In moments, she was in his arms, hugging him fiercely. Joy surged through her as she pulled back to look at him, noting the sad disrepair of his clothing and the lack of flesh on his bones.

His gaze took in everything about her, too. Apparently he was satisfied with what he saw, for he continued to smile broadly, making a lump catch in her throat.

Then his gaze turned to Garett. "I see you didn't lie to me, my lord."

His tone and the familiar way he looked at Garett reminded her of what the king had said. So Garett had known all along that her father lived.

"You didn't tell me," she accused him, her voice laced with hurt.

Remorse shone in his face. He moved to her side to take her hand. "I couldn't be certain he still lived, sweetling, until I spoke with the king. I was returning to tell you when I found the soldiers there."

She shook her head in mute disbelief. Garett seemed to have hidden a great many things from her, and she hardly knew how to react.

Another in the room also seemed to have difficulty adjusting to the new turn of events. Sir Pitney stood in dumb shock as he apparently realized what it might mean.

Then a sneer replaced his amazement. "A touching scene, but it hardly proves anything. He's still guilty of treason, and his daughter with him."

"Is he?" Garett asked. "Another awaits outside who

might have something to say about that. With His Majesty's permission—"

The king nodded. From the other end of the room entered a soldier accompanying a pale woman, whom Marianne recognized as Sir Pitney's wife, poor Lady Tearle.

This time Sir Pitney went as white as his hair before he recovered himself. "Why do you bring her here? She's in confinement. She shouldn't be dragged about the city with no concern for the child she bears!"

The king gazed at Garett. "Well, Falkham?"

Lady Tearle seemed wretchedly frightened, but at the sound of her nephew's name, her eyes sought him out, and she ventured a timid smile.

Garett gave her a reassuring smile of his own. "She, too, may help us unravel this tangle. You see, Your Majesty, when I questioned Sir Henry, I threatened to turn Miss Winchilsea over to the guard if he didn't confess."

How could he have done such a despicable thing? She'd meant nothing to him! Marianne tried to jerk her hand from Garett's, but he wouldn't relinquish it.

"Sir Henry was understandably upset," Garett continued, "but insisted that he was innocent. I found that odd. Even the most reprehensible father would hesitate to sacrifice his daughter for his own good, and Sir Henry is no such man. So I could only believe he spoke the truth."

So he'd done it to test Father. Still, it had been terribly wicked of him.

"This is all nonsense," Sir Pitney muttered.

The king ignored him. "Go on."

"Yet one thing puzzled me," Garett said. "Sir Henry himself insisted that Miss Winchilsea prepared the potions and then gave them to him the morning he went to court. He carried them on his person the rest of the day until he started to administer them and accidentally spilled them. His story corresponded with the one Miss Winchilsea told me as well. So if Sir Henry didn't commit the crime, who did, and how?"

Charles leaned forward eagerly. "Yes, who and how indeed?" he remarked as his gaze rested briefly on Sir Pitney.

Sir Pitney stood there stone-faced.

"Then I recalled a trick I played on my uncle as a child," Garett went on. "I coated the inside of his ale mug with soap. Later, when it was filled, he had a terrible surprise." Garett turned his gaze to his aunt. "Do you remember that, Aunt Bess?"

She glanced nervously at Sir Pitney, but nodded.

"He was very angry after that," Garett said. "He used to check every mug, every box . . . every pouch brought to him to make certain it was truly empty before he used it."

Every pouch. Marianne began to shake as she realized what Garett was leading up to. She'd filled the pouches, but she'd never checked them before doing so. Why should she have? They'd been washed days before. There had been no need to believe they might have contained other additional powders—like poison.

Her father leaned close and took her arm, squeezing it reassuringly.

The king, too, seemed to recognize what Garett implied. He sat back in his chair, his brow furrowed in thought. "If someone had entered Miss Winchilsea's chambers and filled her pouches beforehand—"

"The pouches were of white satin, and she filled them early in the morning," Garett remarked. "She would never have noticed arsenic dusted on the inside. Anyone with access to her house could have—"

"This is absurd!" Sir Pitney said with a shaky laugh. "All this talk of pouches and soap. If indeed someone else did as you say, you still have no idea who might be guilty. It could have been anyone."

Garett turned to fix Sir Pitney with a piercing stare. "Ah, but it wasn't anyone, was it, Uncle? Who else is a known Roundhead who doesn't particularly like His Majesty? And who else wanted Falkham House so badly he would have killed to get it? If Sir Henry were eliminated—"

"All speculation and idle flummery," Sir Pitney protested. "You've no proof, my lord."

Garett turned from Sir Pitney to look at Lady Tearle. "I suspect others here could provide us with proof enough if they were so inclined, eh, Aunt Bess?"

Sir Pitney stiffened. "Bess, don't let him persuade you to spout lies about me, do you hear?"

Lady Tearle looked decidedly ill, and Marianne

pitied her. Yet she couldn't find it in her heart to make Garett stop what he was doing. She needed too badly to prove her father's and her own innocence.

"Have you anything to tell us, Aunt Bess?" Garett asked gently.

When Lady Tearle glanced in Sir Pitney's direction, an expression of pure terror crossed her face. Garett left Marianne and her father to stand beside his aunt. "Don't let him intimidate you," he told her, taking one of her hands in his. "He can't hurt you now, I swear it. No matter what happens here and what is revealed, I won't let him harm you."

She hesitated, her free hand resting on her stomach. Then she looked at Sir Pitney again. She swallowed, and her gaze swung back to Garett, but she wouldn't meet his eyes. "I-I don't know anything, my lord," she whispered.

The king stood to his full height. "Lady Tearle," he said in somber tones. "You are in the presence of your king. Lies will not be tolerated."

She seemed desperately torn. At one point, she looked to Marianne, and Marianne gave her a reassuring smile.

"Aunt Bess?" Garett asked again.

Then Sir Pitney bellowed, "I'll not have you harass my wife in this fashion, Falkham! She's with child. If she loses her child because of this absurd assertion—"

"Just as I lost my father and mother because of your greed?" Garett bit out. Everyone in the room began to whisper. Even the king seemed stunned.

"Think you that I don't know who killed them?" Garett continued, his eyes boring into his uncle's. "I well remember Father telling me that you had suggested the route because it was so swift. You were the only one who knew. You were the only one who could have betrayed them to the soldiers."

Lady Tearle gasped and went limp, but Garett caught her up swiftly. "Garett," she muttered, so low that the room fell silent as everyone tried to catch her words. "H-he told me he didn't know they were even leaving until after they fled."

"He knew," Garett asserted. "I thought you knew as well."

That seemed to shock her out of her faint. "No! I knew nothing of this until now!" She walked clumsily to the center of the room and pointed at her husband. "You killed them, didn't you? You always wanted Richard's lands. I heard you say so often enough even before they were murdered. You killed my own brother! What kind of monster are you?"

"He's lying, Bess. Don't listen to him," Sir Pitney said in steely tones. "Remember what I told you! Think of the babe!"

"You'll never see that babe! The child isn't even yours!" she spat. "And I'll not have him raised by the likes of you!" She faced the king. "Your Majesty, my nephew speaks the truth, as does this poor innocent man here and his daughter. My husband planned the poisoning so he could regain my family home. I only learned of it recently, however—"

"She lies!" Sir Pitney shouted. "She had as much to do with it as I! She took part in it, I swear!"

"And have you proof?" Garett asked. "Nay, I think not. She's just another innocent you'd have take the punishment for your crimes."

Lady Tearle continued, her eyes dark with hate. "I have proof, Your Majesty, of my husband's treachery. If you'll send your guards for a man named Ashton in my husband's house, you may persuade him to confess how it was done. He's my husband's servant, and I heard him say he planted the poison himself."

"I'll kill you for this, you ungrateful bitch!" Sir Pitney cried.

"Seize him!" His Majesty ordered the guards, and they started toward Sir Pitney.

Before anyone could stop him, Sir Pitney withdrew a short sword and lunged toward Marianne where she stood beside her father. In seconds, he had his arm about her waist and the sword at her neck.

"If anyone tries to seize me, she dies!" he bellowed as he began dragging her toward the door.

Marianne leaned back against Sir Pitney, away from the threatening blade.

Garett unsheathed his own sword with a loud clang. "Harm one hair of her head, Uncle, and I'll slice you into so many bits they'll never find them all! Let her go!"

Marianne felt the sword point quiver at her throat.

"Nay!" Sir Pitney called out, backing away with her until he neared the door. "I'll see her dead before I let them take me, you worthless cur!"

He tried to pull Marianne back more, but she planted her feet, fighting him. If he took her from the room, all hope was lost. "Kill me now, then," she hissed.

"No, Mina!" Garett and her father shouted, but she ignored them. Forcing his hand was her only chance.

"I'll not go anywhere with you," she told him when she felt him hesitate. "Go ahead, kill me. But be prepared to die afterward, for you know Garett will never let you live."

Garett stood poised, his face pale as death as he kept his eyes on the sword at Marianne's neck.

"Don't be a fool," Sir Pitney muttered, then pressed the blade against her flesh so it bit into the skin, and blood trickled down her neck.

Garett's face contorted with rage, but Marianne remained calm.

"That's just a prick!" she taunted him. "Kill me. Kill me, I say, for you'll not get me out of here otherwise!"

For one terrible moment, she thought he would. She held her breath, wondering, as his arm tightened on her waist and the sword pressed even closer, if she had risked too much. Then, without warning, the blade left her neck and she was pushed hard in Garett's direction. She stumbled to the floor as Sir Pitney lunged for the entrance. But two soldiers stepped to block his path, their swords at the ready.

Sir Pitney whirled around and darted toward another door, but this time it was Garett who blocked his path.

"Time to give up the fight," Garett said, brandishing his sword.

"Never!" Like a cornered rat, Sir Pitney thrust at Garett.

Marianne screamed, but she needn't have worried. Garett sidestepped his uncle's thrust easily, throwing his uncle temporarily off balance. But Sir Pitney regained his footing and held his sword once again before him with grim purpose.

"I wish they'd murdered you instead of that servant," he spat. "You should have died with your parents. I don't know how you escaped, but you couldn't have been there, or you would have been killed, too. Haven't you ever wondered if they suffered? I could tell you—"

Garett's angry thrust cut off Sir Pitney's taunts, but Sir Pitney parried it with ease.

"Your mother begged at the end," Sir Pitney continued. "They told me that she begged and begged."

Oh, Lord, he was attempting to make Garett slip and let down his guard if only for a second, but apparently Garett realized the same thing, for his face suddenly grew expressionless.

"Mother never begged for anything," he retorted. "But when I'm through with you, you'll beg. Like you've been begging at the doors of every merchant in town, every moneylender, every—"

Sir Pitney lunged wildly, his face mottled with rage. But Garett sidestepped the thrust, at the same time falling to one knee and bringing his sword up through Sir Pitney's chest.

For a moment, the two seemed suspended in space, Sir Pitney gazing at Garett with shock and horror as the sword tumbled from his fingers, and Garett staring at him with the same frightening expression.

Then Garett withdrew his sword, and Sir Pitney fell to his knees.

"A wretch to the end," Sir Pitney croaked out, and Marianne wondered if he meant Garett or himself.

Then he collapsed lifeless on the floor.

Chapter Twenty-two

There's nought but willing, waking love that can
Make blest the ripened maid and finished man.
—William Congreve, *Love for Love*

Chaos ensued. Soldiers swarmed around Garett and the body at his feet. Lady Tearle stood in shock as the king started from his chair and went to her side. And Father moved quickly to enfold Marianne in his arms.

"It's all over now, Mina," he murmured, pulling her limp form against him.

She let him hold her a moment, wanting to soak up the comfort he offered. But she couldn't long keep her gaze from Garett, who stood surrounded by soldiers. His face showed no relief—only a deep, dark pain.

The king motioned for a soldier to lead Lady Tearle from the room, and she went willingly. Then he went over to Garett and the captain of the guard. They spoke a few moments in hushed tones. After that, two soldiers carried Sir Pitney away as servants scurried to clean the blood from the marble.

Tears slid down Marianne's cheeks. So much blood. So much sorrow, for Garett more than for her. She watched Garett as he scanned the room until his eyes locked with hers, a tender light replacing the sorrow on his face. What was to become of their love? Garett had said he'd never leave her. Still, he'd never promised to marry her, either.

He made his way toward her and Father. As he reached them, he looked lost, as if he thought he didn't belong there. Father loosened his hold, although he kept one arm protectively about her waist.

"Thank you for bringing my little girl back to me," he told Garett. "I nearly died when I thought she'd been killed."

Marianne felt a quick stab of remorse. "I wouldn't have let you believe such lies, Father, if I'd known you were alive. I would never have left you alone in the Tower."

"Then 'tis a good thing his lordship didn't tell you about me," her father said in a voice choked with emotion. "Otherwise, we'd both be there together now."

"I doubt that," the king said behind them. "I could never have imprisoned your pretty daughter. Once the soldiers brought her here for my questioning and she turned that innocent clear-eyed gaze on me, I'd immediately have known she spoke the truth."

Marianne pulled back from her father to flash the king a shy smile. Darting a sideways glance at Garett, she said, "Your Majesty is kind, but I don't think 'twould have been that simple. It certainly wasn't with Lord Falkham. He had trouble believing me even when I did confess the truth."

The flash of contrition that crossed Garett's face made Marianne wish to take the words back.

"Miss Winchilsea is right," he said. "I'm afraid I've grown suspicious of everyone through the years, even innocent young noblewomen. But it was unkind of me not to tell her about her father. I should have trusted her with that much."

The intent gaze with which he regarded her warmed Marianne to the bone. For a moment, she forgot about anyone else in the room. "'Tis of no consequence now, my lord."

"You realize you've all put me in a terrible quandary," the king interjected with a wry frown. "Lord Falkham and Sir Henry both legally own Falkham House now that Sir Henry has been cleared of all wrongdoing. So who will retain it?"

"That should be no problem, Your Majesty," Father said with a wink at Marianne. "Lord Falkham and I solved the matter before he left my jail cell."

"Oh?" the king asked. "And what solution do you propose?"

"I think first I should speak with—" Garett began.

"I only intended to keep the estate as my legacy to my daughter," Father went on. "I prefer to remain in London if Your Majesty will allow me to return as your physician. His lordship can retain Falkham House, which in any case is rightfully his. What's more, I need not worry about Marianne's legacy, because his lordship has agreed to marry her, which should take care of the problem admirably."

Marianne's mouth went completely dry. Her eyes widened as she glanced at Garett in clear surprise. Garett watched her, a guarded expression on his face.

"We've already briefly discussed the settlement," her father continued, "and I believe we can come to some amicable agreement without much problem."

"Now that is an expert solution," the king remarked. "And I must say it would please me to see one of my favorite subjects married to such a beautiful, brave young woman."

Marianne scarcely noted the compliment, for her heart was pounding. Marry Garett? That would be as close to heaven as she could reach.

Then the rest of her father's words sank in. Garett would have Falkham House, of course.

Doubt assailed her. Surely that had played no part in his agreeing to marry her. Then again, Garett always got what he wanted, and he wanted Falkham House very badly.

"Have I no say in this, Father?" she asked. "Am I to be married just like that without even being consulted, merely to solve the problem of an estate with two owners?"

Her father looked instantly uncomfortable. Another man might have told her she would do as he said because he was her father, but Father had always been a more lenient sort. "But I thought—"

He broke off at the sound of the king's loud chortle. "This is very interesting, Falkham. Apparently the lady doesn't care about your superior title and ever-increasing wealth." He turned to Marianne. "Don't you wish to marry Lord Falkham?"

She reddened as Garett's face turned stony. She hadn't meant to embarrass him, but she couldn't marry him if he wanted her only for the estate.

The king's eyes darkened, and his smile vanished. "He didn't force his attentions on you, did he?"

"Attentions?" her father queried with a frown, for he hadn't been present during the earlier discussion about her being Garett's mistress.

"No, no, Your Majesty," she hastened to assure him as she avoided her father's gaze. "Of course not. But I would have wished—"

"Your Majesty," Garett interrupted. "If I could have a moment alone with Miss Winchilsea, I believe we could clear up any misunderstandings."

"Could you indeed?" the king remarked, immensely amused. "All right, then. That is, if the lady so wishes to remain with you here."

"Marianne?" Father asked. "May his lordship speak with you alone a moment?"

"Of course." If Garett spoke of the financial advantages their union would bring, it would destroy her. Yet the way he looked at her . . .

She would eternally regret it if she didn't allow him to state his case.

The king accompanied her father from the room, speaking to him in low whispers interspersed with the occasional chuckle. Then she and Garett were alone, the room completely silent.

She gazed down at her hands, uncertain where to begin. "My lord, you mustn't feel it's necessary to marry me to keep Falkham House. I know what my father said, but I don't want it, and I'd be more than content to live here in London with him."

"Would you?" Garett said in a husky rasp as he took a step toward her. "You could be happy here, living for no one but your father all your life?" He hesitated. "Or perhaps you don't intend that," he added, a tinge of bitterness in his voice. "Perhaps you've an eye for some other gentleman—someone more lively, like Hampden."

Tears flooded her vision so she could hardly see. "No, no one else."

He closed the distance between them and pulled her into his arms. "Don't cry, my gypsy princess. You'll break my heart. And I can't afford that, for I only have one, and it belongs to you."

She lifted her gaze to his. "Please don't say such things if you don't mean them."

"Ah, but I've never meant anything more." He brushed her tears away with one finger. "I know you're angry with me for not telling you of your father. You have every right to be hurt, but I swear I'll make it up to you if you'll just marry me. I want you to be my wife, Mina. And not because I wish to keep Falkham House, either."

"Then why?" she asked, needing the words, feeling as if she'd die if he couldn't speak them.

He smiled then. For the first time since she'd known

him, she could truly say he looked like the boy Garett she'd imagined all those years before.

"Because you're sweet and kind. Because my tenants adore you, and my valet and your aunt would undoubtedly kill me if I left you here."

She couldn't suppress a quick smile.

His eyes darkened to the color of midnight rain. "And because I want you more than anything I've ever wanted in my life. More than my estates or even my revenge against my uncle." He swallowed hard. "But most of all because I love you. I didn't realize it until today when I talked to your father, but I felt it long before."

Her heart swelled with joy. At last she'd found a way through all the barriers to his heart. After all the distrust, all the fear, he was hers.

"Well?" he asked as she stared up at him with shining eyes. "Can you find it in your heart to love a reprobate like me, with scars and old wounds always giving me something to grumble about?"

She raised herself on tiptoe to press her lips sweetly to his. "Perhaps in time, my lord—" she teased.

He growled and forced her mouth back up against his, kissing her with such passion that he left her weak in his arms. "Say it," he whispered when he'd torn his lips from hers. "Say it, Mina!"

"I love you," she admitted. "I've loved you so long, my poor, dear exile."

"And you'll marry me," he added in a tone that brooked no argument.

"And I'll marry you," she repeated.

Then her mouth was once again smothered by his.

At that moment the king and her father thrust their heads inside the room to see how matters were coming along. Father bristled immediately, ready to put an end to what he saw, but the king pulled him back with a smile on his face.

"Don't worry," the king whispered. "I think they have matters quite in hand." Then he nodded Father from the room and followed him out, shutting the door behind him.

Epilogue

"Father! Mother! Look what me and Aunt Tamara found!"

Garett turned to see his daughter, Beatrice, come skipping across the grass toward where he stood beneath an apple tree.

Tamara followed more slowly behind the four-year-old, who clutched something black in her tiny fist and waved it like a banner over her head.

"What is it?" Marianne asked from her seat on the ground next to where Garett stood. Her face was wreathed in smiles.

Garett felt his breath catch in his throat as he gazed down at her tawny hair and her face aglow with the knowledge that her next child—*their* next child—would soon arrive.

Beatrice stopped before her parents, all out of breath. She looked up at Garett, the winsome smile on her face reminding him so much of Marianne that he instantly felt the same stab of protectiveness he always felt for his wife.

Gently he ruffled his daughter's hair. "What have you there, poppet?"

Her soft blue eyes alight, she held out the crumpled piece of black silk. Garett smiled as he recognized it, then glanced at Marianne.

"My mask," Marianne murmured. "Where did you find it?"

Kneeling beside her mother, Beatrice laid it on Marianne's lap, smoothing it out reverently. "'Twas in a box of old clothes. Aunt Tamara said I could play with them 'til Uncle Will came to fetch her. Then we found this!" She looked up into her mother's face. "Aunt Tamara said it was yours once."

"Aye," Garett told his daughter. "Your mother wore it the first time I saw her." An image flashed before him of Marianne in Mr. Tibbett's shop. How vividly he remembered his first glimpse of her defiant hazel eyes through the slits in the mask.

Marianne looked up at him now and smiled. She, too, remembered. He laid his hand on her shoulder, pleased when she laid her hand on his.

"Why did Mother wear a mask?" Beatrice asked him.

"She didn't want me to see her beautiful face, dearling," Garett answered with a chuckle. "She knew the minute I saw it I'd want to marry her."

Tamara's snort reminded Garett of her presence. "She knew you'd be wanting something else, I'm thinking," she said dryly.

The quick blush that suffused Marianne's face brought forth another chuckle from Garett. "Aye," he agreed and squeezed her shoulder.

"You two shouldn't say such things in front of Beatrice," Marianne protested as she tried to smother a laugh.

But Beatrice had hardly noticed the exchange, let alone understood it. One of the dogs from the rebuilt kennels went racing by, and she jumped to her feet to run laughing after it, the mask suddenly forgotten.

"I'll get her," Tamara muttered as she lifted her skirts and walked briskly after Beatrice, scolding her all the way.

Garett knelt beside Marianne and plucked the mask from her lap. Marianne's eyes locked with his as he held the mask up to her face.

"You may not believe this," he told her as he surveyed her critically, "but the entire time you were treating my sword wound that fateful night, I couldn't bring myself to believe your lie about the smallpox. I felt certain your face had to be as captivating as your voice."

She looked skeptical. "My voice? But my words to you were harsh."

He dropped the mask into her lap. "Not all of them. You spoke of flowers when all that grew in my heart was weeds. That's when I knew I had to have you. I wanted the flower you hid beneath your veils of mystery."

Settling onto the ground beside her, he took her hand. "It took me some time to unveil you, didn't it? Thank God I managed it at last." His other hand cupped her cheek; then his thumb began rhythmically stroking her lower lip.

"And did you find the flower you sought?" she whispered, her breath quickening.

"That and so much more," he murmured. "I found a garden. The garden of my heart in yours."

Then he swallowed her smile of delight with a kiss.

Turn the page
for a special look at
the first delightful romance in the new
Duke's Men series

WHAT THE DUKE DESIRES

by *New York Times* bestselling author

Sabrina Jeffries

Coming Summer 2013 from Pocket Books

L isette had serious trouble feigning sleep once Mrs. Greasley started talking again.

"Forgive me," she asked, "but what does a land agent do, exactly?"

Holding her breath, Lisette waited to see how the duke would manage this. He'd been stubborn about taking up *her* choice of profession, and now she couldn't even help him with his choice without giving up her pretense of sleep.

"He collects the rents," Lyons answered easily, to her surprise. "He makes inventories. He surveys the farms, keeps a terrier of the common lands . . ."

As he continued to list an impressive number of duties, Lisette marveled at his knowledge. She could not have helped him with this, to be sure. Papa had always just said that his land agent "managed the estate," indifferent to what the man actually did. And Papa had only been a viscount. She'd assumed that a wealthy duke with vast properties would have even less need of such knowledge, and would know little about the inner workings of his estates.

In Lyons's case, she'd been wrong. Mr. Greasley asked more questions, and the duke answered every one easily. Astonishing.

As the two men began to talk of leases and enclosures and things that were far beyond her ken, the rumble of Lyons's voice and the swaying of the carriage began to lull her into a doze. She *had* been up very late and had risen very early. And they wouldn't reach Brighton for some time . . .

She came slowly awake a while later to find the coach dark and the duke's arm about her shoulders. Her head had slid down to the center of his chest, and her hand was on his waist.

Horrified, she jerked herself upright, embarrassment filling her cheeks with heat as he pulled his arm from around her shoulders. "Where are we?" she asked, trying to get her bearings.

"On the outskirts of Brighton," he said in that low timbre that did something unseemly to her insides.

She couldn't look at him. She'd been practically on his lap! How mortifying. He must think her the most vulgar creature imaginable.

"You were sleeping very sound," Mrs. Greasley offered. "You must have been tired, deary."

It was said so kindly that Lisette winced. She felt a little guilty about how her fake tiff with her "husband" had led to a very real tiff between Mr. and Mrs. Greasley. Still, they seemed to have patched it up. The woman was leaning companionably against him, and he didn't seem to mind.

Lisette turned her face to the window. Thank God this nightmare stretch of the trip was almost over. The incident with the Greasleys had proved only too well that she couldn't necessarily travel with impunity.

The duke had known it, too, and tried to take advantage. She couldn't fool herself that she'd gained the upper hand with her little performance. She'd just gained a reprieve, that's all. He could have chosen to drop the facade the moment he realized he might get the truth out of the Greasleys. He could have revealed that she was *not* married to him, and asked them flat out what he wished to know. And in one fell swoop, he would have ruined her and possibly Dom's business.

Why hadn't he? Because he was a gentleman?

More likely it was because he could tell that the Greasleys didn't know enough to help him. Thank God she'd mentioned both Toulon and Paris to them in the past, and thank God the two cities were in very different parts of France. Otherwise, she was almost certain Lofty Lyons would have abandoned her in Brighton to hunt down Tristan in whichever one they'd named definitively.

She'd made a narrow escape. Too narrow.

Fortunately, she had little chance of encountering more neighbors. So once they parted from the Greasleys she ought to be safe from discovery, at least until they were on their way to Paris.

Surely Lyons would never abandon her in France. That would be most ungentlemanly, and he was nothing if not a gentleman.

Most of the time.

A shiver skittered down her spine as she remembered the feel of his strong arm about her shoulders. And worse yet, the way his hand had toyed with hers earlier. She should have tugged hers free. Why hadn't she?

Because it had been so . . . intimate. No man had ever held her hand in such a fashion, boldly but tenderly, too. It had utterly unnerved her. Even now, with her hand still tucked in the crook of his arm and his thigh pressed against hers, she felt that same quivering in her belly that she'd felt when he'd caressed her hand.

She stiffened. Skrimshaw was right. She'd better take care. The duke had been the one to assert he was her husband, and that shifted everything. Now there was no reason for him to treat her like a sister, no reason for them to have separate rooms . . . anywhere.

Her pulse gave a flutter at the thought of spending several nights on the road alone in an inn room with him.

Lord save her. She'd better be careful.

She slanted a gaze up at him. He was looking entirely too unreadable. After her little display, she'd expected him to be a good deal angrier. But he'd conceded defeat and acted as if nothing had happened. It had put her on her guard again. He had something up his sleeve. What could it be?

They reached the coaching inn a short while later. As the Greasleys took their leave, Mrs. Greasley surprised her by murmuring, "Don't let the man bully you, deary. If you don't stand up for yourself at the beginning of the marriage, he'll be no good to you for anything but grief."

The sage advice, coming from a woman who clearly had her own husband tied neatly in knots, bemused her. Had Mrs. Greasley noticed more about their relationship than Lisette had given her credit for? Or was that just the woman's usual advice to newly married couples?

It didn't matter. Lisette had to survive the duke's presence only long enough to extricate Tristan from this trouble. And standing up to Lyons when he tried to bully her wasn't the problem. She could manage that. It was when he was being sweet that he was most dangerous.

Was that his current course—to kill her with kindness?

Trying to figure out his game consumed her throughout the next hour, while he went off with the innkeeper to arrange for their room and their passage to Dieppe, have their bags sent up, and ask that a meal be provided. So much for traveling as a regular person. Clearly he had no idea how a regular person traveled.

Then again, he'd changed the rules by claiming to be a land agent. Such men did have some money—they would be able to afford a decent room in an inn, and they would be used to giving orders.

She had to admit it had been rather clever of him to hit on that role. It put him in that nebulous land between gentleman and tradesman. He worked for a living, but it required a certain amount of polish and skill. It meant that his accent wasn't *too* odd, nor his knowledge of certain things too unbelievable. And clearly he had realized that he knew the role well enough to play it.

She only wished she knew the role of a wife half as well. Would a real wife let him handle all the arrangements without voicing an opinion? Would she complain that the rooms they were led to were too small?

Thank God there were two of them—a bedchamber and a sitting room. That somewhat eased her fear of being alone with him. One of them could sleep on the settee while the other took the bed. They wouldn't be quite as much in each other's pockets as she'd feared.

He must have planned it that way, and for that she was grateful.

As soon as the innkeeper left, scurrying off to arrange for their dinner, the Duke of Lyons walked over to the ewer, poured some water in the basin, and began to wash his hands.

The silence stretched maddeningly between them. "I imagine that you find the public coaches very dirty, Your Grace," Lisette said.

"I find traveling very dirty regardless of the coach, Miss Bonnaud." He dried his hands, then faced her, leaning back against the sturdy bureau that held the wash basin and crossing his arms over his chest.

His unreadable stare made her feel the first tendrils of alarm.

"It is, that's true." She walked over to her bag and opened it, determined to appear as nonchalant as he.

"That was a very enlightening performance you put on in the carriage," he said at last. "I was impressed."

She didn't suppose "Thank you" was the appropriate answer. "You pushed me into a corner," she said defensively. "I didn't have a choice. We agreed that I would help you find Tristan if you would let me go along. You couldn't expect me to jeopardize his safety by telling you too soon where he is."

She shot him a veiled glance. Her voice grew stronger the longer she talked, but it didn't seem to change his stance any. He just kept staring at her with a piercing gaze. An oddly compelling gaze.

It was most unsettling. "Because you know very well," she went on, "that the minute I do, you'll abandon me and go off on your own."

"True."

She gaped at him. He didn't even bother to deny it. "Well, I can't have that. I have to protect my brother."

"Do you?" He pushed away from the bureau. "I'm beginning to think you have a darker goal."

That took her completely by surprise. "Darker goal?" she asked, her blood freezing in her veins.

"When I first met you, I assumed you weren't part of his scheme. But your play-acting today proved that you are masterful at pretense. How do I know that our entire conversation this morning wasn't a pretense? That you aren't leading me away from London at this very moment for some devious purpose?"

Devious purpose? Masterful at pretense? He thought she was some sort of swindler! "That's a vile accusation! I would never do such a thing!"

"And why should I believe you?" He strode nearer,

his face dark with threat. "You've proved yourself very good at dissembling. For all I know, you and your brother cooked up this plan together."

"B-but why? Why would I do that?"

"That's what I want to know." He loomed over her. "I ought to have you tossed in the gaol until you tell me the truth."

"Because I *cry* well?" she squeaked.

"Because you are attempting to defraud me," he said in an ominous tone.

He was going to throw her in irons, just because she could do some acting in a pinch!

"I swear I'm not doing any such thing," she said, her heart in her throat. "You know why I insisted on your taking me with you. You do! I don't know where you've got this daft idea that I'm some swindler, but nothing could be further from—"

He started laughing. She gaped at him, now all at sea.

That merely made him laugh harder, and he gasped, "You're not . . . the only one . . . good at pretense."

And suddenly she understood. This was revenge for her play-acting this afternoon.

Planting her hands on her hips, she glared at him. "You are a horrible, horrible man! How dare you terrify me like that? Why, I ought to—"

He dropped onto the settee, laughing so hard he could scarcely speak. "If you . . . could only have seen . . . your face . . . when I mentioned . . . gaol . . ."

She walked up to hit him on the arm. "That was not remotely amusing!"

"I . . . beg to . . . disagree . . ." he choked out, holding his stomach in mirth.

Glowering at him, she strode over to the ewer, brought it back, and poured its contents on his head.

He jumped up off the settee, sputtering, "What the devil was that for?"

"For making me think you were going to pack me off to gaol, you . . . you . . . oaf!"

"Oaf?" he said as he removed a handkerchief from his pocket and began to wipe his face. "That's the best you can do?"

She narrowed her gaze to slits. "Cretin. Devil. Arse."

He smirked at her. "Careful now. Aren't you supposed to be a respectable married lady?"

"You nearly gave me heart failure!"

"You deserved it, after all that crying and nonsense." He mimicked her. "*M-my brother was right. I sh-should never have m-married you!*"

Tossing the empty ewer onto the settee, she crossed her arms over her chest. "The words might have been feigned, but the sentiment is still valid."

"It wasn't my idea to do this," he reminded her.

"And it wasn't *my* idea to pose as a married couple. Thank God *that's* pretend." She headed for the other room.

"Oh yes," he said irritably as he followed close behind her. "You would hate being married to a wealthy duke who could buy you whatever you wanted and show you the world you so obviously crave to see."

That he had noticed her love of travel vexed her

immensely. She whirled on him in a temper. "I would hate being married to any man who would own me. Who would want to tell me what to do, when to do it, how to do it, and with whom. No, thank you."

He slicked back his wet hair. "Is that really how you see marriage?"

"As a prison for women? Yes."

"And you see no advantage in it," he said as he came right up to her.

"None."

"What about children?"

"My mother had two. She wasn't married." Though Lisette would never follow that example, she wasn't about to admit it to His High-and-Mighty Grace.

He lifted one imperious brow. "And you ended up in poverty as a result."

"So did my half brother, and *he* is legitimate. The fact is, in this country, unless you're the eldest, you inherit at the whim of your father. Marriage is no protection against that, especially if a woman is marrying far above her, as Dom's mother did."

"What about companionship?" he prodded.

"I have two brothers who will never abandon me. That's companionship enough for me."

"And love?" he asked softly. "What about that?"

She glanced away, not wanting him to see her ambivalence on *that* subject. "Love is the chain men use to hold a woman prisoner. They offer her love and in exchange for her devotion, they give her none. I learned that well from my mother's example." Forcing a bright smile to her face, she met his gaze once more. "So you see, Your Grace, I find no advantages to be had in marriage."

"You're forgetting one more," he said, his eyes locked with hers.

"Oh, and what might that be?"

"Desire."

She fought a shiver at his provocative tone. She hadn't forgotten that one. She'd ignored it. "Desire is only an advantage for the man." She'd been telling herself that for years, but it somehow rang hollow when she said it to *him*.

"You can't be that naive." His voice was now a low thrum. "Surely your mother enjoyed her nights in your father's arms."

"I wouldn't know. Maman didn't talk about such things." Her mother had been determined to act respectably outside the bedchamber, probably thinking that it would convince Papa to marry her. Obviously it hadn't worked.

"And you? No man has ever tempted you with desire?"

Not to any great extent. Until he had come along. And she wasn't about to admit *that* to him. "No."

Something flickered in his face. The thrill of a challenge? Or something darker, more visceral? "Then it's about bloody time someone did."

He grasped her face between his hands and sealed his lips to hers.

Develop a PASSION
for the past…
Bestselling Historical Romances
from Pocket Books!